Ann Gosslin was born and raised in New England in the US, and moved overseas after leaving university. Having held several full-time roles in the pharmaceutical industry, with stints as a teacher and translator in Europe, Asia, and Africa, she currently works as a freelancer and lives in Switzerland.

The Shadow Bird is Ann's debut novel. Her second novel, *The Double*, will be published by Legend Press in 2021.

Visit Ann
www.anngosslin.com

Follow her
@GosslinAnn

ANN GOSSLIN

The
Shadow
Bird

Legend Press Ltd, 51 Gower Street, London, WC1E 6HJ
info@legend-paperbooks.co.uk | www.legendpress.co.uk

Print ISBN 978-1-78955-1-150
Ebook ISBN 978-1-78955-1-167
Set in Times. Printing Managed by Jellyfish Solutions Ltd
Cover design by Rose Cooper | www.rosecooper.com

'Human madness is oftentimes a cunning and most feline thing. When you think it fled, it may have but become transfigured into some still subtler form.'

Herman Melville

1

The Meadows
Lansford, New York
February, Present Day

The dark hair, hacked off with a kitchen knife, was the only sign of anything wrong. Asleep in the narrow bed, her face scrubbed clean of make-up, she could be any ordinary girl, dreaming of boys and Saturdays at the mall. But once the drugs wore off, she would surely resurface to whatever nightmare had brought her here.

Erin pressed her fingers to the girl's wrist and waited for the flutter of blood. Like any good doctor, she tried to keep her emotions in check, but some patients distressed her more than others. If one of the staff going off their shift hadn't spotted the girl's body in a snowbank by the gate, she would not have survived the night. In her shoulder bag, they'd found a four-inch paring knife, a handful of hair, and two keys on a plain metal ring. But no ID, and six hours later still no news from the police.

During those first frantic minutes in the clinic's emergency bay, after they carried her inside, Erin had stripped off the glittery top and torn tights, desperate to rub some life into the girl's frozen limbs. Only to find that the skin on her arms and thighs had been cut and re-cut. A network of hash marks, intricate as fish scales.

Pellets of snow ticked against the window. Erin turned her head, sensing rather than seeing the snowdrifts banked against the glass. Too dark to see much of anything beyond the spectral shrubs, shrouded in snow.

A commotion broke the silence. High heels smacking the stone floor like gunshots. Erin stepped into the hall to see a young nurse hurrying towards her, a panicky look in her eyes.

'We've got trouble. I paged Dr Westlund, but he's not here yet.'

At the far end of the reception hall, a woman in a short coat and black leather boots was arguing with the duty nurse. She slammed her palm on the counter, hissed through her teeth. Tall, taffy-blonde hair, the mouth a red slash.

Erin froze. *Could it be?* No. She hesitated in the shadows, her heart bumping her ribs.

'I want to see my daughter. Cassie Gray. Where is she?'

Cassie. And this was the girl's mother. Not the warm, suburban matron Erin was hoping for.

The duty nurse seemed to have the situation under control, but where was Niels? They had a protocol for cases like this. But he wasn't here, and this couldn't wait.

Erin straightened her shoulders and approached the desk. 'I'm Dr Cartwright. Your daughter is out of danger, but she's sleeping now. If you could perhaps keep your voice down…'

Spiky earrings, cheap perfume, that hard red mouth. The woman towered over her like a Valkyrie. 'What are you looking at, Tinkerbell?'

Tinkerbell. Was it her size or the British accent that set the woman off?

A retort sprang to mind, but Erin stifled the urge. She was used to dealing with angry parents. 'I'm sure this is all very upsetting, but if you'll just try to stay calm—'

'Calm? I get a call from some punk in the middle of the

night that my daughter's in this nuthouse, and you want me to stay calm? Screw you.' She shoved Erin hard on the shoulder and pushed past.

Pain shot down Erin's arm and she gasped. Before she could react, the woman had clattered halfway down the hall in those ridiculous boots. If someone didn't stop her, she'd wake the entire clinic.

But there was Niels at last, striding through the vaulted atrium, jaunty and alert at six in the morning. His blue Oxford shirt and tan chinos were perfectly pressed, the parting in his hair razor-straight. Was that where he'd been, standing in front of a mirror combing his hair?

As he approached Cassie's mother, his broad face was wreathed in the appropriate degree of concern. 'I'm Dr Westlund.' He extended his hand. 'Please be assured your daughter is getting the very best care.'

The woman jerked back before he could touch her. 'If you think I'm going to let you people mess with her head, you've got another thing coming. I want to see her.'

'Let's wait until she's awake, shall we?' Niels flicked a piece of lint from the sleeve of his white coat. 'If it were up to me, Mrs Gray, I'd let you have a quick peek in her room, just to ease your mind. But I don't make the rules.'

'I have a right to see her. I'm her mother.' Her face was deathly pale in the muted light.

'I'm sorry.' He shook his head. 'Why don't you go home now and get some rest. We'll call you as soon as we know more.'

With a determined look, she pushed past Niels and continued down the hall, shouting her daughter's name. But she didn't get far before a security guard emerged from the shadows and blocked her path. For a moment, she seemed poised to lunge at the guard's throat, but stopped short and whirled to face them.

'All right, I'll go. You can call off your thugs.'

That mouth, that sneer. Erin's heart missed a beat. Only

after the woman was escorted to the door and through the front gate could she breathe normally.

Cassie.

She hurried to the girl's room. Still asleep, her wan face framed by the sad tufts of hair. Erin smoothed the blanket under her chin. 'You're safe here,' she whispered. 'I'll protect you.' A prickling sensation needled her palms.

You wish. No one is safe.

That voice again – whose?

She covered her ears to smother the sound. Cassie *was* safe. Of course she was. As long as she remained within the Meadows' sheltered embrace. Out in the world, that's where the trouble began.

* * *

Curled in the window seat in her office upstairs, Erin studied the snowy grounds, silent under an oyster-coloured sky. It was quiet enough to hear a clock ticking, but there were no clocks here, nothing to show the passage of time. The scarlet flash of a cardinal provided the only bright spot in the wintry landscape. In the stillness, the stone manor felt more like an English country house than a psychiatric hospital.

Her eyelids drooped. What little rest she'd managed to get last night was on the hard leather sofa in the corner of her office. Not an auspicious start to what was supposed to be a day of celebration. After three months of intensive treatment, one of her patients, a girl named Sara whom they'd almost lost, was well enough to go home.

'Knock, knock.' Niels stood in the doorway, waving an envelope like a flag. 'This came yesterday. I meant to drop it by earlier, but with all the ruckus last night and this morning, I plain forgot.' In two quick strides, he crossed the space between them. 'I had a heads-up on this last week. Pre-approved by the board.'

Erin rose from the window seat and took the envelope

with a twinge of foreboding. It must be one of those *pro bono* things she'd agreed to when they hired her. A worthy initiative, at least in principle, but so far she'd managed to avoid any cases. What with settling into the clinic's routines and her own patients to care for – wasn't that why the board had wooed her away from London? – there was little time for anything else.

She glanced at the return address: Greenlake Psychiatric Facility, Atherton, New York.

Greenlake? The name rang a bell, but it wasn't always called that. Atherton State Asylum for the Criminally Insane, that's what it was, back in the day. Before asylums were repackaged as psychiatric hospitals to lessen the taint of notoriety, though the name change was often little more than window dressing. 'Isn't that a forensic facility?'

'Sure is.' He cocked an eyebrow. 'Right up your alley.'

She dropped the envelope as if stung. 'I don't handle criminal cases.' She busied herself with some papers on her desk to avoid his eyes. 'Not any more.' Certainly not if they involved violently disturbed men.

'Do me a favour and say yes to this one.' He popped a breath mint in his mouth. 'The board meets next week. It will be awkward to tell them you haven't signed onto a project yet.'

He had a point. A certain amount of community outreach was a condition of her employment, and she'd already turned down three requests. But nothing in her contract mentioned anything like this.

'If it helps, the director at Greenlake asked for you personally.' Niels parked his hip on her desk and crunched the mint between his teeth.

'Me?' Who even knew she was here?

'Some guy named Harrison. Said you'd be perfect for this.'

A muscle twitched near her eye. She didn't know anyone named Harrison.

She waited for Niels's footsteps to die away before carrying the Greenlake file to the window, where the light was better. She hadn't meant to read it straight away, but thought it best to know what she was in for. With a letter opener, she sliced through the flap, nicking her finger. A bead of blood formed on her skin, and she licked it away.

Dear Dr Cartwright… On behalf of the State of New York, I am writing to request your services in the matter of a patient.

It was worse than she thought. A forensic patient up for release required an independent psychiatric evaluation. White male, aged 43. Incarcerated since 1978 for the murders of his mother and two sisters. The letter was signed by a Dr Robert K Harrison. How could he claim to know her when she'd only been back in the country a few months? The name meant nothing.

She sank onto the window seat and leaned against the glass. Set amongst the shimmering snowfields, the wrought-iron gazebo resembled a colossal birdcage dropped from the sky.

White male, 43. Mother and sisters brutally slain. A patient with that particular history was out of the question.

It was unlikely Niels knew about her role in the Leonard Whidby case, though it might have been notorious enough to reach the newspapers in the States. And she had no intention of telling him. Why dig up old wounds? One thing was certain, though. She hadn't returned to America after twenty years to work with the criminally insane.

2

A knock on the door jolted Erin back to the present, just in time to greet Sara Henley as she was ushered into the room by her case manager. She shoved the Greenlake file under the desk blotter and greeted the young girl with a smile.

Close to dying three months ago, Sara had made a spectacular turnaround. Along with the entire staff, Erin was thrilled, but also relieved that her groundbreaking treatment, Family Identity Therapy, had delivered as promised. But what should have been a joyous occasion was tainted by the looming spectre of the Greenlake case.

'Come on in, Sara.' Erin guided the girl to a pair of oversized armchairs upholstered in a cheerful apricot paisley. Though fragile still, with legs like pipe cleaners in her tight pink leggings, Sara had made great progress at the clinic. A curated programme of music and bodywork, nourishing meals from their in-house chef, and Erin's own brand of therapy, had pulled her out of danger.

A residential patient's last day was always an achievement to celebrate. Though Erin couldn't help but worry that Sara's hard-won health would start to unravel, one strand at a time, the moment she left the Meadows' cloistered domain. Fraught with taboos and tacit expectations, not to mention anxious parents who often did more harm than good, the home environment could pick apart months of careful work.

As Sara settled in the chair and tucked her legs beneath her, Erin's thoughts drifted to the Greenlake file, lurking under the blotter like a scorpion poised to strike. *White male, 43. Mother and sisters brutally slain.*

She forced her attention back to the girl in front of her. Whatever she said to Sara during the all-important discharge meeting would set the tone for the rest of her recovery. She exhaled slowly. *Do not blow this.*

'This is a big day for you.'

Sara's lip trembled. It was clear she was struggling not to cry as she clutched a squashy blue pillow on her lap.

At Sara's age, where had she been? A locked room with stained walls. The stink of despair. Disembodied faces peering through a narrow pane of glass. No soft pillows or smiling therapists.

Erin folded her hands in her lap. 'What are you looking forward to when you get home?'

Sara's eyes were the soft grey of a pigeon's wing. 'Hugging my dog. Art class with Mr Mulder. He's the coolest teacher at school.' She blushed and plucked at a loose thread on her sleeve.

A blast of wind rattled the windows, startling them both. Erin hurried to close the curtains against the darkening sky. Alert to the mood in the room, a shifting tapestry of anxiety and optimism, she touched Sara on the shoulder before returning to the chair.

'We've been on an extraordinary journey, haven't we?' Battling ogres, outwitting demons, slaying dragons. Or so it seemed.

Together, they stared at the flickering candle between them. On discharge day, it was a challenge to strike the right note. Some of her colleagues opted for a matter-of-fact approach, hoping to avert a full-on meltdown. But Erin relied on intuition as her guide, and it was clear Sara needed something more than a pat on the back and a cheery 'off you go'.

Though a final send-off it wasn't. For the next six months Sara would continue as an outpatient, travelling once a week to the clinic from her home on Long Island. A dangerous time, the first few weeks back with the family, when the risk of relapse was high. *Going home*. It shouldn't be so hard, but it always was.

As she blinked away her tears, Sara's glance shifted to the bookcase, though there was little of interest to see. No photos. Nothing of a personal nature. Better to be a blank slate, Erin felt, lest her patients assign her qualities or quirks she didn't have.

Was Sara reliving the events that had brought her here? Sick since she was twelve, a quarter of her body weight lost in a single year. Her mother furious (*just eat!*), her father distraught. Packed off to the Meadows in desperation, where she was placed in the care of Greta Kozani. A costly mistake. Under Greta's clumsy ministrations, Sara had failed to thrive. Though she hadn't any proof, Erin suspected that Greta's treatment methods involved an odious form of shaming.

As if reading her thoughts, Sara said, 'I'm glad they switched me to you.'

That Sara wasn't ready to leave them was clear. But it was time.

'I have something for you.' From her desk, Erin retrieved a black velvet box. Gifts to patients were against the rules, but this was such a small token, she didn't think anyone would make a fuss. A corner of the Greenlake file poked out from under the blotter. *Mother and sisters brutally slain.* Erin shoved the file out of sight. She placed the box in Sara's hand. 'Go ahead, open it.'

Nestled on a scrap of white satin, a green and gold bird of paradise, its wings aloft, glinted in the light. Sara lifted the fine gold chain and held it in the air. 'It's pretty. Shall I put it on?'

'Better wait till you get home.' Erin smiled. 'It's meant to remind you how far you've come. How strong you are.'

On a chain round her neck, hidden under the navy wool jumper, Erin had a talisman of her own. A silver pendant in the shape of a quetzal, a gift from a Mayan healer she'd met at a street market in Córdoba. *Por qué estas triste?* Why are you so sad? he'd asked, pressing it into her hand. Seventeen and on the run. She never took it off.

* * *

At reception, a man in a blue-striped shirt was chatting with Greta Kozani. Stuffed into a black crepe dress better suited to a funeral than a clinic, Greta tapped the man flirtatiously on the arm. Erin felt a twinge of annoyance. Where was Sara's mother? That she couldn't be bothered to collect her own daughter was a bad sign, but not a complete surprise. During family counselling sessions, she had come across as rigid and withholding. Erin could only hope the father provided the love and acceptance Sara so desperately needed.

'I can't thank you enough, Dr Kozani. You and Dr Cartwright, of course,' he said, when he caught sight of Erin. 'It's wonderful to see Sara like her old self again. My wife and I are so relieved.'

Heat flooded Erin's face. It was childish to care, but how typical – and shameful – of Greta to take the credit for Sara's recovery. If Erin hadn't taken over, Sara would have died.

* * *

Erin looked through the peephole of the observation room. Cassie was awake. Her dark eyes flicked from the window to the door. Was she hoping to make a run for it? But there was no way out, not from this room. No dangling cords or sharp objects, and the window fitted with safety glass. It would be difficult for Cassie to harm herself in here. By law, they could hold her for seventy-two hours. But thirteen were already gone, and the clock was ticking.

A wintry sun cast a weak light into the room. Out in the hall, a resounding tone from the brass Tibetan bowl signalled the start of the midday meal.

Erin pulled a chair close to the bed.

'You gave us quite a scare last night.'

Cassie coughed and struggled to sit. 'Where am I?'

She handed her a cup of water. 'You're in a clinic called the Meadows.'

Shock marred her features. 'You mean I'm locked up. Like, with crazy people?'

It was a good thing Erin had the foresight to remove her doctor's coat. White coats tended to upset new patients. Hadn't they all seen their share of horror films? Defenceless souls spirited away in the dead of night by white-coated men.

'You're not locked up. And no one here is crazy.'

'I heard someone shouting.'

Erin cast about for an excuse. 'One of our staff slipped on the ice and sprained her ankle.' It sounded lame, even to her own ears. She'd always been a terrible liar.

'Right, whatever.' Cassie fell back on the pillow. 'Did Lonnie put me in here?' Her hand jerked to the cropped hair. 'She's going to kill me.'

'Lonnie? You mean your mother?'

'*Foster* mother. She gets a kick out of claiming she's my real mother. Like she's Mother effing Teresa or something.' Cassie picked at the raw skin on her thumb. 'Always threatening to have me locked up.'

Erin tensed. If Cassie was telling the truth, this Lonnie woman was worse than she'd thought. She reached for her hand, but Cassie flinched and pulled away.

'Can you tell me about last night?'

Silence. She might have been talking to a stone.

Cassie squinted at the chipped blue polish on her nails. 'So, if I'm not locked up, I can go home, right?'

'Not quite yet. We need to understand what happened first.'

'I was totally wasted. Obviously.' She exhaled noisily. 'But I'm fine now.'

To give her some space, Erin moved to the window and considered her next move. Getting anyone to admit they needed help was the difficult, but essential, first step on the road to recovery. Unless Cassie chose to let Erin in, she'd continue to resist any attempt to reach her.

'You're not fine.'

Cassie refused to meet her eye.

'You were found passed out in the snow by the front gate. It was only dumb luck that one of our staff spotted you.' Erin allowed this to sink in. 'If he hadn't…'

Silence, thick as fog.

'Did you want to die?'

'No.' Her eyelids snapped open. 'Can I go home now?'

From her spot by the window, Erin watched the clouds move in, bearing a fresh cargo of snow. 'You mixed alcohol and pills.' She paused. 'A dangerous combination.'

Cassie closed her eyes and turned away.

This was the hardest part. Waiting for the brittle shell of denial to crack and fall away. Without a connection to the patient, however fragile, she'd get nowhere. Much of her work involved watching and waiting. For a bridge to appear in the mist, a light to blink on.

But Cassie was done talking. As she slid under the blanket and turned her face to the wall, Erin felt a pang of disappointment.

At the door, she hesitated, waiting to be called back. If the clock ran out before they got through to her, Cassie would walk out the front door and slip from their grasp. Any chance to save her would be gone.

3

Erin jotted a few notes in Cassie's file. *Awake, angry, won't talk. What's she hiding?* In the music room, someone was plonking out discordant notes on the piano. It was impossible to think straight. Not with the Greenlake file trapped under the desk blotter. She slid it free and snapped it open. A grainy photo, like a bad mugshot, was stapled to the inside cover. Muddy-brown hair. Deep-set eyes of an indeterminate colour. A sickle-shaped scar high on the left cheek. A summary of the patient's arrest and trial followed, accompanied by a medical history.

Over the years, the patient's diagnoses had managed to hit all points of the compass – *reactive psychosis, schizoaffective disorder, schizophrenia, paranoid personality disorder, paranoid schizophrenia*. As if his doctors were a band of wanderers struggling to find a path through the darkness. The patient, Timothy Warren Stern, Jnr, was scheduled to appear before a judge on the 30th of June, as the final step in his petition for release.

With a flicker of unease, Erin tossed the file on her desk. Why this, why now? Nearly four months back in the country, and her anxiety about returning to America was finally on the wane. It helped that everyone thought she was born and bred in England. A risky strategy, but a means of avoiding bothersome questions about her family and a past she wished to forget.

Her new role at the Meadows was any therapist's idea of a dream job, and she'd been conscious in the first weeks of the need to make a good impression. With the clinic's vast endowment, they could treat any girl in need, regardless of the ability to pay. Unlike the Thornbury in London, with its fiscal hardship and penny-pinching ways. And what a relief to be freed from working under the thumb of the Thornbury's director. Not that Julian was a tyrant. More like a martinet who never failed to remind her of her place in the pecking order and that she'd better think twice before challenging him.

She should be overjoyed, but the Greenlake case threatened to torpedo everything. She angled the photo towards the light. Pale skin. A blank stare. It was the Whidby case all over again. Her instincts were off that time, when youth and inexperience had given her an overconfidence she hadn't earned. Faced with a similar scenario, how could she be sure her instincts wouldn't be off again? She hadn't even met the patient and already her inclination was to keep him locked up. A clear conflict of interest, surely, and the perfect excuse to refuse the case. Niels couldn't argue with that.

She turned to the window. In the middle of the vast grounds, the branches of the big copper beech swayed and creaked in the cold. After locking the Greenlake file in a drawer, she opened the blinds wide to let in more light. The clouds sweeping in from the river shed a few flakes of snow that soon became a torrent.

Three o'clock. She would give Cassie until five to consider her options. Then, ready or not, she would have to talk.

* * *

By the time Erin hurried into the coffee house, half-frozen from battling the snow, Niels was already seated by the window. A short walk from the clinic, the newly opened establishment was a beacon of warmth in an otherwise deserted street. For Niels to suggest they meet here to discuss Cassie Gray wasn't all that unusual – he liked to mix things up a bit – but in this case, it seemed like a ploy. Erin had a feeling she wasn't going to like what he had to say.

She shrugged off her parka and slung it over the back of a chair. Other than an elderly woman in a red scarf, warming her hands on a mug of coffee, they were the only customers. Niels closed his notebook and slid it into the pocket of his shirt.

'Tough case at St Vincent's.' He rubbed his eyes. 'Sixteen years old. Poor girl thought one of the staff was her father and she practically tore the place down. It's her second psychotic episode, with no signs of mania, so I'm pretty sure we're dealing with schizophrenia.'

While she studied the menu, Erin listened with half an ear to his rundown of the case. Twenty types of coffee with all the bells and whistles, but only a single choice of tea. With any luck it was a proper blend, and not a stale teabag scrounged from the back of a cupboard.

'It always goes back to the parents, doesn't it?' she murmured, placing the menu on the table.

'Not with psychosis.'

His tone was sharp, and she suppressed a sigh. *Here we go again*. When it came to mental illness, Niels leaned heavily on the side of biology. Brain chemistry first, psychodynamics second. Which put them in opposite corners of the therapeutic map. Though family wasn't the only source of their patients' woes, it played a significant part. And much of their work, whether Niels cared to admit it or not, involved protecting their patients from the very people meant to nurture them.

'Though in this case,' he said, flicking a crumb off the table, 'it does appear that childhood trauma is a factor.'

Across the street, the abandoned warehouses and woollen mills from the city's industrial past imparted an aura of desolation to this section of the riverfront. A plough rumbled past, heaping dirty snow across the pavement. A barista with a painful-looking eyebrow piercing set a mug of hot water on the table, with the inevitable bag of Lipton balanced on a saucer. How Erin longed for a proper cup of tea, a rich blend of Assam and Ceylon brewed in a pot.

Niels pointed to the mug. 'A tea drinker in the land of coffee addicts.' He slurped his cappuccino. 'You miss London?'

'Sometimes.' She poured milk in her tea. 'Not the rain, though. Or the Tube breakdowns. But a good pot of tea, yes.' Had she hit all the right clichés? Bad weather, the London Underground, afternoon tea. Anything else might unleash a rash of unwelcome questions.

He wiped a spot of foam from his lip. Freckles dusted the back of his pale hands, the nails clean and neatly trimmed. Not the hands of a Nebraska farm boy, although mucking out stalls and driving a tractor may not have been on his roster of chores.

'But you've been to the States before, right?'

Her face grew hot. 'Sure. Medical conferences, mainly. Chicago, San Francisco.' She made a show of rummaging through her bag to shut down the questions. Amongst the crumpled receipts and tubes of lip balm, she located a notebook and snapped it open. 'Can we talk about Cassie Gray now? We're running out of time.'

'Time for what?' His face was blank, but then the light dawned. 'You mean put her on a hold?' He stirred more sugar in his cup. 'She said the pills were an accident not a suicide attempt.'

'She talked to you?' Erin felt stung. Why would Cassie open up to Niels and not to her? Her ability to bond quickly with a patient had always been a source of professional pride.

'Sure. I couldn't get her to stop. Said she was at a friend's, where they took some pills from the mom's medicine cabinet. Later on, they snuck into a club, where they drank a bucketload of tequila.'

'Did she say what happened to her hair?'

'A joke that got out of hand.' He popped the rest of a

brownie in his mouth. 'As for the home situation, she claims she and her mother are the best of friends.'

'*Foster* mother.'

He licked chocolate from his thumb. 'Foster mother? She didn't mention that.'

What was Cassie playing at? 'Okay,' Erin said. 'Let's say, for the sake of argument, she's not a suicide risk, but she still needs help. If not for the drinking and pills, then for the cutting. Did you see her arms? If that's not a clear sign of something wrong, I don't know what is.'

'I didn't say she doesn't need help.' Niels knocked back the last of his coffee. 'But it's not enough to put her on a hold.'

'I know that, it's just… I have a bad feeling about what might happen if we send her home.'

Niels paid the bill and pocketed the receipt. 'If it makes you feel better, I'll have Janine contact social services for a copy of her file.' In a hurry to leave now, he stood and zipped his parka to his chin. 'Was there something about Cassie's mother that bothered you?'

Foster mother. 'Nothing specific,' Erin said, gathering her things. 'Just the shock, I guess, what with her charging into the clinic like that, all teeth and claws.'

'Teeth and claws?'

'You saw her.'

'What I saw was a frightened parent.'

Clearly, she and Niels operated on a different playing field. If it were up to her, she'd place Cassie on a temporary hold, and then admit her to their three-month residential programme. But her hands were tied. As the clinic's director, Niels had the final say.

Out on the street, the air was sharp as glass. Together, they turned into the wind and plodded through the drifting snow.

'What's the word on the Greenlake case?'

'I haven't decided yet.' She drew her scarf over her frozen lips.

'Look, I know it's a hassle, but it's part of the deal. If the Mr

Moneybags supporting the clinic expects a little community work, who are we to complain?'

By the time they arrived at the Meadows' wrought-iron gate, flanked on either side by a towering yew hedge, Erin could no longer feel her fingers. Through the bars, she could just make out a corner of the glass conservatory, built as an extension on the east wing, an enticing sanctuary in winter, with its profusion of orchids and potted palms. The library and music room, the oil paintings and private chef, the exquisitely decorated patient rooms, all of it paid for by a mysterious benefactor, who preferred to remain anonymous.

She shivered in the biting cold. 'I'll let you know on Monday.'

'Great.' He slipped his key into the lock. 'I'm looking forward to giving the board the good news.'

* * *

Cassie was out of bed and standing by the window, the sheets and blanket in a tangle on the floor.

'You're up,' Erin said, hanging back, afraid to do anything that might spook her. 'You must be feeling better.' The silence lengthened. 'Cassie?'

'I'm fine.' She whipped around, her face taut with anger. 'When can I go home?'

'I can't help you if you won't talk to me.'

'Who says I need help?' Her knees buckled, and she grabbed the windowsill.

Erin hurried towards her, but Cassie waved her away.

'I'm not getting back in that bed.'

'How about a compromise?' Erin dragged the armchair to the window. 'You sit here, and I'll back off.' She perched on the bed, trying to make eye contact, but Cassie kept her face turned away. 'What's at home that you're so anxious to get back to? A boyfriend? Your foster mother?'

'Lonnie? Uh, no.' Cassie curled her lip. 'The minute I walk through the door, she'll probably beat the crap out of me.'

Erin stiffened. 'If she's abusing you, we'll need to file a report with social services.'

'You want to help me?' Cassie bent over and yanked off the clinic's white socks. 'Don't do anything stupid like call social services. Lonnie's got her problems, but she's better than some. It could be much, much worse.'

Lonnie of the slitted eyes and acid tongue. Erin shuddered to think of the life Cassie had led. Neglected. Abused. Shunted from one foster home to another. A copy of her file would give them a better idea what they were dealing with.

'I'll let you rest now.'

'Whatever.'

At the door, Erin turned back. Slumped in the chair, Cassie's face was slack with fatigue, but her eyes were watchful, alert to the smallest sign of danger. A posture Erin knew well.

'How long have you been in the system?'

'Forever.' Cassie opened her eyes wide and cocked her head. 'I was a dumpster baby. Happy now?'

4

Hunched against the wind, Erin stumbled on the blocks of frozen snow at the edge of the car park. How easy it would be to slip and break her neck out here. And who would find her in time? The green bobble hat and mittens she'd bought at a Christmas market in Galway offered poor protection from the freezing air. The driver's seat creaked with cold. By the time Erin inched her car through the icy streets and pulled in front of her building, it was after eight.

The three-storey Victorian house, welcoming enough in daylight, looked bleak and deserted in the dark. A dim bulb on the front porch provided the only light. Long since divided into flats, the house had entered what appeared to be the final stage of its demise. Had it been an option, she would have jumped at the chance to live on the grounds of the Meadows, like Niels, who had a flat in the former carriage house at the edge of the estate. She'd never been inside but imagined it as spacious and light-filled, with a sleek modern kitchen and expansive view of the gardens. How wonderful that would be, freed from the daily battle of the snowy streets. She'd forgotten how brutal the winters were in this part of the world.

The porch railings shuddered in the wind. Moss-green paint flaked off the window frames. But if Erin ignored the scabby paint and neglected garden, the flat ticked all the boxes on her wish list. A private entrance, windows on all sides, and an unobstructed view of the river. A young couple from Honduras, with a baby on the way, lived in the flat below. Her own section of the house spanned the entire top floor, with nothing above her but an empty attic. Mrs Deptford, the elderly widow who rented out the upstairs flats, was thrilled to have Erin as a tenant.

'How I love an English accent,' she'd said when they first met. 'You sound just like Mary Poppins.' Her eyes had lit up when Erin told her why she'd come to Lansford. 'What a marvellous thing, helping young girls in need. I've always wondered what went on over there, behind that great big yew hedge. Though I still remember when it was a private home, back in my schooldays. Some bigwig from the city would spend summers there with his family. Oh, the parties they held out on the lawns… I would lie in bed and listen to the band play into the wee hours.' She passed her hand over her eyes. 'What was their name? Harkness, Hartford. Something like that. I'm afraid my memory's not what it was.'

Easy enough for Erin to imagine what the house was like as a wealthy man's summer retreat. The gloss and the glamour. 'It's been a private clinic for nearly ten years now,' she'd said.

'Well, all I can say is, it's nice to know the old manor is being put to good use. So many of those homes from the glory days of the robber barons have fallen into ruin. Have you driven by the old Bennett estate up the river? Such a lovely place that was. A family home from way back, and then a girls' college in the fifties. But the only thing it's fit for now is the wrecking ball.'

* * *

Under the mournful gaze of her landlady's cocker spaniel, Erin checked the letter box on the front porch, though there was never any post. Except for the phone company, no one had her home address, and she preferred it that way. In her first few weeks back in the country, reeling with culture shock and tinged with an uneasy dread, she'd lost confidence in her ability to pull off her pose as an Englishwoman. Though her accent came naturally after twenty years in Britain, ever since moving to Lansford, the cadence and vocabulary of American speech threatened to return. Though no one had doubted her story so far, she instinctively kept her distance. How shocked the Meadows' staff would be if they discovered she was American as apple pie, born and raised in a small town not three hours' drive away.

Before passing through the narrow strip of dirty snow that led to the entrance to her flat, she glanced back at the street. No shadows lurked in the shrubbery, no car idled at the kerb. Safe to scurry to the door and unlock the deadbolt she'd installed on the day she moved in.

As she climbed the stairs, her thoughts shifted from the day's worries to the pleasures of a hot bath and an early night.

Once through the double-locked door, Erin set her bag down and shut the curtains, before turning on the lights. Only after a quick peek in the closets and under the bed was she able to relax. That she sometimes felt compelled to check the flat twice or three times before going to bed was bothersome, but not enough to do anything about. Long ago she'd sworn off anti-anxiety drugs of any kind. The furred tongue and foggy brain. *Never again*.

In the kitchen, the cupboards were bare. A box of crackers, a handful of black olives, and a wedge of cheese too small to satisfy a mouse were all she had to eat. She'd meant to shop yesterday but had stayed late at the clinic to comfort one of her patients.

Running out of food was a bad sign. She usually kept the pantry well-stocked. A holdover from childhood, where locked kitchen cupboards were the norm, and her portions strictly monitored. At least there was a bottle of Cabernet in the fridge, still half-full. She poured out a glass and carried it to the window. Through a gap in the blinds, she scrutinised the darkened house across the alley. Her neighbour, a large man with a penchant for plaid shirts and tracksuit bottoms, kept odd hours. On nights she couldn't sleep, she liked to stand by the window, waiting for a sign of life. The blue glow of the television or the flare of a match.

Stuffed into her shoulder bag, the two items she'd been avoiding all day called out to her. The Greenlake file and a thick envelope from Julian that arrived in yesterday's post. Which was the lesser evil? She placed them side by side on the heavy oak table. Door number one or door number two?

Physician, heal thyself.

Hannah's voice. Wise counsellor, fairy godmother. It was Hannah who'd pulled her back from the ledge when Erin, a university student in Bristol, was still reeling from the demons that had chased her across the Atlantic. When had they last spoken? Tomorrow, without fail, she would send a detailed missive to her friend.

With Hannah's voice urging her on, she pulled the tab off the bulky envelope from London. A cascade of glossy reprints spilled out onto the table. Copies of her latest publication. Always a thrill to receive them. But what was this? At the sight of Julian's name listed as first author, a flicker of rage spread through her chest. Once again, he'd given himself top billing for her work. Did the man have no shame? One of the many reasons she'd been more than ready to put the Thornbury Clinic behind her. A piece of paper, torn from a yellow notepad, fluttered to the floor.

Hello E. – I hope you're settled in by now and are happy in your new role. How do you find life in America? I do hope they're treating you well over there. I'm sure I don't need to tell you again how sorry I was to see you go, but it's good to know you're continuing our work on the other side of the pond. I've no doubt the Board of Directors at the Meadows recognises what a coup it is to have a Royal College of

Medicine honouree on their staff. Rather impressive, indeed, and they're lucky to have you.

I've enclosed reprints of the Anorexia *paper for your files. I meant to get them to you sooner, but things have been rather chaotic around here. On the home front, Amanda has finally moved out, after months of wavering, so there's that as well.*

Congrats once again on an excellent publication (and don't think I've forgotten you contributed the lion's share on this). Keep me posted on your new life.

Warmest wishes, J.

P.S. You're sorely missed around here – the clinic isn't the same without you...

She dropped the note on the table. *The lion's share?* When he'd done nothing beyond his minimal role as supervisor. The man was infuriating. And what was that annoying 'J' scrawled at the bottom of the page. A misguided attempt at intimacy? How like Julian to wait until she was safely on the other side of the Atlantic to make his move. Not that there was the slightest chance she'd ever reciprocate.

Out front, the street was empty, the cracked pavement rimed with frost. Shadows flickered on the ground by the rubbish bins. *Rats?* Or some other unsavoury vermin. Snowflakes drifted through the air. Across the street, the windows were dark. Before closing the curtains, she checked the pavement again. The shadows by the rubbish bins were gone.

The Greenlake file was next. Though she had no intention of taking the case, it was essential she come up with a plausible excuse for Niels. She carried the file and a glass of wine to the sofa.

Timothy Warren Stern, Jnr. Born July 18, 1960, in Brookline, Massachusetts. The murders of his mother and sisters were committed on August 26, 1977, in the family home at 44 Easton Road, Belle River, Maine.

Belle River? She squinted at the photo. Timothy Warren Stern. *Tim Stern.* A chill snaked down her spine. She knew him, or of him. Scenes from childhood summers in Belle River vaulted through her head. She dropped the file and closed her eyes. But this was good news, wasn't it? She was off the hook. That she knew the patient, however marginally, was an obvious conflict of interest. Now she could decline the request with a clear conscience.

Except she couldn't. How could she admit a connection to a patient from Maine when Niels thought she'd grown up in England? And that bogus story she'd told him about her family. An only child, her parents happily retired and living in a seaside village in Sussex. All lies. If she came clean, she'd be reported as a fraud, struck off the register, and hustled onto the next plane to Heathrow. An ignominious end to a stellar career, of everything she'd ever worked for.

Deep in the cellar, the ancient boiler grumbled to life. *Tim Stern*. She closed her eyes, trying to conjure a face. A shaggy-haired boy… in some kind of hat? Lurking behind a counter. Amongst a tangle of synapses, the apparition briefly sparked and faded away.

She'd have to invent another reason to refuse the case. Her history with Leonard Whidby might be something she could work with, though she'd hoped to keep that notorious blot on her record under wraps. In the morning, when her head was clearer, she'd formulate a plan. In the meantime, an invisible force drove her back to the file on the table.

The Stern murders. Impossible to summon a clear-cut memory of the crime, having only learned about it years after the fact. Belle River was a small town, so she must have seen Tim Stern before, even if she couldn't remember his face. She flipped to the photo – slack jaw, hooded eyes – before taking the plunge and reading straight through.

August 1977. The mother and sisters brutally slain. Tim's flight across the state. His arrest and trial. The verdict of not guilty by reason of insanity. Incarceration at Greenlake, formerly Atherton State Asylum, a maximum-security psychiatric facility in upstate New York. The father, out of town on business when the crime occurred, had not testified at the trial. When it was over, he'd sold the family home and moved out West. Where exactly, the file didn't say.

And while all that was going on, where was she? Trapped in that house on Gardiner Road, struggling to survive. She rested her head on her arms and listened to the tick of snow on the window. Was it a mistake to come back? Twenty years ago, she'd bolted from the country, like a frightened deer fleeing a fire. Would the new life she'd created from the ashes of those early years, one painstaking day at a time, come crashing down, just when she thought she was free?

From under her jumper, she pulled out the silver quetzal, totem bird of the Mayans, and held it in her hand.

Please, let me be okay. Please.

An appeal to… what, or whom? A confirmed rationalist, she didn't really believe anything – or anyone – was listening. But praying to something, however vague, was a childish habit she'd yet to relinquish. Even though, in her heart, she knew that a lump of metal, however cherished, could not keep the past where it belonged.

She switched off the light and peeked through the blinds at her neighbour's flat across the alley. All was dark.

In the morning, she would tell Niels she wasn't taking the case.

5

The observation room was empty. The bed freshly made with a clean white sheet and the clinic's monogrammed green blanket. That could only mean one thing: that Cassie had agreed to treatment and was transferred to one of the rooms upstairs. Erin was giddy with relief. Whatever she'd said to her yesterday must have got through.

At reception, Janine was on the phone and signalled for her to wait. By the time she hung up, Erin was fizzing with adrenaline, already designing Cassie's treatment programme in her head. When was the last time she'd felt this keenly about a patient?

She leaned over the counter, trying to catch a glimpse of the intake list. 'Where have they put Cassie Gray?' Erin hoped they'd given her the Larkspur room on the second floor. With its walls of primrose yellow and large windows overlooking the river, it was the nicest of the patient rooms upstairs.

'Cassie Gray?' Janine scrolled through the roster. 'I don't see her on the list.' She leaned closer to the screen. 'It says here she was discharged this morning.'

'Discharged? On whose orders?'

'Dr Westlund's.' A worried look clouded Janine's eyes. 'Is something wrong? I'm sure he said—'

But Erin was gone, sprinting up the staircase to Niels's

office. She rapped on the door and flung it open without waiting for a reply.

Perched behind an outsized mahogany desk, Niels stared at her, open-mouthed. One of his patients, a tiny, freckled girl from Ohio, who suffered from agoraphobia along with a host of other anxieties, sat primly in one of the big leather chairs.

Erin hesitated. Interrupting a patient session was a grievous flouting of the rules, but this couldn't wait. 'Sorry to interrupt, but I need to speak with you.'

Niels's face was rigid. 'I'm with a patient.' Each word bitten off like thread.

'I only need a minute.'

He turned to the girl in the chair. 'Hold that thought, Lisa. I'll be back in a flash.'

Niels hustled Erin into the hall and closed the door, his lips pressed into a thin line. But if he was annoyed, she was boiling with anger. What right did he have to discharge a patient without consulting her?

'Why did you send Cassie home?'

'Is that what this is about?' He gave her an exasperated look. 'It was time. And there was no clear indication she's a suicide risk.'

'She's at risk of something. What about the foster mother? Cassie said the woman hit her. I can only imagine what else she does behind closed doors.'

'Foster mother?' He rocked back on his heels. 'Oh, right. Janine called social services for a copy of Cassie's file, and get this, they've never heard of her. She's not a foster kid. Not adopted. Lonnie Tyler is Cassie's real mother.' He looked almost gleeful as he imparted the news. 'Quite a little tale she spun for you.'

A pain bloomed in Erin's chest. The hints of abuse. That bit about being a dumpster baby. All lies. And to what purpose?

'Even so,' she said, struggling to regain her composure, 'you could have given me a heads-up before sending her home.' But her words fell flat, even to her own ears. *I'm an idiot*. How easily she'd been duped. And yet… that Cassie felt compelled to lie could be taken as a cry for help. 'I just hope the next time we see her,' Erin said, trying for one last shot across the bow, 'it won't be in the morgue.'

'Unless she seeks help on her own, there's nothing more we can do for her.' He met her look head-on. 'We did everything we could.'

Blood rushed to Erin's face. She was in no mood to be reasonable. 'Just so you know,' she said, 'I won't be taking the Greenlake case.'

He had opened the door to his office, but pulled it hastily closed. 'Why? It's just a formality. Two or three days of your time, tops.'

'A formality?' Three people were brutally killed. And the man responsible could be released into the community on her recommendation. It was hardly a formality. Not when lives were at stake. 'I have a conflict of interest.'

His mouth twitched. 'Then take it up with the head at Greenlake. If he's got a problem with it, I'd like to have it in writing. In the meantime, I'm going to tell the board you're taking the case.'

* * *

Too upset to return to her office, Erin escaped to the soothing hush of the conservatory, hoping the tropical air and lush greenery would calm her down. Lately, Niels seemed to take pleasure in pushing her buttons. When they'd first met during the hiring process, his dedication to patient care, coupled with an affable nature, made for a winning combination. She thought they'd get along famously, but his handling of Cassie's case revealed a side of Niels she hadn't seen before.

She closed her eyes and allowed the enticing scent of citrus blossoms to transport her through time. A long-ago summer holiday in Crete, where she'd wandered through a lemon grove under a coppery sun, the blue Aegean glittering in the distance. Through half-open lids, she scanned the sky with its darkening clouds. More snow was forecast for the afternoon. She pressed her palm to the cold glass and shivered.

White male, 43. Mother and sisters brutally slain.

The branches of the chestnut trees scrabbled against the sky. Near the fountain, the naked limbs of a clump of hydrangeas shook in the wind, while the bronze dolphins and leaping sea sprites, glazed with ice, seemed oblivious to the weather.

Cassie was gone. Sara, discharged. Her three remaining patients, all suffering from various degrees of anorexia, were settled into their treatment programmes. She could afford to take a day and drive upstate to Greenlake. Once she'd met this Dr Harrison, she would invent a story to explain her connection to the patient – over from England with her family for a holiday in Belle River, the same year as the murders. Small world, isn't it? – and excuse herself from the case. As long as the threatened storm didn't block the roads, she could leave for Greenlake first thing in the morning and return to Lansford by late afternoon. Up and back in a single day. And that would be the end of it.

6

Belle River, Maine
August 1977

A kinetic knot of pre-teen girls hover by the ticket booth, passing around a tube of cherry lip gloss. Cascades of hair gleam under the lights. A girl with a pageboy haircut lingers by the door, plump arms clamped across her chest. She sneaks longing glances at the other girls, but they smirk and dance away.

Their shrieks of laughter hurt his ears. The light stabs his eyes. Four hours and sixteen minutes to go till his shift is over.

He's dumping popcorn into a carton when a gang of local boys swagger in. Denim jackets glazed with rainwater. Sly flasks of whisky shoved into the waistband of their jeans.

Rat-a-tat-tat. A pewter ring in the shape of a skull whacks the counter. Eyes like silverfish. Wild blond hair. The one they call the Viking.

'Can I get some service over here, or what?'

A curvy, sloe-eyed girl in a yellow sundress is clamped to the boy's side. *History girl.* Angela. His heart teeters from its perch… and dies. On a pollen-filled afternoon in May, she'd smiled at him once.

'Hey, dickhead.' Stubby fingers stained with engine oil snap in his face. 'You on something? Gimme two Cokes and a box of popcorn. Make it a large, on the house.' The furtive smirk turns sour. 'You lookin' at my girl?'

Like a whipped dog, he lowers his eyes and hands over the popcorn. Later, he'll put the money in the till from his own pocket. He wouldn't want Mack to think he was stealing.

In a haze of cigarette smoke and laughter, the gang disappear into the dark. That skinny boy from biology class, his greasy brown hair tied back with a rawhide cord, who everyone calls the Duke, turns back and snickers. 'Moron.'

Angela tosses him a shy look over her shoulder. He signals with his eyes, *I will save you.* But she slips through the red velvet curtains, forever lost.

He blinks and turns away, hoping to settle the storm in his head by studying the coming attractions. A cheesy horror film about a group of teenagers on a camping trip. Astronauts lost in space. A prehistoric Tarzan knock-off. On the stylised movie poster, a squadron of pterodactyls, their wings spread against the sky, darken an angry sun.

Rain spatters the pavement. Gusts of humid air sweep in through the open door. Except for the mousy girl hiding in the shadows, the lobby is empty. She's staring at the door like she wants to flee. The previews have already begun, but the film won't start until seven on the dot. He beckons her over.

'It's your lucky day. Sodas are free till the movie starts.' He cocks his head at the dispenser. 'What'll it be?'

A scared rabbit, she's frozen to a spot on the floor. Poor kid.

The lyrics of a pop song, about a girl adrift in the night, ping through his head. Eyes closed, he sweeps his fingers over the levers on the soda dispenser, tapping out the beat. Dr Pepper. She'll like that. Dark liquid foams into the paper cup. The sweet stench prickles his nose, the ceiling lights dazzle his eyes. One of those weird headaches is coming on.

He sets the cup on the counter. 'Here you go. But you'd better hurry, the movie's starting.'

A mottled flush, like a port wine stain, creeps up the girl's neck. She takes the cup and lifts it to her lips, but the embryonic smile vanishes at the sight of a green sedan pulling up to the kerb.

'I have to go.' A strangled whisper. She drops the cup on the counter and bolts.

'Get your fat ass in the car!'

A woman with a face like a raptor reaches across and yanks the girl into the passenger seat before screeching away, red tail lights dissolving in the rain. He digs his thumb into his temple, closes his eyes. Crap family. He can relate. But he's glad the girl is gone. With that scared-rabbit look, she's a dead ringer for his sister Izzy. Creeping about the house like a wraith, subsisting on air. As if all she wants is to disappear.

Three hours and forty-nine minutes till he can switch off the popcorn machine and head home. *Don't forget the lights, son. And lock up the doors. You're in charge.* Mack's voice. Good old Mack, his cheeks flushed the high colour of a dedicated boozer. Clumsily patting Tim's shoulder, as if he were the son Mack never had. Though he's wary of such fatherly overtures. One old man impossible to please is enough.

Five minutes before the movie ends, he busies himself with wiping the counter and sweeping up the smashed popcorn underfoot. Anything to avoid seeing Angela draped around that boy again. Rumour has it that instead of crawling back into whatever hole he's come out of, that jerk will be going to the high school in September. Senior year will be hell.

The jabbering crowd surges into the wet street, dashing for the shelter of their cars. The air blowing through the door is ripe with the peculiar mix of pine sap and fish brine he's known all his life. At the sound of the Viking's honking laugh, his head snaps up. The gang are in high spirits, hopped up on something. Adrenaline maybe, or the latest cocktail of drugs.

'Where to next?' Someone suggests Ted's house, whoever that is. 'Yeah, he'll have some decent weed.'

They pile into a blue Camaro, with Angela curled in the

passenger seat, her hair luminous under the street lamp, and roar away.

The thought of something happening to her is like a punch to the gut. A violent crash, her bloodied body flung to the side of the road. Or that psycho, Mister Golden Hair, forcing himself on her.

A sharp pain blooms behind his eyes. He's desperate for sleep. But there's one more film to roll before he's released into the night.

* * *

The rain is coming down in buckets. He splashes through puddles to reach his mother's blue Pontiac, borrowed for the night so she won't have to pick him up. The blasted thing's as big as a boat, but soon he'll have enough dough saved to buy his own set of wheels, something sleek and sporty, built for the open road. On a calendar in his bedroom, he's marking off the days. Soon, very soon, he'll hit the highway and leave boring old Belle River in the dust.

The streets are deserted. The only other driver on the road some lady in a silver Dodge, idling at the intersection. The lit end of her cigarette flares in the dark. As she turns onto the beach road, he accelerates past her, sluicing through a puddle.

* * *

At home, the lights are out, everyone asleep. He shrugs off his sodden coat and flops onto the couch, too tired to kick off his mud-spattered shoes, though there'll be hell to pay tomorrow. Rain drums on the roof. What a washout the summer's been. He roots around in the pocket of his jeans for the pills he filched from his mother's night table and rattles them in his hand. Bright orange Seconal. Quaaludes, bluer than blue. The old lady's got enough pills in there to stock a pharmacy. He pops them in his mouth, swallows them dry, too tired to get a glass of water. Closing his eyes, he awaits the blessed void.

* * *

Scritch, scratch.

Through layers of sleep, he swims upwards, surfacing in the swampy air. Scrabble, scrabble, scratch, whine. Must be the dog, clawing at the door.

How long has he been out? Ten minutes? An hour? His head feels stuffed with cotton. Rain hits the roof like buckshot. He checks his watch. Not yet midnight. What's Maggie doing out in the storm?

He lurches upright and stumbles to the kitchen, slips and falls. There's a puddle of something on the linoleum. The dog is frantic, clawing at the door to get in.

His foot bumps against something soft. The laundry bag? He reaches for the light, switches it on.

Blood, everywhere. On the walls, on the floor. A body lying in a crimson lake. Shaking, he crouches against the wall, arms hugging his knees. Thunder rumbles overhead. He inches forward, pats the matted brown hair soaked in blood. Blank eyes stare at nothing. He scrabbles for the light, switches it off.

A creak on the stairs. His blood freezes. Was that a footstep?

Rain lashes the window. His head throbs with the crack of thunder. In the electrified air, the molecules seem to vibrate in a minor key. On the stairs, the scrape of a shoe. He holds his breath. Run? Or stand his ground?

Blood. On his hands, on his clothes. He crawls to the kitchen door, prepared to flee, when a branch hits the roof and a flash of lightning sears his eyes. The light above the stove grows dark, as if a great carrion bird is passing overhead. Or the shadow of a pterodactyl stretching its wings. He hears a rustle of feathers as the sharp beak pierces his neck, and the massive wings enfold him in a choking embrace, dragging him down to the centre of the Earth.

7

Greenlake Psychiatric Facility
Atherton, New York
March, Present Day

Two miles before the turn-off to Atherton, the engine emitted an unusual noise that grew into a furious screech, like a rodent caught in a trap. When the oil light blinked twice and stayed on, Erin pressed the accelerator, urging the car, purchased second-hand from a dodgy dealer in Lansford, to reach the next exit.

The last thing she needed was to break down out here. When the sign for the off-ramp appeared through the gloom, she veered from the motorway, fighting to stay in her lane as a lorry thundered past, and coasted onto an industrial estate.

Amidst the jungle of neon, she spotted a potential saviour: Reggie's Jiffy Lube, jammed between a pizza joint and a used-car dealer. As she pulled into the forecourt, the engine, right on cue, seized up and died. Her appointment at Greenlake was in thirty minutes. Whatever was wrong with the car, it would surely take longer than that to fix. Could she get a taxi out here? Despite the jarring neon, the barren estate, pockmarked by winter storms, looked desolate and abandoned.

A blast of wind shook the car. Sleet hammered the roof. She tapped on the horn and waited. A kid with grease-stained hands slunk out of the garage and peered at her through the windscreen. When she didn't react, he motioned for her to pull into the service bay. She hesitated before rolling down the window.

'The engine's stopped.'

The boy's grin revealed a mouthful of crooked teeth, and he had a nervy look about the eyes.

'What'sa matter? Car died?'

A shadow appeared in the frosted glass door of a walled cubicle. A man with a military buzz cut and two-day stubble on his chin stepped outside and jerked his thumb at the boy. 'Scram.'

Quick as a weasel, the kid vanished into the shadows of the service bay.

Erin pulled up the hood of her parka before stepping into the driving sleet.

The man exhaled noisily. 'Whatever the kid said, just ignore it.' He held open the door to the office. 'Come on in out of the weather. I've got coffee on if you need a warm-up.'

She slid past him and into the overheated room. A metal desk and row of filing cabinets took up most of the space. On the pocket of the man's grimy overalls, the name 'Reggie' was stitched with scarlet thread.

'Pull up a chair,' he said. 'How about that coffee?'

'Actually, I'm going to be late for an appointment.' Erin tugged off her gloves and fanned her face. The cramped office was like a sauna. 'What I really need is a taxi. I've got to be on the other side of the city in half an hour.'

'Where on the other side?' He pinched the bridge of his nose, his nails rimmed with grease. 'Can you be more specific?'

'Atherton.' She paused. 'There's a psychiatric facility—'

'The nuthouse?' He tossed her a surprised look. 'So, you're what...' his face took on a sly cast, 'visiting someone? Husband, boyfriend?'

'I'm a psychiatrist.'

'A shrink? Say no more.' He held up his hands. 'But you won't get there on time with a taxi. Those guys hate coming out here.' He twisted round to squint at the wall clock. 'Hey, kid.' He snapped his fingers. 'Kenny! Get yer butt in here. I'm going to run this lady into the city.' He fixed the boy with an 'I-mean-business' stare. 'Don't go scaring off the customers while I'm gone. And no messing around on the computer, either.'

Kenny looked shifty, Reggie aggrieved, as he hustled her out of the office and herded her in the direction of a battered pickup.

Erin stuffed her hands in her pockets, her shoulders hunched against the wind. 'Are you sure it's no trouble?' It was a long way, and the roads were slick with ice.

'Nah, I can tell it'll be slow today. Besides, I wouldn't feel right keeping a doc from her patient.' He let the words hang in the air, as if hoping she'd reveal a salacious detail he could repeat to his mates.

Strapped in the passenger seat, she studied the skeins of ice forming on the windscreen as the truck fishtailed on the macadam. Reggie turned on the defroster and switched the radio to a pop station.

'It's not often I get away from the garage.' He wiped the fogged glass with his hand. 'Most days you'll find me under the chassis like a regular grease monkey. Not for long, though. I've got my eye on a little place in Florida. Right on the water, where the fishing's good,' he said, drumming his fingers on the steering wheel. 'About time I retire. My back's shot, and the economy's all gone to hell.' He peered through the gloom. 'We're dying up here.'

Too keyed up to respond, she let his words pass over her.

He flipped the dial on the radio and glanced at Erin. 'Visiting a patient, huh? That must be something. Regular folks like me can only imagine what goes on over there.'

Silence filled the cab. Long silences were her stock-in-trade, though he wouldn't know that. Naturally, he was curious. They all were. In any town with a psychiatric hospital, especially one for the criminally insane, rumours about what went on behind the razor wire must run wild. *Nuthouse. Loony bin, psycho ward, insane asylum.* She wondered what the other good citizens of Atherton called it.

'It's not what you think,' she said, holding her chilly hands close to the heating vent. 'The patients are usually well cared for, even in a state facility like Greenlake. Straitjackets and manacles… those things are only in the movies.'

'If you say so.' He scratched the stubble on his jaw. 'Sure was a panic around here a few years back. One of those, waddya call 'em, *inmates* escaped. Took the cops more than a week to find him. Axe murderer, was what I heard. Some of the parents wanted to keep their kids home from school till he was found. Finally caught the guy skulking around some lady's garbage cans at night. Not a half a mile from my house. Gave my wife the whim-whams. It all turned out okay in the end, but folks were pretty shook up at the time. I thought the crazies were locked up for good, but turns out they can get out on a day pass and roam around the city, just as they please. Who knew?'

She shifted in her seat. An escapee from Greenlake? She could only hope it wasn't Tim Stern. They passed a cluster of derelict buildings on the side of the motorway, faintly illuminated by the yellow glow of the sodium lights.

Her fingers were still cold, and she pulled on her gloves. 'How long will it take to fix my car?'

Reggie made a sharp turn to the right and coasted down the exit ramp through the gloom. 'Can't say till I look under the hood.' He pulled a card from his shirt pocket and handed it to her. 'Give me a call when you're done. With any luck, you'll be back on the road this afternoon.'

A red light appeared in the mist, and Reggie braked hard as a huddled mass of pedestrians, shapeless in their parkas, shuffled across the intersection. When the light changed, he turned right and skirted around the fag end of an industrial estate. In the distance, a crenulated shape emerged in the mist. Shipwrecked in the middle of a wasteland, the gothic edifice couldn't be anything other than what it was: an asylum for the insane. But not in the good sense. Nothing about the place suggested sanctuary. More like the end of the road in a madman's vision of Hell.

'Almost there,' Reggie said. 'Didn't I tell you I'd getchya there on time?'

* * *

At the massive front gate, a guard examined her ID with exaggerated care before waving her through. It was a good hundred yards from the guardhouse to the main entrance, and by the time she traversed the gritty path, Erin managed to complete a relaxation technique she liked to do before entering a locked ward. A few minutes of focused breathing and mindful visualisation designed to shield her psyche from whatever madness awaited.

We're all mad. Did you think you could escape?

She jerked around. But there was no one there. She closed her eyes and counted to ten, trying to calm the thump in her chest. At the base of the stone steps, she refastened the knot of hair at the back of her neck and approached the steel doors, reminding herself she was a doctor consulting on a case, not a woman about to meet a man who had a connection, however remote, to her past. The blackened bricks and barred windows towered over her, blocking out the sky.

With any luck, she'd be finished in an hour and back on the road to Lansford. If her car was up and running, that is, and the forecasted snowstorm failed to arrive. She didn't relish the thought of spending the night here.

8

In the narrow entry hall, not much bigger than a coffin, Erin showed her ID to a guard seated behind two inches of Perspex. Before passing through a metal detector, she emptied her pockets and placed the contents in a plastic tray. An attendant in a stained smock with a face the colour of boiled beef arrived to escort her to the office of Dr Robert Harrison, Greenlake's director and the psychiatrist in charge of Tim Stern's case.

Last night, unable to sleep, Erin had gone online to ferret out whatever details she could about this man who claimed to know her. Not a fan of surprises, she wanted to arm herself with as much information as possible. In the pre-dawn darkness, she had dressed with care. Grey trousers and a plain navy jumper. Bright colours and patterns could be disturbing for some patients. No jewellery, except for her quetzal pendant, hidden underneath her clothes. Anything that could be grabbed was just asking for trouble.

The attendant led her through a rat cage of tunnels that must have been added to the original nineteenth-century building. Each time they passed through a locked door, an ear-splitting buzzer shattered the air and rattled her teeth. Erin's heart beat faster and her palms prickled with sweat. Patches of mould bloomed on the plaster walls. Moisture from a ceiling pipe dripped onto the back of her neck. Two right turns and then a left. Where was he taking her? An unearthly shriek split the air, followed by shouts and the drumbeat of running feet.

At last, they entered what looked like a ward. A large dayroom, opposite a Perspex-enclosed nursing station, was filled with a dozen men, clad in the motley cast-offs of the asylum. A few were positioned round a television like potted plants. Others had staked out various sites around the room. Crouched in a corner, a man with dirty blond hair and glittering eyes gabbled wildly, snapping and flicking his fingers before his eyes. On the far side, near the windows, a skeletal man, naked but for a grubby tunic, stood on one leg, shrieking like an enraged ibis.

As Erin passed in front of the nurses' station, a woman with cat-eye glasses glanced at her through the partition. She was led through another locked door and into a narrow corridor, this one with better lighting and a fresh coat of paint. The attendant rapped on a half-closed door. He had yet to say a word.

'Dr Cartwright, do come in.' A tall man with a long thin nose and a halo of grey hair dashed from behind the desk to remove a stack of files from a worn leather chair. At the sound of his voice, Erin stopped short. He was an older version of the man she'd found online, but the Oxbridge accent was a surprise. Her sleuthing had revealed a medical degree from Johns Hopkins University in Baltimore. But nothing about being British. Her cheeks flushed. Would her Home Counties accent be good enough to fool him? It was one thing to fob herself off as English in a city like London, with its cauldron of accents and ethnicities, but quite another to fool a native Englishman on foreign ground. If she slipped up, she could always blame it on the corrupting effect of four months in America.

Over the top of his wire-rimmed glasses, he gazed at her with an air of confusion. Perhaps he'd realised his mistake and didn't know her after all. On the wall behind the desk, three framed photos of snowy Alpine peaks, dazzling in the winter sunshine, provided a personal touch to the otherwise austere room.

He gestured to the leather chair facing the desk. 'Thank you for coming. I realise I'm taking you away from your regular duties, but it's our policy to convene a panel that includes outside experts.' He tapped a file on his desk. 'And you come highly recommended.'

She hesitated before taking a seat. Recommended by whom? Had she met Harrison at a conference and simply forgotten? Though it was unlikely. Names sometimes slipped her mind, but never faces.

'You look puzzled, Dr Cartwright, so I won't keep you in suspense. You trained in forensic psychiatry under Gordon Hobart, am I correct?'

Alert now, she tightened her grip on the arms of the chair.

'Wonderful fellow, Gordon. We were students at Imperial College together but lost touch after I moved to America. A couple of months ago, I had the pleasure of meeting up with him at a medical conference in Boston. While chatting over coffee, your name came up. The way he sang your praises had me convinced you'd be the best person to evaluate Tim.'

Surprised by the connection to her former mentor, Erin tried to keep her face impassive. Harrison might simply be conveying his awareness of her role in the Leonard Whidby case as a junior doctor under Hobart's supervision. Or perhaps it was a ploy and, right from the start, Harrison was counting on her skittishness to deliver his preferred outcome: that Tim Stern remain in an institution for the rest of his life.

'He's doing wonderful work at Sheffield, as I'm sure you know,' Harrison continued. 'Thirty-three years I've lived over here, but I still get bouts of homesickness.' He looked at her keenly. 'By the sound of it, I'd say you aren't from Sheffield, though, not originally.' His unspoken question hung in the air.

She met his eyes. 'I grew up in Reading.'

He flipped open the file in front of him. 'Well, it takes some getting used to, America. But it's not a bad place to live.'

He smiled. 'I, for one, am very glad you're here. As Tim's treating psychiatrist, I'm too close to the patient, so I'm just as anxious as our review board to have an unbiased opinion of his readiness to rejoin the world.'

Erin struggled to sit properly on the slippery leather, wishing she'd worn her fake glasses, so she would appear less like an awkward teenager and more like a bona fide psychiatrist. 'I can certainly understand that,' she said, 'though, I'd like to mention upfront that I might not be able to take the case.'

His eyebrows rose slightly, though he didn't take the bait. 'Understood. But why don't you meet the patient first, before taking any decisions?' He looked at his watch. 'Tim should be in the dayroom now. He keeps very regular habits.'

9

Harrison slid his arms into a starched white coat and led her along the corridor. 'This ward is one of four in Unit B,' he said, punching a code into a panel on the wall. A buzzer sounded as the door swung open. 'A high-security unit, though not as restrictive as Unit A. That section houses our most violent patients.'

The stench of bleach and something else – cooked cabbage, spoiled meat? – stung her nose. Before they reached the dayroom, Harrison unlocked a door and herded her into a space that was scarcely larger than a broom cupboard. A monitor bolted to the wall provided a bird's-eye view of the patients in the dayroom.

'I thought it best if your first impression of Tim was on the screen. He tends to tense up when he meets someone new.'

Erin stepped close to the black-and-white image. Would she recognise him? Perhaps a fractured memory from a long-ago summer. She peered at the monitor. In the dayroom, the windows were fitted with bars. No one sat in the scattering of plastic tables and chairs, bolted to the floor. An elfin man, not much more than a boy, with translucent skin and hair like chick fluff, crouched on the linoleum, shaking his fist at someone who wasn't there. Another man, round as a beach ball, pressed his face against the scratched acrylic box that protected the TV.

Erin indicated a dark-haired man seated on the floor. 'Is that Tim?'

'No, that's Alan. Tim's sitting at a table by the window.' Harrison tapped the keyboard. 'I'll zoom in a bit, so you can get a closer look.'

A heavyset man swam into view. Lank brown hair, a pale, slack jaw. She blinked hard, waiting for the flicker of recognition that failed to arrive. Instead, the photos of the crime scene flashed through her mind. The mother, her head cleaved in two, splayed on the floor in a pool of blood. Great splashes of blood on the walls and splattered across the cooktop. The two girls stretched out on the beds. Pillows pressed over their faces, and their throats cut with surgical precision.

Alone at the table, Tim hunched his shoulders over a paperback book, pressing the spine flat with his right hand. With his left hand, crabbed around a pencil stub, he made little stabbing motions on the paper.

'What's he doing?'

'Sudoku.' Harrison smiled. 'He's quite good, actually. Rather amazing how quickly he can solve them. Whenever he's not eating or sleeping or in group therapy, that's what he does.'

Erin studied the angle of Tim's shoulders, his iron grip on the pencil. She turned away from the monitor. 'To your knowledge, has he ever shown any sociopathic tendencies?'

The surprise on the older man's face seemed genuine.

'What I mean is,' she said, back-pedalling, 'have you ever thought that Tim might be… faking his symptoms?'

Harrison tugged his ear. 'Not in the fifteen years I've been treating him.' He examined a patch of scaly skin on his wrist. 'From the time of his arrest, he's always maintained he has no memory of the murders. A sociopath would be more inclined to brag about what he'd done.' As if anticipating Erin's next question, he pressed on, 'If he'd been deemed a violent psychopath on admission, he would have gone straight into Unit A with our more dangerous patients. Since I've been here, I've never known Tim to be anything other than docile. But that's why you're here, isn't it?' His smile looked strained. 'To provide a fresh perspective. I may be too close to Tim to see all the ways he might be manipulating me. To you, he's a blank slate.'

Surely, there was no such thing. Not in a case like this, where a crime of such brutality cast an epically long shadow.

A glance at the monitor showed Tim still madly scribbling. 'In the file I received there was no mention of Tim's eligibility for release prior to this.' Erin studied his rigid posture, the intensity of concentration. 'Is this the first time his case has come up for review?'

'Indeed, no.' Harrison looked at his watch. 'There were two previous occasions, but with no one to take him in, or space in a suitable group home, there was little point in petitioning the state.'

'What's different this time?'

'Improved readiness, for the most part.' Harrison pulled a handkerchief from his pocket and dabbed his forehead. The air in the cramped room was uncomfortably warm. 'More importantly, we have a sponsor.'

A sponsor? Erin pictured a well-meaning but misguided do-gooder, or an older, churchy woman, coming forward to save a fallen man's soul.

'Tim's father.'

It was impossible to hide her surprise. This was more than she'd bargained for. Why would an elderly man take in the person, filial relation aside, who'd brutally murdered his wife and daughters? Even with Tim's mental health as a mitigating factor, it was still a shock.

She dropped her gaze, keenly aware of Harrison's eyes boring into her skull in a poorly disguised attempt to probe her mind. *What made her tick? Where was she wounded?*

A movement on the screen caught her eye. Tim closed the

book of Sudoku and shambled towards the window. While his back was turned, a man with the face of a ferret leapt from his spot in the corner and made a beeline for the Sudoku. As soon as the man reached the table, his hand above the prize, Tim turned and pegged him with an Arctic stare. For several seconds they faced each other, predator and prey, before the ferrety man stepped away and slunk back to his seat.

What was that? A prickle of fear needled her gut. She stared at the monitor. It looked like Tim had been seconds away from lunging at the other man's throat. 'Did you see that?'

'Oh, that's just Darryl.' Harrison chuckled. 'Tim will leave something on a table in the dayroom – the Sudoku, a pencil, or a piece of paper – and as soon as Darryl thinks Tim's not looking, he slinks over and makes as if to touch it. They've been doing this for months. Darryl has yet to take anything. It's never gone quite that far.'

'So you don't know how Tim would react if Darryl actually grabbed the book?'

He kept his eyes on the screen. 'No.'

The air in the room had grown unbearably close. As always, when trapped in a tight space, Erin experienced a flutter of panic.

'Are you ready to meet Tim? Instead of telling him the reason you're here, I thought I'd introduce you as a colleague from downstate who's visiting our facility. That way he won't feel put on the spot.'

* * *

A sharp rap on the door and an attendant prodded Tim into Harrison's office. Erin hovered by the bookcase, nervous he would recognise her, though the chance was remote. She looked nothing like the girl she once was. The only possible giveaway was the unusual colour of her eyes. Celadon, a man had told her once. Mermaid eyes. But the thought that Tim might notice something familiar about her, however slight, was enough to quicken her pulse.

Harrison motioned to the chair opposite the desk. 'Have a seat, Tim. I'd like to introduce you to a colleague from downstate. Dr Cartwright is here to tour our facility. I've given her permission to talk to some of our patients. After we finish our session, you'll have a chance to meet with her. Is that all right with you?' He spoke in a normal tone of voice, though with longer pauses between sentences. Looking Tim in the eye and affecting a hearty manner, as if the two of them were mates meeting over a pint, rather than doctor and patient. Tim avoided the attempt at eye contact. Not unusual in a paranoid schizophrenic.

'Okay.' A mumble, scarcely audible, his eyes focused somewhere to the left of Harrison's desk. He hadn't looked at Erin when he came in the room, but he glanced at her now from his spot near the corner. A flick of the eye, as if measuring the distance between them, or assessing a threat. Like a fox in the wild, easily spooked.

She tried not to look directly at him. So far, nothing about his face or form was familiar. She exhaled, relieved. He was a stranger to her, and she to him.

Tim edged towards the leather chair and slid into it sideways, shoulders sloped, legs sprawled. His lank hair showed a hint of grey at the temples, but otherwise he looked younger than his forty-three years. His face and hands were pale and unlined. Years spent indoors and idle would do that to a person.

'Hello, Tim,' Erin said. 'I look forward to speaking with you later.'

At a nod from Harrison, she backed out of the office, nearly bumping into the attendant waiting outside, a solidly built woman with her black hair scraped into a topknot and a no-nonsense demeanour.

'I'm to take you to the staff lounge,' she said tonelessly, as if Erin was one more thing to check off a list. 'You can wait there till someone comes for you.'

The staff lounge, an unadorned box of a room at the far end of the ward, was equipped with two threadbare sofas, a tottering pile of outdated medical journals, and a coffee maker. Helping herself to a chipped ceramic mug from the cupboard, Erin poured coffee from the pot, thick as treacle. Cradling the mug in her hands, she looked out the barred window at the car park. A gust of wind blew bits of plastic and tattered newsprint across the frozen ground. The sky was a sickly shade of grey. All she needed now was for some freak storm to trap her here. The warm lights and familiar routines of the Meadows seemed impossibly far away.

The coffee was too bitter to drink, and she poured it down the drain. Behind her, someone coughed. She turned to find the attendant standing in the doorway, a dour look on her face.

* * *

At the far end of a narrow corridor, a dim bulb protected by a metal grille provided the only light. The attendant pointed to a half-closed door. 'He's in there.'

Before Erin could step inside, the woman gripped her arm.

'There's a panic button on the wall behind the desk.' She looked Erin in the eye. 'Don't be afraid to use it.'

Erin nodded and shut the door behind her, testing the handle to be sure it opened from the inside. A battered desk and tattered chair. A single barred window, smeared with handprints. Tim stood in the far corner, his back pressed to the wall. Panic buttons and body alarms were standard equipment on high-security wards. But the attendant's warning… Was that normal procedure, or was she trying to tell her something? So far, nothing Erin had seen suggested that Tim was ready for life outside the hospital.

Through his bedraggled fringe of hair, he squinted at the fluorescent tubes fixed to the ceiling.

'Do the lights bother you? I can turn them off if you'd like.' She hit the switch by the door, plunging the room in shadow. With only a square of wintry light from the window, the room took on a subterranean hue, more suitable to interrogation by hooded operatives, than a friendly chat with a doctor. To improve the atmosphere, she switched on the small lamp bolted to the table. 'That's better. I don't like fluorescent lights either. Too bright.' She smiled in a way she hoped was reassuring.

But Tim had turned his face to the window. On the other side of the razor wire, an abandoned factory with shattered windows and blackened bricks squatted on a barren patch of land. Three large crows, the colour of soot, pecked at the frozen ground.

In the slanting light, the sickle-shaped scar stood out on Tim's cheek. His arms hung at his sides, and his shoulders slumped forward, as if standing upright was an effort not worth making. 'A murder of crows.' His voice was muffled.

A murder... of what? Erin's neck tingled. 'Why don't you take a seat, Tim.'

The sour smell of defeat hung in the air. She checked her watch, anxious to get this over with and back on the road before the weather blocked her in.

He turned away from the window and focused on a point just beyond her left shoulder. His eyes, the colour of pond water, were blank. 'My name is Timothy.'

'Timothy?' She scribbled a note. 'I heard Dr Harrison call you Tim.'

'I told him to call me Timothy. He forgets.'

'Is there a reason you don't want to be called Tim any more?'

He pivoted back towards the window and pressed his hands against the glass. 'My father's called Tim. I used to be Timmy. But I'm too old for that now.'

In the still air, the only sound was the scratch of her pencil on paper. 'Is there anything special you'd like to talk about?'

He edged close to the chair and dropped into it like a

sack of flour. 'You're not a visitor,' he said, looking at his shoes. 'You're part of that… review, something. Board. Panel. People. I know about it.' He rubbed his hands across his chest. 'I can't leave until another doctor says it's okay. Someone who doesn't know me.' His eyes shifted to the general direction of her face, then skittered away. 'You don't know me.'

Erin was startled but tried not to show it. Maintaining a neutral face was part of the trade. How did he know this? Listening at doors? Or was Harrison's ploy of introducing her as a 'visitor from downstate' so transparent that even to a patient doped up on meds, it was an obvious charade?

'That's right.' She studied his face. 'I'm sorry Dr Harrison told you that. It's always better to be honest. It's true I'm here to get to know you better. But it's not a test you need to pass, like in school. If it turns out that I'm the right doctor to help with your case – and that hasn't been decided yet – then we'll meet with each other a few more times.' She fiddled with the cap on her pen. 'But it could be that we only meet today, just this once. Is that okay?'

He rubbed a stain on his jeans with his thumb.

'You mentioned your father just now,' Erin said. 'Would you like to talk about him?'

Tim's hand twitched. 'Why?'

'You told me about the name change to Timothy, so I thought you might want to say more about what he's like, your father.' She was treading on fragile ground. Harrison had warned her about Tim's refusal to talk about his family, or anything to do with his hometown and the past. But it was her job to test the boundaries. Wasn't that why she was here?

He tugged the book of Sudoku from the waistband of his jeans. As he riffled the pages, a scrap of paper fluttered to the floor. Erin caught a brief look of the pencilled scrawl.

Hey Timmy, Timbo. I'm talking to you. Cat got yer tongue? Mister Golden Hair surprise. Too cool for school. The Viking. Rat-a-tat-tat. Movie night. History girl mystery girl. Three across one down.

Before she could make sense of the jumble of words, he snatched the paper off the floor and stuck it between the pages of his book. What was this? Delusional nonsense? Or possibly snatches of memory. Who was history girl? The Viking?

A chill passed through her. *No. It was impossible.* Across a desert of time, a memory bloomed like a noxious weed. Could there have been more than one? She knew of only one person who called himself 'the Viking'.

Afraid of breaking the spell, she kept utterly still, hardly daring to breathe. 'Is that a poem you wrote?'

'No.'

Hailstones clattered against the window, and she jumped as if struck. When a blast of wind rattled the glass, the desk lamp flickered. She stared at it, expecting the electricity to cut out, plunging the ward in darkness. As it flickered again, she tensed, praying for the gods to be kind. In that moment, hands clasped in her lap, desperately hoping the lights stayed on, the role she was meant to play in Tim's life clicked into place.

She couldn't walk away. Not after stumbling upon a doorway, however narrow, into Tim's damaged psyche. Any other doctor would have dismissed that jumble of words as the product of a delusional mind. But to Erin it was a coded missive from Tim's past, of his life before he killed his family. Impossible to turn her back on him now.

Her mind fizzed with a million questions, but if she pushed too far, it might scare him off. *Take a breath, tread carefully.*

Tim picked at the loose skin on his thumb. When a bright spot of blood appeared, he rubbed it away on his sleeve. 'You talk like Dr Harrison.'

So, he'd noticed. That meant he was paying attention, alert to body language and intonation.

'I'm from England, like Dr Harrison,' Erin said. 'But I only moved here a few months ago. I didn't know Dr Harrison before. We met for the first time today.' Best to spell it out now, before his paranoia ballooned into panic.

He heaved himself from the chair and approached the

window. The icy sleet had turned into snow, big wet flakes that spun out of the sky and stuck to the glass. Before long, the roads would be a mess.

'I want to leave the hospital,' Tim said. 'They tell me it's time to go now.'

'Who tells you?' Was he hearing voices? She jotted the letter *V* in the margin of her notes.

He mumbled. 'No one. Just people.'

'Have you been hearing voices today?'

'No.'

She made another note, *no voices (today)*.

'Dr Harrison mentioned that you didn't want to leave the hospital before when you had the chance. Can you tell me why?'

'Miss Leena said I would live with people like me.' He tapped his skull. 'Crazy people. Strangers. Strange.'

Tim's gaze ping-ponged from the wall to the door. He drummed his fingers on the windowpane, plucked at his sweatshirt, his agitation growing. It might be wise to end their session. But he hadn't clammed up yet, and it was an opportunity she couldn't waste.

'Why are you ready to leave now?'

'My father has a farm. A farm with a barn. A red barn. Chickens, goats, rabbits.' He accompanied each word with a finger tap on the window. 'I like rabbits.'

For the first time, Tim's expression showed a ripple of life.

She was desperate to ask him about the Viking, but if he grew suspicious and shut her down, it might take weeks to regain his trust. 'Does your father come here to see you?'

The room had grown dark, the window obscured by patches of snow.

'He called me one time. No, two times. Two.' He scratched his ear. 'He sent a Christmas card once. Mrs Belmont said it was long ago. Ten years, twenty. From California.' He made a sound, like a bark. 'Palm trees, surfin' USA. California made him mellow. Mellow yellow. Blue eyes, blue.'

Her ears pricked up. 'He wasn't mellow before?'

Tim pressed his whole body to the window until he was spreadeagled against the glass. 'Fly away. Like a bird.'

Through the flocked snow, she could see the trio of crows, dark as paper cut-outs against a field of white.

Tim muttered. '*Scopus umbretta*. A mustering.'

Scopus what?

She held her breath and counted two beats. 'So, your father... he's mellow now. But he wasn't before?'

He made a noise again, deep in his throat, like water running through a cavern.

'People start here, go there.' He traced a line across the glass. As if something had caught his eye, his chin snapped up. In a single motion, he turned and launched his body across the room.

Terror gripped Erin, but it was too late to scream. She covered her head with her arms as he lumbered past and stomped his foot on the floor.

'Cockroach.' He examined the sole of his shoe. 'He's dead now.'

Her heart banged against her ribs. As she pressed her hand to her chest, trying to slow her erratic breathing, he raised his head and looked at her. Straight into her eyes. A white-hot, electric stare.

'The doctors have fixed me. I feel it in my blood. It's humming.' He pushed up his sleeves to show her the network of veins under the skin. 'Like bees. Bees in the trees. Bees in the blood.'

10

An anaemic sun traced a slow arc to the mountains in the west. Standing outside Greenlake's front gate, Erin shivered inside her coat, anxious to start the long drive back to Lansford. But Reggie from the service garage had already given her the bad news that her car wouldn't be ready until morning. She would have to spend the night here after all.

But rather than stay in nearby Syracuse with its bustle and commerce, she pleaded with the taxi driver to take her to a hotel near the motorway she'd spotted from Reggie's truck. He was right about the reluctance of taxis to go so far out of the city, but it was the perfect place to hide out and think. In the back seat, she lowered the window and breathed in great gulps of frigid air, hoping to wash away the sour odours and disturbing sounds of the ward. Loosened from its knot, her hair blew around her face.

Mister Golden Hair. The Viking. Was she looking too hard for a connection? How often had she been counselled to avoid attaching any meaning to a patient's delusions? But from the early days of her training, she'd rebelled against the belief that specific, and often highly intricate, delusions arose from nothing. A basis in reality, however tenuous, surely created the spark for whatever thoughts – however bizarre – sprang forth.

By the time the cabbie pulled up to the entrance of

the Roundabout Motel, a squat brick building next to the motorway, a fresh batch of snow was spinning through the air. The torrent of flakes filled the sky like Arctic moths, swirling in the fading light.

At the reception desk, she collected her key and climbed the dingy stairs to room 19. Beige carpet, polyester bedspread. The cheap air freshener failed to mask the odour of stale smoke and the whiff of other people's bodies. She yanked the shiny orange and brown bedspread to the floor and stretched out on what she hoped was a clean sheet, her eyes gritty with fatigue. With her attention fixed to a spot on the ceiling, she waited for her impressions of Tim to settle into a pattern. *Diffident (shy?). Flat affect (schizophrenia or meds? Institutionalised?). No eye contact. Poor hygiene. Possible schizophasia.*

He seemed articulate enough, though brain-fogged and slow. But that could be a side effect of his medication. The doses they had him on would topple a rhino. His responses to her questions were mainly coherent, with little to none of the jumbled speech or 'word salad' some schizophrenics displayed. No eye contact either, except for that one brief moment at the end of their talk. Plenty of staring out the window, picking at his shredded cuticles. On their own, none of those things pointed to active psychosis.

Her thoughts drifted to the famous experiment in the early seventies that shook the bedrock of the psychiatric community. A prominent psychologist, along with seven other mentally healthy volunteers, was able to get himself admitted to a psychiatric hospital when he complained of hearing voices. Once inside the ward, the volunteers were instructed to act normally and report to the staff they felt fine. All were diagnosed with schizophrenia and prescribed multiple antipsychotic drugs. Nearly two months passed before they were released. When the results of the experiment became known, the psychiatric community was thrown into uproar. Especially provocative was the researcher's conclusion: that once labelled psychotic, it was impossible to be viewed as mentally well.

Tim was admitted to Greenlake a few years after the findings were published. Could he have been misdiagnosed? During the pre-trial investigation, he'd admitted to hearing voices off and on in the months prior to the murders. A true symptom? Or was he coached on what to say to avoid a prison sentence for life? She'd have to look at the trial transcript, or speak to the lawyer on the case to be sure.

As for sociopathic traits, at no time during their brief interaction had Tim tried to challenge her or stare her down. No hint of grandiosity. No attempts to beguile or charm. Not a glimmer of anything other than what he appeared to be: heavily medicated, befuddled, confused. A man who knew almost nothing of life beyond the stultifying routines of a state institution.

In the room next door, a television was switched on, with the volume cranked up. Screeching tyres, shouting and gunfire. Earplugs would have been a good idea, but she hadn't anticipated the need to spend the night. She hauled herself off the bed to look out at the car park, covered in a growing layer of snow. The storm showed no signs of stopping. In the bathroom, she washed her hands and studied the tired set of her mouth. As she coiled her dark hair and fastened it with a clip, she could see a narrow strip of lighter hair, barely perceptible, coming through at the roots. She'd have to visit the hairdresser soon.

Stretching out on the bed, Erin turned the day's events over in her mind. The proper assessments would help her form a more accurate picture of Tim's mental state. Based on today's meeting, he appeared functional enough. Placid. Probably harmless. Provided he continued to take his meds.

Just like Leonard Whidby.

She shut her eyes and pushed the thought away.

* * *

The motel cafeteria smelled of damp wool and bacon grease. Erin slid into an empty booth by the window with a view of the motorway. Heedless of the weather, a stream of lorries thundered past, as the snow continued to fall in the deepening dusk. She might be stuck here for days, but with any luck, the roads would be clear by morning. She had a full day ahead of her, and a roster of patients to look after.

A waitress with sallow skin and vacant eyes set Erin's coffee on the Formica table, along with a wedge of apple pie.

'Anything else for you, hon?'

Erin shook her head. 'I'm fine, thanks.'

'Enjoy the pie. Fresh made today.' The woman's smile snapped into place like a rubber band. Was she on something? Erin's first guess would be Valium, though it could be any number of things. Oxycodone, Xanax. So easy to get these days from unscrupulous doctors or dodgy websites flogging black-market pills.

She tasted the coffee, surprisingly good, before ferrying a piece of pie into her mouth. An older man at the table next to her, with heavy jowls and rheumy eyes, folded his newspaper and struggled into a threadbare coat.

Unsure of her next move, and wary of venturing onto the treacherous path this case would lead her on, her first inclination was to daydream of escape. A cobbled, sun-drenched village in the mountains of Spain where no one would find her. She could get a job at a local café. Spend her free time lounging under a hot sun. Anything other than face what lay ahead. But now that she was no longer just a doctor, but a potential conduit to Tim's past, walking away from his case was not an option any more.

Dread pooled in her gut, but if she was certain about anything, it was this: those scrawled words of Tim's were not the by-product of a diseased brain. *The Viking?* That was her brother's nickname.

11

The Meadows
Lansford, New York
March, Present Day

Niels had vanished. He wasn't in the staffroom or his office, but he hadn't signed out, so he must be somewhere in the clinic's main building. As Erin passed through the vaulted central atrium, trying to track him down, she nearly bumped into Greta, lurking behind a potted palm as she polished off a slice of chocolate cake.

'We missed you at the staff meeting yesterday,' Greta said, brushing crumbs from her lips. 'Not playing hooky, were you? Niels was out, too. Some family emergency, so I ran the show. We allocated group assignments and the on-call schedule for April. You'll find them posted in the usual place.' She waved a heavily beringed hand and swept past.

Notes from the piano drifted through the half-closed door of the music room. Erin peeked in to find a slender woman at the bench, her posture supple as a ballerina's. It took her a moment to remember who she was, the woman who came in twice a week to accompany the girls in their Music & Movement classes.

As if sensing she wasn't alone, the woman paused in her playing and looked up.

'Sorry to disturb you,' Erin said. 'I was looking for Dr Westlund.' She tried, and failed, to recall the woman's name. Karen was it, or Katy?

The woman propped her glasses on her head. Her hair, a sleek bob of chestnut mixed with grey, curved around her cheek. In her fawn trousers, mauve cardigan and sensible flat shoes, she blended easily into the background. *Like me*, Erin thought.

'I haven't seen Dr Westlund since this morning.'

The sun slanted through the windows and pooled on the waxed floor. Erin hung back in the doorway, reluctant to disturb the peaceful mood. The woman's neat figure and quiet grace suggested someone caught between two realms. One in this world, the other inside her head.

'What was that you were playing?' Erin asked. 'It's lovely.'

'Haydn's Piano Sonata 33.' Her smile was warm. 'One of my favourites.'

Erin apologised again for the disturbance and backed away. Niels might be in the conservatory, a desired spot on chilly days. But as Karen, or Katy – she'd have to ask Niels – resumed her playing, something tethered Erin to the floor. What she wanted, more than anything, was a little music therapy of her own. To enter that inviting room of golden light and stretch out on one of the floor mats, close her eyes and sink into the embrace of the piano's soothing melody.

* * *

At first glance, the conservatory appeared deserted, though it was hard to say with the exuberant masses of foliage filling up the space. Erin held still and listened. A rustle of leaves in the far corner provided a starting point, and she followed the blue and yellow mosaic path through the forest of ferns.

After rounding a corner, she spotted Niels, half-hidden behind a soaring plant with large indented leaves.

He dipped a cloth into a brass bowl and wrung it out, wiping down one of the leaves with steady strokes, front and back. His expression was blank, his movements mechanical. She hesitated before approaching him.

'Niels?'

He wet the cloth again and wiped down another leaf. When she drew closer, he spoke. 'In another life,' he said, leaning in to flick something from one of the glossy leaves, 'I might have been a gardener.' He dabbed another leaf gently, as if cleaning a child's face. 'I find it soothing.' He rubbed a stem between his fingers. 'And they seem to like the attention.'

They? Erin perched on a brocade ottoman under the boughs of a date palm. 'Do you talk to them?'

'Not usually. But sometimes I come in here when I can't sleep. Mostly I like to listen to them breathe.'

Erin was taken aback. What could she say to this? Niels, always dependable and a stickler for rules, communing with the foliage in the dead of night. Apparently, there were layers to his character she had yet to discover. Or did his odd mood have something to do with that woman she'd seen him with last week? Erin had been at the coffee house near the clinic when Niels passed by the window, his progress dogged by an angry woman in a red parka, her blonde dreadlocks streaming from a grimy knit cap. She was shouting at him as she punched her fists in the air. Erin had ducked down, so he wouldn't see her through the glass. Though Niels seemed oblivious, his eyes fixed on the pavement, and his face creased with exasperation.

'I'm just back from Greenlake. I wanted you to know I've decided to take the case.'

'Good. The board will be pleased.' He leaned in to examine a yellow spot on a particularly large leaf. 'I was afraid you might back out.'

She fingered a tassel on the ottoman. 'I thought I might,'

she said, leaning in to sniff a bright red flower. 'But we seemed to make a connection, the patient and I.'

'A connection? With a schizophrenic?'

'It happens.'

If Niels wasn't acting so strangely, she would have welcomed his thoughts on the case. What, for instance, would he make of the fact that the patient's father had stepped forward to take in his son? Or about Tim's claim he had no memory of the crime? Or that three days after the murders, he was found two hundred miles away, stumbling along a logging road on the New York–Vermont border? Was it psychosis, a fugue state, amnesia? All these things and more she would have liked to discuss with Niels, but as he appeared to have entered a fugue state of his own, it seemed prudent to say nothing.

She tried another tack. 'Any news about Cassie Gray?'

'Cassie Gray?' Niels scanned the vaulted glass above their heads as if trying to recall the name. 'Not that I know of. But, come to think of it, we've had a couple of phone hang-ups. One late last night, the other early this morning. Probably just kids fooling around.'

Last night and this morning? How annoying, exactly the time she was away. She hated hang-ups. It could have been Cassie, or someone else in need of help who lost their nerve. Or, worse, someone looking for her. But that was a train of thought she didn't care to follow.

When she glanced over at Niels, his face was placid as a pudding, his eyes unfocused. Whatever was wrong, he wasn't going to tell her.

* * *

That evening, Erin pulled into her street to find an ambulance parked in front of the house, its red light flashing like a beating heart. She stopped the car and rushed over to find her pregnant neighbour strapped to a gurney, moaning in pain. Her distraught husband hovered by her side.

'Is she okay?' Erin said, touching his arm. '*Qué pasa?*'

His eyes were wild with fright. '*Accidente.* Baby coming.'

The paramedics bundled him into the back of the ambulance with his wife and sped away in the dark, lights flashing, siren wailing. Only after they'd gone did Erin notice her landlady standing on the front porch in a dressing gown, shivering in the cold.

'Mrs Deptford, you should go in. It's freezing out here.' Erin pushed open the front door and herded her inside.

Her landlady dropped into a chair, her face distraught. 'Poor thing. She slipped and fell in the kitchen, apparently. I heard a tremendous clatter above my head. A pan knocked off the stove, full of hot soup. I do hope she'll be all right. She was so excited about the baby. Not that I could talk to her all that much. Her English is poor, and I don't know any Spanish.'

Erin laid her hand on Mrs Deptford's shoulder. 'I'm sure she'll be all right. The doctors will take good care of her. Shall I make you a cup of tea?'

'You're a dear for asking, but I'll be fine. It's that poor girl I'm worried about.' She patted Erin on the arm. 'Go on upstairs. By the looks of you, you've had a long day.' She stood shakily and turned to go. 'Oh heavens,' she smacked her forehead. 'Silly me, I almost forgot. A letter came for you the other day. It was put in my mailbox by mistake. Completely slipped my mind, but I'll give it to you now.' She pulled open the middle drawer of the hall table, stuffed with receipts and old bills, and handed Erin a square envelope, bright hyacinth blue, with her name and address written in block letters on the front. US postage, but the cancellation mark was smudged, so there was no telling where it came from. The cheerful stamp, orange and yellow butterflies, seemed to mock her.

'Is there something wrong? You're terribly pale.' Mrs Deptford peered at her with concern.

'No, I'm all right. Thank you.' Erin passed her hand over

her eyes. Her knees had turned to jelly. 'Just a bit tired, is all.' She tucked the envelope into her bag and hurried through the door.

Outside in the freezing air, she shuffled along the icy path to the entrance of her flat, fighting to keep her unease from ballooning into panic. Had she given Julian her home address? Anyone in London? She didn't think so. But you could find everything on the internet these days. Privacy was a thing of the past, all boundaries dissolved. Like living in a fish bowl. Or, worse, a bell jar, gasping for air.

As soon as she entered the flat, Erin hurried to close the curtains, shutting out the darkness and the vacant windows across the street. Her mind somersaulted as she switched on the lights. Who would send her something? After she'd fled America, her few contacts had dwindled, fading to nothing as the years went on. Even her dear friend Hannah didn't have her home address. They kept in touch by email.

She sloshed wine into a glass and drank it down before retrieving the blue envelope from her bag. The handwriting on the front gave nothing away. Block letters, black biro. She tore open the envelope and pulled out the card. A cartoon drawing of a cake decorated with burning candles. Chunky gold letters spelled out Happy Birthday. *Birthday?* Her knees gave out and she sank to the floor. Her birthday was a week ago. A day she always allowed to pass without notice.

She picked up the card and flipped it over. But there was no note, no signature. The thought that her presence back in the country had been discovered made her feel ill.

Working fast, she stuffed newspaper into the fireplace and struck a match. As the flames leapt higher, she tossed in the card and watched it burn. Greedy for fuel, the fire roared, and in seconds the card was reduced to ash.

Go back to your room!

That voice, long quiescent, hissed in her ear.

12

Belle River, Maine
May 1977

He squints into the sky above the treeline, wishing he'd worn his baseball cap to shade his eyes from the Sun. But Jeremy says it makes him look like a dork.

Clouds of golden dust from the trees billow in the air. He sneezes and rubs his eyes. On the playing field, the girls flash and shimmer like a flock of jays, scrambling after a little white ball, their striped skirts swishing around their thighs. When the team captain thwacks the ball into the opponent's net, it sets off a frenzy of jumping and screaming. *Way to go, Jilly! High five over here.*

He hates sports. Wouldn't have cut his last class and be out here at all if it wasn't for Angela, the new girl in his American History class. Dark eyes and dimples. Hair that smells like raspberries. He hasn't pictured her as one of the girl jocks, but there she is, gliding and swerving with the rest of them. He used to snooze through Mr Vinelli's class, lulled by the teacher's droning voice, but with Angela six feet away, his nerves are fired up for the full fifty minutes, a chorus line of dancing bees. Heart beating out of his chest, *ba-boom*, like a cartoon character, the second she walks in the room.

If he could just work up the courage to talk to her. School's out in two weeks, so he doesn't have much time to get her attention.

Fat chance. His father's voice booms in his ears.

But he's not a loser. Just last week he won second prize for a sketch of a great blue heron he drew for art class. Not that his father would ever see it. Or care.

The light shifts and he turns his head. Three guys are ambling across the open field, heading towards the woods, probably to smoke weed or smirk at porn mags.

'Hey, pervert. I'm talking to you. Watchya doing, getting an eyeful? Scat, scram.'

The tallest of the three boys, that idiot from out of town with the wavy blond hair, curls his lip. 'You guys smell that?'

His two lackeys, Fat and Slim, smirk and bob their heads like puppets. The skinny boy from biology class, in frayed jeans and a lime-green polyester shirt, theatrically holds his nose. 'You stink.'

'Get along little doggie.' The blond guy takes a step towards him, his hands curled into fists. 'You're stinking up our air.'

He shoves his hands in his pockets and slinks away, ashamed of his cowardice, but what can he do? One wrong move and those three will beat the crap out of him.

He sneaks a last look at the girls on the field. Angela stands apart from her teammates, her eye on the three boys hanging on the metal fence. They make a big show of lighting their cigarettes. *Too cool for school.* He can see the blush rise to her hairline. She giggles and scurries back to her friends.

A hard knot calcifies in his ribcage. If Mister Golden Hair has his sights on Angela, there's no hope for him. A pain stabs his left eye and the world shimmers. He squeezes his head between his palms, riding a wave of nausea before it rights itself again.

When he looks up, Angela is smiling at him. But before he can smile back, she flits away in a flash of green to join the other girls, a shimmer of hummingbirds in the golden light.

13

Greenlake Psychiatric Facility
Atherton, New York
March, Present Day

Seated near the window in the dayroom, his shoulders hunched protectively over his Sudoku, Tim chewed on a pencil stub as he drummed his fingers on the table. A skeletal man with a shaved head stood like a sentinel in the back corner, his arms flung out, dark eyes fixed on the water stains on the ceiling.

A male attendant with a pockmarked face strolled over to the table, repeating himself twice before Tim closed his book and reluctantly stood. In response to Erin's greeting, he mumbled something indistinct and turned away. Wearing the stained green sweatshirt and baggy jeans from the week before, his unfortunate aroma reminded her of an overripe Camembert.

They followed the attendant, single file, down the corridor to the visitors' room, with its tube lighting and smeary window. Tim dropped heavily into the chair and stared at his shoes. A carbon copy of their first visit, though he seemed more withdrawn this time, less willing to engage. Had something happened since their last meeting?

'So, Tim. How are you today?'

'My name's Timothy.'

'I'm sorry.' She tried again. '*Timothy*. Did you sleep well?'

Collapsed inside his body, Tim was a picture of dejection. He stared at the wall behind her, his mood even flatter than last week. Was it a side effect of his meds? A poor night's sleep? Or had his personality been erased by years of living in what amounted to a rat cage. He was a cipher. Anything was possible.

'Can you tell me how your thoughts are this morning?'

His chin lifted a fraction of an inch. 'Thoughts?' He patted the side of his head. 'You mean in here?'

'Yes, in your head. Are they quiet, or do you have racing thoughts?'

'Racing? Like cars?' She nodded. 'They don't race like cars.'

'Have you been hearing voices since we last met?'

He stood and moved to the window, pressing his hands against the glass.

Outside, a flock of starlings squabbled on the frozen ground. Tim tapped the window as if trying to get their attention.

Erin removed the workbook for the MMPI-2 from her bag. The standard amongst personality assessments, this would be her first formal evaluation of Tim's mental state.

'Okay, Timothy.' Perched on the edge of the straight-backed chair, she balanced a clipboard on her lap. 'We're going to play a kind of game, now. I'll say a series of statements out loud, and for each statement, you'll answer true or false. For example, if I say the sky is blue, you'll say…'

He peered through the window. 'False.'

The sky was indeed a sullen grey. Bad example. 'Excellent.' She smiled. 'Just like that. If you feel tired, or need a break, just let me know and we'll stop. Okay?'

With more than five hundred items, the Minnesota Multiphasic Personality Inventory could take up to four hours to complete. Her plan was to administer the assessment over the course of two days, in four short sessions, with a break in between.

She asked Tim to take a seat, noted the time and launched into it. He was surprisingly cooperative, and she marked his answers as they progressed. Twice before, he'd undergone an earlier version of the same assessment. The first time, soon after his arrest, and the second, five years later. It would be interesting to compare his score with the previous results. As she worked her way through the items, she spoke in a neutral voice, and kept her face as expressionless as possible, so as not to bias the result.

'Most people are liars.'

He shifted in the chair. 'True.'

'Sometimes the top of your skull feels painful.'

A shuffling of feet. 'True.'

'All food tastes the same.'

'True. No, false. True.'

'Your sleep is fitful and disturbed.'

His eyes flicked about the room. 'I don't know. Sometimes.'

The five hundred items and ten different scales were designed to prevent faking. Deliberately false answers would show up like red poppies on a field of green. And a whole section was dedicated to teasing out psychopathic traits. Any time Tim hesitated or changed his answer, she made a note.

After he completed a hundred and twenty-five items, Erin marked the time and closed the booklet. 'Great work, Timothy. We're done for now. Would you like a glass of water?'

He held his watch, a chunky octagon of cheap plastic, close to his face. 'It's almost time for lunch. Nineteen minutes.'

She studied his face. 'Did Dr Harrison mention that I'm taking you out for lunch today?

Tim's head jerked up. His hands twitched. 'You mean, go outside?'

'Yes. Didn't he tell you?' That was odd. How could Harrison have forgotten? Though it might be deliberate, to see how Tim would manage outside Greenlake's walls without mentally preparing beforehand.

'You've been given a day pass for the afternoon,' she said,

in the bright voice of a camp counsellor. 'I thought we could have lunch in town, and maybe go for a drive afterwards, depending on the weather. The countryside is pretty up here.'

Tim tugged at the frayed edge of his sweatshirt. She could practically see the words 'lunch' and 'countryside' scuttle through his brain. He clenched his hands in his lap, his face slick with sweat. As the minutes ticked by, her doubts about the wisdom of this arrangement grew. Like a runaway train, his anxiety could derail at any point. Harrison had provided her with a pager in case of trouble, but with neither an attendant nor an emergency sedative on hand, what could she realistically do if he decided to bolt?

She smiled broadly, hoping to put him at ease. 'So, lunch for two it is then.' With a matter-of-fact air, she stood and busied herself with her papers. 'I'll meet you in the dayroom in ten minutes. Is that all right? You'll want to put a jacket on. It's chilly out.'

Tim examined his watch. '11:43. What time do you have?'

'My watch isn't digital like yours,' Erin said, holding out her wrist, 'but it looks like 11:43 to me. So, we're all set. I'll see you in ten minutes.'

14

At five to twelve, Tim was standing in the doorway of the dayroom, holding his wrist close to his face. 'Two minutes late.' He tapped his watch.

'Sorry,' Erin said, as she pulled on her coat. 'I was held up. I wanted to speak to Dr Harrison before we left.'

A shadow clouded his eyes. 'Why?'

'No special reason.' She smiled again, though her jaw was starting to hurt from all the smiling. Perhaps she should try a different tack. Less cheerful air hostess, more white-coated professional with a medical degree. Detached, clinical, poised. She buttoned her coat. 'Shall we go?'

Tim had changed out of his stained sweatshirt and into a dark maroon jumper, only marginally frayed at the collar and cuffs. He'd also swapped his trainers for a pair of heavily scuffed leather Oxfords, as if some distant memory had triggered the appropriate dress code for lunch in a restaurant.

An attendant in a white smock led them through the series of locked steel doors to the front entrance. *Buzz. Screech. Crash.* As each door swung open and clanged shut behind them, Tim flinched.

The attendant, a squat man with a barrel chest, reached out and patted Tim on the arm. 'Going out on the town, huh,

Timmy? Lookin' pretty spiffy. Give my regards to Broadway and all that.'

Tim refused to engage, not even to remind the man to call him Timothy. His face gleamed with sweat, and his panicky look shifted from the walls to the floor. With his feet rooted in place, he turned his head to look back down the corridor from which they'd come.

Another ear-splitting buzzer, a flashing red light, and the final barricade between the ward and freedom swung open. Erin stepped into the fresh air and motioned for Tim to follow. But he hung back, squinting against the light. Outside, his skin was an even whiter shade of pale, nearly bloodless. Strands of hair hung over his eyes. Sluggish as a lizard in the cold, he tilted his face towards the Sun, mouth slack, eyes closed.

'We're outside.' He opened his eyes and turned in a slow circle.

Such a simple boundary to cross, Erin thought. Inside, outside. And yet a minefield for the incarcerated.

She tightened her scarf around her neck. 'Take a deep breath. Doesn't the air feel good?'

'I guess.'

'Don't you ever go outside?'

He shook his head.

'What about the courtyard, or out on the grounds? Aren't you allowed to walk there?'

He shivered in the corduroy jacket, too thin for the cold. 'I like to be inside.' Tim remained rooted to the front step. Out in the daylight, the sorry state of his fingernails, bitten and raw, was clearly visible. Under his breath, he began to count. 'Thirty-seven,' he said, breathing out. 'That's a good number.'

Erin was mystified by the number's significance until it came to her. He had counted the cars in the car park.

She started down the front steps. Tim followed behind, obedient as a child. He was showing more evidence of obsessive-compulsive disorder than reported in his file. Though the symptoms might be aggravated when he was nervous.

A stiff breeze chased dead leaves across the ground. Mounds of dirty snow from a recent storm were piled up along the crumbling asphalt. As they passed through the gate, a wild thought spun through her head. What if she revved the engine and raced to the border? Set Tim up in a flat in a village in Ontario with a job flipping burgers. The idea was so absurd, she nearly laughed. One glance at Tim's clenched jaw and wide-eyed terror was enough to set her straight. Leaving the confines of the ward for the great outdoors was not a cause for celebration.

* * *

It took her three attempts to find Summer Street and the Adirondack Café, the lunchroom Harrison recommended. Conveniently located two blocks from the local police, should anything go wrong.

The minute she parked and cut the engine, Tim consulted his watch. '12:23,' he announced, 'and 17 seconds.'

Was that a good number, a favourable moment in the space-time continuum? Or would they have to wait in the car for the clock to reach a more auspicious time? But he unbuckled his seat belt and folded his hands in his lap.

Erin gathered up her things. 'You can open your door now.'

A group of young people, students from the local college by the looks of it, in jeans and bright parkas, crossed the street in a burst of chatter.

Tim lumbered out and stood fixed to the square of pavement next to the car. He looked so ill at ease, she was tempted to suggest they skip lunch and go for a drive instead, pick up a bag of burgers and fries at a drive-through and hit the open road.

But he moved in the direction of the restaurant, careful to avoid stepping on any cracks in the pavement. At the door to the café, he turned his head, his jaw working, eyes unfocused. Was he thinking of making a break for it? Twice her weight, if not more, he could knock her flat and be halfway across town before she picked herself off the ground.

'Number 11. That's a pretty good number.' He traced it with his fingers.

Thirty-seven cars. Number 11 Summer Street? Was there a pattern or connection? None she could discern. But it seemed to fit with his counting behaviours.

A girl with purple-tipped blonde hair pointed to their table. The place was only half-full. Students. A couple of stressed-out mothers and their fretful children. Tim glanced nervously at the other diners, a rabbit in a field of hounds, before dropping into the chair that faced the exit.

'This is a good table,' he said. 'Close to the door. Five steps.'

The waitress slapped two laminated menus in front of them and rattled off the specials in a bored voice, before walking away to clear another table.

Tim held the menu close to his face. 'What's a... Cobb salad?'

'Chopped apples, raisins and walnuts mixed together with mayonnaise.'

He placed the menu in the corner of the table, adjusting it with his finger and thumb, a little bit here, a smidge there, until the edges were perfectly aligned.

'I'm going to have the lasagne,' Erin said. 'Do you know what you want?'

He turned his head in her general direction. 'Turkey.'

She scanned the menu. 'You're in luck.' A turkey sandwich was on the list. Best not mention the selection of white bread or brown, mustard or mayo. Too many choices.

When the waitress returned, pencil poised, Erin prompted Tim to give his order. He mumbled, looking at the floor. 'Turkey. And a... Coke. Coca-Cola. Not too cold, not too warm.'

'White bread and mayo on his order,' Erin said, lowering her voice, 'and I'll have the lasagne and a cup of tea.'

The waitress gave Tim an odd look before turning on her heel and scooting away. Her face was easy to read: one of those crazies from the loony bin down the road.

From under the strands of hair hiding his eyes, Tim shot quick glances at the other diners. 'Twelve. Odd numbers are better.'

Two girls breezed inside, bringing with them the metallic chill of the outdoors.

'Fourteen.' Angling his body away from the window, Tim stared at a crack in the floor tiles, then his ragged cuticles, and finally the soles of his shoes, left foot, right foot. With a furtive, sideways tilt of his head, his eyes flicked to the two girls who'd installed themselves at the next table. With their long silky hair, bright faces and animated chatter, they must seem as exotic as toucans.

It was a relief when the waitress arrived with their order. Tim leaned over his plate and sniffed. With the flat end of a spoon, he lifted a corner of the bread and examined the contents, then transferred the tomato and lettuce onto a paper napkin. With the sandwich reassembled, he sniffed again and took a bite.

'Turkey always makes me think of your Thanksgiving,' Erin said, her voice bright. 'It sounds like a fun holiday.' *Liar.* She'd loathed Thanksgiving as a child. Holidays in her home were an unceasing nightmare. Alcohol-fuelled rages, humiliation, tears. Worse after her father died. 'What was Thanksgiving like at your house?'

He made a clicking sound, deep in his throat. On a paper napkin, he sketched with a pencil stub he'd taken from his pocket the skull of a large bird, with teeth the size of tombstones.

What was this?

His face was closed down like a shop after hours, lights off, the window shuttered. But what had she expected? That he would prattle on about happy family holidays? Except for the horrifying deaths that marked a gruesome end to his adolescence, his past was a blank slate. For all she knew, happy times in the Stern home were few and far between. *Join the club*. Though he claimed no memory of the murders, he'd been told repeatedly what he'd done. Surely the details were lodged somewhere in the caverns of his mind.

Tim fidgeted in the chair. Next to his plate, the paper napkin with the bird skull lay in strips. He tapped his fingers on the table, muttered under his breath. *'Rat-a-tat-tat, they're at it again, at it again. Too cool for school. History girl, mystery girl.'*

Erin stopped short, fork suspended. It was the string of nonsense words she'd glimpsed on that scrap of paper. Slowly, so as not to disturb the air around them, she placed her fork on the plate.

'You know,' she said, resting her chin in her hands, 'it's so much easier for two people to get to know one another if they talk about things they like. Shall we make it into a game? Let's pretend that you and I have just met. At a party, for instance, or maybe a… baseball game.'

A muscle jumped in his jaw. Was she asking too much? She looked away, not wanting to spook him with eye contact.

'Why don't I start?' Erin continued. 'Let's see, I like… butterscotch ice cream, but I don't like… loud noises. My favourite colour is yellow, and I like the way it smells outdoors after a rainstorm.' She scanned his face. So far, so good. 'Now it's your turn.'

She had his attention now. Around his plate, he'd arranged the uneaten bread crusts like the spokes of a wheel.

'I like…' He stroked the sickle-shaped scar under his eye. 'I like… birds.'

'Great. What's your favourite colour?'

'Pink? No. Pink is for girls, blue is for boys. Blue, moo, boo. I like blue.'

'And what about when you were young. Did you have a favourite toy or book?'

His eyes shifted to the floor.

'Or a favourite place?' Silence. 'I know what mine is.' She took a breath and ploughed on, blithely ignoring Harrison's concerns. 'It's this little town on the Maine coast I visited one summer with my parents. There were these colourful lobster boats in the bay, and a place by the docks that sold really good ice cream.'

Tim's chin snapped up, his eyes wide, a deer in headlights. 'Is this a… a trick? I won't go back there. Dr Harrison said I never have to go there again.' He struggled to his feet, upsetting his water glass. A breadknife clattered to the floor. 'I want to go back to my room now.' His raised voice was ragged with fear. The other diners turned to stare.

'Timothy. It's all right.' She tried to catch his eye. 'Look at me. It's not a trick. I didn't mean to upset you. Look at me. Deep breaths. You don't have to go back there. I promise. Look at me.'

Sweat streamed down his face. His pupils were huge. 'I want to go back to my room now.' He wrenched his coat off the back of the chair and bolted for the door. She'd never seen him move so fast.

No time to signal the waitress. She tossed some bills on the table and ran after him, wondering what she would say to Harrison if he got away from her.

But he hadn't run away. Crouched on the pavement next to her car, Tim was curled into a tight ball, shaking like a tree in a windstorm. The moment she opened the door, he stumbled in and strapped himself into the passenger seat, his chest heaving.

Chastened by her stupidity, she waited for his breathing to slow. *Damn*. Would he ever trust her again? If he didn't, she would have to apologise to Harrison for her unprofessional conduct and excuse herself from the case. Or, she could lie.

She glanced sideways at his clenched hands and rigid posture. Unless Tim said anything, there was no reason for Harrison to know.

15

Erin slept badly in the cheap motel by the motorway, tossing and turning on the sagging mattress, only to rise from uneasy dreams just before dawn. Ten minutes early for her debrief with Harrison, she was groggy and in need of caffeine. As she waited for him to arrive, she tried to gauge the damage she might have caused to Tim's case by her bungled attempt to form a connection.

Harrison hurried into his office a few minutes late, juggling a battered briefcase and a cup of coffee in a red mug bearing the logo of a drug company.

'Would you care for a coffee?' He lifted the mug. 'I can ask Gloria to bring you a cup.'

She nodded her thanks and waited for him to settle into his chair. His manner was unruffled, if a bit distracted.

After his assistant set the coffee on Harrison's desk, Erin reached for the cup and clutched it with both hands. It wasn't warmth she needed, but courage. Though she knew it was ridiculous to feel like an awkward schoolgirl facing a stern headmaster.

She cleared her throat. 'Did you speak to Tim yesterday afternoon?'

He polished his glasses with a handkerchief and settled them on his nose. 'I'm afraid not. After he came back from your outing, he went straight to his room. I was a bit worried when he failed to show for group therapy. One of the attendants said Tim wasn't feeling well. Curled up in his bed and running a slight fever.' He examined her over the top of his glasses. 'Did anything happen during your lunch?'

'Nothing out of the ordinary.' She struggled to find the right tone. 'Though Tim was agitated as soon as we left the hospital. I noticed some obsessive-compulsive behaviour. Counting. A fixation with particular numbers.'

Harrison opened a drawer and took out a pen. 'Tim does have an excessive attachment to his routines. Though that's true of many of our patients. If he's released, he'll certainly require a great deal of support, and time, in establishing new ones.'

As he patted his pockets for the spectacles on his nose, she made a rapid decision. If absolutely necessary, she would admit to alluding to Tim's hometown, but not her connection to it. That was a risk she couldn't take. If he were to consider it a conflict of interest, he'd remove her from the case. And she couldn't abandon Tim. Not now.

* * *

On the monitor in the observation room, Erin spotted Tim at his usual table, bent over the book of Sudoku. As far as she could see, her ill-considered allusion to Belle River had caused no lasting harm. But Harrison had yet to address the question of how Tim would cope with the facts of his past if he were to leave Greenlake to live with his father. Wouldn't the daily contact with his only living family member provide enough reminders of Belle River, and the bloody crime he claimed not to remember?

She could feel Harrison's breath on the back of her neck and shifted away. 'We haven't discussed this before, but do you have any concerns about Tim living with his father?'

Harrison's attention was focused on the monitor. 'A few.'

He cleared his throat. 'It's only natural, I suppose. Tim's been my patient for nearly fifteen years, and what becomes of him will always be of interest to me. Strictly professional of course.' He pressed a switch and the monitor went blank. 'With regards to his father, though, I wouldn't want to say anything that might prejudice your assessment.'

But he already had, she thought, by refusing to say anything at all. Clever man, sending such a clear shot across the bow. Would he prefer that Tim remain institutionalised for the rest of his life? For all she knew, Tim was Harrison's pet observational project, with the ongoing case study all but written up. That was the vibe she was getting. But her concerns were valid. If she were to recommend Tim's release, how would the two men, father and son, yet practically strangers, manage to live out their days together? By pretending they were just two ordinary people sharing a home? Each day ignoring the giant elephant in the room, that one of them happened to have killed the other man's wife and daughters. It was beyond comprehension, and there still remained some missing pieces of the puzzle, including the nature of their relationship before the crime. Did father and son get along, or were their differences a daily source of friction?

She had a lot more digging to do.

16

The Meadows
Lansford, New York
March, Present Day

The clock ticked towards midnight as Erin scraped the dried remains of butterfly pasta and Parmesan cheese into the bin. Though sleepy, she was not yet ready for bed. Still to come were a hot bath and warming glass of brandy, her just reward for having survived a hectic day. The bath was where she did her best thinking, and along with everything else on her list, she needed to consider her next move with Tim.

In the draughty bedroom, she stepped out of her clothes and pulled on a robe, treading lightly on the chilly wooden floor in her bare feet. Lamplight glanced off a silver-framed photo on the nightstand. A slip of a girl, with a wide grin and windblown hair. Behind her lay the deep blue sea and empty sky, but for a trio of gulls, banking against the wind.

Nicky, wild and free.

As inmates at Danfield, they had spun outlandish dreams of running away together the moment they were out. Nicky had gone home first. Two months later, she was dead. Blood swirling in the bathtub, her wrists sliced to ribbons. Erin's unrelenting grief from her failure to save her friend had carved a hollow space in her chest. She looked at the photo for another minute, before turning off the light.

Padding through the flat in her socks, she checked once more that the curtains were closed and switched on the radio to a classical station, before pouring a generous slug of brandy into a glass. With two candles flickering on the table, the stage was set for romance. But Erin was alone, and no one was coming.

Me, myself, and I. Just the three of us. A silly joke amongst shrinks with a certain type of humour.

'*We're fine, thanks. How are you?*' She spoke the words aloud, wondering if the shroud of madness, ever threatening, was preparing to descend.

A light flicked on in the flat across the alley. The tenant returning home. His shadow crossed the window, and she ducked from view. Was he watching her, watching him? From her crouch on the floor, she waited to catch a glimpse of her mystery neighbour, but there was nothing to see but shadows. The light snapped off, the blind was drawn.

Flakes of snow drifted through the narrow opening to the sky. Tomorrow was the first day of spring, though there was little sign of winter's end. To celebrate, she planned to get up early and drive over to the old community centre by the river. A former hotel in its glory days, and later a care home, it was now largely abandoned, except for the rooms on the ground floor that catered to AA meetings and church socials. But the gem of the place, and Erin's greatest find in the city, was the Art Deco swimming pool in the basement.

Built in the 1920s, the pool had the feel of a subterranean grotto. Glazed tiles of turquoise and pink, a midnight-blue ceiling studded with fairy lights. The caretaker, an old man with a limp from a long-ago gunshot wound, allowed Erin to use the pool for free. Gliding through the warm water under the celestial lights, alone with her thoughts, was the closest she'd ever come to paradise on Earth. Having learned to swim late in life, she'd taken to it like the proverbial fish to water.

In her bathroom, she slipped off her clothes and into the tub, sinking down until the water reached her neck. Reflexively, her fingers sought the scar on her chest and traced its length from collarbone to sternum. So much blood was lost, she'd nearly died. A warning carved in her skin by a dangerously mad girl who wanted her dead. *No one gets out alive.* It was impossible to put Danfield behind her. Not when she'd been marked for life.

Eyes closed, she sipped the brandy and tried to calm the anxious beat of her pulse. But tonight, the bath and brandy weren't working their magic. The house was still and no sounds came from the street or her neighbours below. As her breathing slowed, her fevered mind loosened its grip on her churning thoughts and slid into the cool waters of a placid lake. So still, she almost missed it. A shift in the atmosphere. Subtle as dust motes on a current of air.

At the sound of a creak on the stairs, her eyes snapped open. She held her breath and listened. Definitely a creak. Could someone have gotten in? Did she forget to lock the door?

A scrape was followed by a thud. Rigid with terror, she could scarcely move. Trapped in the bathroom, the window was too small and high off the ground to escape through. Knees shaking, she scrambled out of the water and into her robe. With her ear pressed to the door, she strained to listen, until the beat of blood in her ears mirrored the sound of footsteps. *Breathe in, breathe out.* Cowering in the bathroom like a trapped rabbit was not a viable option. She eased open the door and sprinted to the fireplace to grab the iron poker. It was the only decent weapon in the house. No knives, no scissors. Never anything sharp.

She scurried to the entry hall, snapping on lights as she went. At the front door, she pressed her ear against the heavy oak, her heart loud as a drumbeat. Above her head, a scrabbling sound made her jump. It took a moment for her brain to process what it was. A high-pitched squeak and chatter, followed by a thump.

Squirrels. Her knees buckled, and she slid down the wall. *No one was there.* Just harmless creatures in the crawl space, seeking shelter from the cold. She closed her eyes and hugged her knees. Would she always be this frightened? Too wired and alert to every creak and rustle, she'd never sleep now.

She pulled the plug in the bathtub and watched the water drain away. In the bedroom, she pulled on a tracksuit and a pair of old plimsolls. Using cushions and a blanket from the sofa, she made a nest in the front hall and settled down with a book and a flashlight, the iron poker by her side. With her nerves a mess and her knees like jelly, it was the safest place to wait for dawn.

* * *

Hunched behind his desk, Niels looked up from a stack of patient records, his face washed out with fatigue. Dark smudges had appeared under his eyes. Apparently, he hadn't slept last night either. He pointed to the coffees in Erin's hands. 'Is one of those for me?'

She handed him the cup with milk and two sugars and raised the other to her lips.

He rubbed his eyes. 'We had two transfers late yesterday. I don't think I got more than a couple hours of sleep last night.'

Join the club. 'Who's come in?'

'A fifteen-year-old honours student. Swallowed half a bottle of sleeping pills – her second suicide attempt in the past six months. The other girl's seventeen, with a record of histrionic behaviour and a failed suicide attempt. She was discharged from Hillcrest a couple of months ago, not much improved, apparently. Her parents are hoping we'll offer her a more tailored treatment programme.'

Erin shook her head. 'Hillcrest?'

'A psych hospital in Massachusetts. It used to be called

Danfield. But it was closed down by the state about ten years ago and revamped.'

'Danfield?' Erin gripped the chair to keep her hands from shaking.

'Yep. Lots of bad stuff going on behind closed doors. Things are better now, but they don't have the services we offer here.' He pushed aside a stack of papers on his desk. 'The fifteen-year-old's from Chesterton. You'd be a good fit for her. The family situation's a bit delicate. Wealthy parents, pillars of the community. They want this kept quiet. Could be the girl's bipolar, but I think there's a lot more going on there. We'll need to do a complete history and meet with the family. The whole works.' He leaned back and gulped the coffee. 'What's happening with Greenlake? Are you ready to wrap things up?'

Erin drained her cup. 'I'm giving the patient a break for a few days.' She walked to the window. A solitary clump of purple crocus had pushed through the frost-heaved soil. Soon the grounds would be awash with colour. Primroses, daffodils, tulips. Spring couldn't come soon enough. Though the room was warm, she shivered. Her head felt feverish and her nerves jumpy from the caffeine. 'I'll look in on the Chesterton girl before lunch. What's her name?'

'Meghan.'

She returned to the chair and perched on the arm. 'I'm supposed to be on call this weekend, but something's come up. A personal errand. Would it be all right to switch with someone? Andrea, perhaps?'

He checked the schedule on his computer. 'Andrea's not available. But Greta's free. I'll see if she can switch with you.'

Erin inwardly groaned. An emergency was unlikely, but she hated the idea of Greta going anywhere near her patients. Having convinced Tim's caseworker, a woman named Lydia Belmont, to let her tag along on the home study to Stern's house, she couldn't back out now. She only hoped the trip to Vermont would be worth it.

* * *

After lunch, Erin drove across the city to the Riverside Mall. For weeks she'd been carrying around a list of things she needed for the flat. With two new patients, today might be the last break she'd have in her schedule for some time.

She pulled into the car park to find it nearly full. She disliked crowds and her resolve faltered. As she scanned the signs for the nearest exit, a flash of colour attracted her attention. A group of schoolgirls lounged in the weak sun by the entrance to the mall, their bright puffy jackets unzipped to reveal tight jeans and cropped tees. Cheap earrings caught the light. Holding their cigarettes in exaggerated poses, they exhaled great plumes of smoke into the air. A slender girl with short spiky hair tinted pink at the ends threw back her head and laughed. *Cassie.*

Erin gripped the wheel. Should she wave or call her over? Better not. It would only embarrass the girl in front of her friends.

As if sensing her presence, Cassie turned her head and caught sight of Erin through the windscreen. She appraised her coolly before punching the girl next to her playfully on the arm. With the nonchalance of a thirties screen siren, she took a drag on her cigarette and tilted her chin to release a stream of smoke.

Did Cassie recognise her? Or had Erin been tossed on the rubbish heap of bad memories, best forgotten?

17

Matlock, Vermont
March, Present Day

'Do you think that's it?' Erin pointed to a lone white farmhouse, situated on a gentle rise and wreathed in morning mist. As instructed, they'd driven four miles east of the tiny hamlet of Matlock, through long stretches of forest and farmland, in the direction of Stern's home.

'It must be.' Lydia Belmont, Tim's caseworker, peered through the windscreen at the house. 'We haven't seen anything else that fits the description.' They were a few minutes early and she pulled the car to the side of the road.

Erin cracked the window. The smell of decaying leaves and damp earth filled the car.

'Pretty countryside,' Lydia said. 'Though it wouldn't be my first choice to retire up here. Too cold in winter for my old bones.'

Forest and farmland spread to the horizon. In the distance, plum-coloured mountains poked through the mist. A picture of bucolic charm, or it would be, once spring showed its face. But Erin shuddered to think what it was like here in the dead of winter, famous for its paralysing ice storms and the blizzards that cut off lonely houses like this one for days.

She slid her glasses on her nose and coiled her hair into a knot. The glasses were a silly affectation, but they gave her a confidence she didn't feel. The prospect of meeting Tim's father had set her nerves on edge. 'Thanks for letting me come along,' Erin said. 'I realise it's a bit unusual.'

Lydia pulled up to the house and switched off the engine. 'It's an unusual case.'

* * *

The front door swung open, and a man stepped out. In his pressed khaki trousers and moss-green jumper over a white-collared shirt, he could have strolled out of a menswear catalogue.

'Good morning, ladies.' Belying his age, he bounded down the steps to greet them, exuberant as a Labrador. 'I hope you didn't have trouble finding the place.' Behind the horn-rimmed glasses, his eyes, wreathed in lines, were a lively blue. 'Most people make a wrong turn on Hunter's Creek Road and get lost in the forest. One of you must have excellent navigational skills.' He winked. 'It's a pleasure to see you again, Ms Belmont.' He clasped her hand and held it for a fraction longer than necessary, before turning to Erin. 'And you must be Dr Cartwright,' he said, giving her a searching look as he shook her hand. His palm was smooth and dry, the nails spotless. Not the hand of someone used to manual labour.

Lydia hefted her satchel of files. 'Thank you for seeing us, Mr Stern.'

'Call me Warren,' he said. 'Mr Stern sounds much too formal, don't you think?'

Warren? Erin wondered when he'd changed it. Tim's insistence on being called Timothy might all be for nothing.

As Stern turned to usher them in, she caught a glimpse of his profile, and a wave of something akin to déjà vu ran through her. Could they have met before? Not likely, even in passing. It must be Tim's features she saw in the man's face. Though there was little of Tim in Stern's finely cut jaw and clear aqua eyes, a hint of a common genetic heritage was evident.

The smell of freshly baked bread greeted them in the front hall. After herding them into the spacious kitchen, with its black granite countertops and butter-yellow walls, Stern made straight for a chrome espresso maker on the counter.

'Can I interest you ladies in a cup of coffee?' He gave the espresso machine an affectionate pat. 'Retirement gift from my firm.' His eyes crinkled. 'I was a Folgers man for thirty-odd years. Vacuum-packed coffee in a can, that's what I liked. But then we got one of these babies at the office, and I couldn't believe how good the coffee was. Can you imagine? My whole life I was drinking owl's piss – 'scuse my French – when I could have been having the real thing.' He rubbed away a smudge on the chrome. 'This little machine does everything but shine your shoes. Espresso, cappuccino, latte. What's your pleasure? Don't be shy.' He waggled his fingers above the controls, like a magician poised to pull a rabbit from a hat.

Lydia lowered her satchel to the floor. 'We stopped for coffee on the drive up, so I'm fine, thank you.'

Erin considered following Lydia's lead but decided it would be more interesting to play along. 'I'll have a coffee,' she said. 'A cappuccino.'

'One cappuccino, coming up.' As he pushed buttons and pulled levers, the machine steamed and gurgled. When the noise stopped, he bowed with a flourish and handed her a frothy cappuccino in a glass mug. 'Ms Belmont, may I tempt you with some freshly squeezed orange juice?'

Before Lydia could answer, a woman appeared in the doorway. Erin started. She'd thought the three of them were alone in the house.

As the woman stared at the threesome in the kitchen, her

startlingly youthful eyes, the handiwork of a surgeon with questionable skill, were at odds with the rest of her heavily lined face. 'Sorry to disturb, Mr Stern,' she said, 'but I'm on my way out to do the shopping. Is there anything else you're wanting that's not on the list?'

He barely glanced at the slip of paper she showed him. 'Looks fine to me. Thank you, Mrs Gallagher.'

The woman retreated and tapped smartly down the hall. Stern waited until they heard the front door close before showing them into a spacious sitting room, where a fire was lit in the hearth.

'My housekeeper,' he said, gesturing for them to sit on the pale suede sofa. 'Couldn't keep this place shipshape without her.' Grasping an iron poker, he prodded the smouldering logs until they burst into flame.

Erin briefly closed her eyes, trying to catch hold of the distant memory triggered by the smell of burning apple wood. A camping trip at the height of summer, before her father died. A cabin in the woods, the crinkle of pine needles.

Over the rim of her glass, she discreetly inspected the room. Polished oak floor, damask drapes, a Persian carpet in pale blue and grey. A distinct absence of family photos or other personal effects. Not terribly surprising, considering Stern's history. Perhaps Mrs Gallagher was responsible for the décor and believed in a light touch. Somehow, Erin couldn't picture Stern selecting throw pillows and window treatments from a shop.

A log collapsed into coals, sending up a shower of sparks. Stern sat in the slate-grey wingback chair by the fireplace, while she and Lydia settled on the brushed suede sofa.

'I can guess what you're thinking, Dr Cartwright,' he said, after a lengthy pause. 'Why would I, after such a terrible tragedy, offer to take in my son? A man most people view, I imagine, as some kind of monster.' He held Erin's gaze. 'Since I'm not one to beat around the bush, allow me to answer your question.' Stern leaned forward and clasped his hands. 'Do you believe in God, Dr Cartwright?'

She stiffened, her cappuccino halfway to her lips. His eyes, lit by an inner fire, were fastened on her own. 'Pardon?'

'God, Dr Cartwright. The Great Almighty. Divine creator of this marvellous world, of all creatures great and small.' He swept his hand towards the window, as if the creator himself might be lurking in the garden.

'I'm not particularly religious.'

'That's a pity now, isn't it?' His expression turned to one of sorrow. 'Not that I'm making any judgements, mind.' He raised his hands, palms out. 'In fact, I used to be a non-believer myself, as confirmed an atheist as you'd ever find. But then, a few years ago – seven, to be exact,' he said, pointing his finger at the ceiling, 'I was awakened one night from a deep sleep and the Almighty appeared before me in a ray of light.' He looked searchingly into their faces. 'Ever since that miraculous occurrence, I've given myself over to His will.'

Erin cast a sideways glance at Lydia. Ever the professional, her face was impossible to read.

'And let me tell you what a transformation it was,' Stern was saying. He stood and approached the window. When he spoke again, his voice nearly boomed, as he raised his arms to the ceiling. 'As if a choir of angels had illuminated the dark corners of my soul. And every last one was singing the Hallelujah chorus. Since that day, the light of God has flowed through my very being. Every moment of every day. I don't know how I lived without Him before.'

His eyes glittered, his cheeks were flushed. Erin said nothing.

'And how about you, Ms Belmont. Are you a believer?'

Lydia set her untouched orange juice on the table by her side. 'Indeed, I am, sir. I attend the First Methodist church in Albany every Sunday morning.'

Stern beamed. 'Then you, madam, know what I'm talking about. Didn't Jesus say, "hate the sin, not the sinner"? So, who are we, as mere mortals, to pass judgement on others? Only God can do that.'

Erin regarded Stern with a twinge of doubt. This was the big reveal? An evangelical epiphany. Tim being the sinner, and the sin… the murder of Stern's wife and daughters. Or was it a means of pre-empting the one burning question he knew they would ask? *Why?*

In two strides, he returned to his chair, where he leaned back and crossed his legs at the ankle. Lord of the manor, master of his realm.

'Dr Cartwright, you look sceptical.' Stern's eyes pinned her to the sofa. 'I'm happy to tell you anything you'd like to know.'

When she set her half-drunk cappuccino on the table, the click of glass on the polished stone was loud in the stillness. Another log collapsed into coals. Their visit was meant to be a home study, not an inquisition, but Erin was bursting with questions. She glanced at Lydia, who gave her the go-ahead with the briefest of nods.

'All right,' she said, trying to keep her tone light. 'After twenty-seven years of no contact with your son, why have you suddenly offered to take him under your roof?' They eyed each other across the distance. 'Why give shelter to the man who murdered your wife and daughters?'

Lydia sucked in her breath, but Erin refused to pull any punches. If Stern couldn't handle a little tough questioning, he had no business taking on Tim, regardless of his motives. To paint a rosy picture of sharing a home with a mentally disturbed and long-institutionalised man would be a grave disservice.

The skin round Stern's eyes tightened, but then his expression turned earnest, and he leaned forward. 'I found God, Dr Cartwright. It's as simple as that.'

'You said you found God seven years ago. Why the delay in contacting your son?'

He stood and poked at the glowing embers in the hearth.

'When God came into my life, I was married to a lovely woman named Margaret. As kind and loving a wife as any man could ask for.' He bowed his head and passed his hand over his eyes. 'May God rest her soul.'

Erin couldn't help but picture the first wife. Hadn't she been kind and loving?

'When Margaret and I first met,' he continued, 'I'd been alone for nearly ten years, wallowing in the black hole of my grief. For months I was too much of a coward to tell her about my family. I even started using my middle name after the move to California. But I wasn't a complete cad. Before I asked Margaret to marry me, I sat her down and told her everything.' He searched their faces as if seeking absolution.

'The poor woman was devastated. To her, Tim was the devil incarnate. She didn't believe in mental illness, just good and evil. And she couldn't understand why he wasn't locked up in a prison for life rather than some cushy psychiatric hospital. Or that he might walk out of that hospital in the future. She wouldn't agree to marry unless I severed all contact.' His eyes brimmed with tears. 'So, I did. I married Margaret and let Tim go. Last spring, after fifteen happy years together, she passed away from cancer. A remarkable woman. I miss her every day.' He closed his eyes and mouthed a silent prayer, taking his seat once again.

Erin and Lydia waited.

'So, after your wife died,' Erin prompted, 'you were released from your promise, and free to contact your son?'

'That's right.' His face brightened. 'Six months ago, I called the hospital and spoke to this Harrison fellow. He told me about Tim, and how he could petition the state for his release. I understand he's been eligible for quite a while now, but with nowhere for him to go, there was little chance of him getting out. Well, let me tell you, when I heard that, a light bulb went on. Here was a chance to do God's work.' He leaned back in the chair and beamed. 'Now that I'm retired and on my own, I can offer a place of refuge to my son.'

Erin waited for Lydia to chime in, but she was busy making notes for Tim's file.

At the back of the house, a phone rang. Stern let it ring five times, then six. 'I suppose I should get that.' He made a sign of apology. 'If you ladies will excuse me.'

His Italian loafers skimmed silently across the polished oak. In the hall, a floorboard creaked. Stern's cheery 'hello' was clearly audible, but the rest faded as a door was closed. Impossible to make out any words, but the timbre of his voice seemed to change. He sounded angry.

She ventured a whisper. 'What do you think?'

Lydia shook her head. *Not now*.

Erin jumped when she caught sight of Stern in the doorway. She hadn't heard him return. He crossed the room and tossed a birch log on the fire. With a sharp crackle, it burst into flame.

18

'Dr Cartwright, another cappuccino? Or perhaps you'd prefer tea? Though I can't claim I've ever been to your neck of the woods, my idea of English folks is that they live on tea and scones.'

'We have to be on our way soon,' Lydia said, cutting in smoothly, 'but before we go, it would be helpful to get a tour of the house and grounds. With your permission, I'd also like to take some photos for our files.'

'Glad you mentioned it.' Stern's face split into a smile. 'I was just working up to the grand tour. And feel free to take all the photos you need.'

After leading them into the hallway, he expounded for several minutes on the house's history, the provenance of the fanlight over the door, and the origin of the furniture, special-ordered from a Shaker community in upstate New York.

With a prickle of impatience, Erin listened with half an ear as Lydia snapped a couple of photos. They didn't need an architect's tour of the house, just a sense of its suitability for Tim. And it wasn't the house that concerned her, but the location. The sense of isolation was acute, and they must be miles away from the nearest neighbour.

'This room here is my den,' Stern said, opening a door partway at the end of the hall, while keeping his hand on the knob. A mahogany desk faced a sash window, with the rattan blind half-drawn. On the bookshelf stood a row of hardbound law books.

Erin glanced in briefly and turned away, only to be caught up short by a faded photo tacked to a corkboard. Something about the configuration of the group struck a chord. Two men in patterned shorts and a blonde woman standing on a rock-strewn beach. Behind them, a boy crouched at the water's edge. Something about the woman's pose and the design of orange and white diamonds on her dress looked familiar. A gold medallion in the shape of a sun glinted on her deeply tanned chest.

'Not much to see here,' Stern said, closing the door, just as Lydia pressed the shutter. He gave her an aggrieved look, before bouncing back into the gracious mode of host. 'Tim won't be interested in anything here. It's the barn he'll like, and the grounds. And his bedroom, of course.'

They climbed the wooden staircase to the floor above. On a table by the hall window, a jade-green ceramic bowl held a dozen pinecones, artfully arranged.

He pointed across the landing. 'Tim's room has a wonderful view of the barn and the duck pond.'

The three of them stood in the doorway. Maplewood floors, blue walls the colour of a robin's egg. Two sash windows looked out on the surrounding hills and the red barn, the one bright spot in the landscape. A single bed, covered with a patchwork quilt, appeared ready for its intended occupant. Paradise, after Greenlake, Erin mused. Or hell. So much space to contend with. Given Tim's behaviour when they lunched in town, and his skittishness about venturing onto the clinic's grounds, it was clear he had a fear of open places.

After a cursory look into Stern's bedroom, hotel bland with its beige carpet and utilitarian furniture, they trooped downstairs to the kitchen. 'Oh, look, there's Lulu,' Stern said, 'wondering when I'm going to quit yakking and take her on our walk.'

Through the window, Erin spotted a sleek Irish setter standing in the yard, brown eyes hopeful. The three of them pulled on their coats and headed outside.

Lydia took a few snaps of the barn and the duck pond, where a cluster of mallards eyed them nervously. As they moved around the property, Erin discreetly checked the signal on her phone. Poor, fading to nothing in the hollows.

As they circled back to the house, Stern fell in step beside Lydia. 'May I ask you, Ms Belmont, if you're from the islands?'

She gave him a puzzled look as she buttoned the collar of her coat against the chill.

'I thought I detected the hint of an accent.'

'I was born in the Bronx,' she said, primly. 'Not long after my parents immigrated to New York from Trinidad.'

'Ha!' He smiled. 'What did I tell you? I've always had a knack for accents.'

Erin stiffened. She'd seen enough. It was time to make their escape.

Back in the brightly lit kitchen, she couldn't help but notice the shadows under Stern's eyes, and the sagging skin on his cheeks. All this hopped-up enthusiasm had clearly worn him out.

'There's a powder room down the hall, if you need to freshen up before you go,' he said. Just the excuse she was looking for. Erin was itching to get a closer look at that photo, and this might be her only chance.

Near the den, she listened to be sure Stern was still in the front room with Lydia. She eased the door open and in three quick steps stood before the photo. A much younger Stern held a cocktail glass in the air, while his other arm was slung around a dark-haired man in checked shorts and a lime-green polo shirt. The blonde woman in the orange and white diamond-patterned dress gazed at Stern, her eyes hidden by sunglasses, her mouth open in mid-laugh. Was that the murdered wife?

A memory flashed and faded away, slippery as a trout.

She tried to haul it back. There was something about the design of the woman's dress, and the white headband around the candyfloss hair, shining in the sun. Around her neck, the gold sunburst pendant glinted in the light. Erin had seen that necklace before.

'Can I help you?'

Her heart stopped.

When she turned to face Stern, their eyes locked. 'I was just looking for the bathroom.'

For a fraction of a second, the televangelist bonhomie vanished in a spasm of anger, before the smile flashed again. 'It's the door on the left. Easy to get lost when you don't know the house.' He beckoned her to follow and closed the door firmly behind him.

* * *

Erin and Lydia were silent as they drove away from the farmhouse. Halfway on the road to tiny Matlock, with nothing to offer but a general store and a lunchroom, a gunmetal-grey sedan barrelled past, nearly forcing them off the road. The woman at the wheel held a phone to her ear. Erin couldn't be sure, but it looked like Stern's housekeeper.

They didn't speak until they turned onto the main road, a narrow artery through the forest, and headed west. Lydia adjusted the rear-view mirror and switched on the heater.

Erin massaged the tight muscles in the back of her neck. 'So, what did you think?'

'He seems to have made rather a charmed life for himself.' Lydia dabbed her nose with a tissue. 'Though I dare say the poor man deserves it after what he's been through.'

'I suppose.' Erin cracked the window for some air and closed her eyes, drained by Stern's high-octane enthusiasm. Like a carnival huckster flogging tickets to the greatest show on Earth. Why try so hard? If he'd been dishevelled and the house a dump, the state would still be happy to send Tim there. The home visit was merely a formality, as far as the state was concerned. 'Are prospective carers required to take a drug test?'

Lydia puffed out her cheeks. 'You think he's on drugs?'

'I'd like to rule it out,' Erin said, turning to look out the window. It was a habit of hers, difficult to break, to guess what medications someone might be on. Endless stands of dark spruce scrolled past. 'What I really want to know,' she said, closing the window, 'is what the family was like when Tim was young.'

Lydia swerved sharply to avoid a pothole, pitching Erin against the door. 'Sorry about that.' The clove-scented air freshener wafted through the car. 'But who're you going to ask? Tim won't talk about it. The father will say everything was fine, and the others are dead.'

True. The immediate family was gone, but there must be someone. Aunts, uncles, cousins. But even if she tracked them down, they might refuse to talk to her. Neighbours and former classmates, anyone with no emotional stake in what happened, might be a better bet. But digging into Tim's past had a dark side. It would mean returning to Belle River. Something she'd vowed never to do. Just the thought of seeing the town again made her blood run cold.

The sky had darkened, and a few flakes of wet snow splattered against the windscreen. So much for spring. She shut her eyes again as a wave of fatigue swept through her. That photo in the den. The diamond-patterned dress and sunburst pendant had sparked a distant memory. And there was something about the dark-haired man with his arm around Stern. With only hazy recollections of the man who'd died when she was nine, and no photos to remind her, how could she be sure? But somehow, she was. Clear as a mountain stream.

The man in the photo with Stern was her father.

19

Belle River, Maine
June 1977

Smoke from the barbecue drifts through the kitchen's screen door. Why they can't eat off paper plates on the patio like normal people is a mystery, but the old lady's pulled the plug on that idea. Too buggy or something. An hour ago, she disappeared to lie down, so he's stuck in the kitchen with Izzy making the potato salad and devilled eggs. While he chops onions with a cleaver, Samurai-style, Izzy cuts the potatoes in perfectly uniform slices. He looks at her sideways, at the curious creature she's become, hoping to catch her popping a potato in her mouth or licking mayonnaise from her fingers. But not a crumb crosses her lips. Delicate as a sandpiper, with skinny legs to match, a tiny blue vein throbs at her temple. He can't remember when it began, his sister's strange relationship with food.

At a quarter past six, his mother appears in the kitchen, wearing some floaty kaftan thing that looks like a nightgown. Tangerine. The colour makes her skin look bad. Her hair is flattened on one side and her eyes are glassy. Nervously, he checks the clock. At six-thirty sharp, his father will pull into the driveway, stone-faced and pissed off about something. After dropping his briefcase in the hall, he'll head straight for the drinks cart to pour a double Scotch. If dinner's not ready and on the table two minutes after he walks in the door, there'll be hell to pay.

But it took ages to get the coals started, and time's running out. The last day of school and it was his idea to celebrate with a barbecue. But nothing's ready, and he's a mess of nerves. Already in the doghouse, and another screw-up won't help.

Coughing from the greasy smoke, he grabs a pair of tongs and transfers the meat onto a plate. Two burgers slither free and drop on the grass. The chicken looks dried out, and the burgers are charred. When he stumbles up the back steps and into the kitchen, his mother is leaning against the sink, a cigarette in one hand, a highball in the other.

She looks at the pile of smoking meat in bewilderment. 'You kids did all this?'

Off in la-la land again. Not much point in talking to her when she's got that glazed look in her eyes.

'Clara, come on! Help set the table.' He stands at the top of the basement steps, holding the bowl of potato salad. It's 6:25.

His sister drags herself up from the cool nether regions of the house and into the steamy kitchen. She grabs plates from the cupboard and carries them to the table, her eye on the clock. Two minutes to go and the table is set, a paper hat at each place. The meat's in the oven keeping warm. Outside, a party of blue jays cackle and scold in the branches of the dogwood tree.

They wait in the kitchen, nervously eyeing the clock. His mother pours another drink. At six forty-five, his father still hasn't come. No sign of him at five to seven when his mother suggests they sit down to eat. But as soon as they've filled their plates, his father bursts into the kitchen.

'Dorrie! What the hell…?'

He looms in the doorway, half-moons of sweat under his

arms. Tim nearly chokes on the piece of chicken in his mouth. If thunder had a human face, this would be it.

'You couldn't wait ten lousy minutes?' He flings his briefcase onto a chair. 'I'm at the office all day busting my ass for this family, only to come home and… What the hell is this?' He eyes the platter of barbecued meat.

'We only just sat down,' his mother says, looking anywhere but at her husband. 'The food was getting cold.' She stands from her chair, wobbling, to fix him a drink. 'It was the kids' idea, the barbecue. To celebrate the last day of school.'

His face is the colour of putty, and he sways on his feet.

'Whatever.' He drops into a chair. 'Give me that,' he snaps, grabbing the bottle of Scotch from Dorrie's hand. 'Christ, what a crappy day.' His father pins his mother with a look. 'He's out, you know.' He tosses back his drink and pours another. 'Since last Friday.'

'Who's out? Oh.' Her cheeks flush.

Tim wants to ask who they're talking about, but the look on his father's face could slay a dragon.

'Well, we knew it was coming. What a weasel. How I rue the day I ever…' His father pokes at one of the charred burgers in disgust. 'But he won't bother us.' Ice cubes rattle in his glass as he knocks back another drink. 'I can assure you of that.'

20

Belle River, Maine
April, Present Day

The scent of seaweed and brine drifted through the air. Out in the bay, brightly painted lobster boats in yellow, blue, and green bobbed on the water, and a raft of gulls rode the swell. As she drew close to the town line, time collapsed, and Erin was twelve again, dejected and afraid. Perched on a bluff, trying to work up the courage to plummet to the rocks below.

On the road since dawn, every time she passed a turn-off, it was a struggle not to wrench the car around and turn back. But as the miles scrolled past, and her courage grew, the one clear memory she had of her father flickered like a filmstrip in her head. Standing at the helm of a motorboat, wind-tossed and bouncing in the chop, his face pink with sunburn. When he'd turned to say something over the sound of the motor, his voice was snatched by the wind. Three months later, he'd skidded off the coast road on a rainy October night. The car had caught fire on impact, and his body was burned beyond recognition.

Her family had driven up to Belle River for the Columbus Day weekend, where they'd slept at a motel instead of Aunt Olivia's house because she was having her kitchen painted, or some such excuse. That weekend, the rain fell non-stop, but her father went off with some friends to go duck hunting up the coast. When the news came of the car wreck, she was hustled off to bed with a glass of hot milk. No doubt spiked with something to make her sleep. If there was a funeral, she hadn't gone to it. When she asked to see his grave, the answer was like a slap. No grave, no plaque. His ashes scattered offshore.

That none of his family had travelled from England to pay their respects was another mystery. Stranger still, no framed photos were ever displayed in honour of his memory. It was as though he'd never been. Floppy dark hair, kind brown eyes. Lime aftershave, and the sharp scent of gin during the cocktail hour. Though she wanted to believe it, with so little to go on, she couldn't be sure the man in the photo at Stern's was her father.

Welcome to Belle River, pop. 3,719.

At the first crossroads, she turned right to avoid the house on Gardiner Road. Prison and refuge in turns. This trip was fraught enough, and she wasn't quite ready to travel down that particular memory lane. Seven years had passed since her aunt Olivia's death, and for all Erin knew, Vivien had inherited the house. Perhaps, even now, not two miles away, she was holding court in the big front room with its view of the sea.

The weight of the past squeezed her chest. At the first stoplight, her heart thumped like a rabbit in a trap, and she considered turning back. If there was such a thing as a fool's errand, this was it. What could she possibly hope to find here?

A stiff breeze blew the wind-tossed sea onto the rocks at Nelson's Cove. The tang of salt filled the air. Saturday morning, but the streets were nearly empty. Tourist season was still three months away. A woman with a head of pink curlers covered by a polka dot scarf wrestled a loaded trolley out of the Stop & Shop.

As Erin crested a rise, the bay came into view, glinting like a fistful of tossed coins in the morning light. Farther out, near the point, two fishing boats churned towards shore. In the town, patches of dirty snow crusted the pavement where the sun didn't reach.

At first glance, little had changed in twenty years. The stone edifice of the First National Bank looked solid as ever. On the corner stood the newsagent where she'd once bought cherry Lifesavers and packs of bubblegum. But a closer look showed the face of change. Where the hardware store used to be was a coffee house called the Dream Bean Café. The bookstore had morphed into an antiques shop, its front window crammed with dark furniture and foxed mirrors. Always a little forlorn in the off season, the town would blossom in June, when the summer people brought a little gloss and glamour to the streets.

She fingered the quetzal pendant and reminded herself to breathe. *Nothing to be afraid of.* A model New England town, and despite the chill of early spring, it played the part well. Even the wind in the trees seemed to whisper: *spend your holidays in bucolic Belle River, where nothing bad ever happens.*

Except that one unfortunate incident, quickly hushed up, when a family was slaughtered in cold blood.

* * *

At the Moosewood Inn, Erin parked out back and dragged her suitcase along a gravel path to the front door. A pale-eyed woman in a lilac dress and grey cardigan greeted her at the front desk.

'First time in Belle River?'

'My first time in Maine,' she said. *Liar.* She took her wallet from her bag. 'Is it all right if I pay for the room in cash? I only need it for one night.'

The woman gave her an odd look. 'Sure, okay, if that's what you want.' She accepted Erin's money and handed her the room key. 'We serve coffee and tea in the lounge every afternoon at three. Breakfast starts at seven.' She looked at Erin, uncertainly, as if expecting another odd request.

Up on the second floor, the room boasted a canopy bed and two large windows, one with a view of the bay, the other facing the forest. Erin stood at the window for several minutes, studying the dark sweep of hemlock and pine. Nothing moved amongst the trees.

* * *

Before heading back into town, she made herself a cup of tea in the lounge and settled into a chair by the window. After changing into a pair of navy trousers, Erin had tied her hair into a ponytail and planned to wear a baseball cap while she wandered the streets, though the chance that someone might recognise her was small. The only likely giveaway might be her eyes, but they were easy enough to hide behind dark glasses.

The tea and hushed atmosphere of the inn had soothed her jitters, and she felt ready now to drive by the house on Gardiner Road. Even if Vivien had taken ownership of the property, it was unlikely she would be up here at this time of year. To be on the safe side, she took the long way round through the forest, skirting past blueberry farms and potato fields, as a way of sneaking up on the house through the back roads.

Lulled by the drive on the empty road through the woods, she rounded a sharp curve and there it was. A modest frame house set back amongst dense stands of hickory and birch trees. The white clapboards were dingy, and it was much smaller than she remembered. Squinting at the letter box at the end of the drive, it was a relief to see the name stencilled in chipped paint: Thompson. So Vivien hadn't got the house after all. She smiled. Good for Aunt Olivia. *Olivia the good.* Olivia the godsend, who'd offered Erin sanctuary after the horrors of Danfield. A roof over her head and a private tutor to make up for lost schooling. It was Olivia who'd obtained a copy of her father's birth certificate so Erin could apply for a British passport, her escape route to another life. *Ian Marston. Born September 8, 1932, Birmingham, United Kingdom.* RIP.

Midday, and the town centre was showing signs of life. In front of the Rite Aid drugstore, a woman in a pink puffy jacket with bright blonde hair was herding two children in front of her. *Was that Becca?* Erin glanced back as she passed. Though she hadn't seen her old friend in two decades, there was something familiar about the woman's face. The desire to stop and call out was like an ache in her throat. How wonderful it would be to chat over coffee, and to find out how life had treated her over the years. A good friend during a difficult time, Becca would surely be glad to see her, wouldn't she? Even though Erin had disappeared without a trace.

But it was a door she couldn't risk opening. When Erin caught sight of the woman's face in the rear-view mirror, she was relieved to see it wasn't Becca, and tried to focus on the task ahead. This trip wasn't about her own history, it was Tim's life she'd come to excavate, mining the town for whatever nuggets of truth remained.

* * *

In the library, all was quiet. As she closed her eyes and breathed in, the familiar scent of old books, worn leather and wax polish pulled her back in time. The woman at the front desk with frizzy dark hair was too young to be Ruth Davis, the librarian who'd been kind to Erin as a child. How many times had she sought refuge here amongst the stacks of books, while everyone else was at the beach or on the water? The library had been a sanctuary and Ruth Davis a lifeline.

When the woman glanced up for the second time, Erin thought fast. Who was she supposed to be? A tourist, a history buff, a writer? She couldn't be herself, or reveal she'd spent summers in Belle River as a child. Any mention of a past connection would unleash a flood of questions – what was her name, who were her parents, where had she stayed? But it was too late to mumble an excuse and back out the door. A writer would be a good enough cover. A freelance writer researching coastal towns of northern New England.

'Can I help you?' The accent was pure Maine.

Erin cleared her throat and approached the desk. 'I was… I'm looking for information on the history of local fishing villages. Do you have any books I could start with, or perhaps the local paper on microfiche?'

The woman's face brightened. 'You're a long way from home.'

'Pardon?'

'England, right?' She pushed a stray lock of hair behind her ear.

'Um, originally, yes. But I live in New York City now. I'm researching an article on the fishing industry.'

'Well, okay.' She stood and eased her plump figure from behind the desk. 'Are folks in New York City interested in that kind of thing?' She beckoned Erin to follow. 'The *Belle River Gazette* is digitised back till 1987. If you want anything earlier than that, it's all on microfiche.'

She opened a door to a small room crammed with archives. Ring binders lined the shelves. A filing cabinet with rows of narrow drawers occupied the corner.

'That's the card catalogue by the back wall,' she said, flipping on the light. 'You look in there for the year you want, and then cross-reference to the binders on the shelf.' She crouched down to switch on the microfiche reader. 'This old clunker needs a good five minutes to warm up. For the more recent issues, you can access our online archive with the computer over there. The log-in code and web address are taped to the desk.' She swiped at the dust on a shelf. 'My name's Gail. Give me a shout if you get stuck or need anything else.'

Erin waited until she was alone before flipping through the card catalogue for copies of the *Gazette* for the years 1976 and '77. The microfiche records weren't searchable, so she'd have to scroll through every issue for any mention of the Sterns. She settled into the straight-back chair and began with the August issues for 1977. But the murders were given scant coverage, just a three-line item buried on a back page. *In the early morning hours of August 27th, local police responded to a disturbance at 44 Easton Road. No further details are available at this time.*

She scanned through the issues until the end of the year, but there was nothing more on the Stern murders. Surely, a brutal killing in a small town was major news. Why keep it quiet?

She leaned closer to the screen as she scrolled back through 1977, pausing to study the pictures under the *School News* section. June, May, April, nothing. In the March 19th issue, a headline jumped out: *Science Fair Team Triumphs*. A group of boys with the shaggy hair and wide shirt lapels of the 1970s held awards certificates against their chests as they smiled for the camera. *Congratulations to the Team! Raymond Hopkins, Gary Nelson, and Timothy Stern, members of the junior class at Belle River High, win first place in the Chemistry Division at the regional Science Fair in Fremont.*

The photo was blurry and Tim, looking sheepish in a knitted V-neck vest, was focused on something to the right of the camera. But it was the two boys next to him, Raymond and Gary, who were of interest. She wrote down their names, before scrolling back through the issues to the beginning of the year. But there was nothing more about Tim.

Her eyes burned from squinting at the tiny newsprint, and she was desperate for a glass of water. But she pressed on, loading the microfiche for 1976 and skimming through the months. Girl Scout cookie sales, a Junior League charity drive, new parking meters on Main Street. On the inside pages of the special bicentennial issue for July 4th, 1976, she paused at the double spread of photos. A collage of the town picnic and parade, fireworks and boat races. A man in a white baseball cap looked vaguely familiar, and the caption confirmed it – *Master of Ceremonies, Timothy W. Stern, Snr, poised to start the relay race.* He held aloft an American flag before a row of runners toeing the starting line.

In another photo, without a caption, Stern appeared again in the same baseball cap and aviator sunglasses, his arm around a dark-haired boy with his face in shadow, wearing a matching cap and tie-dyed T-shirt. She made copies of the photos and stuck them in her bag. It wasn't much, but at least she had a lead. If she were lucky, at least one of the two boys pictured with Tim in the science fair photo still lived in the area.

21

Sunday morning, and the only place open was the newsagent on the square. A bell tinkled as Erin pushed open the door. An elderly man with a weathered face and comb marks in his thinning hair popped up from behind the counter.

'Morning.' He slapped his hands together as if brushing off dust. 'Cold out there, isn't it? Mother Nature sure is making us wait for spring this year.'

She froze, a deer in headlights. It was the same man who ran the newsagents all those years ago, the one who sold her packets of Wrigley's spearmint gum and cherry Lifesavers.

Too late to back out, she plucked a copy of the local paper from a pile by the door and placed it on the counter.

She lowered her eyes and pretended to examine the goods below the cash register. 'Do you have maps of the area?'

'Ay-uh. Right over there.' He jerked his chin at the metal rack to Erin's left. 'I've got the whole state if you're feeling ambitious, but if you just want the local area,' he leaned over and grabbed a glossy folder, 'this one's for Belle River and Fremont. Does that work for you?'

She nodded and pulled out her wallet.

'Up here for the weekend?' He squinted at her over his bifocals. 'It's a mite early for tourist season.'

'Just passing through.' Her eyes met his for a fraction of

a second before cutting away. She could sense him flipping through the photos in his head, a sharply honed Rolodex of everyone who'd ever come through his door. 'I'll take the map and a bottle of water.' From the candy display, she selected a roll of cherry Lifesavers. 'And this too, thanks.'

He dropped her purchases in a plastic bag. 'Ever pass through here before? Back in the fall, maybe?'

Was it her eyes that gave her away? The man must have a memory like a steel trap. Nothing she could do now except stick to her story.

She cleared her throat. 'I just moved here from London. Not here, New York City. This is my first time in Maine.'

He waited a moment before handing her the bag. 'Huh, I could've sworn I'd seen you before. Never forget a face.'

She escaped into the street and ducked round the corner, waiting in the shadow of Barry's Lobsters & Crabs for her heart to slow, as she worried about who else might recognise her. Clouds had moved in, and wearing her sunglasses would draw even more unwanted attention.

Back in the safety of her car, she ran her finger down the list of streets on the town map until she found Easton Road. She hadn't planned on visiting Tim's old house. A cursory drive-by wouldn't tell her much. But having come this far, it would be silly to return to Lansford without getting a look at the scene of the crime.

* * *

On the drive out of town, she glanced at the bay. A pair of gulls, hovering above the pewter sea, folded their wings and plummeted into the water like stones. The raft of dark clouds mustering on the horizon threatened more rain.

Not long after she turned onto a narrow road through the forest, a battered pickup roared up behind her, aggressively close, and honked twice before speeding past.

Her shoulders tensed and she regretted her errand. What

did she hope to learn from seeing the house? Pure voyeurism was all it was. She'd already examined the photos of the crime scene in all their gory detail. The bodies and blood. Toppled furniture. The bloody cleaver and kitchen knife sealed into evidence bags. Surely that was enough.

As the dark spruce gave way to birch saplings, shafts of light filtered through the boughs and the layer of mist above the loamy ground. A dilapidated house set back in the trees showed no signs of life. By the time she turned onto Easton Road, her hands ached from clenching the wheel. After rounding a bend, where the dark evergreens grew right up to the road, she came upon the house. Number 44. The name on the letter box was Gilbert.

Tall stands of hickory and sycamore dwarfed the white clapboard house. When the Stern family lived there, it was painted a pale grey with a dark green door. In summer, with the trees in leaf, the house would be largely invisible from the street. Farther down the road, Erin could just see the nearest mailbox, a good hundred yards away.

A man in a yellow rain slicker rounded the corner of the house, pushing a loaded wheelbarrow. He stopped in front of a sprawling rhododendron hedge at the edge of the lawn, the pink buds just coming into bloom, and began to shovel dark soil on the ground.

Erin parked on a soggy patch of grass in front of the house and stepped out. The cool air was pungent with damp earth and rain-washed pines.

Grasping the shovel, the man looked up and squinted. 'Not selling anything, are you?' He pointed to a sign by the driveway. *No soliciting*.

She shivered in the chilly breeze. 'No, nothing to sell.'

'Glad to hear it. I don't mean to be unfriendly, but a man likes his quiet, and these door-to-door snake oil peddlers and Jehovah's whatsits have got all out of control.'

She wondered how long he'd lived here. If this man bought the house soon after the murders, he'd probably had his fill of curiosity seekers and busybodies gawking through the windows. Or kids spooking each other on Halloween.

'My name is Erin... Carson,' she said, exaggerating her British accent. 'When I was a child my family came over from London to spend the summer holiday here.' She paused, inventing as she went. 'My father spent some time in Maine as a boy and he wanted to visit again. Memory lane and all that.'

The man had yet to relax his grip on the shovel or move out from behind the wheelbarrow.

'I met a girl who lived here. Lucy Tomlin,' Erin said, pulling the name out of the air. 'There was a trampoline out back, the star attraction in the neighbourhood.'

What neighbourhood? The question was clearly stamped on the man's face. 'Is that so?' He knocked a clump of mud from his boots. 'Well, I don't know anything about a girl named Lucy. Only one other family lived here before we bought the place. There were two girls, I believe, but my memory's not what it used to be.'

A gust of wind rustled the damp boughs of the trees. Erin hugged her elbows for warmth. 'I wondered if I might have a brief look inside the house. For old times' sake.'

Pushing his hat off his forehead, he fixed her with a gimlet eye. 'Sure you're not selling something? Religious pamphlets, a plot at the local cemetery? I already got one of those and my own beliefs too, so I'll thank you to keep yours to yourself.'

She raised her hand. 'No plots, no pamphlets.'

'All right then.' He scanned the sky. 'I guess the rhodies can wait a few minutes.'

He turned abruptly, and she followed him round the back of the house, where the thickly planted spruce trees, fronted by more rhododendrons, cast a deep shade on the scraggly lawn. She made a mental note of the distance from the back door to the driveway. Fifteen yards, perhaps twenty. No more than that.

They entered the mudroom, where a green duffel coat and black parka hung on hooks. The man levered off his boots and peeled off the rain slicker.

'Go on in through the kitchen. I guess you know the way.'

Erin stepped through the doorway. Scuffed linoleum in a starburst pattern of mustard and brown. An avocado-green cooker and fridge. Not much changed in here. The photos from the forensic report flashed through her head. Tim's mother on the floor. Streaks of blood on the walls. She squeezed her eyes shut, trying to jar the scene from her mind.

'Are you okay, Miss? Looks like you're having some kind of spell.' Mr Gilbert folded his arms, as if waiting for her to drop the charade and wave a sheaf of religious tracts under his nose. 'I'll get you a glass of water.'

'No, I'm fine. Please don't go to any trouble.' She passed a hand over her eyes, hoping she wouldn't faint. *Get a grip.* The buzzing in her ears faded to a dull whine. 'I'll just have a quick look around and be out of your way.'

'Suit yourself. Though I hope you're not planning on pocketing a souvenir or two from your glory days with... What was your little friend's name?

'Lucy.'

'Right. Lucy.' His eyes rested on her face. 'Go on, have your look around.' He shooed her out of the kitchen. 'There's a nice view of the bay from the front bedroom upstairs, though I guess you'd remember that.'

Relieved he wasn't going to trail her round the house, Erin escaped into the front hall. No fool, the man would see straight away she'd never been here before. She peeked into the living room, gloomy with heavy drapes and a distinctive musty smell. A yellow and green crocheted Afghan was draped over a faded chintz sofa. A thin layer of dust coated the walnut sideboard. Sliding glass doors led onto a wooden deck out back, stained black on the edges with mould. Mr Gilbert appeared to live in the house alone. There'd been no mention of a wife.

An alcove off the living room contained a narrow bed, a cracked leather recliner, and an ancient television, boxed in a fake mahogany veneer. A well-thumbed paperback mystery, with a raven-haired woman in a ruby dress on the cover, lay on the bedside table. Black-capped chickadees swooped around a feeder hanging from the branches of a dogwood tree, its white petals ghostly in the mist. She held her breath. Other than the ticking of the grandfather clock, the house was silent as a tomb.

As she climbed the stairs to the upper floor, she counted the steps, trying to picture Tim, his mind intent on the deed to come, approaching the bedroom where his sisters slept. She reached the landing to find all the doors closed. On a scalloped-edge table, a vase of dried flowers gathered dust in the stillness. When she blinked, the crime scene flashed like a strobe light in her head. The sisters laid out on the twin beds in the room to her left, blood covering their chests.

A shadow passed over her like a living presence, and she grabbed the bannister. *Don't be stupid.* There was nothing behind that door. No evil in the air, or traces of the horror. And certainly no ghosts of the two girls in their white summer nightgowns. Erin placed her hand on the tarnished brass knob, cool under her damp palm. The hinges squeaked when the door swung open. Bunk beds pushed against the wall, a poster of a hockey player and a rock band she didn't recognise. She breathed out and shut the door.

The other bedroom had pale pink walls and a white bookcase filled with children's books. A stuffed giraffe lay on the pillow with its legs splayed. An empty stage set, waiting for the actors to appear. Directly above her head, something scraped along the ceiling. Faint at first, then growing louder. *Scritch, scratch*, punctuated by an unearthly yowl, and the scrabbling of fingernails on the floorboards. She held her breath and waited. A desperate whimper erupted from above, then faded into silence. Her instinct was to bolt.

A man's voice boomed from below. 'Find what you're looking for?'

22

Mr Gilbert stood at the bottom of the stairs, his neck stuck out like a snapping turtle. Erin shrank from his blunt stare. It was time to make a hasty exit.

In the kitchen, she retrieved her bag and pulled on her jacket, not bothering with the buttons.

'Thank you so much,' she said, moving towards the door. 'But I should be going now.'

He rinsed a coffee mug in the sink and dried it with a tea towel. 'Notice anything different from when you were here before?'

'Not especially.' She gripped the strap on her bag.

'Well then,' he returned the mug to the cupboard and swivelled to face her, an amused flicker in his eyes. 'You might want to get yourself checked out by a doctor. The house that used to be here was destroyed in a fire.'

Her cheeks flushed. *Destroyed?* He'd known all along she was lying.

'Six months after we bought the place,' Gilbert said, running a damp sponge over the countertop, 'the whole thing went up in flames. The police suspected arson. My wife didn't care either way. A blessing in disguise, is what she said, and that if the old Indian gent hadn't banished the bad spirits from the house, the fire surely did.'

Indian gent?

'You'd make a terrible poker player, Miss… Carson, is it?' He dropped the tea towel on the counter. 'There never was any Lucy, was there? It's the murder house you came to see.' He chuckled. 'I can spot 'em a mile away. Though we don't get many these days. The last one was three, maybe four years ago. Some nosy parker claiming he was writing a magazine article. Don't know if anything ever came of it, and I don't care. But I could see it in your face, plain as day. Fascination, fear, horror, whatever you want to call it. My wife wouldn't let them inside. But I figured, what's the harm, just this once.'

She dropped her bag and sank into a chair, embarrassed at having been caught in a lie.

'You look like you've seen a ghost. Cup of coffee'll fix you right up.'

'No, I'm fine.' Erin cleared her throat. 'Thank you.' She stood. 'I'll be on my way then.'

'I was already planning to make some for myself, so it's no trouble. You've come this far, and I have yet to see any pamphlets.' He rubbed his jaw. 'Weekends are awfully quiet since I sold the store.' At the sink, he scrubbed his hands with a block of white soap and filled an enamel kettle with water from the tap.

Clearly, the poor man was lonely. The least she could do was stay for a coffee.

She perched on the edge of the chair. 'You owned a store?'

'Sugar's on the table. You take milk?' He removed a carton from the refrigerator and gave it a sniff. 'I did indeed,' he said, when they were seated across from each other, the steaming mugs between them. 'Gilbert's Hardware. Nineteen years, right smack in the middle of Main Street. It was supposed to be Gilbert & Sons at some point, but neither of my boys wanted anything to do with it. Three years ago, I sold it to a young couple from New York City. Wish I'd known they were going to turn it into a coffee place, or I might not have done it. Poked my head in there a while back,

126

thinking maybe I'd get a cup of joe. But all they've got are these godawful... *confections* that nobody's ever heard of, least not in my day. Hazelnut swirl delight.' He wrinkled his nose. 'Viennese amaretto thingamabob. Whatever that is. Well, good luck to them.'

A clock chimed the hour. A deeply resonant tone from another age. They drank their coffee in silence.

'I was eleven when Tim Stern murdered his family,' Erin said, glancing up to meet his eye. 'I was staying in Belle River with my family the summer it happened, I didn't lie about that.'

He looked at her steadily before setting his cup on the table. 'I've got a tin of ginger snaps somewhere,' he said, hauling himself from the chair. 'Gift from the ladies at the care home.' After a brief rummage in the cupboard, he pulled out a round tin, gaily patterned with blue and yellow pansies.

Care home? She took one of the proffered biscuits. Was that where his wife was?

The warm kitchen, a kindly old man, coffee and ginger snaps. Such a homely tableau. When was the last time she'd done anything like this? A spasm of grief passed through her, for what she'd lost, or never had. She turned away and blinked back tears.

'We bought the place in the winter of '79,' he said, dunking a ginger snap in his coffee. 'Didn't know about the murders at the time, though Milly and I were surprised the asking price was so cheap. Just a couple of yokels from the Midwest, so what did we know? That realtor lady sure kept her lip zipped. Didn't take long for us to find out, what with the neighbours busting to spill the news in all its gory detail. They trooped over here with their welcome casseroles and their gossip.' He added another splash of milk to his coffee. 'Poor Milly. She wanted to move out before we'd unpacked the boxes, but we'd sunk all our money into the house. And given the history, who would buy it?'

Erin turned her head towards the window. If he'd bought

the house in 1979, then she might have passed Mr Gilbert on the street a few years after that. But in those days, newly freed from Danfield and under the protection of her aunt, she had kept close to Olivia's house, terrified of being plucked off the street and spirited away.

'But Milly was so spooked by what happened here, she couldn't sleep,' Mr Gilbert was saying. 'The local librarian, a sweet old gal and smart as a whip, understood our dilemma, so she suggested we do some kind of cleansing ritual. If nothing else, it might make Milly feel better. So, Milly got hold of some old gent from the Penobscot tribe. He came in with a lot of gewgaws and whatsits. Burned a bunch of feathers and switchgrass, with plenty of chanting and dancing to go along with it. When he was done, he claimed the spirits of the dead had agreed to leave the house. *Agreed*, that's the word he used. Can you believe it? Stuff and nonsense. But after that, Milly did feel better, so who was I to scoff?'

He looked round the kitchen. 'Funny how the house burned down while we were out of town. A little road trip to Ohio to visit Milly's family. Got back to find the place charred to bits. 'Course, the police came around asking questions. Did we have any enemies? Shady business connections? The insurance money paid to build this place.' He cocked his head at the door to the hallway. 'Sometimes I hear things that go bump in the night, but usually it's squirrels or raccoons that get into the attic.' He gave her a sly wink. 'Scared you, didn't it, all that hullabaloo up there? Family of raccoons set up camp about a month ago. Don't have the heart to move them, even though they make a godawful racket when the mood strikes.' He glanced out the window, as if he'd just remembered his rhododendrons and the threat of rain. 'My wife's got the Alzheimer's now.'

'I'm sorry to hear that.'

'Yes, well. Our kids visit when they can, but they've got their own lives, and their own families to worry about.' He stood and craned his neck to scan at the sky. 'I'm going to have to get back to my rhodies soon. Milly loved her garden and I try to keep it going for her sake.'

* * *

Out front, he examined the sodden lawn. 'You know, I think about that boy sometimes,' he said, as he walked her to her car. 'Wondering what kind of demons drove him to do such a terrible thing. Hard to make sense of, isn't it?' He tugged a canvas hat over his head. 'Back in high school, our younger boy got in with a bad crowd. Drinking, drugs, breaking into houses. There was a time Milly and I thought the best thing that could happen was for him to get arrested. We thought that a spell in juvenile hall, or even jail, would knock some sense into him. But he managed to straighten himself out in the end. When I think about that boy who lived here… there but for the grace of God. It could have been my kid.'

He picked up the shovel and started across the lawn before turning back. 'You got any children, Miss Carson?'

She shook her head.

'Well, if you ever do have any, keep in mind that it isn't always a rose garden. Raising kids, I mean.' He turned his head away. 'And speaking of gardens… I best be getting on with it.'

* * *

On the road back to town, Erin thought about something Mr Gilbert had said. How the local librarian had been a help to them. Ruth Davis it must have been. To Erin, Mrs Davis had been a wellspring of warmth and wisdom, and it was nice to know someone else appreciated her kindness and sharp mind. She'd be retired now, and it was anybody's guess where she might be living, but if anyone had inside knowledge of the town's secrets, it would be her. And after a whole day of wandering around town without incident, Erin's fear she might be recognised had faded to nothing but a whisper.

23

Greenlake Psychiatric Facility
Atherton, New York
April, Present Day

Greenlake's steel gate swung open to allow Erin through. Two weeks had passed since the ill-fated lunch at the Adirondack Café. With any luck, despite her blunder, Tim wouldn't have lost the delicate trust she'd managed to foster between them, and they could pick up where they left off. In the morning, she would conduct another unstructured assessment, and in the afternoon complete the final evaluation mandated by the state. That would give her plenty of time to write her report and send it to the review board. Whatever happened after that was out of her hands.

The mild weather put a spring in her step that not even the incessant buzz and clank of the ward could dispel. But after being ushered into Harrison's office by an attendant, one look at his distracted expression and deathly pallor was enough to puncture her buoyant mood.

She hung back by the door. 'Is everything all right?'

'I'm afraid not.' Perspiration dotted his forehead. 'Tim suffered a relapse in the early hours of the morning. A rather severe psychotic episode, I'm afraid. We had to put him in restraints and forcibly sedate him.' He pulled off his glasses and rubbed his eyes. 'It's been chaos around here. Just last week, a patient in Tim's ward was found dead with his throat cut.'

A chill passed through her, and she waited for him to say more.

'I've been up all night,' he continued, sinking back into his chair. 'I should have cancelled your appointment today, but it completely slipped my mind.'

Distracted and distraught though he was, it was imperative that Erin hear the details. This new development in Tim's case could change everything. She set her bag on the floor. 'Can you tell me what happened?'

'The death? Or Tim's relapse?'

'Are they related?'

'Possibly.' He motioned for her to sit. 'It was Darryl who was killed.'

She settled in the chair. 'Darryl?'

'The man who liked to pretend-steal Tim's Sudoku.'

Erin felt a wave of unease as she slipped her arms out of her coat. 'Do you know who's responsible?'

'Not yet. Though I have my suspicions.' He shuffled some papers on his desk. 'Two of our attendants are being questioned by the police. One might be arrested. He's a fairly new hire, with a record of violence, apparently, though I'm not sure how he slipped through our vetting procedure.' He made a note in the file in front of him and snapped it closed. 'When I took over the reins here fifteen years ago, the first thing I did was to institute a number of reforms. The abuse of inmates that went on in this place would make your blood curdle. Though it hasn't always been smooth sailing, I've been proud of our record since then. But now this.'

She examined the extreme pallor of his skin. If anything, he had grown even paler, as if he'd lost a great deal of blood. 'So, Tim's not under suspicion?'

Harrison looked startled. 'Indeed, no. We've definitely

ruled him out.' He paused. 'Though I can't say it didn't cross my mind.'

* * *

They passed through the ward and its series of locked doors. The air was especially stale, as if the whole place was in lockdown. Erin paused as they walked by the dayroom, where a dozen or more patients milled about, but there was no sign of Tim. In the staffroom, Harrison poured out the old coffee and started a fresh pot.

'It began last night,' he said, picking up the narrative he'd begun in his office, 'when Tim refused to turn his light off. He was quite insistent it stay on. When the attendant switched it off anyway, Tim launched himself off the bed, howling with outrage.'

This was a side of Tim she hadn't seen. 'Did he attack the attendant?'

'Fortunately, no. But he was clearly distressed. And the attendant was rattled, to say the least. He's never known Tim to be violent. Not in his five years on the ward. In the end, he told Tim he could sleep with the light on. But the attendant who came in for the late shift must have turned it off, because the room was dark when Tim began shouting around two in the morning. It took three attendants to restrain him long enough to get a needle into him. About an hour ago, we moved him to an isolation room.'

Poor Tim. He must be terrified. But Erin's heart sank at the thought of another delay. As for Harrison, he seemed not only dispirited, but physically ill. Making a mental note of the date and time, she couldn't help wondering if they were back at square one. 'Shall I suspend my assessment?'

He finished his coffee and poured another. 'I think we should proceed as planned. We've adjusted his medication, and there's still plenty of time. Your report's not due until the end of May. In a week or two, your schedule permitting, we can start again.' He glanced at the barred window overlooking the car park. 'Oh, now that you're here, I heard you accompanied Lydia Belmont on the home study visit.' He grabbed a sponge to scrub at a stain by the sink. 'I understand the house is rather isolated. That's a worry, of course. But at least Stern has a mobile phone and internet access. They won't be completely cut off.'

Erin said nothing, but she couldn't help thinking that, given the isolation, the phone and internet would offer little help in a crisis. 'Would you consider allowing Tim to see the house, before anything is decided?' If he didn't like the place, it might have an impact on her assessment.

'Normally, I would, but what Tim thinks about the house won't make any difference now.' Harrison loosened the knot on his tie.

'I don't understand.'

'Greenlake has become another fiscal casualty, I'm afraid. We're slated for closure at the end of the year. Any patients not fit for release into the community will be transferred to other secure facilities in the state.' He sat on one of the worn sofas and rubbed his knee. 'If it were up to me, Dr Cartwright, he would remain at Greenlake for the remainder of his natural life. Since that's no longer an option, we should all be grateful that Tim's father has stepped forward.'

The news was like a blow. How long had he known? And why wait until now, when her evaluation was nearly finished, to drop the bombshell? If Tim were declared unfit for release, he would be shipped off to another facility. Even more crowded and grim than Greenlake, surely, with a different warden and staff and a new set of rules. So, regardless of her concerns about sending Tim to his father, she had no choice but to advocate for his release.

The room was stifling and she fanned her face. When her eyes met his, she saw sympathy in his look. In that moment, a light blinked on. *Of course, he knew*. He'd known all along about her role in the Leonard Whidby case. Hobart must have told him. So, he understood her dilemma, and that a heightened concern for the father's safety was a significant factor in her decision.

* * *

As they walked back through the ward, Erin was beset with painful memories of the Whidby case. Two days after Leonard was released, on Erin's recommendation, from the psych ward of a hospital in Sheffield, she had arrived home at her flat in the evening to find him standing in the bedroom, wielding one of her kitchen knives, blood seeping from a wound on his hand, and his eyes glinting with malice.

Erin had stood in the doorway, frozen in terror, until her training kicked in. She remembered to make eye contact and speak in a calm voice. 'You seem upset, Leonard. Why don't you put the knife down so we can talk about how you're feeling.' Trying to sound friendly and supportive, while agonisingly aware he might kill her if she made a sudden move. Putting on a bright voice, she had announced she was hungry and would like to order a pizza. He was welcome to share it with her. She'd smiled at him as she dialled the number of a psychiatrist friend. While fake ordering a cheese pizza, she had said their emergency code word, gripping the phone to keep her hand from shaking. That one word, *heavenly*, had saved her life.

After the police stormed through her door and took Leonard away, she had fallen to the floor in a heap, unable to stop shaking. Later, she learned that after savagely gunning down his parents in their home, he had dismembered the bodies with a butcher's knife.

As a newly minted doctor, she'd been taken in by Leonard's winning smile and beguiling charm, too naive to understand she was dealing with a psychopath. A skilled chameleon, he reflected back whatever she wanted to see and believe. After the Whidby case, notorious throughout the country, and her name in all the papers, she'd abruptly ended her career in forensic psychiatry.

No more criminally violent men.

Until now. Stern's blood on her hands would be more than she could bear.

'Yours is not an easy position to be in, Dr Cartwright,' Harrison said, when they reached his office. 'If it's any consolation, it helps me to remember that we're not gods but mere mortals with little control, if any, over the fate of our patients. Particularly after they leave our care.' He laid a paternal hand on her shoulder. 'Our best is all we can ever do. Everything else must be given up to fate.'

* * *

An attendant with a spider tattoo on his neck was Erin's mute companion on the long trek to the isolation room. The paint on the heavy steel door, once white, had been scratched and clawed away. She stood on her toes to peer through the observation window, no bigger than the width of her hand. *Welcome to Hell.* She closed her eyes, waiting for darkness to descend. But for Tim's sake, she bit her lip and pulled herself together.

The room appeared empty, and her heart skipped a beat. Could he have escaped? But in the corner, she spotted what looked like a pile of rags. It was Tim, in white hospital garb, curled into a ball, rocking to and fro. A vision of despair.

Behind her, the attendant stood uncomfortably close. She could smell the stink of alcohol on his breath.

'How long will he have to stay in there?'

The man grunted. 'That's for the docs to decide.' He jangled a fistful of keys and unlocked the door.

She hesitated. Her last meeting with Tim didn't end well. In the grip of a paranoid delusion, he might see her as the enemy, a co-conspirator behind his loss of freedom.

'In or out?' the attendant said. On his neck, the spider jerked with each beat of the man's blood.

She stepped into the room, and the door slammed shut behind her. No going back now. Mould, stale urine, unwashed feet. The smell made her gag.

'Hello, Timothy.' The rocking continued. 'It's Dr Cartwright.' She hung back against the closed door. 'I wanted to make sure you were all right.'

From the corner came a high-pitched, insistent humming, like a wasp.

'Dr Harrison told me you were upset last night. Would you like to talk about it?' No response. Perhaps a distraction would help. 'If you're feeling up to it, we could play a game. Something with numbers.' She removed a pencil stub from her pocket and sketched a triangle on the padded canvas. In the middle, she wrote the number nine. 'It's called a magic triangle.'

Tim's face remained buried in his arms.

'Take a look, it really is like magic.'

Slowly, he raised his head, and she gasped at the condition of his face. Eyes like bruised plums. An angry swelling disfigured his jaw. Did they have to be so rough? His eyes were fixed on a rust-coloured stain on the floor.

'A triangle...?' Alert, but wary.

'Yes. I've drawn one on the wall.'

Tim tightened the grip on his knees, but his battered face showed a flicker of interest. Whatever had happened, he was still in there.

'This one's easy,' she said. 'All you need to do is come up with three numbers on each side that add up to nine. Do you want to try it?' She held out the pencil. Too short to be used as an effective weapon. But still. If she cried out, no one would hear her. She could only hope someone was watching them on the monitor.

His eyes flicked from the pencil to the floor. She stayed still, though her arm was beginning to ache. Like a wax figure coming to life, he loosened his grip on his knees and staggered upright. The room, no more than ten by twelve feet, was worryingly small, and she tensed. When she stepped forward and placed the pencil in his palm, her fingers grazed his skin. Gripping the pencil stub in his fist, he shuffled to the wall. In a matter of seconds, the puzzle was completed, the numbers jagged as chicken scratches on the dirty canvas.

'Great, Timothy.' She relaxed a little. 'You're a master at this.'

In his right hand, he clutched a wad of paper.

'What's that you've got?'

'Sudoku.' It came out as a croak.

'You tore pages out of your book?'

'No books allowed. No pencil. I can have three pages.'

She stepped away and sketched two more magic triangles on the wall. Tim completed them as effortlessly as breathing. Now she was stuck. Off the top of her head, she couldn't think of another one.

'Shall we try a different game? This one uses words instead of numbers. But before we start, I want you to close your eyes and take a few deep breaths. Like this.' She placed her hands on her belly and breathed in and out.

Tim copied her, hands on his abdomen, and sucked air noisily into his lungs. His breathing was laboured and slow.

'Okay, here's how the new game works,' she said. 'I'll say a word, and then you say the first word that comes into your head. Ready?'

Tim pressed his back against the wall and slid to the floor. 'I'm tired.'

'That's okay, it won't take long. When we're finished, it'll be easier for you to sleep. Ready? Sky.'

Silence. The only sound was the gurgle of water through the pipes in the ceiling.

He breathed out. 'Clouds.'

'That's great, Timothy. Let's try another one. Ocean.'

'Cold.'

'Eagle.'

'Free.' He loosened the grip on his knees.

'Rainbow.'

'Parrot.' He lay on his side and closed his eyes. 'My head hurts.'

'I'll let you rest, then,' she said, backing towards the door. 'Later, when you're feeling better, I'll come back and we can do some other games.'

'You're leaving?'

'I can stay a little longer, if you'd like.'

His eyes were half-closed, his breathing ragged.

'I don't want to go back to my room,' he said, his voice thick with fatigue. 'Not if that man is there.'

'You mean the attendant who turned your light off?'

'No. That man on my bed. He had a mean face. I yelled at him. But he wouldn't go away.'

A man on Tim's bed? Harrison hadn't mentioned anything like this. Was he delusional, hallucinating? Or was it something else? She was afraid to move and break the spell.

'What did the man look like?'

Tim peered at her from under the fringe of hair, his eyes in shadow. 'Like me. Exactly the same.'

* * *

During the long drive back to Lansford, Erin mused about this latest development, Tim's mysterious hallucination about a man who resembled him, lying on his bed. Like a doppelgänger. A malevolent twin conjured up by a delusional brain, though it could be something neurological, like temporal lobe epilepsy – in medical school, she'd once read about a similar case. Or it could be a Fregoli delusion, that oddest of neurological quirks in which the affected individual believes that everyone they meet is the same person in disguise. But Tim's medical history made no mention of visual hallucinations, only auditory ones: voices, ringing bells, whispers. The formal assessment she'd signed on to, and should have taken two weeks at most, had mutated into an endless labyrinth, full of false turns and dead ends.

By the time she reached the turn-off to Lansford, she was no wiser as to her next move. If Tim missed his court date, it could be another year before a new one was scheduled. Neither of them had time for that kind of delay.

The road to Lansford High School was coming up on her right. On impulse, she turned onto it and drove through a neighbourhood of modest brick homes with pickup trucks or rusty vans parked in the drives. She'd scoped out the high school twice before, without any luck, hoping to catch a glimpse of Cassie. Almost four o'clock, and school would be out for the day. But it wouldn't hurt to swing by.

As a precaution, Erin pushed her hair under a cap and hunched down in the driver's seat. A pity she didn't have a pair of binoculars, though that would peg her as a stalker, and she was already crossing the line.

On the school's front steps, a few students larked about in the spring sunshine. But nobody who looked like Cassie. As she reached for the ignition, a girl with short dark hair and Cassie's slender frame waltzed through the door, her arm draped over a boy in a leather jacket. She stopped and nuzzled the boy's neck, playfully pushing her knee between his legs.

As Erin started the engine, the girl turned her head in her direction. Cassie, no question about it. She glared at Erin for several seconds, her posture rigid, a sullen look on her face, before whispering something in the boy's ear. He smirked and wrapped her in a bear hug. Behind his back, Cassie shoved her middle finger high in the air, before stepping away, hands balled into fists. 'Stop stalking me.' She fixed her eyes on Erin, her face tight with fury. 'Or I'll call the police.'

24

Belle River, Maine
July 1977

He stumbles on the rocks above the beach, nearly dropping
the crate of lobsters. A leaden sea sloshes in the fading light.
It's taken him twenty minutes of slogging through the woods
to reach his father's so-called secret cove. The town beach
isn't good enough for one of his famous parties. Ruined by
out-of-towners with their fat wives and smelly egg salad and
tinny radios. Or so he claims.

The rock-strewn spit of sand is a far cry from the yacht club,
but even here the old devil manages to hold court. Master of
ceremonies in his mirror sunglasses and a sky-blue polo shirt
with the neck unbuttoned. Green and yellow checked shorts
ride up over his father's sunburned knees as he kneels to dig
a bottle of Löwenbräu from a plastic cooler. His white teeth
flash as he salutes his guests, though the smile sours when he
catches sight of Tim. There'll be hell to pay later, though who
knows what he's done this time. It's always something. But
he's safe for now. The self-proclaimed wizard of the cocktail
hour won't let anything spoil his party.

As he trudges down the sand with the poor beasts struggling

to escape the crate, the guests' faces swim into view. The yacht club crowd. Summer people, mainly, though he recognises one of the fat-cat lawyers from the Portland office. The blonde lady with the frosty smile and tinkly laugh is making a 'poor you' face at his mother, who's developed an ugly rash from something she ate. Swanning across the sand, the blonde lady flashes her long legs in an orange and white mini-dress. Next to her, his mother looks dumpy and glum. The jingle-bell titter grates on his nerves. *Give it up, lady.* No one wants to see your wrinkly knees.

'The prodigal son, here at last.' His father's voice rises above the water slapping against the rocks. He smiles for his guests, but the words are tipped with ice.

He's late. Before picking up the lobsters, he'd stopped by Jeremy's for a couple of hits off his friend's bong. His eyes, a tad bloodshot, might give him away, but he doesn't care. All summer his father's been treating him like his own personal slave, and he's sick of it.

'Ooh, lobsters. How marvellous,' the blonde woman says in a fluty voice. 'You clever man.' She tilts her chin and taps his father playfully on the arm. 'You'd think there wouldn't be a single lobster left in the state after last week's regatta. And what a triumph that was.' She bats her mascaraed eyes. 'People will be talking about it for years.'

'I happen to have a top-secret source,' his father says, clinking his bottle of beer against the woman's cocktail glass. They giggle like teenagers.

Perched on a piece of driftwood, his mother squirts a blob of white cream from a tube and smears it on her arms.

He picks his way down the rocks, hugging the crate to his chest. Poor beasts, scrabbling in their cardboard prison. Do they know that death is imminent? When school starts, he's going to swear off meat and let his hair grow out. That'll piss off the old man. You'd think he'd invented filet mignon and prime rib, the way he goes on about the benefits of a bloody steak. Washed down, of course, with liberal amounts of Scotch or gin. From now on, he'll stick to carrots.

Near the fire pit, he drops the crate and tries to rub some life back into his arms. From the other side of the headland, a boy his age clambers into view, clutching a basket of seaweed against his bare chest. *Crap.* It's the skinny kid who hangs around with that Viking asshole. What's he doing here?

His father salutes the kid with a bottle of Löwenbräu. 'There's the man of the hour.' A grin splits his face. 'Without this marvellous harvest of seaweed, ladies and gentleman, there would be no steamed lobsters. So, let's all give Louie a round of applause.'

As the boy lowers the basket to the ground, he's got a stupid grin on his face, as he basks in the light of the old man's praise.

Tim snorts in disgust. Does his father know that his skinny-assed hero is the biggest hophead at school?

With plenty of backslapping, and joking around, the kid and his father set to work lining the fire pit with seaweed. As the coals spit and smoke, the rich smell of the seabed, with its fish bones and scuttling claws, billows in the air. At long last, the lobsters are ceremoniously lowered to their deaths, antennae waving in a final plea for mercy.

His father slips a wad of folded notes into the boy's hand and slaps him on the back once more.

'Thanks, Mr Stern.'

The Boy Scout grin is bogus. *Christ.* If his father only knew.

'Don't mention it. And, hey, why don't you stick around? There's plenty of grub. No need to rush off if you don't have to.' He slings his arm around the boy's shoulder.

Tim spits on the sand in disgust, but the sour taste in his mouth remains. He turns and heads up the beach to retrieve his bike.

'Look at that sunset.'

It's the blonde lady, waltzing across the sand. She places a hand on his father's shoulder as she leans over to adjust the strap on her sandal.

'A photo, that's what we need.' He snaps his fingers.

'To commemorate a stupendous evening, and this glorious gathering of friends.'

Tim has grabbed the handlebars of his ten-speed and is just about to hop on when his father shouts, 'Hey, get back down here. I need you to take a picture.'

When he turns and squints, the Sun is a huge ball, suspended above the horizon.

'Come on, hop to it, or the light will go.'

He considers telling his dad to take a hike, but that'll make things worse. Like a whipped dog, he scrambles down the rocks, scraping his hand on a patch of barnacles.

Without looking at him, his father hands over the Instamatic.

'Come on, fellow revellers. This one's for the history books.'

But two of the couples have wandered to the far side of the cove, taking their drinks with them. So, it's just the blonde lady and her husband who get hustled in front of the fire pit. His father positions himself between them. 'Dorrie, come on, get in the picture.'

She shakes her head. 'Not with this.' She points to the rash on her arms and chest.

'No one will care.' His face is flushed, and his eyes snap with impatience. He waits for his wife to join the group, though she keeps to the edge, standing as far from the blonde lady as she can get.

He turns to Tim, his face dark with sunburn. 'Come on, come on! Take the picture. And make sure you get the sunset. Okay, gang, this is for posterity. Say *cheese*.'

Tim lifts the camera and squints through the viewfinder. The Sun is going fast. If he doesn't move quickly, it'll be too late. One more thing he'll have screwed up. But the skinny kid's in the frame, crouching down to look at something on the sand. *Move, jerk*. But if he waits any longer, the Sun will be gone. The four adults, burnished by sun and loopy with drink, flash their teeth.

His hand twitches, and he presses the shutter.

25

Norfolk, Rhode Island
April, Present Day

A woman with a halo of soft white hair peered through the gap in the doorway. Her skin was deeply lined, but her eyes, the colour of toffee, held a familiar spark. It was the warmth of her smile Erin remembered. Not to mention Ruth Davis' canny ability to take your measure at a glance, before plucking a book from the library shelves to suit the mood.

She looked searchingly at Erin's face before ushering her into the tidy flat. A large bay window, crowded with airy ferns and pink cyclamen, looked out onto a vast tract of marshland. The far wall was lined with books.

'Thank you for taking the time to see me,' Erin said, setting her bag on the floor. 'You've got a lovely place here.'

'Please make yourself at home.' She motioned to a plush green armchair before heading into the kitchen. 'And do call me Ruth. Otherwise,' she smiled, 'I'll feel like an old lady.' Within minutes, she returned with a tea tray. 'Does it expose my ignorance to assume the English prefer tea? Years ago, a dear friend from Devon taught me how to make a proper pot of black tea, and I've been a devoted tea drinker ever since. I've got coffee, if you'd prefer, but afternoon tea is so much more civilised, don't you think?' She poured out the tea in delicate china cups with a spray of violets painted on the rim.

Erin added milk and took a sip. Perfectly brewed. 'Proust would approve.'

'Ah, Monsieur Marcel.' Ruth's eyes twinkled.

The enticing citrus odour of the freshly baked lemon cake was irresistible, and Erin helped herself to a slice.

'So, you're a journalist then, or a writer doing a story on Belle River?' Ruth regarded her over the rim of her cup. 'I didn't quite catch what you said on the phone.'

Erin squirmed at having to lie to the woman who'd once saved her sanity, if not her life, when the Belle River library provided an island of calm in a sea of chaos. The memory of the much-thumbed pages of *Anne of Green Gables* and *Little Women* still lived in her fingertips. Even now, she had only to close her eyes to project herself into the March family's cosy parlour, a twin to the feisty Jo, and cast an adoring eye on Marmee. On many a gloomy day, she hungered still for that fictional family's love and the warmth of the firelight.

'Actually, I'm a doctor,' Erin said. 'A psychiatrist.' This time, the lies wouldn't come. Some cake crumbs had lodged in her throat and she coughed. 'I work at a private clinic for girls in upstate New York.'

'How rewarding,' Ruth said, dabbing her lips with a napkin. 'Helping young girls in need.'

Their eyes met briefly over the teacups before Erin looked away. If she wasn't careful, she would dissolve into floods of tears.

Ruth murmured something and crossed the room to open the balcony doors. A lively breeze carried the scent of the salt flats into the room.

'As a side project, I've been working on a series of case studies,' Erin said, when Ruth returned to her chair. 'One concerns a former student of yours, and I was hoping you could help me fill in some gaps in his background.' She returned the teacup to its saucer and straightened up. 'His name is Tim Stern.'

Ruth's face grew pale. 'Oh my.' She fiddled with the emerald ring on her left hand. 'Tim Stern,' she murmured. 'That poor family. It was a terrible shock when we heard what happened. The tail end of the summer vacation, it was, and Don Hickey, he was the principal at the high school, called all the teachers at home to give us the news.'

Only after Erin started to dig into the details of Tim's case, did she remember that Mrs Davis, in addition to her role as town librarian during the summer, had taught English at Belle River High School.

'Shall we go for a stroll?' Ruth's eyes looked troubled. 'I could do with some fresh air.'

* * *

A flock of terns swooped and squabbled at the water's edge. The air, wonderfully fresh and alive, carried the sharp, briny scent of the sea. After guiding Erin through the bracken, Ruth led her onto a well-trodden path that wound through the marshland.

'Brisk today, isn't it?' Ruth said as she fastened the buttons on her coat. 'Not cold, are you?'

Erin shook her head.

They walked in silence for several minutes before Ruth cleared her throat. 'So, Tim is one of your… case studies, is that it?'

Admitting the truth would be a breach of ethics, but she didn't have the stomach to lie any more than she already had. Posing as a born-and-bred Londoner to colleagues and strangers, and relating stories about growing up in Britain, was one thing, but Ruth had always loomed large in her imagination, to the point where Erin had fantasised as a child about what it would be like to have Ruth as her mother. Yet here she was, prepared to relay another outrageous falsehood. *Ethics be damned.*

'Actually, I've been asked to provide an assessment of his case,' Erin said, tucking her windblown hair into the collar of her coat. 'It's standard procedure for psychiatric patients in the criminal justice system who are eligible for release.'

Beside her, Ruth bent her head into the wind. 'You mean he's been in a mental asylum all these years?'

On the far side of the salt flats, a fleet of sailboats, white canvas billowing in the wind, tacked through the channel.

'I've completed most of the formal assessments,' Erin said, 'but I wanted to speak with someone who knew Tim as a child. Before the crime.'

Ruth adjusted the scarf around her neck. 'It was a terrible shock, of course.' She briefly met Erin's eyes. 'Tim was a quiet boy. Rather awkward. The kind of person you couldn't imagine hurting a fly. He rarely spoke in class and when he did he would sometimes stutter from anxiety, what with everyone staring at him. He wasn't a particularly good student, at least not in my English Literature class. Rather than take notes, he used to doodle in the margins of his paper. Once, I remember catching sight of a list he'd made of the collective nouns for different types of birds. A quarrel of sparrows, a conspiracy of ravens, that sort of thing. But I heard he was good at maths, and something of a talented artist. One time, I passed his desk and looked down to see he'd made an absolutely exquisite sketch of a great blue heron. So lifelike, I felt it might fly off the page. Since he was supposed to be taking an exam, I couldn't exactly praise him for his work, but it was truly lovely.'

Erin pushed her hands into the pockets of her coat. 'What about the father, did you know him?'

'Tim's father? Oh my.' Ruth brushed the windblown hair from her face. 'That poor man. I can't imagine how he went on living after what happened.' She plucked a tissue from her sleeve and dabbed her face. 'I didn't know him socially. But he was quite the man about town in my day, so everyone knew who he was.' She looked up and shaded her eyes against the pale sun. 'Shall we press on? There's a wonderful view of the bay from the lighthouse.'

Erin marvelled at Ruth's vigour. She must be in her mid-seventies, but showed no signs of slowing down.

'I remember the first time I saw him,' Ruth said, bending down to collect a piece of blue sea glass from the sand. 'The summer of 1956. I was on my lunch break with one of the library volunteers. Babs Greeley, her name was. Gosh, I haven't thought about her in years. Anyway, we had just bought ice-cream cones – it was so hot that year – and were heading to the docks. Babs had her eye on a lobsterman, and she was looking out for his boat when someone else caught her eye. She grabbed my arm and said, "Who's that?" I was trying to keep my ice cream from melting all over my hand, but when I looked up, I saw this absolutely gorgeous man. Wavy chestnut hair, eyes like the Aegean, and a smile from a toothpaste ad. The spitting image of Senator Kennedy, only better looking, if you ask me. The whole town was abuzz, so it was easy enough to find out his name. He was a local boy, just graduated from law school in Boston and home for the summer.' Ruth pointed to the sailboats, plunging through the whitecaps. Sunlight sparkled on the water. 'Isn't that a pretty sight?'

A familiar snapshot, blurred by time, surfaced in Erin's head. Her father at the tiller of a Sunfish, his ruddy face turned happily into the wind. This memory of the two of them, one of the few she possessed, had begun to appear at odd moments, ever since her trip to Maine.

'Rumour had it he'd come back to Belle River to set up a law practice,' Ruth was saying. 'Why he didn't stay in Boston or head to another big city after law school was anybody's guess.' She turned into the wind. 'A year later, I saw his wedding picture in the paper. He'd married a girl from Philadelphia. Quite a number of hearts must have been broken that day.' Her lips twitched into a smile. 'Not mine, though, in case you're wondering. Tim Stern *pére* was a bit too flamboyant for me.'

When a shadow blocked the Sun, Erin looked up, surprised to see the lighthouse looming above them. She'd lost all track of time. Her mind was in Belle River with Stern, gallivanting about town, a cocktail glass in hand, holding court at the yacht club.

'Would you look at all those gulls,' Ruth said. 'There must be a school of herring out there.'

As they rested on a nearby bench, Ruth's eyes took on a faraway look. 'After his marriage, I don't recall seeing much of him. At one point, I heard they'd moved to Boston when Mr Stern took a job at a bigger firm. I thought they were gone for good, but they only stayed for a few years, and I still remember my surprise at seeing his wife at the grocery store, pushing a lively little boy in a stroller. I don't know why they left Boston. But by that time, I was married to Marvin and busy with my own life.

'The Sterns had bought a house quite a way out of town. The few times I saw his wife she was no longer the vivacious girl she used to be. Still attractive, but something wasn't quite right. Being a pharmacist, Marvin was bound by confidentiality, and couldn't say, but I suspected those prescriptions she had filled were some kind of sedative. "Mother's little helper", we used to call them. Mr Stern was working for a law firm in Portland then, and he seemed to be out of town a lot.' She hesitated. 'There were rumours of affairs.'

* * *

Back at Ruth's flat, Erin pulled out her notebook and flipped through the pages. *History girl, mystery girl?* She'd been so caught up in Ruth's memories of Tim's father, she'd forgotten to ask. 'Do you remember if Tim had a girlfriend, or maybe a girl he was especially fond of?' She carried the tea tray into the kitchen. The least she could do was help with the washing up before heading home.

Ruth pulled off her walking shoes and slid her feet into a pair of carpet slippers. 'A girlfriend? Not that I'm aware of. He was on the shy side and, as far as I could tell, something of a loner.'

'Were you aware of any trouble at home?'

Ruth pinched off a yellowed leaf from one of the cyclamens. 'Not at the time, though I suppose, in retrospect…' Her voice fell away. 'Isabel, the older sister, was in my freshman English class. A darling girl. Everyone doted on her, the father included. In fact, it was Mr Stern who came to parents' night the year Isabel was in my class. He didn't come to Tim's, which I thought was strange at the time, but he was keen to ask me about his daughter's progress. His eyes shone when he spoke about her, as if she were the light of his life. The other girl too… What was her name? Carla, I think, or maybe Carol. Anyway, I would sometimes see him in town with the two girls, buying ice creams or coming out of a movie matinee. A devoted father, at least where the girls were concerned.'

And Tim? Erin was anxious to learn more about the relationship between father and son. While she washed the cups and set them on the rack to drain, she thought how nice it would be to linger for a while longer. Perhaps whip up something in the kitchen and share a meal at Ruth's table. She dreaded the long drive back to Lansford, where nothing awaited but the empty flat and the grey fog of loneliness that had dogged her for weeks.

Dusk brought shadows into the room and Ruth switched on a lamp. 'Is that a quetzal?'

'I'm sorry, what?'

'The pendant around your neck.'

Usually tucked inside her clothing, Erin wasn't aware the quetzal had swung free.

'I was travelling in Mexico last year and saw something

similar in a village market,' Ruth said. 'They were everywhere, in fact. Carved in wood or silver, painted on ceramic bowls. I wish I'd seen a live one, with their magnificent jewelled plumage. Sacred bird of the Mayans. Symbol of freedom.' Her eyes crinkled. 'Though I'm sure you know that. Listen to me peppering you with trivia. An occupational hazard, I'm afraid.'

Erin hastily buttoned her coat, as the bottled-up tears threatened to overwhelm her. In the narrow vestibule by the door, Ruth clasped Erin's arm and sought her eyes. When Ruth spoke, it was scarcely above a whisper. 'I'm so glad to see you're all right.'

Erin stood rooted to the floor.

'Those two summers you didn't come into the library,' Ruth said. 'I was worried something had happened to you.'

The room tilted, and she grabbed the coat rack for support. *Ruth knows who I am?* But how…? Erin could barely meet the older woman's eyes.

'I was confused by the name at first,' Ruth said, holding Erin's hands firmly in her own. 'Not to mention your English accent. But it struck me you might have made a new life for yourself.' She looked away, as if to give Erin a chance to recover. 'When summer rolled around that one year and I didn't see you, I made a few discreet inquiries.' Ruth's eyes were sad, her hands trembled. 'You were such an anxious child. Terrified of something, that much was clear. I remember once dropping a dictionary on the floor, and you leapt up like a scalded cat. Petrified. Like you were being chased by a pack of wolves. When I found out you'd been sent away, and where, I was devastated.'

Erin's palms tingled. Would her aunt Olivia have said something? It was a small town. Perhaps the two women were friends.

'So, what a relief to have you turn up at my door, after all these years,' Ruth said, wiping her eyes. 'Right as rain.'

At a loss for words, Erin blushed with shame that she wasn't straight with Ruth from the beginning.

'That awful woman…' She cupped Erin's face in her hands. 'I'm so glad to know you're okay. Better than okay. Good for you, for getting out.'

* * *

Niels was leaning against the reception desk, chatting with the duty nurse. 'There you are,' he said, as Erin came through the door. 'I left two messages on your phone. Didn't you get them? You just missed her.'

'Missed who?'

'Cassie Gray. She left ten minutes ago, very upset. But we couldn't convince her to stay. I think she came here to talk to you.'

Erin stopped short. Cassie had come back to the clinic and she'd missed her. *Damn*. 'What happened? Did she say how I can reach her?'

'She didn't. But the home number's in her file.'

But that was no use. Twice Erin had tried calling Cassie at home. Both times the mother had hung up on her. She could pretend to be one of Cassie's school friends. But Lonnie Tyler was surely too clever for that old ruse.

Regret washed over her. She should have been here. All this chasing around the country for clues about Tim's past was running her ragged, not to mention stealing time away from her patients. And now this. Cassie had sought her out, looking for help, and where had she been? On a wild goose chase. If that wasn't a sign it was time to stop, she didn't know what was.

Except there was one lead she couldn't ignore. The boy who'd won the science fair prize with Tim. One more foray into Tim's life before he killed his family, and then she was done.

152

26

Manhattan, New York
April, Present Day

'Tim Stern? Sure, I remember him.' Ray grabbed a pile of laundry off the divan. 'How could anyone forget?' He trod barefoot across the floor, picking up newspapers and stacks of mail and dumping them on a table in the corner.

The air in the flat reminded Erin of a Middle Eastern bazaar. Cardamom and cloves and another scent she couldn't quite put her finger on. Dramatic black-and-white photographs of the city covered the far wall. Across the room, a bank of windows showed a sliver of Riverside Park. She wondered what Ray did for a living that he could afford a place like this.

'That's better.' He swept his fingers through his hair. 'I'm a terrible slob.'

Erin bit back a smile. The flat might be a mess, but not the man himself. His crisp burgundy shirt was perfectly pressed, his face clean-shaven. And there was something charming about an untidy flat. A sign of someone too caught up with living to worry about the mundane details of housekeeping. As he passed close to her, she studied his face. If she'd seen him before, no trace of it remained.

As soon as she was settled on the low-slung couch, Ray slipped into the kitchen and returned with a bottle of wine.

'Care for a glass?' He showed her the label. 'Friend of mine's got a superb vineyard in Mendoza. This one's an excellent Pinot Noir. He sent me a case, all the way from Argentina, for my birthday last week.'

It was a bit early to start drinking, but perhaps a little wine might take the edge off her nerves. When he handed her a glass, their hands briefly touched.

Sprawling next to her, Ray spread goat's cheese on a cracker and popped it in his mouth. 'Olive?' He passed her a bowl, but she shook her head. This wasn't a social call. 'So... Tim Stern, huh? Talk about a bolt from the blue.' As he looked at her, his eyes, the warm colour of hazelnuts, seemed to change with the light. 'Are you writing a book or something?' He propped his feet on a brightly coloured floor cushion. 'True crime is hot right now. I know some people in publishing. If you'd like, I could put you in touch with them.'

'Not a book, just an article.' Heat rose to her face. To hide her unease, she stood and carried her glass to the bank of windows. Five storeys below, the street was jammed with yellow cabs, and the pavement teeming with Saturday shoppers. A woman juggling a baby and a sack of groceries flung her arm out and smacked her other child, a tiny toddler, on the cheek. The little girl's face crumpled and she let out a howl. Erin instinctively touched her own face and winced. *Poor kid.*

'I hope I didn't give you the wrong impression on the phone,' Ray was saying as she turned away from the window. 'It's true that Tim and I were assigned to work on a science project together. But other than that, I barely knew him.' He swirled the liquid in his glass. 'We didn't exactly move in the same circles.'

She returned to the divan, woozy from the wine already. In her rush to catch the train into the city, she'd forgotten to eat lunch.

'After I graduated high school,' he said, 'I couldn't get away from Belle River fast enough. But I've got my old class yearbook around here somewhere, if you want to see Tim's photo.' He gestured to the wall of books across the room. 'Funny what we hang onto.' Ray jumped up and ran his fingers across the hardbound volumes on the bottom shelf. 'Nope, not here.'

He disappeared into the back of the flat, where Erin could hear the sound of furniture being dragged across the floor. Out in the street, a siren blared and faded away.

He rejoined her, hefting a blue and white book above his head. 'I knew I had it.' Sitting cross-legged on the floor, his back against the divan, he flipped through the pages. 'There's your man.' He tapped a photo with his finger.

She scooted closer until her knee touched his shoulder. *Timothy W. Stern, Jnr, Junior class of 1977, Belle River High School.*

So, that was Tim. Before committing the bloody crime that sent him to Greenlake.

'May I?'

As he passed her the yearbook, their hands touched again and she felt a distinctive tingle. She moved her knees away and studied the photo. Tim at seventeen, in a corduroy jacket and knit tie, cinched up tight around his neck. A thick pelt of dark brown hair, not quite long enough to cover his ears, was combed over his forehead and to the side. His eyes were shifted away from the camera's lens. Under the photo was a brief quote, from some long-ago rock star, about the inevitability of death, and the need to live one's own life.

Ray joined her on the divan. 'I haven't looked at this thing since high school.' He held it to his nose. 'Ah, *eau de mildew*.' A riffle of pages, followed by a groan. 'That's me.' He pointed to a photo in the top row. 'Can you believe what a total dork I was?'

As she leaned in to look, her hair fell over her shoulder and she brushed it back. *L. Raymond Hopkins*. Wavy brown hair, longish sideburns, serious eyes. A wide-collared shirt, topped with a striped knitted vest. He was the only boy on the page not wearing a jacket and tie. No activities were listed under the picture. Just a string of nonsense words and symbols. A code, she imagined, known only to the in-crowd. Though a quick glance confirmed that most students had strings of coded messages under their photos, some with a forest of exclamation marks, or other symbols, impossible to decipher. A few of the girls had included a tiny heart followed by a set of initials. She wondered if one of the girls was history girl. Ray's entry ended with a George Orwell quote about how you could only break the big rules if you paid heed to the minor ones.

He turned back to Tim's page and read aloud the Jimi Hendrix quote. 'Holy crap. That's eerie. It's like he knew, or something.'

It would be rude to point out that the sentiment under Ray's and Tim's photos was not all that different. Both suggested rebellion, or at least the need to make one's mark on life. But look how things turned out: Tim was locked up in a high-security psychiatric ward, while Ray lived in a spacious, light-filled flat on the Upper West Side.

L. Raymond Hopkins. 'What's the L stand for?'

'Lewis. My dad's name.' He tossed the yearbook on the floor and refilled their glasses.

Erin shifted her legs. 'What about friends, did Tim hang out with anyone in particular?'

'Not that I know of.' His eyes clouded over. 'Wait. There was this one kid. Frizzy blond hair, coke-bottle glasses, acne. No idea what his name was, but his face might ring a bell.' He grabbed the book and flipped through the pages.

Out in the street, a jackhammer started up. Sleepy from the wine, Erin wanted nothing more than to stretch out on the divan, with its heap of squashy cushions, and close her eyes.

As Ray pored through the photos, a lock of hair flopped in

his eyes. 'Aha.' He stabbed the page with a finger. 'Jeremiah Sowka. I'm pretty sure that's the guy.'

In the photo, the boy's unruly hair appeared to have been tamed with a thick hair gel. No signs of acne. Someone had done a good job with the airbrush.

'Did you know Tim's parents?' Erin shifted on the couch to put some distance between them.

Ray knocked back the last of his wine. When he offered her more, she shook her head. 'His parents?' He jumped up and headed to the kitchen. 'I might have run into his mother the couple of times I was at the house. But the dad?' He appeared in the doorway with a bottle of Perrier and shook his head. 'Never met him.'

In need of air, she moved to the open window. The angle of light filtering through the plane trees and the familiar urban symphony reminded her of London. How she missed it. The bustle in the streets. Red double-deckers glistening in the rain. The bluebell wood near the Thornbury Clinic where she used to wander during her lunch break.

Little more than an hour in Ray's company was enough to expose the hard kernel of loneliness lodged in her chest. Since returning to America, he was the first person she'd met who made her feel perfectly at ease. The moment she crossed into his light-filled flat and heard the warm timbre of his voice, something inside her had shifted. She longed to suggest they continue their conversation at some lively bistro in the neighbourhood. But it was time to shake off her musings and catch the train back to Lansford. She touched the cool glass with her fingers.

Looking for something?

Erin whirled around, but the room was now empty. When her phone rang, she jumped. Anonymous caller. Though Ray was in another room, she stepped into the front hall before answering. 'Hello?'

Dead air, followed by the sound of something heavy scraping across the floor and a ragged intake of breath.

'Hello? This is Dr Cartwright.' The click of a door closing. 'Who's there? Hello?' But the connection was cut, and she clutched her phone, waiting for the caller to ring again.

'Everything okay?' Ray stood in the doorway.

'Fine.' Her face burned. 'Wrong number.' She struggled to keep her voice casual, but her throat was tight. It could have been Cassie. But there was no way to know, and now no chance to reach her.

She turned away from Ray's quizzical gaze. She'd told him her name was Carson. Had he heard her say her real name when she answered the call? The endless lies were exhausting. But it didn't matter, it was unlikely she'd ever see him again.

27

Greenlake Psychiatric Facility
Atherton, New York
April, Present Day

Hunched over a stack of paperwork, Harrison barely glanced up when Erin entered the room. 'If I'm not mistaken, today is your last formal session with Tim?' He stuck his glasses on top of his head and rubbed his eyes.

Erin nodded. 'If things go as planned, I'll be submitting my full report to the review board by the end of next week.' Ahead of the deadline, she might have added, despite the earlier setbacks.

'Well, that's good to hear.' He fussed with the papers on his desk. A nervous gesture she'd come to recognise. 'How did you fare on your visit to Tim's hometown? Anything of interest come up?'

She hesitated, sorry now she'd mentioned her plan to visit Belle River. At some point, Harrison had transformed from ally to adversary. But when? Two doctors eyeing each other across a hostile no man's land. To deflect the question, she busied herself with some papers of her own. 'It was just a routine look around,' she said, trying not to sound defensive. But she had no desire to describe her visit to the Stern family's former home, or how she'd been so easily duped by the current owner.

Something odd about the space behind Harrison's desk attracted her attention. The middle photo, the one with the largest snowy peak and diamond-bright sun, was missing. She looked round till she spotted it on the floor, leaning against the bookcase. In the corner, a cardboard box was filled with files.

'Did you discover anything of note?' He leaned heavily on his elbows, his forehead damp with sweat.

'Not especially.'

In a show of vigour, Harrison hauled himself out of the chair and began to straighten a row of books on the shelf. But his agitation was apparent.

'Well, it's good to hear things are progressing,' he said, stepping back to survey his handiwork. 'And now that I've met Tim's father, I feel more confident about the situation. He seems like a perfectly decent chap. And quite keen to give Tim a proper home.'

It was impossible to hide her surprise. Harrison hadn't mentioned anything about a visit. Was there a reason for keeping her in the dark?

'Mr Stern arrived yesterday, just after lunch,' he said, answering the question on her lips and returning to his chair. 'We spoke for nearly an hour, before I took him to see Tim in the dayroom, where I kept a watchful eye from the nurses' station. We were all a bit on edge, considering it was the first time the two had seen each other since... well, in twenty-seven years.'

As her mind buzzed with questions, her fingers drifted to the scar by her collarbone, a clear sign of anxiety. What she wouldn't give to have been a fly on the wall of the dayroom. The body language alone would have relayed a treasure trove of information. Her instinct was to pepper Harrison with questions, but she relaxed her grip on the armrests, reminding herself to breathe and tread slowly. An attendant rapped on the door.

'Ah, your chariot awaits.' Harrison's smile looked strained. 'Would you mind coming round again when you've finished your session?'

* * *

The shriek and clatter of the ward assaulted her eardrums. Doors clanged, keys jangled. The shrill buzzer that erupted each time a door opened seemed to have tripled in volume since her last visit. An attendant with a sour expression led her down the long dank corridor. Her skin felt clammy in the foetid air.

In his room, Tim sat upright in a plastic chair. Feet together, eyes front, as if waiting for a bus. He turned his head away as the attendant's bulk filled the doorway.

'Got a visitor, Timbo. Doc here to see you.'

A muscle twitched in his jaw. 'My name is Timothy.'

'Yeah, yeah. *Timothy.* Whatever. But look sharp. Pretty lady wants to talk to you.' As he leaned close, Erin stepped away. 'We don't get many women in here. Should perk the old boy right up.'

She waited until the attendant backed off before turning to Tim.

'Hello, Timothy. Everything okay in here?'

His eyes flicked to the walls and the floor. 'Do you see anyone?'

'I don't see anyone. Only you.' She paused. 'Do *you* see someone?'

He clenched and unclenched his hands, but said nothing.

'There's no one in this room but you, Timothy.' She watched him carefully, wondering if this was the same type of delusion he'd had before when he claimed to have seen a strange man lying on his bed.

'Nobody here.' His breath came in gasps. 'No one?'

Should she go ahead with her evaluation, or was Tim too upset to make sense of the tests? Her heart plummeted. There'd been too many delays already. She was hoping this would be her last trip to Greenlake.

'Do you feel well enough to answer some questions? It won't take long.'

He coughed and lumbered upright. 'I'm ready now.'

Accompanied by a female attendant, they walked single file to the visitors' room at the far end of the ward, with the dim light bulb and flaking paint. A feedback loop of her own incarceration scrolled through her head. The smells and noise. The noxious cloud of despair. She closed her eyes and focused on her breathing, terrified of being sucked back through the tunnel of time.

Inside the room, Tim turned away. She could see the tension in his shoulders as he sidestepped to the window, shielding his eyes. The Sun shone on the scraggy fields and abandoned factory, glancing off the cracked windows. The coils of razor wire splintered the light into tiny shards.

She perched on the edge of the chair. 'Why did you think someone was in your room?'

He leaned his forehead against the window and muttered something under his breath.

'Was it the same man as before, the one you saw lying on your bed?'

'No.' He dragged his sleeve across his face. 'It was nobody.'

She would like to ask him about his father's visit – how it went, what he thought – but that might set off another spasm of panic, a repeat of the lunch fiasco when she'd alluded to Belle River. Only four weeks ago it was, though it seemed like years. Time had contracted to a thin, treacherous stream.

'Okay then, Timothy. I'm going to ask you a few questions and show you a couple of pictures. It won't take long and then we'll be done.'

'My father was here.' He rotated away from the window, pulling his head tortoise-like into his hunched shoulders. 'He gave me a sweatshirt, but I left it in my room.' He ran his hands over the stained green sweatshirt he usually wore.

'Did you and your father have a good visit?' She scanned his face for signs of distress.

'I got a book of Sudoku. And the sweatshirt. He said places like this are always cold.' A chill pricked her spine. *Places like this are always cold*. A perfect mimicry of Stern's voice. Tim turned back to the window. 'Winter's over. Spring is here.' He tapped his fingers on the glass. 'He gave me a picture of his dog. She has silky hair. Her name is…' He squeezed his eyes shut. 'I don't remember.'

'Do you like dogs?'

He pulled a creased photo from the pocket of his jeans and held it out. She touched it with her fingertips, expecting resistance, but he released it willingly into her hand. Lulu, caught in mid-stride, as she lolloped across the lawn, with the pond and red barn in the background. Like a farm in a picture book. She turned it over to see if Stern had written anything on the back. No text, but someone – Tim? – had sketched a large birdlike creature with outstretched wings, its head shaped like an anvil.

'What's this… some kind of prehistoric bird?'

Sweat shone on his brow. '*Scopus umbretta*. Hamerkop.'

The drawing was accomplished, the winged creature so deftly executed it seemed poised to lift off the paper. Ruth Davis was right. As a bird artist, Tim clearly had a gift. He held out his hand, and she dropped the drawing into his palm.

'Can we start now?' He held his watch close to his face. 'I need to get back to my Sudoku. I've done 31 out of 400 and I don't want to get behind.'

He sat and wedged his hands between his knees. Erin noted the time and began the assessment, but with Tim distracted and unfocused, it was slow-going. After fifteen minutes, she suggested they take a break. She had him stand up, and together they did a few simple stretches, hands reaching to the ceiling, bending side to side, followed by a breathing exercise.

When she was ready to begin again, Tim had wandered back to the window.

'Bed shed dead. Dud thud blood.'

She gripped the pencil and listened intently. Symptoms of psychosis? Or had Tim remembered something he'd seen?

'Timothy?'

He turned away from the windows, his eyes flat. 'Can I go now? Eleven more by lunchtime or they won't count.'

Won't count? It was impossible to follow the topography of this mind.

'Twenty minutes. I promise.'

She gamely continued with the rest of the assessment, but struggled to concentrate, as her thoughts leapt ahead to the questions she wanted to ask Harrison about the change in Tim's mood. His meds could have been altered again, or he might have stopped taking them. Patients could be notoriously clever at deceiving the nurses.

* * *

After debriefing Harrison on the day's session, Erin stopped by the records department to check out Tim's medical history from his first ten years at Greenlake. It wasn't easy to persuade the staff to allow her to take the boxes offsite, but after endless promises to safeguard them, she loaded them into the boot of her car.

Bed shed dead. Dud thud blood. Classic clang symptoms of schizophrenia were often meaningless. But not this time, of that she was sure, especially with those particular words. His father's visit had shaken something loose. Tim was starting to remember.

28

Lansford, New York
May, Present Day

Erin shut the blinds and switched on the light before dumping a box of Tim's medical and legal records on the coffee table. She spread out the files and tilted her head to study the labels. Where to begin? The arrest, the police report, or the trial? Running her fingers over the folders, she paused at the police report.

She plumped the cushions and poured a glass of wine. *Just dive right in.* Curled up on the sofa in the living room, she went straight to the plastic sheaf of photos from the crime scene. Many more than provided in the summary of Tim's case she'd received from Harrison. The mother's head split open, her chest and abdomen stabbed repeatedly with a carving knife. According to the pathology report, the first blow was struck in the living room, but the body had been found in the kitchen, following an extended struggle. That meant the initial blow from the meat cleaver wasn't enough to disable her, not if she had the strength to flee.

A logical scenario if Tim was hesitant and pulled back. Did that mean he wasn't in a state of full-blown psychosis at the time? She scribbled a note on the yellow legal pad by her side. To complicate things further, Tim's two sisters were not killed with the same weapons as the mother. They were found in their beds, their throats cut with a fish knife, discovered later by the police, stuffed under Tim's mattress. The coroner's report suggested they may also have been asphyxiated. Probably with the bed pillows. Though the investigation could not conclude who was killed first, Erin could only assume it was the two girls. If they'd been alive during the mayhem and bloodshed downstairs, wouldn't they have run to help their mother when they heard her screams?

The downstairs rooms were marked off with yellow crime-scene tape and chalk from the forensics team. Modern furniture in the living room, a nubby carpet the colour of oatmeal, dark green curtains on the windows. A delicate spun-glass hummingbird with a tiny beak and scarlet throat lay broken on the floor. An amber hanging lamp over the dining table that resembled a flying saucer. Avocado-green appliances in the kitchen, and a brown-glazed cookie jar in the shape of an owl.

A typical suburban home. Except for one thing. Nothing was tacked to the refrigerator with cheerful magnets. No student artwork, notes or party invitations. No magazines or books strewn about, and no evidence of sporting equipment or gym kit tossed in the entryway. Except for the bodies, no signs of family life at all.

In Tim's room, the bed was neatly made, the pillow placed squarely in the centre of the headboard. Had he tidied up before or after the murders? She scanned the police report. It must have been before as no blood was found in his room. Blood from the mother was found on the stairs and in the sisters' room, but the police couldn't determine if it had been tracked in before or after the girls were dead. Tim could have suffocated them first, dispatched the mother, then returned to his sisters' room to slice their throats.

Why? She closed her eyes. What type of paranoid delusion would have driven Tim to massacre his family? Psychosis of such violence couldn't possibly have sprung from a void. To commit such bloodshed, a tidal wave of fear and paranoia must have roared through his veins.

She shut her eyes, but the photo of Doris Stern, soaking in a pool of blood, remained fixed in her mind. The air in the flat was stifling and she leapt up, knocking against the coffee table and banging her knee. Dizzy with fatigue, she opened the window to let in some air.

Across the alley, the light was on and a shadow drifted past the closed blinds. In the stillness, the rhythmic sound of chopping came through the open window. Root vegetables, chicken bones? Or was her mysterious neighbour dispatching a hapless hitchhiker he'd picked up on the motorway? She chided herself for the gruesome nature of her thoughts, closed the window and yanked the curtains shut. Enough crime-scene photos for today. Sleep would not come easily tonight. She stuffed the photos, yellowed with age, back into the plastic folder, and turned her attention to the police report.

According to the coroner's assessment, the victims had died sometime between eleven that night and two in the morning. Tim's father had taken a hotel room down the coast in Portland, in order to meet with a client early the next day. On Saturday morning, a neighbour called the police just after ten to report the crime. The Stern's dog had been barking for hours, so she'd gone over to investigate. Other than the barking, the house was quiet. When she peeked in the front window, it was to find the furniture tipped over and the walls smeared with blood. After running home in a panic to call the police, she barricaded herself in her house, terrified that a maniac was on the loose.

Doris Stern's car, a blue Pontiac sedan, was parked in the driveway. The police made numerous attempts to contact Mr Stern, though, at the time, nobody knew where he was. When he pulled up to the house, shortly before noon, he found his home cordoned off with yellow crime-scene tape and a female officer waiting to deliver the terrible news. They questioned him about Tim. When had he last seen him? Was he known to use drugs?

As for Stern, he was exactly where he claimed to be, in Portland for a business meeting. It all checked out. A woman, whose name was later redacted from the police report, had provided an alibi for the evening before. Two people remembered seeing him in the hotel at breakfast, and an attendant at a Texaco station in Portland confirmed that Stern stopped to fill up his car just after eleven on Saturday morning.

When Stern was asked to identify the bodies, he refused, saying he couldn't bear to see his daughters laid out in the morgue. An old family friend, who lived in Boston, volunteered for the grisly task. *Just the daughters.* It wasn't his wife who Stern couldn't bear to see. Erin scribbled that down.

Three days later, on the Monday afternoon, Tim was picked up just over the New York state line. A motorist spotted him wandering down a rural road cutting through the forest, his T-shirt and jeans stained with dried blood. When questioned by police, he claimed to have no idea how he'd got there or where the blood came from. The officer at the scene would later report that Tim didn't bat an eye when informed his family was dead. He'd merely stared at the wall with a vacant expression. When he finally spoke, he said, 'Even my dad?'

Throughout the arrest and trial, Tim repeatedly claimed he had no memory of the murders, or how he ended up so far from home. He had no drugs on him and his bloodwork was clean. A preliminary diagnosis of dissociative disorder, with possible amnesia or fugue state, was made by the court-appointed psychiatrist. Later changed, after further assessment, to paranoid schizophrenia. Following a brief trial, Tim was declared not guilty for the deaths of his mother and sisters by reason of insanity. Stern did not testify or appear in court. Nor did he see Tim before he was sent to Greenlake for an indefinite period of incarceration.

Erin's back ached. As she stood and paced the floor, a thought came to her. Was there a police record of the suspected arson attack on the house? She rummaged through the box. But it wouldn't be there, of course. The house had burned down after Tim was in custody. With Tim on a locked ward, and the family home destroyed by fire, the case was closed. End of story.

Except it wasn't. At least not to someone like her, pervaded by a floating sense of dread, and the sensation of 'what if?' woven into her bones. She circled the room, paging through Tim's file. But little in those old records had any bearing on his current mental state. Agonising over old police reports and digging for clues would not give her the answer she wanted: what had made Tim snap? Were there drugs involved? Had he argued with his father – or mother – one too many times? Or was it simply a case of garden-variety psychosis, a break from reality with no inciting event, and no real answer? Her only task now was to write up her report and send it to the review board. She wouldn't go to bed until it was done.

She brewed a pot of coffee and switched on her laptop. In dispassionate, formal prose, she filled fifteen pages with information on Tim's history and mental state, the results from her assessments, and her opinion regarding his fitness for release. With each word and every paragraph, she tried to confer her professional opinion in a clear and concise manner, with just enough supposition to leave room for interpretation.

Before typing the final line, she paused a moment before plunging on.

In my professional judgement, Timothy Warren Stern, Jnr, is not a danger to himself or to others. Having completed the full complement of assessments required by the State of New York, and having met with and interviewed the patient on several occasions over the course of eight weeks, to the best of my knowledge, he is fit for release into the community, where he will reside in the home of his father, Timothy Warren Stern, Snr, at 160 White Valley Road, Matlock, Vermont.

When she hit Print, it was two in the morning. At the bottom of the last page, she scrawled her signature with a blue biro, initialled the other pages and sealed the report in an envelope. Resting her head on her arms, she closed her eyes. It was done.

First thing in the morning she would send it by express courier to the review board. The 30th June court date, when the petition for release would be decided by a judge in Albany, was the final hurdle. After that, if all went well, Tim Stern would walk out of Greenlake Psychiatric Facility, a free man.

29

Manhattan, New York
May, Present Day

Saturday night, and Casa Habana was buzzing. A woman in an ivory silk blouse smiled at Ray, as he chatted with the maître d' in rapid Spanish, while slipping a folded bill into the man's hand. Erin tried to avoid the crush by standing against a wall, until a dark-eyed woman in a swishy red dress and gold hoop earrings whisked them upstairs to a table by the window. A bottle of Rioja appeared, followed by a platter of green and black olives, rounds of goat's cheese and crisply toasted bread.

Ray poured out the wine and raised his glass. '*Salud. Qué vivas durante todos los días de tu vida.*' May you live every day of your life.

'*Gracias, igualmente.*' Thanks, same to you.

'You speak Spanish?' His eyes lit up.

She smiled over the rim of her glass. '*Un poco.*' Was this flirting? If so, she was out of practice. Her last time out with a man must have been, what, two years ago? Not since Sebastian, a moody Dane with a penchant for secrets, disappeared from her life in a puff of smoke. On a rainy Friday in March, she'd arrived home to their shared flat to find his things gone and a note on the table. *Sorry. Take care, S.* It had taken months for the sting of his brush-off to fade. After that, she'd sworn off men.

Light-hearted dinner conversation was not her strong suit, so she let Ray do the talking. At the moment, he was singing the praises of the chef, a personal friend of his, before segueing into an animated description of a recent fundraiser his non-profit had organised in support of immigrant engagement.

'Education and job training, mainly,' he said when she asked him what his organisation did. 'Family outreach, integration, community support.' He gestured at the room. 'Half the people who work here have come through one of our programmes.'

Having sent her report to the review board at Greenlake, Erin was more than ready to put Timothy Stern's case to rest. But some things still troubled her. A heap of unanswered questions that kept her up at night.

She hadn't expected to see Ray again, and was surprised he'd responded at all to her rather curt text, *Something's bugging me, re: Tim. Shall we meet for dinner?* But here they were, awash with food and wine, candlelight flickering between them. There was no sign he'd overheard her say her real name and title, that time in his flat, and he seemed to be having a good time.

A uniformed waiter, elegant as a toreador, set more food on the table. Grilled prawns, red snapper, spicy black beans and saffron rice. As she sucked the juice from a prawn, Erin plotted how to steer the conversation to Tim without spoiling the mood. But Ray seemed to have forgotten the pretext for their dinner. Their talk ranged from books and films to food and travel. His eyes shone as he regaled her with tales of Galicia, the beguiling, but little-known, province in the north-west of Spain. Windswept beaches. Old men with craggy faces, herding their goats into the mountains. The bustling markets with their sun-warm tomatoes, fresh cheeses, oranges and cured hams, piled high on trestle tables.

It occurred to her that he might have assumed her text was a ruse for asking him out. Charming though he was, she wasn't ready for a relationship. So rather than confess her own experience of living and travelling in Spain, she kept mum. Talking about herself might lead to the locked door of her past she had no intention of opening.

He popped a glistening prawn in his mouth. 'So, what's the verdict on the food?'

'Perfect.' She wiped her buttery fingers on a napkin and rehearsed the words in her head. *So, about Tim…*

'Best kept secret on the West Side.' As he leaned forward to refill her glass, the candle flame shone in his eyes. 'Though there was a time, soon after I moved here, that I couldn't stand the sight of seafood. Can you imagine? Here I was, surrounded by a mob of Manhattanites clamouring for lobster airlifted from Maine, and I couldn't even look at it, much less eat it.' He grinned. 'Too many summers shucking clams and gutting fish.'

He piled more saffron rice on her plate. 'Funny thing, when I got your text, I was just about to call you. Last week, in the middle of a meeting at work, something about the Sterns popped into my head. Completely out of nowhere.' He motioned to the waiter for a bottle of water. 'Not about Tim, but his folks. I must have blocked it out before, because… you know, the fish thing.' He waggled his brows in a weak imitation of Groucho Marx. 'There was this one summer I bussed tables at the yacht club. Saturday nights, the Sterns would show up for dinner.'

Goosebumps rose on her bare arms. This was more than she expected. During their earlier encounter, Ray had said he'd never met the man. 'Was Tim ever with them?'

'At the yacht club? I don't think so. Just their own friends. It was usually a table for four, sometimes six. I remember this one woman with a tinkly laugh. Used to drive me up the wall. Skinny lady. Blonde bouffant. Always wore this choker of white plastic beads and big sunglasses like Jackie O. I remember feeling sorry for her husband. He didn't say much. I had the idea he might be foreign because he ate like a European. You know, with the fork in his left hand? I remember thinking that was really cool. But she would hiss at him to sit up straight and not eat so fast. How could I have forgotten? The tinkly laugh, the hissing.'

The ghost of a memory flickered, and Erin briefly closed her eyes. The laugh didn't sound right, but the foreign-seeming husband? It could have been them. Or not. With her memories of those years shattered by the drugs she'd been forced to take at Danfield, there were a million ways she could reshuffle the actors from her past.

An attractive woman in a backless dress brushed by their table, trailing a cloud of perfume. Ray didn't give her a glance.

'I remember one night when Stern snapped his fingers at me to bring him some notepaper. He and his friend had just come up with the "greatest idea ever" and wanted to write it down. So, the two started scribbling away, with Stern calling out for another round of cocktails.'

She studied his face, puzzled by the flood of details he so fluently recalled. 'What was the great idea?'

'Beats me.' He gave her a sheepish grin. 'I was something of a stoner in those days. Before going off to work, I'd take a couple of bong hits to get through the evening. The things I can't remember from that time would fill a black hole.'

A stoner? She wouldn't have guessed that, but at least a few details had filtered through the weed-induced fog. *Tinkly laugh, blonde bouffant*. She jammed her thumbnail into her wrist, hoping the pain would silence the alarm bells in her head. There were no photos from those days. All were lost, or so she was told. After her father died, and they moved to Concord. That photo she saw at Stern's house. Was it the same couple? The woman with the annoying laugh and the man who ate with the fork in his left hand? Impossible to return to the house for another look, but Lydia had taken some snapshots of the rooms. There might be something she could work with.

'Before I forget, I brought you this.' She reached into her bag for the Belle River High School yearbook Ray had pressed into her hands before leaving his flat. She'd been planning to send it by post but changed her mind after he'd agreed to meet her for dinner.

His eyebrows shot up. 'Wow, okay. I totally forgot I'd given that to you.'

An awkward silence grew between them. Erin was worried she'd spoiled the mood. But that was the reason she'd contacted him, for information on Tim, not for a date, however pleasant this evening was turning out to be. *In for a penny, in for a pound*. Ever since their first encounter at his flat, she was curious to know if Ray had known her brother.

'Speaking of high school…' She nodded at the yearbook. 'I was going through the pictures and jotted down some names.' Erin made a pretence of looking in her bag. 'I must have left the list at home. Anyway, during my research on the Stern murders, this one name kept popping up.' She sought his eyes. 'Do you remember someone named Graham Marston?'

They had long-since finished their caramel flan, and Ray rose from his chair to signal for the bill. When their waitress arrived, he flipped open his wallet and extracted a card.

'Marston? At Belle River High?' He ran his hand through his hair. 'I don't think so.'

She wanted to ask him about his yearbook picture and what 'eldu#QUEpasa?' meant, but that was surely going too far. What rational person would want the long-buried details of their teenage years picked apart?

Out in the street, Ray seemed to be in a hurry. He hailed a cab and held the door as she stepped in. No kiss on the cheek. No, 'I'll call you.' Not a date then. Was she disappointed? Not in the least, she decided, after examining her thoughts. Just frustrated from grasping at so many straws. As her cab pulled away, he stood on the pavement with his hands stuffed in his pockets. His face was impossible to read.

The storm that had been building all afternoon broke just as her train pulled out of the station. A relief to listen to the rain pelting the carriage roof as they trundled north. Water streamed down the window, blurring the skyline. As they swayed along the track, she was lulled into the feeling of lying in a boat, adrift at sea. But the evening wasn't a total loss. That bit about the Sterns and the couple at the yacht club was interesting. If not for Tim's story, then her own. It could have been them. The few memories she had of her father were slippery as minnows.

The Hudson cut a dark ribbon through the landscape. Her face, reflected in the window, was pale, and faint lines were etched around her eyes. Perhaps she should contact Tim's old school friend, Jeremiah. If nothing else, he would know if Tim had been a victim of Graham's bullying. Foolish to get sucked in, and yet impossible to turn away.

* * *

In the quiet hour after lunch, Erin closed her office door and plugged in her electric kettle. As she waited for the water to boil, she grabbed the file for her newest patient and settled into the window seat. Out on the grounds, the lacework of fresh green leaves shimmered in the sunlight.

Reading between the lines of the case summary, it was clear that the girl had a long history of troubled behaviour. But Erin's concentration was fading, and her thoughts kept drifting to the yearbook she'd returned to Ray, the one from his – and Tim's – junior year of high school. She wished she'd asked him for the one from his senior year, though she might be able to find it online. Everything was online these days. She typed a couple of search terms into the browser on her computer, and in less than three minutes she'd found it. Belle River High School, 1978.

Like a diver poised to jump, she held her breath and scrolled to the Ms. There it was: the scowling mug and stone-cold eyes that had haunted her dreams for years. *Graham Marston*. When the doctor arrived in the dead of night to take her to Danfield, her brother had held her down as she cried out in terror, grinning like a jackal as he pinned her to the floor.

Under his name was the usual string of nonsense. *VmanKingxxxAngeltwjsbr#rip*. The arcane codes of high-school students everywhere. Concocted during a time when he was, what, the king of the world, the Viking conqueror? She read the text aloud, halting at the 'tw'. Tim's first two initials. A coincidence? Surely they'd known each other. That pencilled scrawl of Tim's had clearly mentioned the Viking.

She massaged her temples, trying to ward off a headache. Graham. The Viking. She had no interest in knowing where he might be now. Since her arrival at Lansford, she'd taken great pains to keep her previous incarnation under lock and key.

Out of curiosity, she scrolled back a year to the photo of Ray as a junior. Long, scruffy hair, sideburns, a druggy look about the eyes. Under his name was the Orwell quote, followed by a string of letters: eldu#QUEpasa?777party#docks@ Alcapolco+doree. Impossible to imagine the Ray she knew as this rebellious, drug-addled teenage boy. She scanned the pages of the 1978 yearbook, looking for the picture of Ray as a senior, and almost missed him. Jacket and tie. Short hair, neatly combed. Nothing but a quote by T.S. Eliot under the picture, something about having to accept the terms life offers you if you don't have the courage to impose your own.

In the space of a year, he seemed to become a completely different person. Had he grown out of his rebellious pose, or was it something else?

30

The Meadows
Lansford, New York
May, Present Day

Janine swept into the staff lounge, clutching a cardboard envelope. 'Here's the FedEx package you were waiting for.'

Erin thanked her and tucked the envelope into a stack of files. As she gathered up her things, she spotted Greta Kozani checking her post. She was in no mood to listen to one of Greta's harangues, so she ducked behind the bookshelf until certain she was gone.

With the staffroom to herself, it was tempting to linger with a cup of tea. But the photos in the envelope had her on tenterhooks and she couldn't wait. She slipped into her office without encountering anyone and locked the door. On her desk, she sorted Lydia's photos, placing the exterior shots in one pile and the inside ones in another.

Under the light of the desk lamp, she studied the living room and kitchen for anything she might have missed during her visit to the Stern farm. It was just as she remembered. No photos or anything else of a personal nature. Not even a shopping list tacked to the refrigerator. And the large front room, with its curated colour scheme and designer gloss, could have come straight from a magazine. No knick-knacks on the shelves by the fireplace, nothing but the boxed set of leather-bound classics.

It was the two shots of Stern's study that started her pulse jumping. The first was too dark, but the second looked promising, with the photos tacked to the corkboard clearly in view. The flash had reflected on the photo at the far left, obscuring its subject. But the one she was interested in, of the two couples on the beach at sunset, was fairly clear. If she had it blown up, she might be able to identify the dark-haired man, and the blonde woman with the sunburst medallion. The second woman was not fully in the picture, with only one shoulder and a triangle of her blue dress visible. Behind the foursome, a shirtless boy with brown hair crouched on the rocks by the water.

That sunburst medallion. The mere sight of it made her uneasy, and she tossed the photo in a drawer. How could she focus on her patients with these niggling details from the Stern case pulling her away? Just when she thought she'd put it all behind her, a string of nonsense syllables in a high-school yearbook, and a snapshot of a random couple on a beach, had the power to haul her back.

* * *

The following day, the enlarged snapshots from the photo lab in Albany arrived by courier. Erin shut herself up in her office and spread them on her desk. Both were grainy, and the resolution poor. One was too dark to see much of anything but shadowy figures against a paler background. But in the other, the four figures were clearly discernible, though the faces were a blur of eye holes and dark mouths.

She held the photo up to the light. The medallion worn by the tall blonde woman was slightly out of focus, but the sunburst shape was just about discernible. The diamond-patterned dress, orange and white, showed off the woman's tan. Her teased hair, with ends that flipped up on her shoulders, was held in place by a white headband.

Erin propped the photo on the bookshelf and backed away. If she unfocused her eyes, the configuration of the foursome swam across her vision. She'd seen this photo before. But where? In a magazine, a newspaper? Or someplace closer to home? The man on the far right was clearly Stern. But the man next to him, the one with his right arm slung around Stern's neck in a gesture of camaraderie, and the left hand holding a cocktail glass... With little to go on but a gut feeling, she was sure this was her father.

She leaned in to focus on the sunburst medallion. It could be a coincidence. But Vivien had worn a necklace like that.

Erin closed her eyes and tried to summon up a cohesive picture of her fractured past. An image wavered into focus. The gold rays of the medallion, glinting in the sun, the freckled chest, the smell of cigarette smoke and drugstore perfume. The smirk, the sneer. *Stop stuffing your fat face.*

But the photo was merely a distraction. It had nothing to do with Tim. His court date was coming up fast, and she was running out of time. But she still had one ace up her sleeve. Tim's school chum, Jeremiah Sowka. The one with the acne and frizzy hair. He might have a story to tell.

31

Hartford, Connecticut
June, Present Day

At a corner table in a Dunkin' Donuts, on the outskirts of the city, a balding man in a tan windbreaker blinked under the fluorescent lights. Next to him, a skinny kid with a mop of straight black hair and wearing football kit fiddled with a computer game. Erin squeezed past the scrum of customers, fidgeting like addicts as they queued for their morning fix of sugar and caffeine.

'Mr Sowka?'

'Yep, that's me.' He gave a mock salute. 'Jeremy.' Powdered sugar dusted his lip. 'And this is my kid, Kyle. Sorry I had to bring him along, but his mom's not home yet. He won't get in the way though, will you, Ky?' He cuffed the child playfully on the shoulder, but the boy, intent on his game, didn't bother to look up.

The air was thick with the smell of burnt sugar and cooking oil from the deep-fat fryers. She removed her jacket and fanned her face.

'If you want a jelly doughnut, you'd better get in line,' he said, scratching a patch of eczema on his neck. 'They sell out fast on Saturdays. And while you're up there, would you mind getting me one of those Belgian cruller things and some doughnut holes for Kyle?'

From the back of the queue, she scanned the trays of glistening doughnuts, spackled with pink glaze, or spiky with sprinkles. The binge food of choice for some of her patients. But the thought of all that sugar made her teeth hurt. How she longed for the little tearoom near the Thornbury Clinic in London, with its assortment of colourful teapots and perfectly brewed tea, the fresh-baked lemon tarts and scones. She settled for a poppy seed bagel and a large coffee.

'So, Timmy Stern, huh?' Jeremy plucked the cruller and doughnut holes from the plastic tray. 'Are you a relative or something?' He tore open two packets of sugar and dumped them into his coffee. 'My doc said I should stay away from this place, but we all gotta die from something, right?' He made quick work of the cruller. In a minute it was gone. On his cheeks and jaw, tiny depressions on his skin were all that remained of his teenage acne.

'I'm not a relative,' she said, adopting a serious air. 'I'm researching a book on family murders.' She clicked her pen and wrote Jeremy's name and date in her notebook. 'The Stern case is of particular interest.'

'Whatever floats your boat.' He drained his coffee and stared at the empty cup. 'I sure could use another one of these. Flew in from Chicago last night and didn't get much sleep.' He ruffled his son's hair. 'How ya doing there, buddy, want something else to drink?'

Kyle twitched away from his father's hand, his eyes fixed on the screen.

Erin scraped back her chair. 'I'll get it.' Annoyed at his impertinence, she gritted her teeth and rejoined the queue. But it was simply a matter of singing for her supper. When she returned to the table with a large coffee and two crullers for good measure, she sank into the chair, beset with fatigue. How long would she have to ply him with doughnuts before he said anything useful? This little excursion to Hartford was looking like a massive waste of time.

'Shall we start with your first memory of meeting Tim?'

He blinked rapidly, as if there was something in his eye. 'Sure, that's easy. Timmy and I met in the sixth grade. I was the new kid that year. On the first day, the teacher tells everyone to give me a big welcome. But they kept their distance. Typical kid behaviour, you know? Curious, but cautious, trying to see how I'd fit in. We sat in alphabetical order, so I was put next to Tim. Sowka, Stern. Destined to be friends.' He shrugged. 'Or sworn enemies. It could've gone either way, but it turned out that Timmy had this thing for birds, and guess what? Sowka in Polish means owl. Go figure.'

Owl. She wrote that down. Almost as an afterthought, she scrawled the name of the strange bird Tim had drawn during their last session. *Scopus*… something. She would look it up when she returned to Lansford. 'What were his parents like?'

'His parents?' With his finger, he herded some scattered sugar crystals into a little pile. 'Haven't a clue. Timmy and I mostly saw each other at school. I didn't go over to his house much. He usually came to mine. Come to think of it, I don't remember ever seeing his dad at the house. Just his mom, but not much of her either.'

A group of teenage girls burst through the door, noisy as a flock of starlings.

Jeremy fidgeted and drummed his fingers on the table.

Kyle paused his game long enough to ask where the bathroom was. Erin waited until the boy left the table. Now was the time to ask some of the more delicate questions.

'What was his mother like?'

As Jeremy scanned the room, his gaze rested briefly on the girls in their tight jeans. 'Like I said, I hardly ever saw her. Whenever I was at Timmy's, she was mostly somewhere else. Or lying down in her room maybe. Who knows? She wasn't like my mom, hanging around the kitchen with plates of cookies and glasses of milk. I remember a lot of ashtrays filled with cigarette butts. Pink lipstick on the filters.'

Erin shifted in her seat. This line of questioning was going nowhere. 'What about other friends, or enemies? Was Tim ever bullied at school?'

'Sure. Him and me both.' He rubbed the angry patch of eczema on his neck. 'We were the class dorks, total losers in the eyes of the cool kids. There was this one guy everybody hated. I don't know where he was from, but he would roll into town at the end of June like clockwork, strutting around like he owned the place.'

Her ears pricked up. Was he talking about Graham?

Kyle returned to the table and tapped his father on the arm. 'Can we go now?'

A look of confusion crossed Jeremy's face. 'What time is it?' He scrambled for his phone. 'Damn. I'm supposed to drop Kyle off at soccer practice.' He jerked his chair back. 'Time to go, buddy.' He shot Erin an aggrieved look. 'Are we done here?'

'Not really, but—'

'You can ride along if you want,' he said, heading for the door. 'But we gotta go now, or my ex will have my ass in a sling.'

* * *

With a screech of tyres Jeremy pulled up to a football pitch on the other side of town. Kyle jumped out to join a group of small boys in green jerseys and yellow shorts swerving across the playing field, iridescent as a school of fish.

Jeremy checked the time on his phone. 'Not too bad, only ten minutes late.'

He waved at his son, but the boy had joined his mates and took no notice.

'Okay. Shoot. What else you got?' He made as if to grab the notebook from her hand, but she yanked it away.

Now that they were no longer moving, she could finally identify the smell inside the car. Congealed grease from the empty fast-food cartons peeking from beneath the seats. She cracked the window for some air.

'What about this bully you mentioned,' Erin asked, 'the one who came to town in the summer. What was his name?'

'Huh?' Jeremy dragged his attention away from the boys on the field. 'Can't remember the guy's real name, but he had this stupid nickname. Called himself the Viking. What an asshole.'

She dropped her pen. Graham kept popping up in other people's stories like a bad smell. 'The Viking?' Erin subtly retrieved the pen from her lap and scribbled a note.

'Yep, can you believe it? A summer kid. He was like this… kingpin of a group of toughs. They had these stupid names for themselves, the Viking, the Enforcer, the Duke. Then, to make things worse, he enrolled at Belle River High my senior year. Timmy was gone by then, and I remember thinking he was lucky. Better the loony bin than having to deal with that idiot for an entire school year.' He touched the side of his head. 'I've still got a scar from the time he slammed me against my locker. But his real specialty was forcing your head into the toilet and flushing it. Don't know how many times I had to suffer that. It was even worse for Timmy, though he didn't like to talk about it.'

Erin wondered if the scar on Tim's cheek was another legacy of her brother's bullying. She felt a senseless urge to apologise for Graham's reign of terror. But having been a victim herself, she was on Jeremy's side, hoping that the Viking, in a delicious stroke of karma, had been made to pay for his crimes.

'Did you ever report this Viking person to a teacher or the principal?' She purposely avoided his eye.

'Are you kidding? I was trying to stay alive, not sign my death warrant.'

She ran down her list of questions. 'What about in the

months leading up to the murders, did you have any sense that Tim was unstable, or prone to violence? Did he mention hearing voices or act unusual in any way?'

'Voices?' He scratched his ear. 'Not that I remember.'

'What about drugs?'

'A bit of weed now and then. If Timmy was hitting the harder stuff, he never told me.'

Jeremy's attention was focused on the boys scrambling after the ball. He was fast losing interest. She'd better speed things up a bit.

'Does this mean anything to you?' She handed him the sequence of letters she had copied from under Graham's yearbook photo.

He squinted at the paper. 'In what context? Like a, waddya call it, an anagram?'

'Belle River High School, 1978.'

Jeremy flicked the paper back to her. 'No idea.'

She was running into one brick wall after another. 'One more question,' Erin said, ready to wrap things up. She had a long drive back to Lansford, and a stack of patient files to get through before she could call it a day. Not to mention that her car was across town, and she'd have to find her own way back. 'On the day of the murders, did you see Tim?'

'Nope.' Jeremy rolled down his window. 'Funny you asked, though, as he was supposed to come over to my place that afternoon. He called to say he couldn't make it, that he had to help his dad around the house or something. Later on, I think around nine, he called from the movie theatre. Said he was going straight home after his shift, instead of meeting up to go out. He had one of those weird headaches he used to get. Always described it as like an ice pick in his brain.'

An ice pick. It sounded like a migraine.

'I drove over to his house sometime after eleven to see how he was doing. Tim should have been home by then, but the house was dark. I figured everyone was asleep, so I drove back home.'

Erin's ears pricked up. 'I didn't see that in the police report.'

Jeremy stifled a yawn. 'I took my mom's car without asking. If she found out, I would have been grounded till I was forty. I was going to tell the police eventually, but then the cops found Timmy, and I figured it didn't matter.'

'Did anyone see you?'

'Nah, no one was out. The rain was coming down in buckets. I did pass some lady on my way back into town though.'

That got Erin's attention. 'What did she look like?'

'Couldn't tell. She had a scarf over her hair. I remember the car though. A green four-door. Or maybe grey. Greeny-grey. It could've been a Dodge or maybe a Pontiac, though I couldn't say for sure.'

A green Dodge sedan. A chill ran through her, although there could have been a dozen green sedans in Belle River that summer. Coincidence, perhaps, but it might be something.

32

Manhattan, New York
June, Present Day

Across a stream of yellow cabs, honking and jostling along the rain-washed street, Erin spotted Ray standing in front of the Morgan Library. She waved to catch his eye, but he was looking at something in his hand. She'd taken an early-morning train into Penn Station, and with her brain still sluggish from yesterday's meeting with Jeremy, and the long drive back to Lansford, she was finding it hard to stay focused.

Last night, Jeremy had sent her an email with the layout of Tim's house. A draughtsman he wasn't, but it was better than nothing, and she was hoping Ray would be able to fill in any gaps. Worn out from several nights of fitful slumber, her primary goal was to get through the day without collapsing into a heap.

As if sensing a shift in the air, Ray looked up and smiled as she stepped onto the pavement. Grey suede jacket slung casually over a shoulder, a lock of hair flopping on his forehead. As he leaned in to kiss her on the cheek, his eyes sparked with mischief. Whatever had dampened his mood during their recent dinner had evaporated into the mist.

'Find the place okay?'

She smiled at his concern. It was a few blocks from Penn Station, how could she miss it?

'Coffee?' He tucked the slim paperback he'd been reading into his back pocket.

'Lovely.' Considering how tired she was, a gallon would be welcome.

As if sensing her fatigue, he touched her elbow and guided her along the pavement. 'The place around the corner's got the best *pastéis de nata* this side of Rio. If you're up for it later, I thought we could have a look in the Morgan. There's an interesting exhibition on.'

How easy he made it sound. Breakfast. A stroll through a museum that epitomised old New York. Perhaps, afterwards, a leisurely lunch at a sleek bistro in Tribeca. It was the sort of charmed life she'd once dreamed about.

The aroma of espresso and toasted almonds greeted them as they entered the tiny coffee house, its glass case crowded with pastries, and barely enough space for three small tables. As they carried their coffees and a plate of the famed custard tarts away from the counter, Ray nabbed a table vacated by a woman in clattery stilettos, who left a cloud of perfume in her wake.

'I'm glad you called,' Ray said, pouring steamed milk in his coffee. 'I must admit, though, when I imagined us going out again, it was to a place nicer than this. Dark wood, candlelight.' He flashed a wan smile. 'But something tells me this isn't a date.'

She hesitated. Why burst his bubble? 'Can't a girl come into the city on a whim?' She met his eyes over the rim of her cup. At some point she'd have to confess that what she really wanted from this meeting was to pick his brain about Tim. For now, it wouldn't hurt to let him think this was a kind of date. Why shouldn't they share a coffee and witty repartee like normal people getting to know each other? That she was lying about who she was would have to be dealt with later, if things got personal, but not today.

Revived by the caffeine, she followed Ray into the Morgan, oddly empty, and with the solemn atmosphere of a cathedral. Insulated from the noise of the streets, she breathed in the musty scent of the leather-bound volumes that were kept, like precious jewels, behind protective metal screens.

'Sunday morning's always a good time to come here,' Ray said, lowering his voice to a conspiratorial whisper. 'While the rest of Manhattan is out having brunch, we can have the place to ourselves.'

As they threaded their way through the vaulted rooms, Erin paused to lean over a glass case of fifteenth-century illustrated manuscripts, exuberant with splashes of blue and gold, bright as a harlequin beetle. In the next case, an engraving from the *Book of Hours* depicted in minute detail the laying out of the dead. An emaciated body lovingly cared for as it awaited the next phase of its journey.

Ray appeared at her side. 'Makes you think, doesn't it? *Carpe diem*, and all that. I love it here, though I realise it's not everyone's cup of tea.' He gestured at the books. 'A few years after I moved to the city, my mother came down from Maine for a visit. The first and only time she ever braved the mean streets of New York, and I dragged her here to the Morgan. She stayed for five days and the entire time she was terrified someone would snatch her bag, or that we'd be mugged walking home from dinner.'

'Do you ever go back?' Erin leaned closer to the display case, trying to decipher the medieval French inscribed within a lavishly coloured border.

'To Belle River? No. Me and my folks…' he looked away. 'We're not close. My younger brother's the favoured son. Married with two kids, he works with my dad in his construction business. It was bad enough when I left home for the big, scary city, but after my marriage fell apart, things got a bit frosty. They hate that I'm divorced.' He touched the small of her back. 'Ready to go?'

The warm sun had burned away the morning mist. As they strolled uptown, the urge to confess everything beat in her head like a drum. With the mention of his divorce, things had taken a personal turn, and it didn't seem fair to keep lying to him. They crossed into Bryant Park, where the trees sparkled from the recent rain. A group of city dwellers and tourists alike sprawled on the chairs and benches, enjoying the sunshine. She pointed to a vacant bench. 'Do you mind if we sit?'

He pressed his palms together. 'Madam, your wish is my command.' He seemed to be in inordinately high spirits, and she considered dropping the whole subject of Tim. How much easier it would be to enjoy the day and see where things might lead. As Ray sat on the bench and stretched out his legs, the light filtering through the leaves dappled his face. Near his elbow, a fat bumblebee roamed amongst the dog roses.

'I have a confession to make.' She slipped out of her pale green cardigan and bundled it on her lap, unable to meet his eyes. 'My last name isn't Carson, it's Cartwright. And I'm not a writer either. I'm a psychiatrist.' When she glanced up, Ray's face was still. 'Following his trial, Tim Stern was sent to a maximum-security psychiatric facility near Syracuse. He's been there since 1978. I couldn't tell you the real reason for my interest in his life because...' She sought his eyes. 'My involvement in his case is confidential.'

As Ray turned to look at the far side of the park, a muscle twitched in his cheek. 'Okay. But why tell me now?'

Because I'm tired of lying. She was ready to blurt it out, but what would be the point? He wouldn't want to see her again, not after today. 'I've completed my assessment.'

'So, you're done with the case?'

'In principle, yes.' Her cheeks felt hot. 'I recommended that Tim be released.'

'Released? To what... some kind of halfway house?'

Above their heads, the leaves rustled in a passing gust of

wind. Her skin prickled from a sudden chill. 'No. If the state agrees to release him, he'll go live with his father.'

Ray's chin jerked up. 'Why would he do that?'

She plucked a leaf from a nearby shrub and rolled it between her fingers. 'That's a question I've been trying to answer myself. And I can't get it out of my mind. I mean, Tim killed the man's wife and daughters. Who's to say, once he's under his father's roof, that he won't finish the job?'

Show him the floor plan. What do you have to lose? That voice, a sibilant whisper. 'Go away.'

'What?'

Had she spoken out loud? 'Nothing,' she mumbled. 'I didn't mean you.' A white-hot pain stabbed her temple. The flickering light, coming through the leaves, bothered her eyes. She shifted to the shady part of the bench before pulling the floor plan from her bag. On the backside of the paper, she'd copied some notes from the police report. 'You've been inside Tim's house, right?'

He hesitated. 'Once or twice. For that science project, remember?'

A group of tourists, squinting skyward, bumbled past as they pointed their cameras at random objects and people. Erin waited until they were on the other side of the park before continuing. 'Did you know that the original house burned down?'

'Did it?' He shook his head. 'I never heard about that. But I've hardly been back since leaving home.' His voice was flat, and his face shut down. Here they were, on a beautiful spring day, and she was forcing him to remember a time and place he'd put behind him long ago.

'This is the layout of the house,' she said, handing him the floor plan. 'Could you walk me through the rooms?'

He gave her a searching look before squinting at the sketch in his hand. A ripple of irritation crossed his face. If he wanted to get away from her as fast as possible, she wouldn't blame him. As soon as he gave her the information she sought, Erin would head for the train station and leave Ray in peace.

'So, the police are suggesting… what?' He ran his index finger along the arrows. 'That Tim killed his sisters in their bedroom, and then went downstairs and murdered his mother in the kitchen?' When he looked up, his face was pale. 'Seems very methodical to me.'

'The deaths were close together in time,' Erin said. 'Which makes sense if Tim was in the grip of psychosis. A psychotic breakdown, or drug-induced psychosis, might have triggered a violent response to a perceived threat.' She shifted her legs on the bench. 'From the time he was picked up until now, twenty-seven years later, Tim claims not to remember anything about that night, or the three days afterwards when he went missing.'

'Tim's psychosis was drug-induced?'

'Possibly.' A gust of wind blew a loose strand of hair across her face. 'The brain is complicated. A drug-induced psychosis can mimic a psychotic disorder, such as schizophrenia. No drugs were found in Tim's blood or urine when he was tested, but they could have cleared his system in the three days he was missing. Or he could have taken something a few days, or even a week, before the killings. Delayed reactions are common with PCP.'

'PCP. You mean angel dust? That can cause a delayed reaction?' He leaned back and ran his hands through his hair. 'Plenty of drugs floating around back then. LSD, mushrooms, speed. Not to mention truckloads of marijuana.' His attempt at a smile quickly faded. 'Could Tim have taken PCP without knowing it?'

'It's possible.'

Clouds moved in, blocking out the Sun. For a moment, neither of them spoke. She shivered and pulled on her cardigan.

'Shall we get something to eat?' Ray stood. 'Midtown's dead on Sundays. But we could take a cab up to my neighbourhood.'

She hesitated, surprised by the invitation. But not quite

ready to head back to Lansford, she was happy to follow his lead.

When he took her hand, his palm was warm, and she sucked in her breath, enjoying the feeling of being cared for. After coming clean about her name and profession, and her connection to Tim, she had expected him to send her packing. That he still wanted to spend time with her seemed a mark of character. As they left the park to hail a cab, she felt lighter than she had in years.

* * *

Ten past midnight. By the time Erin pulled up to the kerb in front of her building in Lansford, all was dark. Even the porchlight was switched off. She sat in the car and listened to the engine cool, scanning the deserted street for signs of life. In the silence, she could hear the blood pulsing in her ears.

Inside the flat, she made the usual rounds. Closing the blinds, flicking on the lights, checking inside the cupboards and under the bed. Only then did she collapse on the sofa in the front room, too wired to sleep. A draught crept along the floorboards and rustled the curtains. The lights from a passing car cast shadows on the wall.

The day, which began with such promise, had morphed into a full-on train wreck. After a stroll through Central Park and an early dinner at an Italian bistro, Ray had invited her back to his flat, tucking her arm into his as they walked up Broadway. The glow of the street lights filtered through the leaves, and the sound of their footsteps rang out in the soft air. After opening the door to his flat, and ushering her inside, he'd pulled her into his arms.

Woozy from the wine she'd drunk at dinner, she followed his lead as her coat slipped from her shoulders and onto the floor. Ray had switched on some Cuban music, samba or merengue, and danced her down the hall and over to the bed, kissing her neck and shoulders.

Riding the wave of his touch, his mouth on hers, she grew limp in his arms, until he unbuttoned her blouse and his fingers found the scar. He'd traced its length with his fingers before she realised what he was doing.

'What happened to you?' His voice was soft, but there was a note of something else. Fear. Suspicion. Here was one more thing she'd chosen to hide.

With a start, she pulled away and yanked her blouse closed.

'I can't talk about it,' she whispered. Then she had fled. But there was nowhere to run.

Even now, alone in her flat, clutching a mug of camomile tea, anxiety flowered like a weed. Her fingers slid under her shirt, seeking the scar, familiar as her own face and hands. The terror of that awful time was locked in the past, or should be.

Using an old trick to calm her nerves, she focused on the items in the room, naming each one aloud in turn. *Table, chair, fireplace, window.* But instead of the desired sensation of calm, the floor plan of the Stern house flashed in her mind, the red arrows pointing out the path of the crime, the lifeless bodies, the walls stained with blood. When an errant thought wriggled to the surface, her hands shook so hard she spilled her tea.

What if it was Stern?

33

Matlock, Vermont
June, Present Day

Twelve miles west of Stern's farmhouse, Erin idled her car at a stop sign. Hanover, Vermont, boasted a white-steeple church and tidy clapboard houses clustered round a village green. It was as good a place as any to base her operations. A sufficient distance from Stern's house to avoid running into him, but close enough to get an idea of the local area.

'First time staying with us?' A woman in a pink cardigan placed a room key in Erin's hand. 'In the lounge, you'll find all kinds of information on the area. Hiking trails, local history, and scenic points of interest. We've got an award-winning chef, but if you'd rather dine out, there are two other options in town. Nothing fancy, but popular with the locals. Enjoy your stay, Ms Cartwright.' She snapped her fingers at a uniformed boy skulking in the corner, waiting to carry her bag.

Her room on the top floor boasted a canopy bed and a large bathroom with a claw-foot tub. A world away from the motorway motel in Atherton. For a moment, Erin considered ditching her plans to spy on Stern and treat herself to a relaxing weekend.

In the lounge, birch logs were stacked in the fireplace, ready to be lit. A selection of paperbacks lined the oak shelves. Dark green damask drapes were drawn against the midday sun. After making a cup of tea from the machine on the sideboard, Erin examined the glossy maps and tourist pamphlets. Stern's village was a tiny dot on the county map and she circled it with a pen. Her online search for details of Stern's life had yielded little. Whatever he might have done out in California, he'd kept a low profile. Later on, she planned to drive over to Matlock and have a look around. What she hoped to find was yet unclear, but she would know it when she saw it. This time, unhampered by Lydia's restraining hand and Stern's determined enthusiasm, she'd like to get a clearer picture of Tim's future surroundings.

Fortified with a cup of sweet, milky tea and two lemon biscuits, she headed east in the direction of the mountains. After twenty minutes of driving on a narrow road that snaked through the forest, she reached the town of Matlock, population 628. Tiny, as towns go, but big enough to support a general store, a lunchroom, and a roadside tavern. Before leaving the Black Horse Inn in Hanover, she'd pulled a shapeless grey jumper over her jeans, and shoved her feet into ratty plimsolls. With her hair tied into a long plait and her head covered with a baseball cap, it was unlikely Stern would recognise her, should she be unfortunate enough to run into him.

In the time since her last visit, when the ground was crusty with frost, a transformation had taken place. An impressionist's palette of green and gold bestowed colour to the fields and farmland, and the air was full of birdsong. A lunchroom called the Brightside Café sported pink and white petunias by the door. In front of the food market, the adverts were bleached in the sun.

The village hardly made a dent in the surrounding countryside, with the green hills flowing to the horizon. After twenty-seven years of life in a locked ward, how would Tim cope in this vast open space? Would he accompany his father into town and sit at a table in the lunchroom to eat a grilled cheese sandwich and fried onion rings? Or would Stern choose to keep his son tucked away at home, far from prying eyes and village gossip? If confined to Stern's property, Tim might be happy enough to play with the dog, feed the ducks and collect eggs from the henhouse. A good enough solution in the warm months. But during the long, dark winters, with the land blanketed in snow, how would the two of them cope?

In the gravel lot behind the market, Erin parked her car at an angle so that anyone driving by wouldn't see the out-of-state licence plate. Though New York plates on a weekend in June might not be a strange sight, she didn't want to advertise her presence. From the boot, she lifted out the hired bicycle and locked it to a fence post.

Inside Garry's Food Mart, a shaggy bear of a man dropped the plastic-wrapped cheese sandwich, apple and bottle of water into a paper bag. 'Going on a hike?' His face was easy to read. *City girl, not equipped for the rugged outdoors*. 'Don't get lost out there. Could be a long time before anyone found you.' He took her money and handed her the bag.

Stern's farmhouse was nearly five miles out of town, but the road was mainly level and on the bicycle she made good time. Three hundred yards from the house, she pulled onto the verge and propped the bike against a towering oak. With the high-powered binoculars she'd bought at the mall in Lansford, the Stern farm, pristine in the sunlight, swam into view.

She'd crossed a line now. Spying on a patient's family was an egregious breach of ethics. If she were caught, she could lose her licence. But if anyone were to wonder what she was doing, lurking on the edge of the forest with a pair of binoculars, she could claim to be a bird enthusiast, on the lookout for… what, a red-tailed hawk, an eagle? She'd seen a number of birds of prey soaring overhead, scouting the stubbled fields for voles and mice, but lacked the knowledge to name them. Other than the common garden varieties, what she knew about birds would fill a teaspoon. As of yesterday, though, she could add one more name to her list. The one that Tim had mumbled under his breath. *Scopus umbretta*, or hamerkop, a native of southern Africa and Madagascar. A large brown bird with an anvil-shaped head and mysterious habits. *Scopus*, from the Greek for shadow, and *umbretta*, brown.

A slow pan of the property revealed nothing of interest. The yard was empty, and the windows shut. Nothing to suggest anyone was home. Though Stern could be out in the barn or sipping one of his machine-made cappuccinos on the patio behind the kitchen. A dark blue Audi was parked out front. Stern's other car, perhaps, or it could belong to the housekeeper. She couldn't remember what kind of car the woman drove.

She lowered the binoculars and rubbed her eyes. Having got this close to the house without being seen, her breath came easier. A mosquito buzzed in her ear and she swatted it away. As she turned to mount the bike and pedal back to town, the front door of the house opened, and a man stepped out. Ducking behind the oak, she focused the binoculars on his face, but it wasn't Stern. This man had salt-and-pepper hair and a distinct stoop to his shoulders. His bulky jumper, the colour of porridge, looked too warm for the weather, and the khaki trousers bagged at the knees. Stern stepped through the doorway after him, his face like a slab of granite. He appeared to be shouting.

The man in the beige jumper said nothing, just headed straight towards the Audi. As he climbed into the car, Erin got a good look at his face. Puffy cheeks, ruddy nose, heavy bags under the eyes. Her palms prickled as she scrambled to adjust the focus. Something about the slant of his neck, and the way he lifted his hand with an air of defeat to smooth back his thinning hair. Could she have seen him before? An old crony of Stern's, perhaps, from his Belle River days?

As the man turned the car around, the plates came into view. Massachusetts. But before she could memorise the number, he sped down Stern's drive, scattering gravel as he spun the wheel. Instead of turning left towards town and the road to Massachusetts, he pointed the car in the direction of the distant hills, and whatever lay beyond the ridge of mountains to the east.

Stern stood on the front stoop, arms crossed, shoulders tense. Only after the Audi disappeared from view did he go back inside the house.

What now? She couldn't follow Stern's visitor on the bicycle. And lurking in the shadow of the oak, spying on Stern with the binoculars, was beginning to feel absurd. She straightened her legs from her awkward crouch and headed back to the village. The road had been empty all morning, but as she rounded a curve, a car coming up rapidly behind her honked twice and careened past, nearly running her into a drainage ditch. She squeezed the brakes and bumped to a stop on the grassy verge, looking up in time to see Stern's silver SUV flinging gravel as it roared away.

Her heart slammed against her ribs. Where was he going in such a hurry? She hoped someplace far away. With her car parked behind Garry's Food Mart, it would be easy for their paths to cross.

By the time she reached the village, it was nearly three, and a few locals were out on the streets. She stowed the bike in the boot of her car and drove towards Hanover, keeping a steady eye on the rear-view mirror. But there was no sign of Stern's SUV, or the dark blue Audi.

* * *

Back in Hanover, a farmers' market was in full swing. Around the village green, trestle tables stacked with jams and maple syrup and cranberry bread made a lively sight. From her room on the top floor of the inn, with its view of the street, Erin scanned the green with her binoculars, on the lookout for Stern. Was he mingling with the townsfolk, filling a canvas shopping bag with pots of honey and home-made strawberry jam, as he chatted with his neighbours? That's what she wanted to believe. But the rage on Stern's face as he watched his visitor drive away told a different story. Clearly, the man in the Audi hadn't been trying to sell Stern a magazine subscription. There was a history there.

Seated at a table in the Morning Glory Café, engrossed in an article on a local case of arson, she nearly failed to look up when the door swung open, and a woman sailed in, bringing with her a rush of fresh air. Cropped blonde hair, figure-hugging black trousers. It was Stern's housekeeper.

Erin hid behind the newspaper as the woman carried her coffee to a table by the window. In her suede loafers and peach linen blouse, she clearly hadn't come from cleaning Stern's home. That the housekeeper might recognise her was unlikely, but just when Erin thought it was safe to slip outside, Stern breezed through the open door, his face flushed, his jaw tense. As he joined the woman at her table, he leaned in to kiss her on the mouth. Her expression softened, and she stroked his cheek. Not his housekeeper, it would seem. But lying about his love life was hardly a crime.

The counter girl arrived to clear away Erin's empty mug. 'Anything else for you? We've got some nice sandwiches today and a delicious veggie soup.'

The housekeeper glanced over as Erin shook her head and raised the newspaper to hide her face. Would she have to wait for them to leave? Perhaps, if she was lucky, she might be able to breeze past them undetected. But Stern seemed the type of man who noticed the smallest detail. As a lawyer, he'd be good with faces and body language. Bad luck that she'd removed her baseball cap and sunglasses when she came inside. It would look odd now if she put them back on. During the home study visit with Lydia, she'd worn a charcoal-grey trouser suit and her black-framed spectacles. Dressed as she was now, in jeans and a jumper, and her hair in a messy bun, she could easily pass for a college student. He might not make the connection.

Trapped behind the newspaper, she tried to focus on an article about local politics, but failed to take in anything. As the minutes ticked by, she felt like a mouse trapped in its burrow. When Stern and his companion finally finished their meal and pushed away from their table, she lowered her head and rummaged in her bag. If Stern glanced her way, at least her face would be hidden. He made a big show of joking with the girl behind the counter and turning to call out something to a younger man across the room. Playing the man about town, even in this small village in rural Vermont. Perhaps he was trying to seed the ground with an abundance of goodwill. Splashing money about and patronising the local merchants to show what a good citizen he was. How else was he going to explain to the townsfolk that his schizophrenic murderer son would be living in their midst?

After they left, Erin waited a good five minutes before getting up to pay her bill. When she stepped outside, she hung back under the awning to check the street, before making a beeline for the car park out back. As she hurriedly freed the helmet from the crossbar of the bike, someone behind her coughed.

'Dr Cartwright?'

She stiffened. But by the time Erin turned to face him, she had a smile ready. No sign of his lady friend, or his car. He must have followed her after she left the café.

'I thought that was you.' His smile did not come quick enough to mask the suspicion in his eyes. Not a man she would want to face in a courtroom.

'What brings you to this neck of the woods?' he said, tucking his hands into the pockets of his jacket. 'Did we have an appointment?'

She felt caught out, like a child with her hand in the biscuit tin.

'How nice to see you again,' she said, brightly, hoping her voice sounded natural. 'An appointment? Not at all, I'm up here on a weekend getaway. A friend of mine said this was a nice area to explore by bike.' She gestured at the helmet. 'She also said the farmers' market in Hanover was not to be missed.' She showed him her bag of jam and maple syrup as evidence, like a witness on the stand.

'Where are you staying? The Black Horse? A lovely place. Be sure to give my regards to Jean and Artie. Tell 'em I said to treat you well.' He looked at the helmet dangling from her wrist, then at the bike leaning against the fence post. She could see his mind scrolling backward and putting two and two together. She held her breath and waited, but the moment passed, and she turned to unlock the bike.

But Stern didn't move away. She could hear him behind her, shuffling his feet on the gravel. He cleared his throat. 'Now that we've bumped into each other, may I ask if there's any news about Tim's case?'

In the dappled shade, his face looked strangely opaque. It may have been a trick of the light, but for a moment it seemed as though his eyes could see through her skull and straight into her brain.

'I'm afraid I can't give you any details about Tim or the status of his case,' Erin said, easing the bike round until it was pointed towards the street. The air felt heavy, and she was anxious to get away. 'I'm sure someone will contact you before Tim is scheduled to appear before the judge.'

'That's good to know.' He slapped some dust off the sleeve of his jacket. 'Enjoy your stay in Hanover.' The voice was hearty. But his eyes hadn't changed, and it was his eyes that bothered her. Surely, he didn't buy her story about driving all the way up here to buy jam at the local farmers' market.

The wheels of the bike spun on the gravel as she pulled out of the car park and pedalled away, acutely aware of Stern's cool stare, boring into her back. Some might say those penetrating eyes were the sign of a true believer. A man lit by the flame of a higher power. But Erin would call them something else.

34

Belle River, Maine
August 1977

Music thumps from the stereo in the basement rec room, blocking out the chirrup of crickets in the yard. Jeremy's parents have gone out to a party and won't be back until late. A perfect time to break out a little weed. Jeremy pulls the plastic baggie of Jamaican Gold from the pocket of his jeans and sets to work rolling the sticky buds into a fat spliff. He lights the end and takes the first pull, holding the smoke deep in his lungs before passing the spliff to Tim. He's not all that fond of weed, but he takes a pull, coughs and sputters.

Another toke, and the top of his head shears off. He can feel his blood and bones break away and waft through space to rendezvous with the stars. He closes his eyes and lies back on the orange beanbag, his heart galloping as his spinning thoughts race for the moon. He takes another toke, waiting for the familiar calm to flush through his veins, but this time he feels something different. An urgent, vibrating energy, like a swarm of bees descending through the air. Bees in the trees. Bees in his blood. Jeremy's face balloons to twice its size.

'Man, this is heavy stuff,' Jeremy says. 'Where'd you get

it?' He lies flat on the floor and laughs like a loon. 'I'm totally wasted.'

It was that boy everyone called the Duke who gave Tim the weed. He'd been acting all chummy recently, even slinging his arm around Tim's shoulder when they'd run into each other at the docks last week. Punching him on the shoulder, laughing at his jokes. Like they were blood brothers, or members of some long-lost tribe. Weird, that's for sure. But if Jeremy knew who'd given him the dope, he'd freak out, sure they'd been poisoned. If there was anyone Jeremy hated worse than the Viking, it was the Duke. A snake in the grass was what Jeremy called him.

He sucks more of the oily smoke into his lungs, and tries to focus on his friend's face, but it keeps moving in an out of his sightline, until it detaches from Jeremy's body and floats up to the ceiling like a helium balloon.

Blood canters through his veins and electrifies his fingers. A surge of power blows his body into the size of a giant, while sharp fangs push through his gums. Beset by a furious hunger, he eyes Jeremy's limp form, splayed out on the beanbag, and the delectable, tender skin of his neck, where a blue vein pulses, beating in time to the werewolf thump of Tim's heart. How inviting the pale skin looks. He creeps closer, presses his finger against the beating blood.

Jeremy stirs and opens his eyes. 'Hey, man. What's up?'

35

Lansford, New York
June, Present Day

A stiff breeze, laden with the tang of the river, ruffled the yellow tulips Erin had placed in a vase on the kitchen table. On her way home from the clinic, she'd taken the long way round, to drive by Cassie's house, the third time in two weeks. But the blinds were drawn, and the windows shut. She could only imagine what went on behind those closed doors, and hoped that Cassie was okay. When a man from the house next door stepped onto his front porch, she had started the engine and driven away. First, the weekend in Hanover to spy on Stern, and now this. If she kept pushing it, she'd be in serious risk of losing her licence.

* * *

The phone at the police station in Belle River rang six times before someone picked up.

'How old did you say the case was?' The man had a smoker's gravelly voice.

'August 1977.'

'Hang on a sec.' He muffled the phone to shout something, before coming back on the line. 'Name of the perpetrator?'

'Timothy Warren Stern.' She paused. 'He murdered his mother and two sisters.'

'Stern? Oh, sure,' he said. 'I heard about that case. Long before my time, though. Not much in the way of violent crime around here, so a case like that sticks in your head.'

'If it's possible,' Erin said, 'I'd like to speak to the officer in charge of the case.'

'Don't know what he can tell you that's not in the police report, but I'll have someone dig up the name for you. Call back tomorrow. I should have it by then.'

* * *

The punishing Florida sun glittered in a flat blue sky. After driving for an hour through an unending stream of salt flats and housing developments, the taxi pulled up to a gated community on the water, home of Harry Talbot, the detective on the Stern case. At the gatehouse, a guard checked Erin's name against a list before waving her through. Masses of pink and white flowers from the oleander hedge lined the driveway. On the clipped lawn, date palms were arranged in mathematical precision. Crouching low to the ground, a crew of groundskeepers worked their clippers amongst the foliage, decapitating weeds and snipping errant blades of grass.

In less than a minute, her blouse was damp, her loose cotton trousers stuck to the back of her thighs. She followed the numbered arrows to a lime-green bungalow set on a postcard-sized lawn of prickly grass. It was a long way from the salt-pocked granite and pine forests of Belle River. Her sandals crunched along a path of crushed coral and broken shells that led to the front door. Before she could press the bell, a man with a shock of white hair and a deeply lined face stepped onto the porch. His yellow polo shirt and khakis were rumpled, as if he'd just woken from a nap.

'Come on in out of the sun. It's a sizzler today, isn't it?' He ushered Erin through a tiled foyer and into the living room. White plantation shutters filtered the Sun's rays. 'You must be about ready to melt. Not used to this kind of heat, are you? I can crank up the air con if you'd like.'

She shook her head. The room was as frigid as a meat locker. Erin slipped her arms into her linen jacket as Talbot crossed into the open-plan kitchen.

'Would you like a glass of iced tea? Adele made a fresh pitcher this morning.'

'Thank you, that would be lovely.'

She perched on the couch upholstered in pale peach fabric. On the wall, a clock in the shape of a pelican ticked away the minutes. Talbot returned with a tray and handed Erin a glass before lowering himself into an easy chair. His right hip seemed to be bothering him, but his eyes were lively, with the keen glint of a cop back on the beat.

'You've come a long way to pick the brain of an old man.' He rattled the ice cubes in his glass before taking a sip of his drink.

Outside, a lawnmower started up, slicing through the stillness. 'I've read the police report,' Erin said, setting her glass on the table. 'It was very thorough, but what I'm really interested in is *your* impression of the case.' She struggled to sit up straight on the slippery fabric. 'Whatever you can remember.'

'Well, when it comes to the Stern case, my memory's as sharp as a tack. Though sometimes I wish it weren't so good,' he said, rubbing his eyes. 'The scenes in that house will stay with me to the grave.' He plucked his glasses from a shirt pocket and settled them on his face. 'Where do you want me to start?'

'From the beginning, if you don't mind.'

'That would be when the call came in,' he said, scratching his jaw. 'I was on desk duty. Just after ten it was, when the neighbour called, a widow living on her own. The Stern's dog had been barking all morning, so she walked to the mailbox at the end of her driveway, where she had a partial view of the Stern home. The front door was ajar, that's what she noticed first, and Mrs Stern's car, a blue Pontiac sedan, was parked in the driveway. But there was no one out front, so she waited for a minute or two, assuming that Mrs Stern or one of the children had gone inside to fetch something and would come right out. But no one did, and the dog was still barking like crazy.'

Talbot hauled himself from the chair to close the slats on the shutters. 'When nobody appeared,' he said, running his finger along the sill as if checking for dust, 'she went over there and called out from the front yard. But no one answered, so she looked through the window. That's when she saw the blood splashed all over the walls and fled back to her house. The poor woman was hysterical. I jumped into an unmarked car with a uniformed cop named Danny Calhoun and hightailed it out there. No lights, no siren. We didn't want to alert the perpetrator, in case he was still inside. Hot as Hades that day. I can still remember how the steam was rising off the roads in the sun.

'I was a beat cop in Brooklyn for ten years, and saw plenty of things to keep a man awake at night, but I've never seen so much blood as I saw in that house. Mrs Stern was lying face down in the doorway to the kitchen. I didn't bother to check if she was alive.' He stared into his glass of iced tea, before meeting Erin's eyes. 'I didn't need to.

'After calling for backup, we searched the rest of the house, but there wasn't anybody alive in there. I found the two girls in their beds, the sheets covered in blood. I assume you know the details of how each of them died?'

She nodded. The crime scene would forever be imprinted in her mind.

'Okay, so after seeing the bodies, Danny and I stared at each other, both thinking the same thing, that some maniac was on the loose, and we needed to move fast before he struck again. From the squad car, I called in the forensic unit.

At the time, I had no idea how many people were living in the household, so we couldn't be sure who, if anyone, had escaped the carnage.'

He smoothed the creases on his trousers. 'Mr Stern pulled into the driveway just after eleven,' Talbot said. 'By that time, forensics had arrived and the whole place was taped off. We took him down to the station to break the news and to ask him some questions.' Talbot drained his glass. 'He kept asking about his son Tim, if we'd found him.'

Erin paused in her note-taking and studied his face. 'Tim wasn't a suspect at that point?'

He shook his head. 'It crossed my mind that the kid might've done it, but it was too early to say. Being a small town, I knew who he was, of course. Used to work at the movie theatre on the weekend. Adele and I would take the kids on Saturday afternoons. He seemed polite enough, if a bit shy and awkward. Never would have pegged him as a killer. But then again, it's always the quiet ones, isn't it?'

'How did Mr Stern react when he heard the news?'

'He was pretty calm, considering. He'd only just driven up from Portland after meeting with a client. I didn't think lawyers kept office hours on a Saturday, but what do I know.' He removed his glasses and pinched the bridge of his nose. 'When we questioned him about his whereabouts the night before, Stern said he'd driven down to Portland on Friday afternoon and checked into a hotel. When he called his wife at six, the two girls were at home, and the boy was working his shift at the movie theatre in town. Mrs Stern called him back a couple of hours later. Something about a dress pattern at a local shop. According to Stern, she sounded fine.

'We have the records from the phone company, and it all checked out. Stern said he called the next day around ten to remind his wife to pick up his suits from the dry-cleaner's, but there was no answer. When we asked if that was particularly worrying, he said no. She was often out in the mornings doing errands, and the girls would be at their various activities. Tim usually slept in late.' He stood and massaged his hip. 'Are you a golfer, Dr Cartwright?'

She shook her head.

'We've got this nifty little putting green right here in the complex. Would you mind if we went over there so I can putt a few holes?' He tapped his forehead. 'Helps me think.'

* * *

With a straw sun hat belonging to Talbot's wife perched on her head, Erin hovered at the edge of the putting green. The heat was ferocious, and she wondered how long she'd last before collapsing to the ground. Talbot bent at the knee and swung the putter, missing the little hole by a whisker.

Beads of sweat formed on her upper lip. 'What about Stern's alibi?'

He set up the shot again and got ready to putt. 'Well, like I said, he checked into a hotel in Portland just before six on the Friday, and two of the staff confirmed they saw him at breakfast on Saturday morning. The client meeting checked out too. An older gentleman confirmed that he met with Stern at the firm's office on Saturday morning at nine-thirty.'

In the distance, the pastel bungalows shimmered in the heat. 'What about the woman whose name was removed from the police report?'

Talbot set up another shot and moved his hips into position. 'Her story checked out too,' he said, driving the little white ball cleanly into the hole. 'She confirmed she was with Stern the whole night. After Tim was found and arrested, her name was removed from the report at her request. She was worried the media would get wind of it, and she'd have reporters camped out on her front lawn. Didn't want her children finding out she had shacked up with a married man.'

'Seems unorthodox to me,' Erin said, fanning her face. 'Altering a police report on a murder case.'

Talbot shouldered his clubs and heaved himself into the

driver's seat of the little golf cart. 'Times have changed, Dr Cartwright. But back then, in a place like Belle River, with its small-town morals, a woman admitting she'd spent the night in a hotel room with someone else's husband would have destroyed her reputation. She was only a summer resident but still quite worked up about anyone finding out. She had family living in town, over on Gardiner Road. I could see how it could make things difficult for her, if it got out.'

Gardiner Road? She shivered. It could be any of a dozen houses on that road, but Erin somehow knew which one it was.

'Besides,' he said, manoeuvring the golf cart along a gravel path, 'when the boy was picked up by state troopers, covered in his mother's blood, the issue of Stern's alibi became rather moot, don't you think?'

No, she didn't. When was an alibi ever moot? 'Who questioned Tim when he was first picked up?'

'The troopers who found him took him to the nearest hospital. When the docs there checked him out and pronounced him okay, he was taken into custody at the local sheriff's office. Questioned there too, but he didn't say much. Didn't know how he got over the state line into New York, or whose blood was on his clothes. Disoriented and a bit panicky, he barely knew his own name. Kept saying something about a shadow, or some kind of bird with large wings. Drugs was my first thought, but he was clean when they ran the tests. At the time, he was being treated as a victim, not a suspect. Only after he was brought back to Belle River did we tell him about his mother and sisters. That boy was like a stone when he heard the news. Didn't flinch or show any signs of distress.'

Talbot parked the golf cart under a canvas awning and switched it off. 'He did ask about his father, though. Wanted to know if he was alive. When we assured him his dad was okay, the funny thing was, he looked scared, like a little kid about to be punished. I remember the boy's exact words when we told him his dad was okay: *Am I in trouble?* Later on, somebody mentioned amnesia or delusions. Something about a… what's it called… a fugue state.'

They returned to the house and a welcome blast of frigid air. 'Let's forget about the diagnosis for a minute,' she said. 'I'm interested in your impression of Tim. As a seasoned police officer, what was your gut reaction the first time you saw him, right after he was brought in?'

Talbot puffed out his cheeks. 'Hard to say. Though one thing's for sure. He didn't look like a crazed killer. He looked like a scared kid. Not just lost, but…' He snapped his fingers. 'Haunted. Yeah, that's the word. Like he'd seen a ghost.'

36

Albany, New York
June, Present Day

In an airless courtroom in Albany, Erin took a seat at a table by the lawyer appointed to Tim's case. The judge, a stout woman with black hair coiled into a bun and a permanent crease between her eyes, studied the file in front of her before calling the proceedings to order.

Lydia Belmont and Dr Harrison were seated behind Erin, waiting to be called to give their accounts. For the past twenty minutes, Tim's lawyer had presented the details of the case. In a moment, it would be her turn to provide the results of her assessment. Dressed in a navy trouser suit and black pumps, Erin hoped she projected the proper air of seriousness and restraint the occasion called for. What happened today would change the course of Tim's life.

When asked to speak, she cleared her throat and sipped from a glass of water before standing to address the judge. With her notes on the table in front of her, she launched into it.

Having completed the mandated evaluation process, Timothy Warren Stern, Jnr, remanded to Atherton State Asylum for the Criminally Insane, now Greenlake Psychiatric

Facility, in February 1978, after being declared not guilty by reason of insanity for the murders of his mother and sisters, was – in her professional opinion – neither a danger to himself, nor to others.

As long as he continued to take his prescribed medication and was offered the appropriate social support to assist his re-entry into the community, she recommended he be released into the care of his father.

As soon as she'd said her piece, Erin sat down and folded her hands in her lap, examining the judge's impassive face for a sign of how things might go. Once the ruling was made, they would be informed of the court's decision within three days.

* * *

When Harrison called two days later with the news of Tim's release, Erin was not terribly surprised and also relieved to know that Tim would be living in a beautiful house in the Vermont countryside, and not shunted off to another state facility. But an undercurrent of unease still needled her gut, especially at night while lying in bed, waiting for sleep to release her from the worries of the day.

'Thank you for letting me know,' she said. 'Is there anything else you need from me? Any follow-up?'

'Nothing from our side.' Harrison's voice faded in and out, as if he were phoning her from the bottom of a well. 'But I'd like to extend my heartfelt thanks and appreciation, Dr Cartwright, for the time and care you've put into Tim's case.'

'It seems to have worked out in everyone's favour,' she said, trying to keep any hint of doubt from her voice. Would it be overstepping the bounds to ask him to keep her updated on Tim's status, once the move to Vermont had taken place? Though Lydia might be more sympathetic to her desire to stay in touch.

After hanging up the phone, she sank onto the leather sofa in her office, uncertain whether the feebleness in her limbs was a sign of relief or the beginning of a new wave of worry. Whatever the case may be, her part in the Stern family murders was over. As for Tim, the die was cast. Whatever happened now was out of her hands.

She opened the windows wide to let in the fresh morning air. Sunlight filtered through the canopy of leaves and cast a golden glow on the lawns. In full glorious bloom at last, the celebrated meadows, an undulating tapestry of colour, shimmered in the breeze. If she were to walk amongst the throng of blossoms, they would surely be alive with the buzz and tumult of bees.

Closing her eyes, she tried to teleport herself into the landscape, until she could smell the scent of honeysuckle perfuming the air and feel the flowers brushing her bare arms. She took a deep breath. It was over. Tim Stern was no longer her problem to solve.

Though a few details still rankled. On the plane back to New York, following her meeting with Detective Talbot, she had briefly toyed with the idea of following up on the information he let slip about Stern's alibi. The mystery woman who'd spent the night with Stern in his hotel room, who just happened to have family living on Gardiner Road. A coincidence? Perhaps, but too tantalising to brush aside, and there was only one way to find out. But as her plane touched down at LaGuardia, she had decided to let it go. Why reopen old wounds? Entering the vipers' nest would blow her cover and might even set off a chain of events that torpedoed her job. It was all over now, in the past where it belonged. Time to focus on her patients and to get on with her life

She had a few minutes before her next patient session was due to begin. Admitted three months ago, fifteen-year-old Meghan should have been discharged this week, but she was still struggling with depressive symptoms and suicidal thoughts. Her wealthy parents had been more than willing to extend her stay for another month, if not more. Meghan had responded well to treatment at first, but as the weeks wore on, she seemed to regress, incandescent with rage that her parents had hauled her out of school and away from her friends. At least the girl's anger was a good sign. It meant she'd stopped bottling up her emotions and was experiencing the raw pain of her distress.

It would be a challenge to break through the wall of all that anger, to the hurt and terror smouldering below. But in Erin's experience, the ones who could access their rage were easier to reach. The outwardly angelic girls, wraithlike and luminous as ghosts, who insisted they were perfectly fine, were another thing. Those were the cases that kept her up at night.

With Tim no longer taking up space in her head, she finally had time for other pursuits. Perhaps she could sign up for a cooking class, or something calming, like yoga or meditation. Get out more, make some friends. Perhaps consider dating again. She glanced at her watch. Ten minutes until her session with Meghan. On impulse, she picked up her mobile and punched in Ray's number. When he answered, his voice sounded distracted.

'Hi, it's Erin.'

A muffled cough, the shuffling of feet. Was he with someone? Stupid of her to call. Of course, he wasn't alone.

'Erin?' Ray's voice was hoarse, as if he'd just woken up, or recently taken up smoking. A siren blared in the background, followed by the scrape and bang of a window being closed. 'Is everything okay?'

'Everything's fine.' She smiled into the phone. 'I was just calling to say that Tim's been released from Greenlake.'

'Tim's out?' He coughed again. 'Well, that calls for a celebration. Why don't you come into the city for dinner? Or we could meet somewhere else. Manhattan's a cesspool in this heat.'

She thought fast. Somewhere on the train line would work. 'How about Dobbs Ferry?'

'Perfect. I've been wanting to visit the provinces.' He laughed. 'At least there'll be a breeze up there. Shall we meet on the train platform at seven? I'll be the guy with the red carnation in his buttonhole. In case you've forgotten how I look.' He paused, as if not wanting to end the call. 'It's really good to hear from you, Erin.'

She hung up, smiling. It was good to hear his voice, especially now that her heart felt a hundred pounds lighter. He'd sounded happy to hear from her. A surprise, considering how they'd left things the last time. Fleeing his flat like a crazy person when he'd asked about the scar. Perhaps this ongoing flirtation with Ray – if that's what it was – might actually turn into something.

* * *

True to his word, Ray was waiting for her on the platform at the stroke of seven. Italian loafers, crisp white shirt, a dark blue linen jacket slung over his shoulder. She smiled as she spotted the red carnation in the buttonhole. As she stepped from the train in her strappy, high-heeled sandals, she felt a bit wobbly on her feet. She rarely wore heels, but relished the extra inches of height they provided, and the feel of warm air on her toes.

Ray leaned in to kiss her cheek. 'Success becomes you.' In the soft light of early evening, his eyes were clear as amber.

Indeed. She hadn't felt this carefree in months.

He took her arm. 'Shall we walk a bit?'

For the first time in Ray's company, she could actually let down her guard and be herself. Shed at last the serious demeanour of Dr Cartwright and just be… Erin. No more quizzing Ray about Tim or forcing him to dredge up memories of schoolboy antics from a lifetime ago. Today, they were simply two people, a man and woman, strolling along the river on a summer evening, as swallows swooped over the water, and pleasure boats churned upstream. The sun was deliciously warm on her bare arms, and when Ray took her hand, it felt like the most natural thing in the world.

With no need to keep secrets any more, she could relax a little. Perhaps, the next time they met, or the time after, she would even feel ready to tell him who she was. Haul all those festering lies into the light, until they shrivelled on the vine and blew away.

* * *

The evening with Ray passed like a dream. A perfect meal at a lively restaurant on the water, a shared bottle of wine, an after-dinner stroll as the Sun sank into the bluffs across the river. Whatever awkwardness she'd felt with him on previous occasions had vanished. With the Stern case behind her, they were free to discuss other things. Books, art, travel. A memorable meal, all-time favourite films.

After walking her to the station, Ray pulled her into his arms and kissed her while they waited for her train. In his kiss, she could sense the sorrow of parting. But it wouldn't be for long. They made a date for the following Saturday to visit an exhibition at the Met, and there was a new Sicilian restaurant in the Village he wanted to try. After that, if things went well, she could picture a whole series of outings and weekends in the city. As the train clattered north, her heart thumped with anticipation of all that was to come. For the first time in many years, the future spread before her like an endless plain of possibilities.

The ringing of her phone punctured her dreamy mood. She glanced at the unfamiliar number on the screen and considered letting it go to voicemail. But it might concern one of her patients.

'Dr Cartwright?'

A youngish voice, faint but defiant. 'Who's calling?' Erin asked.

'I've been arrested. I need you to pick me up.'

'Who is this?' Assuming it was a prank, Erin was about

to hang up, but then the penny dropped. 'Cassie, is that you? What's going on, where are you?'

'In Lansford, at the police station.' Her voice quavered.

'I'll be right there.' Erin's heart flipped over in surprise. Cassie wanted her help.

As soon as the train pulled into the station, she ran to her car. By the time she hurried into the police station, thirty minutes had passed. Erin was flushed and out of breath. They would think she was hysterical if she didn't pull herself together, so she bent to sip cold water from a drinking fountain and smoothed back her hair, before approaching the duty officer and stating her name.

He gave her a weary look. 'Are you the girl's parent or legal guardian?'

'I'm her doctor,' Erin said. 'Can you tell me what the charges are?'

In her floaty summer dress and strappy sandals, she didn't look like a doctor, but she had proof, of course, in case he asked.

He hesitated for a moment before turning to consult the booking sheet. 'Trespassing, vandalism, disorderly conduct. All Class-B misdemeanours. No bail's been set. She's got a court date next week. If you're planning to sign her out, I'll need to see some ID.'

As he wrote down the number on her driving licence, Erin could hear the rattle of keys and the clanging of doors. A female officer escorted Cassie from the cell block. When they reached the desk, the sergeant handed Cassie a brown envelope with her things – wallet, keys, shoelaces, belt – and asked her to sign for them.

Cassie avoided Erin's eyes as she grabbed the envelope and retreated to a wooden bench to lace her sneakers. 'Like I'm supposed to, what, hang myself with my shoelaces?' she said when she caught Erin looking at her.

Erin turned away to address the officer. 'Do you need anything else?'

'No, we're done here.' He tossed his pen on the desk. 'But

if you want my advice, Dr… er, Cartwright,' he said, reading her name off the form. 'You might want to scare the crap out of that girl. Kid like that…' He jerked his thumb in Cassie's direction. 'It starts with minor stuff, you know? But then it escalates. Drugs, petty larceny, or worse. I'd hate to see her back here in six months.'

Cassie waited by the front door, arms across her chest in a posture of defiance. Smudged eyeliner, a bruised lip. A tiny gold hoop threaded through her left nostril glinted under the fluorescent light.

Behind the wheel of her car, Erin waited for Cassie to settle in before starting the engine. The lights in the empty car park cast a sulphurous glow on the deserted street.

'I'm glad you called me.'

Cassie was hunched in the seat, her head turned away.

Erin waited. 'How did you get my number?'

Cassie looked down at her hands, examining the fingers black with ink. She sniffed the back of her arm. 'I stink. That cell was gross. Can you take me home now?'

Erin folded her hands in her lap, listening to Cassie breathe. If necessary, she would wait all night. This time, she wanted some answers.

A noisy sigh. 'When they were checking me out of that loony bin of yours, I got a look at the computer screen. Your phone number was right there with your address and birthday, and everything. I'm guessing the lady at the front desk isn't the sharpest knife in the drawer.'

Her birthday? 'Did you send me a birthday card, back in March?'

'Maybe.' Cassie slid down on her tailbone and closed her eyes. 'I'm tired. Can we go now?'

Erin started the car and pulled into the street. 'Where to?'

Cassie snorted 'You know where I live. I've seen you drive by my house like a million times. I could report you for stalking, you know.'

She waited for more, but Cassie seemed deflated. Spending a few hours in a jail cell would knock the stuffing out of anyone.

So, mystery solved. Cassie had sent her the birthday card. No reason to have panicked. It was a good sign. In her own troubled way, Cassie had made the first move in what would undoubtedly be a complicated game of 'catch me if you can'.

Erin couldn't help but smile. That bridge she'd been waiting for? It had appeared at last.

37

The Meadows
Lansford, New York
July, Present Day

'Dr Cartwright? It's Lydia Belmont.' Her voice was muffled by the hum of traffic. 'I'm calling about Tim Stern.'

'Is everything all right?' In the middle of a staff meeting, Erin signalled to Niels that she needed to step outside.

'He's in the hospital.'

'Where? Greenlake?' She felt a twinge of unease.

'No, in Burlington. He was admitted to their psych ward two days ago.' Lydia paused. 'They had to forcibly restrain him. When I called this morning, he was still heavily sedated. I'm on my way over there now.'

The shock of the news struck Erin speechless. How long had Tim been at his father's? Not more than three weeks, or was it four? 'Did he stop taking his meds?'

'I don't know about that,' Lydia said. 'They only mentioned that he was in an extremely agitated state when he was brought in. Nearly incoherent, at first.' She fell silent. 'He said his father tried to kill him.'

A strange paralysis gripped Erin's limbs, and for a moment

she couldn't move. Her worst nightmare, that something dreadful would happen once the two of them were alone in the house, had come to pass. But in spite of her suspicions about Stern, it was *his* safety she'd been worried about, not Tim's. Had Lydia got it wrong? Surely Tim was the wild card in this case. The stress of leaving Greenlake must have tipped him into the swamplands of paranoia and fear.

'Have you spoken to Mr Stern?'

'Not yet, but I did talk to the psychiatrist on call,' Lydia said. 'He thought Tim might have had a panic attack, brought on by the stresses of the move.'

The meeting had broken up and Niels, coming through the door with the rest of the staff, motioned for her to stop by his office.

'Sorry, what was that?' Erin said. She'd missed half of Lydia's side of the conversation.

'I was saying that Dr Harrison isn't able to get away on such short notice. He wondered if you could drive up there to see what's going on.'

She'd have to check her calendar, though it wouldn't be a simple matter to drop everything and drive up to Burlington. A good three hours away, if not more, and there was no telling how long she'd have to stick around once she got there. She had her own patients to think of, and a full diary of responsibilities.

After hanging up, Erin felt an overwhelming urge to skip town. Would this case never go away? But that something had gone wrong wasn't a complete surprise. Nothing ever played out as expected, and Tim's move to Vermont, no matter how seamless on paper, was never going to be all sunshine and roses.

What else could she do but drive up there and help sort things out? If Tim had gone off his meds, paranoid delusions were just one of the many possible effects. It was only later that another, more frightening, thought occurred to her. That Tim wasn't delusional at all. And there was a grain of truth to his claim of attempted bodily harm. Especially if Stern had behaved in ways, both large and small, that Tim viewed as a threat. For all she knew, a hair-trigger temper lurked behind Stern's easy-going smile.

* * *

With a little juggling of her schedule, Erin managed to be on the road to Burlington by four. Three hours alone in the car would give her plenty of time to think. As she wound through the Green Mountains, miles upon miles of dark forest that shifted in and out of the golden afternoon light, the potential scenarios of what had gone wrong piled up in her head. When she pulled into the car park of the Burlington hospital, it was a few minutes after seven.

As the big glass doors slid open to let her in, she wondered if she'd find Stern there, hovering in the lobby like a concerned parent. Or perhaps he was at home in Matlock, rethinking his decision to house Tim under his roof.

She rode the lift to the psych ward on the top floor. The duty nurse, a woman with a no-nonsense expression, glanced at her ID.

'He's out of restraints now,' she said, consulting a chart on her desk.

'Could I speak with the attending physician on call when Tim Stern came in?'

Distracted by a beeping monitor, the nurse tilted her head. 'Who? Oh, sure. Dr Larsen. There he is now, coming out of Room 603.'

Erin hurried to intercept him, aware she looked a mess, with her shirt untucked and her hair limp from the long drive in the heat. 'Dr Larsen?'

The man's eyes swam behind a pair of thick glasses. He blinked as he hitched his belt over a considerable paunch. Erin cleared her throat and asked about Tim.

'Are you a family member?'

'I'm a psychiatrist,' she said. 'His treating physician couldn't get away, so he asked me to represent him.'

Larsen slid a notepad from the pocket of his white coat and flipped through the pages. 'The patient was brought in by ambulance on Sunday, just after two in the morning. He was highly agitated and disoriented. Possibly psychotic. He knew his name, but not what day it was. After taking a blood sample, we administered a sedative as a precaution. His labs showed no evidence of antipsychotics. As of seven this morning, he's back on his prescribed meds. My guess is he stopped taking them soon after he was released from, where was it… Greenlake?'

Stopped taking them. How was that possible? Stern would have been schooled on the importance of Tim's meds, and the consequences of his failure to take them.

'I was about to go off my shift,' Larsen said. 'But I can stay on a while, if you think it'll help.'

Through the observation window in the door, Erin could see Tim lying flat on his back, eyes fixed on the ceiling. 'Thank you, but there's no need for you to stay.' She remained at the window for a few minutes, hoping to see some movement, but not even a twitch emitted from the figure on the bed. Except for the eyes, fixed but clearly alive, he might have been a corpse.

She knocked softly and opened the door. 'Timothy? It's Dr Cartwright. May I come in?'

When he didn't respond, she entered and tiptoed towards the bed.

'How are you feeling?' She pulled up a chair.

The faint rise and fall of his chest provided a hint of life, but nothing suggested he was aware of her presence.

'You're safe, Timothy. You're in a hospital in Burlington. Your father isn't here, and he won't be allowed to see you without your permission. No one will hurt you.'

Her shoulders tensed as she waited for a response.

Breathe in, breathe out. She counted ten breaths as she

held herself perfectly still, until they resembled two statues in the waning daylight.

A tiny movement, a shift of air.

He shut his eyes. 'Go away.'

She waited for him to say more, but when nothing came, she continued. 'I'm on your side, Timothy.'

A ragged intake of breath. 'I have no one.' His voice was a croak. 'Everyone… gone. Hummingbird.' His hand twitched. 'Broken.'

Hummingbird?

Erin pulled the chair closer. Tim's wrists were chafed red from the restraints. How long had they kept him tied to the bed?

'Can you tell me what happened?' A dinner trolley rattled along the corridor. 'Are you thirsty? There's a soda machine downstairs. I can get you a Coke if you'd like?'

His eyes stayed closed, but his mouth twitched. It was something.

She stood and stepped away slowly so as not to startle him. 'I'll be right back. It's so warm in here. A cold drink will make us both feel better, don't you think?' She was babbling, trying to find the switch that would jolt him from his stupor.

The machine in the waiting room was out of Coke. But there was Sprite and Dr Pepper. When was the last time she'd had one of those? She rummaged in her bag for change and carried two Dr Peppers back to Tim's room, pressing one of the chilled cans against her cheek.

Standing at the foot of Tim's bed, she cracked open the flip-top and filled a paper cup, but he showed no interest. She sipped the cold liquid, sickly-sweet, and closed her eyes as it slid down her throat. Something about the taste rattled her vault of stored memories. Marquee lights, popcorn, red velvet curtains… A boy in a red and white striped hat handing her a paper cup, fizzing with bubbles.

I was there.

Her eyes snapped open, and she leapt from the chair, spilling the soda on her clothes.

'Heat. Hot. Hat.' The words erupted from his lips. 'Flask. Cask. Mask.'

She stiffened. *Mask?* 'Did you say something about a mask?'

'Space. Race. Face.' Tim levered himself upright and swung his legs to the side of the bed.

She jumped back as he lurched to the window and placed his hands on the glass. The mountains beyond had darkened to purple.

He slid his fingers along the window's edge. 'Nailed shut. Door locked.' He turned his head from side to side, each movement painfully slow, every word an effort, as he fought the deadening effect of the drugs. 'Key turns. Door opens.' Tim was panting now, fighting for air. 'My father, not my father. His face…' He squinted at his upturned palms. 'Pretend to sleep. Can't breathe. Something dead on my face. Front door locked. Smash window, run to barn.' Sweat streamed down Tim's face. His hands jerked, his eyes rolled back in their sockets.

Erin took a step forward. 'You're okay, Timothy. Try to breathe. Deep breaths, in and out.'

'Blood on his face. Blood on his hands.'

Blood? Lydia didn't mention anything about blood. 'Who was bleeding, Timothy?'

'Blood on his face, blood on his hands.'

'Was someone else in the room besides your father? Did he say anything to you? Ask you if you needed help?'

His eyes flicked, his hands clenched. 'I don't know, I don't know, I don't know.' With a spasm, he slumped to the floor and curled into a ball, trembling so hard his teeth rattled.

Erin ran into the hall and called for the nurse. 'I need some lorazepam in here!'

An orderly rushed to hold Tim down while the nurse stuck a needle in his arm. In a moment, he was quiet, and they guided him into bed. Tim's eyes closed, and his face went slack.

'He'll sleep now,' the nurse said. 'It would be best if you came back in the morning.' Her mouth was set, and her voice held a hint of annoyance.

Not quite ready to leave, Erin hovered in the doorway, watching Tim breathe. Her thoughts galloped ahead. Whatever happened at the farmhouse had triggered something in Tim's mind. A primordial fear or a deep-rooted memory, long buried in the recesses of his brain. Reflexively, her fingers sought the amulet round her neck.

I was there. Friday night. She had snuck out of the house in her best cotton dress to go to the movies. Flouting the rules, but she didn't care. For once she wanted to feel like a normal kid, to be like other girls her age, with their movie nights and lip gloss and long, shiny hair.

She traced the outline of the quetzal with her thumb.

Bloody hands, a broken hummingbird. *The glass hummingbird*. The one in the crime-scene photos, smashed on the living-room carpet.

Tim was starting to remember.

38

In the hospital cafeteria, Erin bought a large coffee and a chicken sandwich and carried her tray over to a window. Except for two orderlies sharing a table in the corner, the room was empty. She shivered in the chilled air. The coffee was weak and the sandwich stale, but she was too tense to eat anyway.

Whatever happened three days ago at Stern's home had caused Tim's brain to skip back in time. He must be remembering details of the original crime. Otherwise, why would Tim say there was blood on his face and hands? Though it could have been a nightmare, a trick of the light, or the delusions of a diseased brain, it was possible Tim was remembering his own actions on the night of the murders. After slitting his sisters' throats, he could have looked in the mirror to see his hands and face covered with blood. Years later, during a panic attack in a farmhouse in Vermont, he'd confused his own face with that of his father's.

She tossed the remains of the sandwich into the bin and stepped outside to call Harrison. When he didn't pick up, she left a message on his voicemail. The soft air was alive with the hum of insects in the tall grass. She sat on a nearby bench and closed her eyes, trying to make sense of the thoughts cartwheeling through her head. That night at the movies, her trepidation and terror, Vivien screeching up to the door, her face black with fury. *Get your fat ass in the car.* What happened afterwards was harder to recall. So many of her memories from that time were smashed into fragments by the doctors and their drugs at Danfield.

Of all the scenarios she'd worried about when recommending Tim for release, she had never imagined that Stern might be an object of terror to his son. During the assessment process, her only fear was that, once the two of them were alone in the house, either Stern would lash out in frustration, or Tim would finish what he'd started that rainy August night in 1977.

Next to her on the bench, her phone vibrated.

'Dr Cartwright? How's our patient doing?' It was Harrison, sounding more upbeat than concerned.

'He's asleep. And heavily sedated. When I arrived, he was awake and alert but extremely agitated.'

'Psychotic?'

'I don't believe so.' She debated whether to tell Harrison that Tim might be remembering the murders. But it wasn't a conversation to have over the phone.

The silence lengthened before Harrison spoke again. 'Did he tell you the same story, that his father tried to smother him with a pillow?'

'Not in so many words.' She hesitated, trying to gauge Harrison's mood by the sound of his breathing. 'With your permission, I'd like to question Tim under hypnosis.' A new approach to a therapy that had been attempted before. She had an argument ready if he insisted it was useless to try.

Harrison cleared his throat. In the background, she could hear the shuffling of papers. 'I suppose it wouldn't do any harm, though I'm sure I mentioned before that we tried several times in the past with little success. The last attempt was about twelve years ago, I believe.' The sound of a window closing, the rattle of keys. 'I can't get away this evening,' he said. 'And tomorrow I have to drive to Albany for a critical meeting about Greenlake's closure.' She could hear the sound of paper being torn in two. 'I do agree it's best not to send Tim home until we get to the bottom of this,' he said. 'It could be something as simple as night terrors or a bad dream, but until we know for sure...'

Erin confirmed she could remain in Burlington for another two days. It would mean admitting to Niels she was still involved in the case. And someone would have to cover her patients for a day or two, but that couldn't be helped.

* * *

After a night of restless sleep at a nearby hotel, Erin fortified herself with a cup of weak tea and a soggy pastry before returning to the hospital. Tim was in bed, exactly as she'd left him, flat on his back and staring at the ceiling.

'How are you feeling this morning?' She hung back by the door. 'I spoke with Dr Harrison yesterday. He's worried about you.' She stepped into the room and pulled up a chair. 'He suggested we try something. It might help you remember what happened the other night.'

Nothing moved. Tim might have been carved from stone.

'It won't hurt. It feels like going to sleep. All you need to do is lie quietly with your eyes closed and listen to my voice. If you don't feel comfortable, we can stop at any time.'

When Tim tried to speak, it came out as a croak. 'You'll put thoughts in my head, like a... seed. Alien seeds.'

She shifted to the foot of the bed, so he could see her. 'I'm only going to ask you a few questions. No alien seeds. I promise. Okay?'

Was that a nod? For ethical reasons, she needed his consent. It looked like a nod, or close enough. In the hallway, a nurse was waiting with a syringe of sodium amytal. Its effect as a so-called truth serum had long been discredited, but it wouldn't hurt to give it a try. If nothing else, it would help Tim relax.

When Erin motioned to the nurse, she approached the bed and smiled. 'A little something to help you feel better, Timothy.' The needle was in and out before he could react.

A slow drip would be more effective, but this was all she had. Erin gave the drug a few minutes to do its work, before moving the chair out of Tim's line of vision. In her lap, she switched on the mini-recorder that would capture anything Tim said while under hypnosis. First, she'd take him through the recent events at the farmhouse and, if the questioning went well, attempt to coax him all the way back to August 1977, and the night of the murders.

'Okay, Timothy, I'd like you to close your eyes now. In your mind, I want you to visualise your arms and legs and imagine how relaxed they are. Now I want you to pay attention to your breath as it moves in and out of your lungs. Your arms and legs are heavy, your breathing is steady. Your whole body is relaxed. Imagine you're floating on a big white cloud. Breathe in... breathe out. Relaxed and floating. Floating and breathing. Your limbs are heavy and completely relaxed.' She went on like this for another minute or so. 'Focus on my voice, Timothy. You're safe here. No one will hurt you.'

She held her breath and waited. Tim's eyes were closed, his breathing steady.

'Now, I'd like you to think of a pleasant place, somewhere you feel safe. In this place you're surrounded by a golden healing light, and nothing can harm you. Are you in that place now?'

'Light. Golden.'

'Yes, that's good. Think about how nice it feels to be surrounded by this warm golden light. You can go back to that place any time you feel frightened.'

With a click and whoosh of air, the ventilation system came on. Erin tensed, but he didn't stir.

'Now, Timothy, I want you to go back to last Saturday. A light rain was falling all afternoon, but it's evening now and the sky is clear. You've finished eating supper in the kitchen at your father's house and have gone to your bedroom. Can you describe it for me?'

'Blue. Door locked… music… window shut. No air.'

'What happens next, Timothy?'

'Footsteps. Door opens. A man with something white… a laundry bag.' Tim's hands twitched.

She held her breath. Nothing about a mask. Or blood. 'It's okay, Timothy. You can go back to your safe place now.'

She waited for him to settle.

'Slow, even breaths, in and out. Arms and legs relaxed.'

She hesitated before taking the plunge, but this might be her only chance.

'Let's go further back in time. It's a Friday night in late August. You're seventeen years old and working behind the concession counter at the movie theatre. Can you tell me what you see?'

Tim's face had gone slack. His chest rose and fell.

Erin waited as she listened to him breathe.

'Friday night. Movie night. Sad girl, frightened eyes… I gave her a soda. The Viking… History Girl, arm around her neck. Rain hitting the roof like stones.'

Erin held her breath, her spine so rigid she was afraid it might snap. At last, a connection. Her brother Graham with his arm around the girl Tim liked.

'Your shift has ended,' Erin continued, 'and you can finally go home. You've turned out the lights and locked the door. Now you're driving home through the rain.'

Tim's face contorted, his hands clenched.

'Breathe in, breathe out. Relax your arms and legs.' She waited. 'Now you've arrived at your home on Easton Road. What do you see?' She tried to synchronise her breathing with his.

'House… dark. Everyone asleep.'

'Your mother isn't waiting up for you?'

'No lights. Tired. I lie down on the couch. Thunder wakes me. No lights. Maggie scratching at the door. Who let her out? Poor Maggie. I go to let her in. Something wet on the floor… lightning flash… blood. Blood on the floor. Blood on my hands. Overhead, a shadow. Rustle of wings. Shadow bird. The beak stabs my neck. Can't breathe.' He clutched at his throat.

Tim's eyes snapped open. 'Face in the mirror. *Him.*'

39

Matlock, Vermont
August, Present Day

The leaves of the big white oak in Stern's front yard hung limp in the heat. Erin cut the ignition and stared at the house as the Toyota's engine pinged and cooled in the silence. Next to her, Lydia released the clasp on her seat belt. Her face looked drawn and her shoulders slumped.

'Shall I wait here?' Erin shifted her legs, hot and sticky from the long hours in the car. 'I don't want to antagonise him.'

On the drive up, she had told Lydia about her little excursion to Matlock in June. How Stern wasn't fooled for a minute that she happened to be spending a holiday weekend in the area. 'What did you expect? You were spying on him,' Lydia had said. 'An inexcusable breach of the man's privacy. Shame on you.'

But Erin didn't feel ashamed, she felt vindicated, especially in light of recent events.

'Well, you can't sit out here,' Lydia said, as she stepped into the sultry air and dabbed her face with a handkerchief.

As they walked up the drive, Lulu bounded over to greet them.

'At least it's not a pit bull,' Lydia said, holding her skirt away. 'Plenty of those in my neighbourhood.'

She sidestepped Lulu and pressed the doorbell. But the house looked shut up tight. Lydia pressed the bell again.

When the door swung open in a whoosh of air, Stern stood aside to let them in. He seemed to have aged ten years since the last time they met. Bags hung under his eyes, and the skin on his face was heavily creased, as if he'd just woken up.

'Are we early? I hope we aren't disturbing you.' Lydia smiled kindly.

'I was going over some papers and forgot the time.' His voice was hoarse, his expression flat. He pointedly avoided Erin's questioning look. The ebullient small talk of their first visit was nowhere to be found.

Seated at the table on the back patio, Stern poured iced tea into tall glasses. In the few minutes it took him to fetch the pitcher from the kitchen, his face had cleared. But something had happened in this house. An echo, however faint, of the violence and bloodshed of the murders all those years ago, and Erin was determined to find out what it was.

'How's Tim doing?' Stern stirred a spoonful of sugar in his tea. 'They won't tell me anything when I call.'

'He's being well cared for,' Erin said, after a pause. She had no intention of confiding any details.

He waited for her to continue, but Lydia broke in smoothly, her voice modulated, as if speaking to a child. 'Perhaps you could tell us what happened the other night.'

A yellowjacket hovered near the sugar bowl, and Stern shooed it away. 'I don't know where to start.' He lifted his glass and set it down again without taking a sip. 'To be honest, I'm completely mystified.' He stood and walked to the edge of the patio, turning his face towards the barn. 'Things were going great. Tim seemed happy with the house and his room, and he loved hanging out with Lulu.'

Erin and Lydia exchanged a look.

'What was your evening routine like?' Lydia asked.

Stern returned to the table and topped up their glasses from the pitcher. 'We ate dinner at six. Usually in the kitchen. Sometimes out here if it wasn't too buggy. After we cleaned up and washed the dishes, Tim would go up to his room with his Sudoku. Mostly, he would turn the light out by nine or ten. I've always been a night owl, so usually I—'

'Did you lock him in his room at night?' Erin hadn't meant to cut him off, but she was losing patience.

Lydia gave her a warning look.

'Lock him in?' His voice was strained. 'Absolutely not.' When he lifted his glass, his hand shook. 'I did lock my own door, though.' He addressed Lydia as if seeking absolution. 'I truly believe Tim's okay now, but I slept better knowing my door was locked.'

Lydia nodded. 'That's understandable.'

'When I spoke with Tim,' Erin said, 'he told me his door was locked, and the window nailed shut.'

The yellowjacket returned, and Stern swatted it away. 'Aren't delusions a symptom of his illness?'

'They can be. But that doesn't mean everything he says or remembers is false, or never happened.' She let this sink in.

Another yellowjacket arrived to join the first, and settled on a drop of spilled tea. Stern squashed it with a napkin and flicked it to the ground.

The photos from the crime scene scrolled through Erin's head. The splattered walls. Stern's wife lying in a pool of blood. Who wouldn't lock their door at night with Tim in the house? Perhaps she was being too hard on him.

Lydia leaned forward and touched Stern lightly on the arm. 'I can only imagine how upsetting this is for you, but it would be a great help if you could tell us exactly what happened on Saturday last week.'

Sweating profusely in the muggy air, Stern wiped his brow with a napkin. Even on the patio, in the shade of the sycamores, the heat was suffocating. The metallic buzz of a cicada broke the stillness.

'The day started out fine,' he said, rubbing his eyes. 'I got up early to work in the garden. Tim was still asleep at nine when I went in to check on him. He likes to sleep late, but I try to get him up by ten. I don't think letting him sleep all day is a good thing, and the social worker from Burlington said it was important to establish a daily routine.'

From her shady spot under a sprawling blue hydrangea, Lulu loped towards them and rested her head on Stern's knee.

'We had lunch here on the patio at twelve on the dot, the time Tim prefers. After lunch, he walked over to the pond with some stale bread and fed the ducks, then he took a nap in his room. Dinner at six.' Stern stroked Lulu's velvety ears.

'In the middle of the night, I woke to hear Tim shouting. When I went into his room and switched on the lamp, he was sitting bolt upright in bed, a look of terror on his face. When he saw me, he started yelling, *go away, go away*. So, I closed his door and locked it from the outside, so he wouldn't hurt himself. Then I called an ambulance. It took nearly an hour for them to get here. The whole time, Tim was shouting and pounding on the door. When the paramedics arrived, they held him down and gave him an injection.' Stern's face was pinched, his eyes bloodshot. 'As soon as he settled down, they took him away.'

Erin studied the trail of sugar crystals on the table before looking Stern in the eye. 'Tim said you came into his room holding a pillow. That you tried to smother him.'

Stern jerked back in the chair. 'Why would he say such a thing?' He covered his face with his hands and shook his head. 'Poor Tim, he was doing so well. Kept his room clean, helped me with the chores, and he really bonded with Lulu.' He patted the dog's head on his knee. 'He was in charge of filling her bowl with kibble and making sure she had plenty of water to drink.' Lulu, upon hearing her name, looked at Stern with hopeful eyes. He rubbed his forehead as if something occurred to him. 'I don't understand why this happened. Do you think his medication stopped working?'

Medication only works when you take it, Erin thought. Surely, he knew that. She was having trouble breathing in the sweltering air. 'Was he taking his meds?'

'Every night, right after dinner. I watched him swallow the pills.'

Lydia wrote something in her notebook.

'I'd like to have a look at Tim's room.' Erin stood up too fast and her head spun.

'By all means.' He led them through the kitchen and into the hallway. A quick glance confirmed that the door to Stern's den was firmly closed. What she wouldn't give to get another look at that photo. Or anything else that provided a clue to what this man might be hiding.

Upstairs, the door to Tim's room was shut. Stern twisted the knob and pushed it open. *See, not locked.* 'Feel free to look around.'

A single bed, covered with a white cotton blanket, a desk and chair, a chest of drawers. Two sturdy rugs, blue and green, on the oak floor. No busy patterns or pictures on the walls. No mirror. Surely the advice of the social worker.

Erin crossed the room to check the window. It opened with ease for a few inches and stopped. Two brass knobs were screwed into the sash, the kind of safety device someone might use in a child's room. The six-inch gap, while allowing the free flow of air, was barely wide enough for a cat to slip through. Directly below, the slate tiles of the patio glinted in the sun.

'The social worker suggested the security pegs on the window,' Stern said, moving next to her, so close she caught a whiff of his aftershave. 'As you can see, it still opens to let air in.'

She turned and looked at the door. No key in the lock. But that didn't mean anything. It could have been removed for their visit.

Stern invited them to look into his own bedroom on the other side of the hall, with an expression that declared he had nothing to hide. The room was as she remembered. Bland as a hotel suite, seemingly unchanged from their first visit. The only new addition was a solid brass bolt fastened to the inside of the door.

As Erin scanned the room, her attention was caught by a row of framed photos on the dresser. The one with three men in camouflage vests jumped out at her. One of the men – a boy, actually – with blond hair and a square jaw looked familiar. But before Erin could get a closer look, Stern ushered them out of the room.

Something about the photo, and the camouflage vests, triggered another thought. 'Are there any weapons in the house?'

'You mean a gun?' Stern shook his head. 'No, wait a minute. I've got an old shotgun in the barn. Used to do a bit of duck hunting in my younger days.' Lydia started to speak, but he cut her off. 'It's in a locked gun safe and there's no ammunition anywhere on the property. But I'll get rid of it, if you think that's best.'

Erin's mind was on the photo. Could the blond guy be Graham? He'd liked to hunt and fish. Though how Stern would have known him was a mystery. Through Vivien, perhaps?

She had a dozen more questions, but he herded them downstairs and towards the front door, clearly wanting this intrusion to be over. Out on the front steps, they made an awkward threesome as Lydia thanked Stern again and they said their goodbyes. The cicada buzzed as thunderclouds gathered above the mountains to the west. Erin hoped the storm would hold off until they were on the motorway.

'If there's anything I can do to help Tim get back home, you'll be sure to let me know, won't you?' Stern said. He kept his back turned to Erin, freezing her out, as he spoke to Lydia. Apparently, he'd told them all he was willing to say. Not just about the recent events that put Tim back in the psych ward, but anything to do with the original crime. Her conviction they were connected had only increased. She would have to get her answers from someone else.

Though the thought filled her with dread, it was time to pay a visit to the Viking.

40

The row of red-brick apartment buildings, darkened with age, squatted under a turbulent sky. Rain lashed the trees and pummelled the streets. Hugging the kerb, Erin inched her car forward, keeping a look out for 98 Morrison Avenue. If she'd ever wondered where former budding psychopaths ended up, drug kingpins or indicted hedge fund managers, it might have been a place like this.

She parked opposite the two-storey building, half-hidden by a row of sycamores, and contemplated her next move.

Her fingers sought the amulet, warm against her skin, though it was ridiculous to be afraid. He couldn't hurt her now.

She waited another few minutes, but the rain showed no sign of letting up. Erin opened the door and ran across the street, soaked by the time she reached the covered area by the entrance. The dingy white paint on the door was cracked and peeling, and the brass nameplates, green and pitted with age, were smeared with fingerprints. Why would Graham live in a place like this? Mr Golden Hair. *The bloody Viking*, with the world at his feet.

Perhaps her online sleuthing had led her astray. But there was his name, G. Marston, taped on the letter box to apartment 2A. It could be another Graham Marston, but to find out, she'd have to go inside.

Her hand shook as she pressed the bell, but the solid weight of the quetzal against her skin gave her courage. *I can do this*.

A moment later, she was buzzed into a gloomy foyer, ripe with the smell of kitchen grease and mildewed carpets.

As she climbed the stairs, dread pooled in her stomach. But before she could even knock on the door to 2A, it swung open to reveal a balding man in stained tracksuit bottoms and a grubby T-shirt, stretched tight across a roll of flab. Sausage fingers ferreted a couple of bills from a battered wallet. He pulled out two tens and raised his head.

'Who the hell are you?'

For a moment, Erin was struck dumb. This man, with his thinning hair and dirty fingernails, could not possibly be her brother. Whatever she imagined he'd become in the intervening years, it wasn't this.

She looked past him to the living room, with its porridge-coloured carpet and saggy sofa. Ratty venetian blinds were drawn against the outside world. The rancid smell of a rubbish bin filled the air.

'Wrong apartment.' He started to close the door, when the street-door buzzer rang again. 'What the hell?'

A skinny kid bounded up the stairs, balancing a box of pizza and a paper bag on his arm. 'Here you go. Still under thirty minutes, even with the rain pissing down.' The boy smiled.

As soon as he'd handed over the money, he started to close the door in her face.

'Graham.'

He squinted at her in the dim light.

'It's Mimi.' She cringed at the sound.

'Mimi?' His eyes roamed her face. A nest of broken capillaries were spread across his nose and cheeks.

'Aren't you going to invite me in?'

He snorted. 'Well sure, why the hell not. What kind of person would I be if I shut the door in my own sister's face?'

He stood aside to let her pass, hugging the pizza box and six-pack of beer in the crook of his arm. It was a tight squeeze, and she panicked at the thought of him reaching out to grab her. Unnerved at the prospect of being in the same room with him after all these years, she'd tossed a steak knife into her handbag before leaving Lansford. No protection at all against this hippo of a man, but it gave her a sense of security. This time she was armed.

He dumped his food on the table. 'Don't mind the mess. It's the maid's day off. Hardy-har, just joshing.' He wiped his hand on his shirt. 'Doesn't hurt to pretend though, right? The lord in his castle, and all that.' He swept a pile of newspapers off the couch. 'Have a seat.'

With her eye on the door, Erin lowered herself onto the edge of the sofa, jumpy as a fox.

A decaying stack of newspapers teetered on the floor by the couch. The air smelled of dirty bed linens.

Not missing a beat, he pried open the lid of the cardboard box and grabbed a slice of pizza, paved with salami and glistening with oil. 'I gotta tell ya,' he said, taking a bite, 'I wouldn't have recognised you in a million years. What's with the hair? Some kind of goth thing?'

Goth? It was true she used to have pale hair. Dishwater blonde is what Vivien called it. But she'd dyed it dark brown after running away, not black. In her blue cotton jumper and linen trousers, she couldn't look any less goth than she did.

As he chomped through the pizza, and glugged a beer, she imagined this might be how an entomologist felt, while observing a particularly gruesome species of arthropod.

Before she could jump away, he reached out and flicked a lock of her hair. 'Remember that time you chopped your hair off as a kid? That was weird. But you were a weird kid, weren't ya?' With his finger, he made a circle near his ear. 'So it kind of went with the territory.'

The cropped hair, how could she forget? Though it wasn't crazy at all, but a perfectly rational, if desperate, act of self-preservation. What else could she have done in the face of Vivien's threats to hack off Erin's long hair while she slept? *Snip, snip*. Vivien liked to terrorise Erin by snapping the sewing shears in front of her face as she got ready for bed. Cutting off her own hair was the only way Erin could think of to put a stop to Vivien's nocturnal reign of terror. That was the idea anyway. Though a fat lot of good it did her in the end.

'Cat got yer tongue?' He took a swig of his beer and smirked as he tore into another slice of pizza. A glob of tomato sauce fell to the carpet. 'Wanna slice?'

She shook her head, hypnotised by the grease on his chin and the piggy eyes. Her mind spun back to an image of herself as a child. Pudgy, awkward, terrified. How Graham used to stalk her through the house, jumping out from behind doors to grab her by the neck, trap her under the stairs, or lock her in the cellar at night. The friction burns, and the bruises from his vicious pinching. Baiting, jeering. She was a fat pig, a retard.

He popped open another beer and tilted his head, slugging down half the can in a single gulp. Munching and slurping his way to some pre-appointed doom. Even if he tried, he couldn't be more a caricature of the boorish sad-sack than he already was. When had it happened, this transformation? Was it slow and steady, or all at once? Golden Boy gone to seed.

He waved a hand round the room. 'In case you're wondering, these aren't my usual digs. I got me a nice house over in Nashua. Or did. But my ex got it in the divorce. Crap lawyer or it would have gone to me. I paid for the damn thing, didn't I? And the last kid's almost out of the house, so it's not as if she needs all that space. It won't be long before she's sitting over there all by her lonesome, wishing old Graham was there to cosy up with on the sofa.'

Erin bit her lip to keep from laughing. Whoever the former

Mrs Marston might be, she couldn't imagine her, or anyone, wanting to snuggle up to this disgusting swine of a man. She'd seen enough, it was time to get the answers she came for and get out.

'Do you remember a guy named Tim Stern?'

'Timmy Stern?' He grabbed a handful of crisps from the bag on the floor and tossed them in his mouth. 'The whack job who axed his family?'

There was no axe involved, but that was beside the point.

'What brought him up?' Graham dropped the empty pizza box on the floor. 'Wait, don't tell me. You're dating him, right?' He glanced at her hand. 'No ring, so at least you're not engaged yet. But in case you're about to tie the knot, you should know that, in addition to him being a murderous psycho, he's a total wanker. But, hey, whatever floats your boat.'

The skin on her neck prickled.

'I've been trying to remember the night of the murders,' Erin said, resisting the urge to bolt from the room. 'Where I was.' She met his eye. 'And where you were.'

He popped the tab on another beer and handed it across to her, but she shook her head. 'Where do you think you were? Home in bed, right. Didn't old Viv have a rule against sleepovers?'

Vivien had a rule against most things. 'So if I was home in bed, where were you?'

'How the hell should I know?' He scratched his neck. 'What are you, a cop or something?'

'I'm a psychiatrist.'

'No shit.' He threw back his head and laughed. 'That's the funniest thing I've heard all year. The loony treating the loons.' He snorted and downed the beer.

'I'm trying to remember if I heard anything. Like somebody coming home very late, after midnight.'

Unless she had the dates mixed up, Erin was sure it was the same night she got caught sneaking out to the movie theatre, and that there'd been a storm, with the rain hitting the roof like marbles. Lying in bed in the dark, tense with the terror of being alone in the house, she had heard someone come through the kitchen door just before two in the morning.

'It was a Friday night,' she said. 'You must have been out.'

He shrugged. 'If it was a Friday, I sure wasn't at home.' He swung his feet onto the coffee table. 'Out with the Duke and that crazy Lenny Simko, probably. I wonder whatever happened to those guys.'

'You don't keep in touch?'

'Nah. Not since I moved out to Ohio. And after I came back here, it seemed kind of lame to look them up. For all I know, they're all in prison. Or dead. The Duke used to do some pretty serious drugs back then.'

'What kind of drugs? Cocaine?'

'Nah. Cocaine's for wussies. The trippy stuff. LSD, shrooms, angel dust.'

'You mean PCP?'

'Sure. Whatever you wanna call it. The one that makes you batshit crazy. If I thought any of that old Belle River crowd would end up murdering somebody, it was the Duke, not that wuss, Timbo.'

'Did this Duke person ever give PCP to Tim, or maybe some marijuana that was laced with it?'

'How the hell should I know? And why do you care?' He puckered his mouth as if biting into a lemon. 'Come on, fess up. You and Timbo are at it.'

An eye roll would have provided welcome relief, but she refrained. 'I'm just trying to make sense of my own memories.'

'Good luck with that.' He grinned. 'Do you even have any left? Didn't they zap your brain like a zillion times at that nuthouse? Probably nothing in there but a big ol' pile of scrambled eggs. Give it up, sis, and move on.'

She'd been wondering how long it would be before he brought up Danfield. Vivien and Graham, thick as thieves, colluding with that quack doctor to convince him she was mad. Poor little Mimi, totally bonkers. Vivien even going so far as to say she was afraid of her, a child of thirteen.

'That night, I remember waking up around two in the morning,' Erin said. 'It was pouring rain. I thought I'd heard someone come home. I don't think it was you.'

He made a noise in his throat. 'If you're wondering about nocturnal shenanigans, you'd better ask Her Majesty.' He reached for the remote and switched on the television. 'She calls herself Vivien Donnelly now. Married some schmuck about ten years back. But he died a few years ago. So now she's a widow twice over, and milking it for all it's worth. Calls me all the time, saying she needs me to fix something in the house. Same old Viv. Hates to be alone.'

The room had grown dark. A blackbird, mistaking the glass for open air, smacked into the window. Erin jumped. She crossed the room to see if the bird was okay, but it was lying on the flagstones, its neck broken.

The locked room, the dark basement. Bloated and pathetic though Graham might be, buried in there somewhere was the savage boy everyone called the Viking. The one who'd pinned her wrists to the floor and laughed when the doctor came to cart her off to Danfield. For the first time since she arrived in the flat, fear sliced through her chest. If he went for her, that steak knife she brought wouldn't make a scratch.

She picked up her bag and edged backward to the door, afraid that any quick moves might cause him to lunge forward and grab her by the arm. Without turning her back, she opened the door and stepped in the hall.

He tore off another slice of pizza and took a bite. 'Leaving so soon?' He smirked. 'And we were having such a good time.'

41

Standing under the metal awning outside Graham's flat, Erin inhaled great gulps of the rain-washed air. Her clothes smelled of dirty socks and pizza grease. If she were smart, she'd get in her car and drive straight back to Lansford. Wash off the stink of the afternoon under a hot shower and treat herself to dinner at a fancy restaurant. But she'd come this far and survived.

Like an arrow shot from a bow, there was no turning back. Concord was little more than a thirty-minute drive away. If anyone had the answers she was looking for, it was Vivien. Time to face the dragon.

But as the miles ticked past, her courage wavered, and the familiar fear snaked through her gut.

This time, she reminded herself, there was no reason to be afraid. No doctor was waiting to knock her out with a hypodermic and bundle her away. She was no longer a child, and Vivien was old. So who had the power now?

In no time, she had reached the outskirts of town. How predictable of Graham to live a stone's throw from his old haunts. Not to mention the woman he professed to loathe, but to whom he was tethered like a balloon to a fence post. Stuffed with pizza and bloated with beer, perhaps even now, he was planning his comeback. Sliding behind the wheel of a sporty new car. Wavy blond hair magically resurrected, Adonis body gleaming with health. The Viking's triumphant return.

She laughed out loud.

But as she pulled off the main road and drove through the centre of town, the tension returned, and she gripped the wheel. Clapboard houses, bordered by strip malls, dozed in the summer haze. As the clouds dispersed, steam rose off the pavement in the heat of the Sun.

On the northern edge of town, where the houses thinned out and the forest began, she turned left onto a narrow street lined with single-storey homes set back in a dense wood of hickory and pine. No children played outdoors. No barking dogs or lawnmowers disturbed the still air. She idled the car in front of the last house on the right.

At night, locked in her room with the lights off, she would peer at the dark woods, sensing rather than seeing the nocturnal creatures lurking amongst the trees. Staring at her with their red eyes and sharp fangs. Smelling fear. On some nights, she used to pray that a kindly wood sprite would emerge from the pines and spirit her to safety.

In the hot car, a trapped bluebottle butted against the windscreen. She opened the window to release it and stepped onto a ratty patch of lawn. No dog bounded across the grass to greet her. No pets had ever lived in the house. Nothing warm-blooded to speak of.

Her sandals flapped on the slate flagstones that led to the front door. Erin's pulse quickened, and her throat felt tight. She glanced round for possible escape routes, gauging how long it would take to run to the nearest neighbour, barely visible amongst the trees. Ridiculous to be afraid. What could possibly happen in broad daylight?

But a vision of a snarling Medea floated before her eyes. Arms raised, kitchen shears poised to deliver the murderous blow. When she touched her pendant for courage, the spectre vanished. With no plan for what she would say, or how she might react when the door opened, she was flying blind. When dealing with a human Rubik's cube, impossible to solve, the best strategy was not to play. Erin would get the information she'd come for, by trickery if necessary, then make a swift exit. After that, she would disappear into the mists, just as she had all those years ago.

Her legs felt stiff as she mounted the steps. Her brain sounded an increasingly urgent alarm. *Run. Run for your life.* But she sucked in her breath and pressed the bell.

42

A woman in a turquoise cotton shift and towering heels opened the door. In her left hand, she held a burning cigarette. Menthol, judging by the smell. The pale, candyfloss hair was swept back from her forehead and fixed with a net of hairspray. At some point, in a misguided attempt to turn back the clock, the woman's skin had been stretched tightly across her cheekbones.

If it weren't for the telltale webbing under the eyes and the spray of liver spots on the deeply veined hands, she might have passed for fifty. At least in the dim lighting of a seedy tavern. But next month, Erin knew, the woman before her would turn seventy-one.

As she scanned Erin from head to toe, the ripple of astonishment was followed by a haughty lift of the chin. 'Interesting what you've done with your hair,' Vivien said. 'Though it's too dark for your skin tone, and it always looked better short.' Her smile was chilly.

'Aren't you going to invite me in?' The words caught in Erin's throat. She pulled her shoulders back, in an attempt to appear taller.

'I have company. Whatever you've come to say, you can say it right here.'

A plump woman in a voluminous pink-flowered dress, her

face flushed with heat, poked her head into the front hall. 'Vivien? Is everything okay? It's not those Jehovah's people again, is it?'

'Everything's fine. Just someone I used to know.'

Sweat broke out on Erin's forehead, but she stood her ground as Vivien took a drag of her cigarette. In the oppressive heat, with the hot sun on her back, she was afraid she might faint.

'All right.' Erin looked directly into the faded eyes, once a dazzling blue, and refused to look away. 'Let's talk about Tim Stern.'

Vivien blanched, but quickly recovered. 'That boy who killed his family?'

'Not the son. It's the father I'm interested in,' Erin said. 'The two of you were having an affair.' She paused. 'On the night of the murders, you provided him with an alibi.'

Vivien's friend reappeared, clutching a straw handbag against her bosom. 'I really should be going,' she murmured, casting an alarmed look at Vivien as she squeezed past them and hurried to her car.

'Lunch next week?' Vivien called gaily, but the woman merely flapped her hand and drove away. 'Still a troublemaker, aren't you?' She exhaled a stream of smoke. 'What are you, a cop?'

Like mother, like son. Perhaps it was a sign of a guilty conscience. 'I'm just looking for answers.'

Vivien narrowed her eyes. 'You'd better come in then. I won't have you making a scene in front of the neighbours.'

The neighbours were too far away to hear anything, but that wasn't the point. It was all for show, and the face Vivien put on for the world, engaging and warm, was certainly not the one she wore at home.

As Erin stepped over the threshold, the cloying scent of Vivien's perfume brought back a flood of complicated memories. *Home.* What should have been a refuge had only ever been a prison.

Vivien hesitated, as if trying to decide where they should

sit. When Erin lived here, the living room, with its spindle-legged furniture and satin upholstery, was strictly reserved for guests. The dining room was poky and dark, and the narrow kitchen claustrophobic.

As they stood in opposite corners of the front hall, like pieces on a chessboard, Erin felt her edges dissolve as the air shifted and the familiar tunnel appeared, offering escape. But she focused on her breathing and held on.

She can't hurt me.

Besides, Erin had the advantage. She was no longer a child, cowering in terror, but a trained psychiatrist, well-acquainted with the many varieties of human suffering. How easy it was to see that behind Vivien's spite and bile lurked a woman terrified of the darkness in her own soul. As a child, grasping for order in the chaos, Erin had been unable to spot the cracks in Vivien's shell. But she could see them now, clear as day.

Vivien pointed a lacquered nail at the living room. 'We can sit in there.' She pulled the drapes closed against the light and settled into the wingback chair by the fireplace. As she crossed her legs and lit another cigarette, she studied Erin through a curl of smoke.

Who was she supposed to be this time? A forties screen siren? A woman done wrong by a no-good man but choosing to wear her pride like a crown? This was the woman who'd stalked Erin's nightmares for years. When Vivien plotted to send her to Danfield, who was she playing then? Conniving mistress, grieving widow, ruthless harpy? The thought that she was ever concerned for her own daughter's welfare had never crossed Erin's mind.

She perched on a chair near the door. No need to get comfortable. She would say her piece and go. 'Tim Stern.'

Vivien flicked cigarette ash into a crystal bowl. 'What about him?'

Was that a flutter of anxiety in her eyes? For the first time, Erin felt she held all the cards.

'On the night Doris Stern and her daughters were murdered,

you told the police you'd spent the night with her husband in a hotel in Portland. The entire night.' She waited for this to sink in, but Vivien didn't so much as blink. 'Did he ask you to lie?'

'Who says it was a lie?' Her voice was cold.

A child's natural desire to please struggled to the surface, and it was an effort for Erin not to back down. After her father died, she'd had little choice but to seek comfort from her sole remaining parent, despite Vivien's deficiencies in that regard. When Aunt Olivia rescued her from Danfield, she used to say that children were wasted on her sister, that Vivien didn't have a maternal bone in her body.

But a clingy, anxious child must have been suffocating for someone with Vivien's restless nature. Ever seeking opportunities to display her charms, she liked to go out on the town at night. But rather than pay for a sitter, Vivien chose the more expedient solution of spiking Erin's bedtime glass of milk. What harm could it do? Curled up on the mattress, fighting sleep, Erin would tremble with fear in the empty house, with its dark rooms and strange noises.

But Vivien rarely stayed out past midnight. How would it look if the neighbours saw her, sneaking home at dawn. A woman raising two children on her own. As a widow, grieving the loss of her husband, she had her reputation to protect. But any relief Erin felt when she heard Vivien coming through the kitchen door was swiftly replaced by a mounting dread. Terrified of falling foul of Vivien's moods, when anything might happen. A cigarette burn on the arm. Her head snapped back by a swift yank of hair. The glint of the sewing shears. *Snip, snip.* Easy to commit, easy to deny.

Vivien stubbed out her cigarette. 'Twenty years without a word, and you've come here to ask me about an old lover?'

'I heard you come into the house that night,' Erin said. 'Just before two.'

'So?'

'Why lie to the police about spending all night in Portland. After Tim was arrested, Stern was no longer a suspect.'

'He asked me to,' Vivien replied, fiddling with her rings. She lit another cigarette. 'It's always the husband, isn't it? Until they found Tim's son, he was the prime suspect. I was in love with him, or thought I was. So it was only natural for me to protect him. And what of it? It's ancient history now.' Her voice had gone flat. 'After they found the son, covered in blood, it didn't matter what I told the police.'

Erin fixed her eyes on Vivien's face, hoping to unsettle her by refusing to back down. 'If it didn't matter, then why the need, two years later, to have me locked up?'

Vivien's mouth was a thin line.

'You were afraid I'd give you away,' she continued. 'When you came home so late that night, I pretended to be asleep, but you weren't fooled. And it must have worried you that I might mention it to someone, a teacher or a friend. Or Aunt Olivia.' She studied the grim mouth. 'That could have been dangerous for you, or your lover, if it ever came out.'

Vivien's eyes were like slits. 'Why all the questions? Or is this an excuse to come crawling back to your family?' She looked pointedly at Erin's left hand. 'No husband, I see. Poor Mimi, all alone.' She stood and turned to the fireplace, where she straightened a picture on the mantel. 'You think you know everything, but it wasn't easy for me, after your father died, raising two children on my own.' She checked her face in the mirror. 'Such a wild imagination you always had, but sending you to Danfield was for your own good. What else could I do? You were crazy as a loon.'

Her eyes had grown misty, but Erin wasn't fooled. She was no stranger to crocodile tears.

'What was I supposed to do?' Vivien said, throwing her hands in the air. 'You were babbling to yourself and sleepwalking at night. And those strange incantations you used to chant before entering the house. Holding funerals for the dead birds in the yard. Communing with *spiders*, for heaven's sake. If it hadn't been for me, you'd be living under a bridge now. If not dead.'

Communing with spiders? Erin bit her lip so she wouldn't laugh. 'There was nothing wrong with me,' she said, looking Vivien in the eye. 'The truth is, you sacrificed your child to save your own skin.'

They stared at each other across the distance. In spite of what Erin had endured, it was worse for Vivien, she supposed, who had to live with what she'd done. And to find new ways, as the years passed, to paper over the cracks in her life. But let her live with her delusions. Whatever Vivien told herself, she had been incapable of giving Erin the love and nurturing she needed. *Blood from a stone.*

It was time to go. Erin stood and walked to the door. In the hall, a floorboard creaked, the old house settling around its sole remaining occupant, living out her days alone.

Before stepping into her car, she glanced back at the house to see Vivien standing at the window, motionless as a department store mannequin.

Lucky for you, Erin mused, *that we're not bound forever to the orbit of the Earth.* Perhaps in her next life, Vivien would have the chance to try again.

As Erin drove away, the weight pressing on her chest faded to nothing. Not only had she faced Vivien and survived, she'd got the information she came for. One more piece of the puzzle slotted into place. With Vivien's confession about lying to the police, another detail had come into focus. Stern not only lied about his alibi, but there were eight hours he couldn't account for. And if he wasn't with Vivien in Portland, he could have been anywhere. Even Belle River.

43

New York–Vermont Border
August 1977

He opens his eyes to a shaft of sunlight, stabbing through the canopy of trees. The ground under his cheek smells of leaf litter, mouldy and damp. Pine needles rustle overhead. When he tries to sit up, the world spins and he falls back. His eyes are gritty. His mouth tastes like the inside of an old shoe. A chorus of birds, flitting through the boughs, shriek and twitter, clamorous as church bells. His head throbs with pain, and he covers his ears to block out the noise. As he closes his eyes, his only wish is to re-enter the void.

He sleeps for what feels like years, gliding above the surface of a dreamscape, searching in vain for a place to rest. But when he jerks awake, the Sun is not much higher in the sky and the birds are as loud as ever. He rolls over and pushes himself up on his hands and knees. Wobbling as he stands, his feet are clumsy and heavy as lumps of clay. His canvas jacket, too warm in the heat, is damp with sweat, and he pulls it off. His T-shirt is covered with some kind of dried paint, rusty brown. He runs his hands over his chest and wonders where it came from or how he got here.

Was he in a car accident, or a plane crash? Abducted by aliens?

The songbirds chirrup, oblivious to his presence. Perhaps he has died, and they can't see him.

For a moment, the birds cease their chatter. All is silent, and then he hears it, the sound of a passing car. So, he hasn't travelled to Middle Earth, after all. Nor was his body flung across space and time. There must be a road nearby, and he shuffles off to find it.

A quarrel of sparrows and a murder of crows mock his progress as he tramps through the undergrowth. Twigs snap underfoot, branches lash his face. But before long, he crashes through a tangle of thorny shrubs and onto the weed-choked verge of a two-lane road winding through the forest.

As far as he can see, there is nothing but trees. Green and more green. The only way out is to follow the road, but his knees wobble, and his mouth is dry as dust. As he sinks into a heap on the roadside to wait for a passing car, he sets off an explosion of grasshoppers that spring like popcorn through the tall grass. Through the fog in his head, he hears the distant hum of tyres on the road and tries to stand. But a darkness passes over him, and he slips away.

When he comes to, a red light flashes in his eyes like a beating heart. The crackle of a radio splits the air. A human shape looms over him, blocking out the Sun.

'What's your name, son? Do you know where you are?' The man crouches down, his face shaded by a wide-brimmed hat. 'Are you in pain? It looks like you've been in some kind of accident.' He stands and scans the area. 'Got a car around here?' On the man's chest, a silver badge flashes in the light.

'Where are we?' His throat hurts.

'You don't know? Have you been drinking or taking any drugs?' He helps Tim to his feet and walks him to the squad car. 'You sit in the back, and I'll call it in. If you're lucky, someone's reported you missing.'

The man guides him into the back seat, where he lies down

and closes his eyes, listening to the crackle of the radio, and a string of numbers he can't decipher.

'I've got a 10-81 here, and a possible 10-58. See if anyone's put out an APB that matches the description. Male, late teens. Five-ten, brown hair, medium build. Over.'

The cop bends and squints through the window.

'Copy that. Over.'

The radio squawks like a demented crow.

'Say again?' He steps away. 'Holy shit. No kidding. Okay, I'm bringing him in now.'

44

Manhattan, New York
August, Present Day

'This is all very cloak and dagger.' Ray smiled at Erin as she emerged from the Dyckman Street subway and into the sweltering air. 'Not that I'm complaining.' He leaned in and kissed her on the lips. 'I was wondering when I'd see you again.'

The week before, she'd had to cancel their date in the city. With the unfinished family business still ahead of her, she hadn't wanted her anxiety to spoil their day. Last night, on impulse, she'd texted him to meet her in upper Manhattan. Perhaps now, with everything behind her, they could start again.

He pulled away and studied her face. 'Nothing's wrong, I hope?'

'No, but I didn't want to explain over the phone.'

While it was true she had come through her encounters with Graham and Vivien unscathed, seeing them again had disturbed her in ways she had yet to sort out. Time would help, but in the meantime, what she needed was a diversion. Something unusual and festive, where she and Ray could relax and enjoy each other's company.

With the help of a city guide, she'd chosen the Cloisters

for their day out. Having first learned about the museum and vast stretch of woodland on the northern edge of Manhattan in a book she'd read as a child, she could only hope it was as magical as described. They slipped through the gates of the park, leaving behind the heated concrete and sticky asphalt of the city streets. Before them stood the ancient cloisters, much of it constructed from carved blocks of stone salvaged from a medieval monastery in the Pyrenees. In the dappled sunlight, the air was remarkably sweet, as if they'd passed through a portal into rural France.

Erin gazed in wonder at the soaring branches of the trees, spackled with sunlight and alive with birdsong.

Ray smiled. 'I haven't been here since I first moved to the city.'

As they strolled through the courtyard gardens, she breathed in the scent of a dozen herbs, laid out in a pleasing pattern of knots and squares. All her favourites were here – bee balm and lemon hyssop, myrtle and sage. The drone of bees filled the air as she ran her fingers over the rough stone walls.

'It reminds me of Granada.'

'You've been to Andalusia?' Ray's eyes lit up as he looped his arm through hers.

'A long time ago.'

The Sun's heat drove them into the cooler air under the stone colonnades that led to the gallery where the unicorn tapestries hung. Under a row of dim lights, the famed panels of painstaking needlework depicted an age-old story. The hunt and capture of the mythical beast. The violent death and rebirth.

Erin paused in front of the tapestry of the unicorn in captivity, restored to life after death, yet still enclosed, its spirit subdued, as it lay under the branches of a pomegranate tree.

'I lived in southern Spain for a year,' she said, leaning in to examine the millions of tiny stitches that had gone into its making. 'That's where I ended up after leaving home at seventeen.' She retraced her steps to begin the tapestry sequence again. 'I found a job as a cleaner, and lived in a tiny shared flat near the Alhambra. The texture of the old stone walls and the scent of orange blossoms are what I remember most.' She turned away from the dying unicorn, bleeding from its breast, and looked up at Ray. 'I miss it, sometimes.'

A barrel-chested man in shorts and leather sandals entered the gallery and looked at them with barely concealed annoyance, as if expecting to be alone.

Ray held her arm and led her into the sunlight. 'Shall we get something to drink?'

They passed under the colonnades through stripes of light and shadow, their feet tapping on the stones, before emerging into the museum's courtyard café.

At a table next to the herb gardens, Ray pulled out a chair. 'Is coffee okay, or would you rather something cold?'

Sapped by the heat, Erin struggled for a moment to remember where they were. She blinked twice, and the scene wavered before her eyes. A shifting crowd of visitors in shorts and T-shirts, chattering in English.

Her heart thumped and she was back in her body. *You're in New York. This is Ray.*

'Sorry,' she said, dropping into a chair. 'I'm feeling a bit dizzy.' Her hands were clammy with sweat.

'I'll be right back.' Ray made a beeline for the counter to get their drinks.

Erin looked round in vain for the toilets, until she spotted a discreet arrow pointing down a passage. In the loo, she locked the door and leaned against the sink, scanning her face in the mirror. *Am I going mad?* It was too much, seeing Graham and her mother on the same day. An avalanche of memories, transporting her back in time. The dark years when she'd been wrestled to the floor and shot full of drugs. Carted off to a locked ward. Abby, the wild-eyed girl with the scarred wrists, who'd attacked her with a piece of jagged metal, barely missing her jugular as she sliced it down Erin's chest. And

Nicky, so full of life. Finally free from Danfield after nearly a year, only to hack open the veins in her arm and bleed to death in the bath at home. No matter where she went or how far she ran, those memories were lodged like a parasite in Erin's brain.

She splashed her face with cold water and returned to the table.

Ray stood and helped her into the chair. 'Everything okay?'

At her place was a glass of iced tea and a chicken salad sandwich.

'It must be the heat.' She fanned her face.

'Drink something. That should help.' He sipped his cappuccino.

She held the cold glass against her cheek before taking a sip. 'Thank you. I feel better already.'

They sat for a moment in silence. Around them, the chatter of tourists and the warble of birds rose and fell as shadows moved across the stone floor. By the time she finished her sandwich, the other patrons had drifted away, leaving the two of them alone.

When Ray returned to the table with more drinks, she decided to tell him everything. At this point, she had nothing to lose.

He handed her a glass of iced tea, and she fidgeted in the chair.

'I haven't been completely honest with you,' she said, unable to meet his eyes. 'I meant to tell you earlier, but the timing was never right.' She lifted her glass and set it back on the table without taking a sip. 'There was another reason for my unusual interest in the Stern case, besides the assessment I was asked to do. A personal one.' She searched his face. 'Cartwright isn't the name I was born with. I changed it when I moved to London. My real name is… Marston.' She studied Ray's face. 'Graham Marston, the guy who bullied Tim at school, was my brother.'

Ray's shock seemed genuine. Either that, or he was an excellent actor.

'Your brother?' He was staring at her now, his upper lip pricked with sweat. 'I don't understand, I thought you'd grown up in England.'

She shut her eyes and breathed in the scent of lemon thyme and bee balm. Light and shadow flickered across her lids. 'When I was thirteen, my mother began telling people I was mentally disturbed. My guess is, she was putting something in my food that made me act strange. Your average garden is full of plant alkaloids that can mimic symptoms of psychosis.' Erin waved her hand at the herb garden. 'Anyway, with my brother's help, she convinced a psychiatrist I was deranged, telling him she was afraid of me, and about how she'd woken to find me standing over her with a knife in my hand. I was taken away in the middle of the night and spent two years in a psychiatric hospital on a locked ward.'

Ray reached for her hand, but she pulled away.

'You've been so sweet to me… and I've done nothing but lie to you.'

His face was creased with concern.

She pressed the cold glass to her throat. 'My aunt saved me. My mother's sister, but the two women are as different as day is to night. When she discovered where I was, she got me out. I went to live with her in Belle River, on Gardiner Road. It's where we used to stay in the summer, except Aunt Olivia would move in with a friend while we were there. They inherited the house when their mother died, but Olivia couldn't bear to be under the same roof with her sister. After she found out what happened to me, Olivia not only barred my mother from the house, she threatened to go to the police if Vivien ever came near me again.

'Two years later, Vivien was still on the warpath, trying to stir up trouble, so I fled to Spain for a year to hide out. After that, I moved to London to start a new life.' Her fingers grazed the back of Ray's hand. 'Erin is the name of my father's mother, long dead now, and Cartwright… I got that off the back of a delivery van.' Her smile felt forced. 'It seemed appropriate at the time.'

The blood had drained from Ray's face. She was sorry now to have dumped this on him, but he deserved to know the truth.

'That's the reason I've been so obsessed with Tim and his family,' Erin said, raising her eyes to meet his. 'At first, it was just the Belle River connection, but when I discovered my own family was involved, what with Graham possibly giving PCP-laced marijuana to Tim, and my mother providing a false alibi to Stern, so many things didn't mesh with my own memories of that time.'

She scooped an ice cube from her glass and touched it to her wrists. 'I heard her come home that night, though I didn't remember it until recently, when she was supposed to have been with Stern. For nearly two years, she lived in fear I would rat her out to the police. That's why she had me sent to Danfield.' The story, locked away for so many years, came out in a rush. Had anything she said made sense?

As the memories surfaced and whirled like a Catherine wheel, Ray swam in and out of focus.

What if Stern did it?

There it was again. That voice, teasing and taunting. But she wouldn't say it out loud.

The nausea returned, and with it an overwhelming desire to lie down. She felt someone pulling her up by the arms and tried to speak, but darkness descended, and she slipped away.

* * *

When she opened her eyes, it felt like hours had passed, but it was still daytime and bars of sunlight slanted through the blinds. The pillow under her head was deliciously cool. A ceramic urn, glazed in a pleasing mosaic of yellow and green, stood in a corner by the bed. On the far wall, a motley collage of photos provided a bright spot of colour.

As she pushed away the damp bed sheet, fragments of the day shimmied to the surface. The confession to Ray, her panic and confusion, the ride through the heat-buckled streets in a taxi, all the way to the Upper West Side.

A knock, and Ray stuck his head around the door. 'Look who's up.' He slipped into the room and sat on the edge of the bed. 'How are you feeling?' He felt her forehead with the back of his hand. 'Much better. You were burning up before.' He handed her a glass of water.

Erin struggled to sit up, embarrassed at feeling so helpless. 'I should get home.'

'Why not stay over? We can order in food or watch a film. Whatever you like.'

Nausea cramped her stomach. She rushed to the bathroom, where she threw up in the toilet. Heatstroke. She'd had it once before, in the cauldron of southern Spain. The mirror gave her the bad news. Sweat-damp hair stuck to her cheek, and her skin was milky pale. She splashed water on her face and yanked a comb through her hair before returning to the bedroom.

It was empty. She could hear Ray in the kitchen, opening cupboards and running water in the sink. The parquet was deliciously cool on her feet, and she paused to look at the photo collage, a pastiche apparently, of Ray's travels. Spain, Greece, Italy. A country in South America that might be Ecuador or Peru. Were there pictures of his ex-wife? She saw no photos of women, but her eyes were drawn to a familiar snapshot, similar to the one she'd seen in the *Belle River Gazette* from the 1976 bicentennial. Further down was a picture of Ray and an older man, both in baseball caps and sunglasses. A beach at sunset, with the surf at their backs and rocky bluffs damp with salt spray.

Ray stood in the doorway, holding a plate of food. 'I made sandwiches. And, if you're up for it later, I can open a bottle of Rioja.'

'Is that Spain?' She pointed to the photo.

He set the plate on the bedside table. 'Nope. Santa Barbara. Me and my dad from a few years back.'

He came up behind her and lifted the hair from her shoulders. His breath tickled the back of her neck, as his lips sought the skin behind her ear. She shivered as he slid the cotton blouse from her shoulders and when she turned to face him, he kissed her neck and grazed his lips along the length of her collarbone. With a pang, she remembered the scar. But this time, it didn't matter. She no longer had anything to hide.

45

Matlock, Vermont
August, Present Day

On Friday afternoon, Erin locked the door to her office and slipped away from the Meadows. While her judicious side urged her to inform the authorities of her suspicions and let them handle it, this trip to Vermont to confront Stern was a piece of unfinished business she needed to deal with on her own. Even if she convinced the police to follow up on the false alibi, Vivien would flat out lie. And if that didn't work, she would wave Erin's records from Danfield in their faces. *Who're you going to believe, me or some crazy girl?*

Not long after she crossed the border and entered the Green Mountains, heavy clouds rolled in from the west. Fat drops of rain slapped onto the windscreen, transforming the landscape into a watercolour painting. By the time Erin turned onto the road to Stern's farm, the rain had slowed, and the sky began to clear.

Stern's SUV was the only car in the driveway. He must be alone in the house with Tim. Or was his woman friend inside as well, the one he'd passed off as his housekeeper? Not that it mattered. She would tell Stern what she had come to say, with or without an audience.

By the time she reached the front door, her clothes were damp from the spitting rain. Heart thumping, she pushed the bell and waited. She must look a mess, but it didn't matter. All she wanted was to see the look on Stern's face when she told him what she knew.

The door swung open. If Stern was surprised to see her on his front doorstep, looking like a drowned rat, he didn't show it. Though he must have heard her car drive up, so it was unlikely she'd caught him off guard.

'Dr Cartwright.' He stood back to allow her to pass.

She crossed into the foyer and stood dripping on the slate.

'If you'll wait here, I'll get you something to dry off with.' He ducked into the downstairs bathroom and returned with a thick white towel. No sign of Tim.

Every day since his discharge from the hospital in Burlington two weeks ago, she had expected to hear he had suffered a relapse, or that Stern was mortally wounded.

'This is a surprise,' he said, showing her into the front room.

The fireplace was clean swept and laid with birch logs, but there was no need for a fire today. Even with the rainstorm, the air was oppressive.

As if he had guessed why she'd come, Stern dispensed with the usual gestures of hospitality, even failing to offer her a coffee from his machine in the kitchen. 'You've come a long way.' He gave her a cool look of appraisal. 'Is this about Tim?'

The room was cast in shadow. Through the glass, she could see a new batch of storm clouds building up on the horizon. With the windows closed, the room was stifling.

'I'll get right to the point,' she said. 'When the police questioned you about your whereabouts on the evening of August 26, 1977, you told them you had spent the entire night at a hotel in Portland. The woman you were with confirmed your story, although her name was later redacted from the police report, at her request.'

Stern waited, arms across his chest. He had yet to bat an eye.

'When I spoke with the woman in question, she admitted she wasn't with you all night. And that you received a phone call around ten in the evening and left the hotel. When you hadn't returned by one in the morning, she left and drove home.' Erin waited. 'She also said you asked her to lie to the police.'

Stern's eyes were flat, his face expressionless. He flicked a spot of lint from his sleeve. 'So, you talked to your mother. It must have been a shock to see you after all these years.'

Her heart bumped. *He knows who I am?*

'I can see you're surprised.' His laugh came from deep within his throat.

When their eyes met, the fury in Stern's face froze her blood.

And, just like that, the mask dropped, sliding away with scarcely a whisper. Wasn't that what she'd wanted all along, to unmask him as a charlatan and a fraud? But nothing about this moment was the least bit satisfactory. Not when he'd pulled a trump card of his own. All this time, he'd been playing her for a fool.

The room grew darker with the gathering storm. Uncomfortably aware she was alone with this man, possibly dangerous now that she'd upped the stakes, she tried to figure out her next move. In the hall, the clock chimed the half-hour.

'It doesn't say much for your ability to read people, Dr Cartwright – or perhaps I should call you Mimi? Seeing as we're old friends.' His smile was thin. 'Not to have noticed, I mean. That a psychiatrist of your calibre wasn't aware I recognised you the moment I saw you. Well, not the very first, perhaps.' He chuckled. 'But I had a strong suspicion. I knew you as a girl, of course. A plump little thing you were, with the dirty blonde hair you inherited from your mother. But I've never seen anyone else with eyes like yours. Such an odd shade of green. Not quite human, I used to think, always watching. Impossible to forget. And when I caught you snooping in my den, taking an undue interest in that photo, I knew it was you. You couldn't have been more than eight or nine when that photo was taken, but it clearly sparked a memory.

'Your mother used to keep a copy of it on her bedside table. Naughty Vivien, rubbing our affair in her husband's face. But, otherwise, a memento of our days as a happy foursome. Until that idiot father of yours got caught with his hand in the cookie jar. Working-class trash to the bone, but what a poser he was.' He sneered. 'Clever of your mother to concoct that cock-and-bull story of Ian's death. But what else could she do? Who would want it shouted all over town that her prim and proper schoolteacher husband had been caught embezzling old ladies' pensions?' He ran his hands through his hair. 'You'd think Ian would have enough sense to keep well away, after everything he's done, but lately he keeps showing up like a bad penny.'

'My father died in a car crash,' Erin said. She struggled to keep the quiver from her voice.

Stern hooted with laughter. 'Vivien deserves an Academy Award for that one, playing the grieving widow. I'd forgotten what a convincing actress she can be. I saw your father about a month ago. He showed up at my door, spoiling for a fight. Still blaming me after all these years for getting him sent to prison. Third time in the past three months he's turned up here, looking for a handout, so, unless I'm hallucinating, he's very much alive.'

The room closed in around her. Her father was alive? She didn't believe him. Stern was just messing with her head. But then the light dawned. The day she'd spied on the house with the binoculars. The man on the doorstep in the beige jumper and baggy khakis.

'You sent my father to prison?'

'Who said it was me?' He pivoted to face her. 'It's your mother who has a habit of sending people away. You of all people should know that.'

A drop in pressure seemed to suck all the air from the

273

room. It was a relief when a clap of thunder broke the tension. Erin fought to stay calm, but her heart jerked oddly against her ribs.

'Who I am isn't relevant,' she said, trying to keep her voice from shaking. 'What interests me is why you lied to the police.'

His mouth twitched. 'You used to be a criminal psychiatrist, am I right?'

She blinked, wondering whether or not to lie.

'Yes, I know all about you, Dr Cartwright. Funny what you can find out these days, just by turning on a computer. So, you don't need me to tell you that in a domestic crime the husband is always the primary suspect. When the police inquired about my whereabouts the night of the murders, I told them the truth. That I had dinner in Portland and then spent the night at a hotel with a woman who was not my wife. When asked if this woman was with me the entire night, I said yes.'

His unwavering stare bore into her skull. Sweat trickled down her neck.

'I was in a state of shock. My wife and daughters had been brutally murdered. My son was missing. At the time, nobody thought he was a suspect. They assumed one of two things: that he'd spent the night with a friend, or he'd been abducted.'

'You weren't concerned for Tim's welfare?'

'Of course I was. I wanted the police to find him. What I didn't want was for the Belle River police department, who hadn't the first idea how to handle a murder inquiry, to waste precious time by treating me as a suspect. After Tim was found covered in my wife's blood, whatever story I'd told the police no longer mattered. But, tell me, is there a point to all this? Your mother's been jerking my chain for years. I don't need more hassle from her daughter.'

'You're still in touch with her?'

The ghost of a sneer crossed his face. 'Only by cheque. She's been blackmailing me for years.'

'What for? You said you have nothing to hide?'

'Vivien's unstable. How could I know what story she'd cook up after the fact? Lobbing a cheque at her every now and then is like tossing a bone to a dog. Better to keep her quiet than have her drop a grenade into my life. And I had my new wife to think about.' He wiped the sweat from his face. 'My family was killed by my mentally ill son, yet it's me who's being harassed. How's that for justice?'

A crack of thunder shook the house, followed by heavy rain that lashed the windows. From upstairs came a thump.

Erin looked at the ceiling. Was that Tim? Did he know she was here? The windows were closed but not locked. Would she be able to escape through one of them if Stern attacked her? She looked to the fireplace for a weapon, but the iron poker was gone.

'Here's what I think,' she said. 'You killed your wife and your daughters and made it look like Tim was to blame. Who would ever suspect you, a successful lawyer and upstanding pillar of the community? You were counting on that to tip the balance in your favour.'

A muscle twitched in Stern's jaw. 'Fascinating, Dr Cartwright.' He clapped twice. 'You have quite the imagination.' He took a step towards her. 'But, tell me this, if Tim didn't murder my family, what was he doing two hundred miles from home, covered in his mother's blood? How did he get there?'

'You drove him there.'

'I drove him?' Stern laughed so hard he began to cough. 'My dear young lady, you're delusional. You might want to consider checking yourself into that asylum again. What was it called... Danfield? Once a raving lunatic...' He raised his eyebrows, allowing the rest of the sentence to hang in the air.

'You could have drugged him and driven him there,' Erin said. 'Dumped him in the woods over the New York state line before turning around and heading back to Portland. It wouldn't have taken more than six or seven hours, there and back. Nobody would ever know. After all,' she said, 'you had an alibi for the entire night.'

Neither of them moved.

Another thump came from upstairs, followed by the sound of a chair scraping across the floor.

'If I'm a cold-blooded killer, then you're mighty brave, aren't you, coming out here to confront me on your own.' He paused to rub his temples. 'But you haven't got a shred of evidence. Everything you've just said is pure speculation. Even if you went to the police, they'd never reopen the case.'

'They would if they had an eyewitness.'

That got his attention. His mouth twitched. Coupled with the greenish cast to his skin, Erin would say he was worried.

'That was the one loose end you needed to tie up, wasn't it?' she said. 'To get rid of the only person who knew what really happened in your home that night. You could make his death look like suicide, or an accident. Who would question it? A mental patient recently released from long-term incarceration, who couldn't cope with living in the world. Hanged himself from the rafters in the barn.'

Before Stern could answer, thunder rolled across the sky.

Erin held her breath and waited.

He turned to look at the storm and when he whirled around, his face was black. 'If anyone's responsible for what happened to my family, it's that pain-in-the-ass mother of yours. She didn't have the sense to keep her goddamn mouth shut. Always needed to be the centre of attention. It's her fault my daughters are dead.'

Erin reeled back in shock. 'My *mother* killed your daughters?'

'She might as well have.' Stern exhaled noisily. 'That bitch told your father about our affair, and he told my wife. She knew Dorrie was unstable emotionally, and that it would push her over the edge if she found out about Vivien and me.

'That night, Dorrie called me at the hotel in Portland to tell me there was an emergency at home. There was something odd about her voice, so I raced back. When I got there, she was doped up or drunk, stumbling around and taunting me. It took me a moment to understand what she was saying, that my girls were dead. She had suffocated them with a pillow and then cut their throats. She'd wanted me to see it, all that blood. She looked at me with those mad eyes and laughed in my face. Revenge, pure and simple. Destroying what I most loved in life. It was the only way, in that twisted mind of hers, that she could get my attention.'

His face, a sickly shade of grey, was streaming with sweat. 'Do you have any idea what I had to put up with? Coping with a wife like that? Do you think that was easy? I was on track to be partner at a prestigious firm in Boston when one of the senior partner's wives found her passed out drunk in the bathroom. I had to slink back to Belle River with my tail between my legs. If word got around that my wife was a junkie, I'd have been finished as a lawyer. My whole life in the toilet after everything I'd worked for. Every night when I walked through my own front door... I never knew what I'd find. But that I would come home one night to discover my beautiful daughters...' He covered his face with his hands and sobbed.

For a moment, Erin felt a twinge of sympathy. It would derange any loving father to find his daughters murdered in their beds by his own wife. That explained the strange discrepancies between the deaths. The two girls smothered in their beds, their throats neatly cut, compared to the blood and gore of the wife's butchered body. Until now, it had never made any sense.

'So, you killed your wife.'

A branch scraped against the window, followed by a flash of lightning. Stern stood in the corner, rigid as a statue.

'You need to leave now.' Each word like the jab of an ice pick.

'When Tim came home that night,' Erin said, 'it must have struck you that he'd make the perfect scapegoat. My guess is you knocked him out with some kind of tranquilliser, smeared his clothes with your wife's blood, and then bundled him into your car and drove to New York. Who would suspect? After all, you were in Portland with an ironclad alibi.'

He seemed strangely calm as he waited for her to say more. But Erin had said her piece, and she slipped past him and into the hall. The front door, though only a few metres ahead, seemed impossibly far away.

Behind her, a floorboard creaked, and a wisp of air prickled the skin on her neck. Before she could react, a hand clamped over her mouth. She struggled in his grasp, but his strength was too much for her. As she went to bite his hand, something sharp pierced her neck. A shadow embraced her, and she slumped to the floor.

46

A scrabble by her ear. The floor against her cheek was gritty and cold.

Erin opened her eyes to the dark. Not even a glimmer of light pierced the blackness. Her head felt woozy, and a dull pain cramped her gut. The dank odour of mildew and damp earth soured the air. She must be in a basement. Whether it was day or night, or how long she'd been out, was impossible to say. When did she arrive? Friday afternoon? By Monday, if she didn't show up for work, someone would come looking for her.

But she'd told no one where she was going, not even Ray.

Her hands were cinched tight behind her back, a rag tied over her mouth. But even if she could call out, who would hear her? No one but Stern, who would only jab her with another hypodermic. Harrison must have given him a supply of knockout drugs in case of an emergency.

Footsteps overhead. She must be in the house, and not in some outbuilding or root cellar under the barn. Her wristwatch was gone, but she still had her amulet, and the weight of the quetzal against her sternum was comforting. Touching it with her fingertips always helped to calm her nerves, but she couldn't even move her wrists.

As she struggled to sit upright, her head spun, and she

nearly toppled over. There must have been something powerful in that syringe. Haldol or lorazepam. Or both. A combo used liberally at Danfield, whether warranted or not, where almost anything could get you the needle. Failing to turn off your light, talking back, begging to be let out. Whatever Stern had planned for her, short of dumping her body in a ravine, it couldn't be worse than what she'd already been through.

At the sound of a scrape on the concrete floor, her heart skipped a beat. Was he coming for her now? Did he plan to kill her and dispose of the body? A shallow grave in the woods or tossed into an abandoned quarry, either would do. But her disappearance would place him directly in the crosshairs, exactly where he didn't want to be, so he would have to be cleverer than that. Nobody just vanished. Someone would trace her whereabouts back to Stern. Unless... The thought made her shiver. Unless he was planning to pin her death on Tim. And why not? It would be easy for Stern to claim that Tim had overpowered him and knocked him out. When he came to, he'd been horrified to discover Erin's lifeless body in the basement. Another death at the hands of his lunatic son. Such a tragedy. As far as the state was concerned, Tim had already killed three people. What was one more?

Her muscles tensed as she cycled through the possibilities, each more grisly than the last.

Another footstep.

Like a hunted rabbit, she kept absolutely still, hoping he would leave. She held her breath and strained her ears for another sound. Had he meant to finish her off with the hypodermic, and was only now coming to see if she was dead? Stern might be desperate, but he wasn't stupid. And letting her go was the one thing he couldn't do. She'd head straight for the police. Even if they couldn't get Stern for killing his wife, they could certainly charge him with kidnapping and grievous bodily harm.

A door scraped open. A shadow appeared in the gloom.

When a dim bulb snapped on, she was momentarily blinded. She squinted and prepared to defend herself.

As the shadow detached itself from the doorway, her throat closed up. But with nothing to lose, she canted her body backwards and got ready to kick.

But it couldn't be Stern. She blinked. The body was too bulky, the shaggy head familiar. *Tim.* His eyes were wide in the dim light, with a look of terror stamped on his face.

She tried to speak, but the gag in her mouth prevented her from making any intelligible sounds. She waited for him to make a move, but he remained stock-still, a tree rooted to the floor. As she shuffled her feet and tried to stand, he looked back over his shoulder in alarm. The seconds ticked by.

He moved closer and crouched down. 'What are you doing here?' The barest whisper, like exhaled breath.

She twisted round to show him her hands were tied, and waited for him to undo the knots.

An agonising minute passed before he edged towards her with a sideways motion, dragging his heels, crablike, across the rough floor. His hand trembled as he reached out to touch her hair, freed from its customary knot, before pulling away fast, as if stung. With clumsy fingers, he struggled to get at the gag's knot on the back of her neck. Blood pounded in her ears. Tim's breath grazed her cheek as he wrestled with the knotted cloth.

Unbearably slow, he loosened the gag at last. She coughed and sucked in a lungful of air. In another part of the cellar, a water heater clicked on, and her momentary elation plummeted. Nothing had changed. She was still trapped.

'Thank you.' She coughed again and sought his eyes, but he turned his head away. 'And my hands?'

Fear darted across his face. He looked at her, then looked away. Something was different, but what? Then, with a shock, it came to her. The dullness was gone, and his usually passive expression was no longer flat. He must be off his meds again. Was that a good thing, or bad? Whatever it meant, he was clearly terrified, transformed from a large man doped up on meds, into a small boy afraid of his father. Untying her might be asking too much. With her hands free, he couldn't be sure what she might do. But at least she could scream, and with the use of her legs, she could run.

'Timothy, do you know what time it is?' Frightened as she was, she remembered to use the name he preferred.

He held his wrist close to his face to look at his watch, the same chunky black model he'd had at Greenlake.

'It's exactly…' He held up a finger and counted under his breath. '2.36.'

'In the afternoon?'

'No.' A puzzled frown. 'It's dark out.'

The middle of the night then. Stern would be asleep. 'What day is it?'

He consulted the watch again. 'SAT. Saturday.'

So she'd been out for more than six hours. Her throat was parched, and her head ached. 'How did you know I was down here?'

'I saw your car from the window. I heard you talking to my father.'

'Why didn't you come downstairs?'

'The bedroom door was locked.' He tilted his head as if listening for movement. 'The rule is,' Tim said, 'I go to my room if anyone comes to the house. My father locks the door, so no one will take me away.' He rubbed his eyes with his fists. 'I saw him drive your car away. Before he fell asleep, he brought me something to eat and forgot to lock the door. So, I came down here to look for you.' He looked frightened. 'This is where he sends me when I'm bad. So I try to be good,' he said, peering at the damp walls and the ceiling draped with cobwebs. 'I don't like it here.'

In a few hours it would be daylight. What if Stern woke and discovered Tim's room was empty? Her mind raced through the possible options. She needed to get out of the house without alerting him. But with no transportation, she wouldn't get far. If she knew where Stern kept his keys, she could drive his car into town and alert the police. But she'd have to do all that without waking him.

'Timothy, listen to me.' She scooted along the floor to close the distance between them. 'I need your help.' She tried and failed to catch his eye. 'But we have to be very quiet.' She dropped her voice to a whisper. 'Could you untie my hands now?'

He chewed the skin on his thumb. 'You won't tell my father?'

'No, of course not. We'll be quiet as mice. All you need to do is let me out of the house so I can get to the village and after that go back to my own home. He'll never know you helped me.'

He gave her a frightened look and backed towards the door.

'I just need some air, Timothy. Nobody likes to be locked up.' She tried to keep her voice light. 'If I can just get outside into the air, I'll be fine. Then you can go back to bed.'

Another moment passed before he looked directly at her. And there it was, the one thing she'd been hoping for all these months. A flicker of awareness, and a clear sense of their shared humanity. Despite the long years of incarceration and the constant cocktail of drugs, he was still in there.

His hands were clumsy as he struggled with the knots. For a moment, she was afraid he wouldn't be able to loosen them. But at last, with a gasp of relief, she was free, though her wrists throbbed as the blood returned.

'Thank you,' she whispered, weak with relief. His face was pale, his pupils large.

'Okay, Timothy, here's what we'll do. You go up the stairs first. On tiptoe, as quiet as possible. Can you do that? And then you'll stand in the hallway, very still, like a statue, and listen. We need to be sure your father is asleep. If you don't hear anything, I'll follow you up the stairs. Then you'll open the front door for me, so I can get out. As soon as I'm gone, you go back up to your room, very quiet, and get into bed. Do you think you can do that?'

His eyes flicked from her face to the door. His skin gleamed with sweat. But he nodded and turned towards the stairs.

The scrape of his trainers on the gritty floor boomed in her ears. She flinched at the sound.

A thought suddenly hit her. *The dog.* Where was Lulu? Was she in the house or asleep outside?

Fear lodged in her throat. 'We need to be quiet, Timothy. Very, very quiet.'

One step, two. Another step, agonisingly slow. As Tim eased his bulk up the stairs, the steps creaked under his weight. Erin held her breath, waiting for Stern to fling open his bedroom door.

At the top of the stairs, Tim stopped and cocked his head to listen. No sounds came from the upper floor. She swayed on her feet as her heart raced, worried she'd faint dead away from the fear alone.

Tim beckoned her to follow. She climbed the steps with care, testing each tread before putting her weight on it. When she emerged into the hall, it was stuffy and warm. No hint of fresh air from yesterday's storm. Every window in the house must be shut tight.

She touched Tim's arm and held her finger to her lips. Aside from Stern, her biggest worry was the dog. Where was Lulu? Would she start barking when Erin, a stranger, fled across the lawn? To keep the dog quiet, Tim would have to come with her, at least to the end of the drive. But that was three hundred metres at least, and he might not agree to accompany her that far in the darkness. If there was a moon, it was obscured by clouds. The hall was pitch black. Only a dim glow came from a light in the kitchen.

She motioned to Tim to follow and crept towards the front door. Under his weight, a floorboard creaked. Panic gripped her chest. She sucked in her breath and counted to ten. Upstairs, all was quiet.

Almost there.

At the front door, she tilted her head to listen before reaching for the handle. But when she pulled, nothing happened. The deadbolt was locked, and the key removed. No way out from here. As she struggled to quell her panic, her breath came in gasps. The logo on Tim's trainers glowed like an iridescent beacon in the darkness. A surge of adrenaline urged her to flee. But how?

47

She leaned close and whispered, 'Let's try the kitchen door.'

With infinite care, they headed towards the light at the end of the hall. Erin winced at each creak of the floorboards, expecting at any moment for Stern to bolt from his bed.

A flash of lightning lit the hall, followed by the crack of thunder. The sudden clatter of rain on the roof was a relief, if only as a cover for her escape. As they moved towards the kitchen, each sound was like a knife at her throat.

At the door to the backyard, she turned the knob, but it was locked from the inside.

Tim peered at her with frightened eyes. 'There's a key.'

She waited. 'Do you know where it is?'

He pointed to a row of canisters for sugar, coffee, and flour. Taped to the lid of the sugar canister was a door key. She peeled the tape away and clutched the key in her hand.

'I'm going to leave now,' she whispered. 'As soon as I'm out the door, you relock it, return the key and go back to bed. Okay?'

He nodded. The yellow glow from the stove light cast a sickly hue on his skin.

Almost there. She eased the key into the lock. Freedom was but a moment away.

When a flash of lightning lit up the room, Tim cried out.

She turned to see a shadow in the doorway. The overhead light flicked on, dazzling her eyes. The key clattered to the floor.

'Are you off then, Dr Cartwright?' He turned to Tim. 'You've been a bad boy, Timmy.' In the sharp halogen light, Stern's eyes were brittle as glass. With his right hand, he gripped a shotgun, wielding it like a truncheon.

'Timothy,' she said. 'Help me.'

But he was looking at the weapon in his father's hand and backing away.

Stern raised his free hand and jingled a set of car keys. 'Since you're so anxious to leave, why don't we go for a little drive. Just you and me. There are some lovely back roads through the forest. The road to the quarry is especially scenic, particularly in a storm. Lots of thrashing pine trees and hairpin turns. Quite thrilling, actually.'

He turned to address Tim. 'Go on up to your room. We'll have a little chat about your behaviour when I get back.'

Her pulse jumped.

Tim dropped his head and scuttled away. As he mounted the stairs, each step felt like a nail in her coffin.

Erin eyed the gun. Though Stern was fit for his age, and a good fifty pounds heavier than she was, he was an older man and, once outside in the darkness, she could probably outrun him.

He stood aside to let her pass. 'Let's go out through the front door, shall we? So much more civilised.'

But fear rooted her feet to a spot on the floor. It was impossible to breathe. The old terror, always lurking beneath the surface, came roaring back. Vivien's cobra eyes, glinting in the dark. The sour smell of Graham's breath. All those hours and days locked in the damp cellar. The threat of the asylum and Vivien's cold sneer. *I can have you locked up, any time I want.*

Erin straightened up and found her voice. 'I'm not going anywhere with you.' Her legs were shaking, but she turned to face him. 'If you're planning to kill me, you'd better do it here. Though you won't get away with it. Several people know where I am and why I've come. If I disappear, the police will show up on your doorstep asking questions.'

Stern snorted with laughter. 'In that case, I would kindly invite them in, like the gentleman I am, and inform them that you came here to thank me for the care I've provided for my son, after saving him from that wretched asylum. And after having a drink with me, you left for home in the middle of a storm, where you must have met with a terrible accident.' He fixed her with a bloodless stare. 'It happens all the time in the backwoods. People disappear. Sometimes they die.'

With her brain reeling, she scrambled to come up with a plan of action, while pretending to give in and follow him to the front door. When they reached the stairs, she could make a dash for Stern's bedroom and bolt the door. There was a telephone in there. If she moved fast enough, she might be able to alert the police in time.

'Coming, Dr Cartwright?'

With an eye on the shotgun, she moved past him and into the hall, her eyes flitting from side to side, searching for a weapon or a way out, but Stern kept close behind. So close, she could smell the alcohol on his breath. If she was lucky, he might be unsteady on his feet.

Halfway there. The hall clock ticked the minutes as rain drummed on the roof. A bolt of lightning lit up the dark hall, blinding her briefly. *This was it.* She spun round and pushed Stern hard on the chest. As she fled up the stairs, fear gave wings to her feet. If Stern had locked his bedroom door, she'd be trapped. But the door was open, and she flung herself through it, scrabbling for the bolt as Stern pounded up the stairs. She shot the bolt closed, a second before he slammed his weight against the door.

She sprang away. Solid oak, but was it strong enough? Could he break it down, or blast through the door with the shotgun?

The room was dark, and she stumbled to the bedside table,

where a white phone gleamed, and switched on the light. At the sound of the dial tone, she was flooded with relief, but as she punched in the emergency number, the line went dead. Erin dropped the receiver and scanned the room for a weapon. He'd lied about the shotgun. So there might be a pistol in the nightstand. She yanked open the drawers and felt around, but there was nothing.

Sprinting to the dresser, she rummaged through his clothing. Nothing. As she straightened up, she came face to face with the row of photographs on top of the dresser. One looked oddly familiar. It was the photo of Ray and his father on the beach in Santa Barbara. But it wasn't Ray's father. The man in the photo was Stern. Why hadn't she seen it before? *Ray and Stern*. Pain squeezed her chest. Everything he'd told her was a lie.

Something hard smashed against the door. She dropped the picture and ran to the window, but it wouldn't budge. By slamming her palms against the sash, she managed to raise it a few inches.

Another crash against the door splintered the wood. He must have got hold of an axe. Terror gave her strength and she wrenched the window wide enough to climb out. Rain hammered the roof tiles, and the wind blew her hair in her eyes as she scrambled onto the steeply pitched roof. The ground was dizzyingly far below, but if she could skirt round the back, she could drop onto the roof of the kitchen, and from there onto the ground.

Rainwater streamed down the back of her neck. Clinging to the slippery roof tiles, she crab-walked away from the window, moments before Stern smashed through the door. She turned to see his face, tense with fury as he raised the shotgun to his shoulder and took aim. Tim loomed up behind him. They locked eyes for a split second before he lunged forward and grabbed Stern around the chest.

She was two storeys off the ground, but there was no time to lose. Her wet hair stuck to her face, blocking her view. For a moment, she was too frightened to move. If she lost her grip, that would be it. *Don't look down.* Sprawled flat, she inched forward, praying the rain gutter would hold her if she slipped.

'There's nowhere to hide.' Stern was at the window, pointing the gun at her head.

Erin pressed her face against the slate. As she scrabbled for something to hang onto, her hand whacked against a metal spike. *Lightning rods.* The roof was lined with them.

Stern fired and missed. She grabbed a rod and then another, pulling herself along, inch by painful inch. Lightning flashed across the sky, followed by a symphonic clash of thunder. The metal rods tingled in her hand.

Stern climbed out the window, leaving the gun behind. Better if she fell, he must be thinking. It would look like an accident.

Move. The ground was far away, but she forced herself forward, one inch, two, risking a glance over her shoulder. Stern, tethered to a rope, was closing the gap between them.

A thump was followed by the crack of splintering wood, and a sharp cry. Erin, spreadeagled against the shingles, looked back in time to see Stern tumble off the roof, the loose rope flailing in his hand.

Tim leaned out the window, his eyes wide in fright, as the rain streamed down his face.

Stern grabbed for the gutter, legs flailing. But the metal groaned and pulled away, sending him cartwheeling through the air. The crack of his skull on the flagstones was like a gunshot.

Tim looked terrified.

She called out to him. 'Grab the sheet off the bed and throw one end to me.'

He disappeared from view. She pressed her face against the roof, desperate to keep her grip as the rain streamed down. A thud sounded behind her. Tim had tossed a rope out. Better than a bed sheet. Lying flat, a starfish splayed against a rock, she stretched forward and grabbed the rope, already sodden and slippery from the rain. Tim leaned out the window to haul her in. Too tired to do anything but hold on, she went limp as he dragged her over the sill, where she flopped onto the carpet, gasping for breath.

Relief lasted only a moment, until panic seized her. Where was Stern? Did he die in the fall, or was he still out there, about to come after her again?

Heaving herself upright, she gasped. 'Timothy. Your father? Is he…?'

Tim leaned out the window. 'He's not moving.'

'We need to call for help.'

He hobbled to the far wall and slid to the floor. 'I think he's dead.'

'We still need to call.'

They eyed each other across the distance, before he dropped his head on his knees and mumbled something.

From where she lay, flat on the floor, her ears pricked up. 'What did you say?'

When he lifted his head to stare at her, the light dawned in his eyes. 'I didn't kill them.'

'No, Timothy,' she said. 'You didn't kill them.'

'I didn't do it.' His eyes, perfectly clear, locked onto hers. 'It wasn't me.' He dropped his head in his hands and burst into tears.

48

Dobbs Ferry, New York
September, Present Day

Ray was waiting for her at the café by the river. Their café, as she'd once thought of it, where they'd had dinner on the terrace on a sultry summer evening in June. But as Erin crossed the street, she looked away to avoid his smile. How easy it would be to get sucked in again by Ray's good looks and charm, when what she needed was to stay clear-headed and in control.

As she approached the table, he leaned in to kiss her tenderly on the lips. She submitted without flinching, but when she pulled away, rather abruptly, he gave her a puzzled look.

Friday afternoon, and the riverside terrace was teeming with the happy-hour crowd. Animated laughter rang out over the water. Faces were flushed with wine and sunburn, as the jubilant patrons, sprung from their office drudgery, got a jumpstart on the weekend.

'Shall we go inside?' Erin said. 'It's a bit noisy out here.' Without waiting for an answer, she stepped through the door and headed to a table in the back. The dining room was empty.

No one wanted to sit inside on a day like today, with the Sun suspended above the river like a jewel.

A waitress hefting a tray of drinks glanced at them in surprise. 'Be with you in a minute,' she said.

Erin pulled out a chair and sat, holding her bag on her lap.

'Why don't I go out and give her our order,' Ray said. 'Faster that way. I don't know about you, but I'm parched.'

'Could you get me an iced tea?' She patted her face with a napkin.

'No wine? Nothing to eat?'

She shook her head. 'I can't stay long.'

His smile faltered.

The waitress brought their order and clip-clopped away in her wood-soled sandals.

Too hot in her long-sleeved tunic, Erin was desperate to push up her sleeves and get some air, but the bruises on her arms would raise questions she had no wish to answer. Not yet. Let's see what he had to say for himself first.

Ray raised his glass of sangria. '*Salud*. I like what you've done with your hair.' He appraised her new look. 'Very edgy. It suits you.'

The day she was released from hospital, she'd gone straight to a salon to have her hair cut. Shoulder-length and two shades lighter, she wouldn't call it edgy, just fresher. She'd been long overdue for a change.

'It was nice to get your message,' he said, fiddling with his glass. 'When I didn't hear from you…' He looked away. 'I hope I didn't do anything to upset you.'

Erin savoured the pleasure of the cold tea as it slid down her throat. When had it ever felt this good to be alive? Edges were sharper, colours more vivid, as if the thin membrane between her senses and the physical world had been ripped away. For a moment, her feelings towards Ray softened. She had lied about who she was, and he forgave her. For all she knew, he had a good reason of his own for hiding his relationship with Stern.

'I have some bad news.' She set her glass on the table. 'Tim's father is dead.'

The shock in his eyes was genuine.

'I thought you'd want to know.'

'Why would I want to...?' He flushed and looked away. 'What happened?' His hands shook as he picked up his drink and abruptly set it down again.

'He died from a fall. Two weeks ago.'

He ran his finger round the edge of his glass. 'I'm sorry to hear that.'

'I imagined you would be.' Erin reached into her bag for the photograph from Stern's bedroom. Lydia had swiped it for her when she went to the house to collect Tim to drive him to the group home near Albany, where a place had become available at just the right moment.

'This was in Warren Stern's bedroom.' She pushed it across the table. 'It's an exact copy of the photo I saw in your apartment, and I couldn't help wondering why he would have a picture of you and your dad. But it's not your father, is it?' She studied his face. 'It's you and Stern.'

When he looked up at her, his skin was the colour of putty. 'What were you doing in Stern's bedroom?'

She nearly laughed, but then grew serious. 'I was running for my life.'

He struggled to connect the dots. 'Running...? I don't understand.'

A stream of chatter from the crowd on the terrace drifted through the open window.

'Tim didn't kill his mother and sisters. When Doris Stern found out her husband was having an affair with another woman, she killed her daughters in revenge. When Stern discovered what his wife had done, he murdered her and made it look like Tim was to blame.'

In front of her eyes, Ray seemed to shrink, until he took on the shape of a sullen boy, angry at the world. 'All this time, it was Stern?'

Erin looked at him, but said nothing. Around them, the air fell still.

He finished his drink, and when he spoke, his voice was hollow. 'My father was a violent drunk. He used to beat the crap out of me when I was a kid. And my mother...' He shook his head. 'To escape the chaos at home, I joined a Little League baseball team, even though I didn't like sports, just so I could get out of the house on Saturdays. Stern was one of the coaches. I was twelve and desperate for any sign of kindness. He took me under his wing, encouraged me to work hard at school. Kept telling me that good grades and a fine character would be my ticket out.'

He signalled the waitress for another glass of sangria.

'By the time I was fifteen, I'd started to pull away from him. When I quit playing baseball, I could tell he was hurt. He's the one who got me the job at the yacht club, though by that time I was a mess. Drugs, skipping school, petty theft.' He paused. 'Even, on occasion, arson.' His crooked smile fell flat. 'If it was bad, or against the law, it was like honey to a bee.'

Arson. A picture of Tim's charred house rose in Erin's mind.

'A year after the murders, before he moved to California, Stern came to see me in New York. I'd gotten a scholarship to Columbia and was over the moon at the chance to escape Belle River. He said he thought of me as family, that with his wife and daughters dead, and Tim locked away, I was the son he was meant to have. It wasn't always a welcome or easy mantel to wear, but we kept in touch. Cards at Christmas and on my birthday, and every couple of years, when he flew out here on business, he'd take me out to some slick restaurant.'

Ray picked up the photo. 'This was taken about ten years ago. He'd remarried by then and the new wife wasn't happy about him keeping up with the old Belle River crowd, such as it was. So, we drifted apart. The last time I saw him was about four years ago, when we met for lunch at a steakhouse in midtown. That's when he told me his wife had cancer. About a year ago, I got a card saying he'd moved back east. Bought a house in Vermont and wanted me to come up for a visit. I never got around to writing him back. By that time, our relationship had started to feel a bit forced.' His voice fell away. 'I didn't know he'd kept this picture in his bedroom.'

In the space of a few minutes, Ray's face had aged ten years. The lines around his eyes were deeper, and his skin an unhealthy grey.

'I called him once, but I never went up to the house. Always had some excuse. Work, travel, whatever. But the truth was, I didn't feel like rekindling the relationship. It was fine when he was out on the West Coast, but with him living in Vermont, it felt like an obligation. It was like he wanted something from me I didn't have to give.' He reached for her hand, but she pulled away. 'When you turned up at my door, asking about Tim Stern… it was a huge shock. The last thing I heard about Tim was that he'd been sent to a state asylum. Stern never mentioned him.'

His tone seemed sincere, but she wasn't convinced. Something told her there was more to the story. Much more. 'Okay, I get that you were surprised, but why lie about knowing him?'

'Habit, I guess.' He rattled the ice in his glass. 'I learned to keep secrets as a kid. Safer that way.'

That she could understand. Two people with miserable childhoods. It should have formed a bond between them. But something didn't ring true.

He tossed some bills on the table. 'Do you mind if we go outside? I could use some air.'

* * *

They walked north along the river, where the swirls and eddies rippled in the light. On the other side, high bluffs cast shadows across the water.

'When you started asking all those questions about the

Sterns, I had the idea you might be a cop, or some kind of private investigator. And that new information about the case had come to light. It made me kind of jumpy, like I might be implicated, just by association.' He touched her arm. 'That's why I lied about knowing him. Plus, all those questions… asking me if I knew Graham Marston. It brought the whole thing roaring back, my crappy family, my misspent youth, and it got me thinking about those cheques he'd been sending me over the years.'

'Stern was sending you money?'

'Not in a regular way,' he said, steering her towards a bench. 'But every now and then, on my birthday, or for Christmas or college graduation, I'd get a card with a cheque in it. A big cheque. I'm not talking piddly amounts here. Two, five, sometimes ten thousand dollars.' Ray shook his head. 'Once, I tried to return the money, but he said he'd made some kind of investment in my name when I was a kid, back in my Little League days, and the money was from that. It did strike me as odd, though. I mean, why would he do something like that? But who was I to complain? I was a struggling student, and then trying to get by with a bunch of jobs that didn't pay well. The money was a huge help. In fact, it changed my life. I used it to buy my apartment.'

He turned to look at the boats on the river. 'It was only when you asked all those questions about Stern that I started to remember… after so many years of trying to forget… about the night his wife and daughters were killed. The memories came rushing back, and those cheques began to seem a lot less like generosity from a man who'd suffered a horrible tragedy, and more like… hush money.'

Erin dropped onto the bench. 'Hush money? Why would you think that?'

'Because I saw him. That night. I was out with some friends, squashed into the back seat of someone's car. We were just cruising around when I saw Stern sometime around midnight, driving on one of the back roads that cut through the forest. At the time, I didn't think anything of it. We never heard any details about what happened that night. It was barely mentioned in the local paper. Plenty of gossip, to be sure, but nobody really knew anything. Stern must have kept the more salacious bits out of the news. He had that kind of pull. Though I did eventually hear that Tim had been arrested and charged with the crime.'

'But you never told anyone that Stern wasn't in Portland where he claimed?'

Ray turned his back to the river. 'Like I said, I learned early on it was safer to keep my mouth shut. I was an awkward, frightened child. My dad was violent. My mom was a mess, and just as scared of him as I was. It got worse in high school. I turned into this sad loner, a bit of a weird kid. Awkward, shy. Kind of like Tim, I guess.'

From her bag, Erin pulled out the copies of Ray's yearbook pictures she'd printed off the internet. With a red pen, she'd circled the string of nonsense letters that had kept her mystified for months, having failed to see, until a few days ago, what they meant: *eldu#QUEpasa?* She passed him the photocopy. 'Someone whose high-school nickname was "the Duke" doesn't sound like a loner to me.'

When Ray looked at the photocopy, his face paled.

When he said nothing, Erin continued. 'I knew my brother had a bunch of friends with a reputation for raising hell. Vandalising property, selling drugs, terrorising other kids.' She watched his face. 'They had these ridiculous nicknames. The Viking, the Enforcer, the Duke. When we first met, I was so charmed by you, it never occurred to me that you were one of them.'

'I really don't know what—'

'It took me a while to make the connection. But your yearbook photo gave it away.'

'Erin, listen…' He tried to grab her hand, but she pulled away.

'All this time… getting to know you, baring my soul. How could I have known I was falling for "El Duque" himself.'

* * *

That night she cried. Though the tears had been building for months, ever since that day at Ruth Davis' flat, when she'd nearly fallen to pieces, it was Ray who broke the floodgates. The look on his face when she'd left him on the banks of the river sliced her in two.

Skilled at seeing through the mask people showed to the world, how had she failed to spot the moral deficiencies lurking below the surface? On the train back to Lansford, she tried to come up with excuses for what he'd done. Not only the cruelty of his teenage years – hadn't they all done things they were ashamed of? – but the lies about the money and his relationship to Stern.

But however she tried to justify it, the facts remained. In the guise of 'the Duke', Ray had tormented boys like Tim and Jeremy. But that wasn't the worst of it. If Ray had come forward about seeing Stern that night, the truth would have come out, and Tim's name cleared. Twenty-seven years in a locked ward. There were no reparations for that.

Two nights later, while she was tucked up in bed at the country inn near Albany, where she'd checked in to rest before returning to work, Erin's mobile pinged.

Can we talk? I'll come to you.

She reached for the delete button. But it was only fair to hear him out.

Saturday 3.00pm. 79 Maple Street, Albany.

She pressed send and switched off the light.

* * *

Erin was waiting in her car in front of a three-storey house with a wrap-around porch when a taxi pulled up and Ray stepped out. Dressed in jeans and hiking boots, he looked prepared for a day in the countryside. He glanced at the house with a puzzled frown.

Be patient. All will be explained.

As he approached the driver's side, she rolled down the window. 'Get in. I don't want anyone to see you.'

Ray slid into the passenger seat. His eyes were dull and his hands shook, as if he hadn't slept in days.

'I'm not here to make excuses or defend my behaviour,' he said, looking straight ahead through the windscreen. 'Not about the awful things I did as a teenager. Or lying to you about Stern, even though that information could have affected Tim's situation.' He turned to look at the house. 'I was a screwed-up kid from a messed-up home, but that doesn't excuse the way I treated Tim, or any of the stupid and vile things I did to hurt others.' He took a white envelope from inside his jacket and handed it to her. 'You can open it later when you're alone.'

The air inside the car was warm, though the oak trees lining the street provided a welcoming shade. Earlier in the day it was cooler, with a hint of autumn in the air. Soon, the canopy of trees would change colour and burnish the countryside with great swaths of red and gold.

He turned to look at the house. 'Is this where you live?'

She cleared her throat, wishing she didn't feel so nervous. 'No, but there's someone who lives here I'd like you to see.'

At precisely three-fifteen, the front door opened, and a man in jeans and a brand-new green sweatshirt stepped onto the porch. From behind him, a dog barrelled past and charged down the steps, before turning to wait for the tennis ball in the man's hand. As he threw it in a clean arc across the wide lawn, the dog barked excitedly and took up the chase, her russet coat shining in the sun. The moment the dog caught the ball, the man took off round the side of the house, while she chased him into the backyard.

When Lydia had called with a report on Tim's progress, she had described this routine – out the front door, throw the ball, scurry round the back – as their new game. Under the care of a doctor, Tim was being weaned off the medication he'd never needed and was adjusting to his new home. With Lulu, a hit with the other residents, the star attraction of the house.

'Is that…?'

'Yes,' Erin said. 'That's Tim, or Timothy as he prefers to be called. He seems to be settling in well.'

Ray fell quiet. But what could he say? An apology wouldn't turn back the clock, nor would it give Tim the years he had lost.

He stared out the window, as if waiting for Tim to reappear, but the front yard remained empty.

'Erin…' He started to say something, then shook his head and opened the door. 'It's all in there.' He nodded at the envelope on the dash. After shutting the door, he leaned through the open window. In Spanish, he murmured a few words about learning from one's mistakes. 'I repeat that quote to myself at night before falling asleep.' His eyes were sad. 'It doesn't make me feel better. But perhaps someday it will.'

* * *

It was her last night in Albany, hiding out in her room at the inn. She hadn't been ready to return to Lansford before, but it was time. In the morning, she would pay the bill and head back home.

She made a cup of tea and curled up in the window seat to read Ray's letter. When she slit open the envelope, a square of stiff paper fell out. She picked it up and turned it over. It was a photo of her and Ray, snapped at that Cuban restaurant, Casa Habana. One of Ray's waitress friends must have taken it. The camera caught them at the moment they'd lifted their glasses in a toast. *May you live every day of your life.* Her eyes shone in the light of the candle as he touched his glass with hers. She looked happy.

From the envelope, she pulled out a letter, handwritten on a single sheet of paper, and a document of several typed pages, printed on the letterhead of a New York law firm.

Dear Erin,

In the summer of 1978, after graduating from high school, I left Belle River for what I hoped would be the last time. The move to NYC was meant to be a fresh start, and a chance to put my demons behind me for good. But I don't need to tell you that whatever demons hound us through life are inside, not out, and no matter how fast we run, we can't escape ourselves or the shadows that haunt us.

I can't make up for the things I did to ruin Tim's life. The bullying and the drugs were the least of it. If not for my indifference to his fate, he would never have been locked away. Someone with more integrity would have gone to the police with what he knew. For the rest of my life I will have to live with the consequences of my cowardice and cruelty.

I can't give Tim those years back, but I sincerely hope that a better future awaits. To my great surprise, and consternation, I was contacted by an NYC lawyer, who informed me that I was the beneficiary of Stern's estate. Even though I turned my back on him in the end, apparently he considered me, much to my shame and regret, to be the son he'd always wanted.

Following probate, the entire value of Stern's estate will be placed in trust for Tim. The enclosed document from Lear, Reinhardt & Barton contains all the details. Though it won't change the past, I hope the money will allow Tim to live in comfort and safety for the rest of his life.

As for me, I'm taking a six-month leave of absence from work and heading to a village in Galicia. In the winter months, storms batter the coast, and the villagers huddle in their homes against the elements. With not much to do and little to see, I plan to walk the hills and tally my debts.

It is unlikely you will ever want to see me again, but I do hope when I return it will be as a better man, and perhaps, should you ever think of me, I will somehow receive your thoughts like a beam of light through the darkness.

Yours ever, Ray

She placed the letter on the table and scanned the document from the law firm. It was all as Ray had written. The money from Stern's estate would be placed in trust for Tim's care for the remainder of his life. He had ended his letter with a quote in Spanish. Something about how the honourable man shall arise one day from the ashes of his mistakes. She could only hope Ray was right.

The document she stowed in her bag. The letter and photo she held in her hands, preparing to tear them into pieces. But then she remembered Ray's downcast look, and the regret in his eyes as they sat together in the car. At the sound of a dog's excited bark, they had both looked up to see Tim standing on the front porch next to Lulu, his face tilted towards the Sun.

She put the letter back in the envelope and tucked the photo in her wallet. It wouldn't hurt to hang onto it. Perhaps in six months, she'd be ready to look at it again.

49

Lansford, New York
September, Present Day

At the top of the stairs, a letter awaited her, helpfully taped to
the door by Erin's landlady. But after everything she'd gone
through in the past few months, the sight of a strange letter
had lost the power to set her heart racing.

Following her meeting with Ray, she'd taken a week's
leave from the Meadows and headed straight for the Canadian
border. In a small village on the shores of a placid blue lake,
she had checked into a modest inn, hoping the quiet landscape
would heal her body and salve her spirit.

Home. A sour smell greeted her as she stepped through the
door. The cracked cornice moulding and dark, poky kitchen,
once so charming, looked shabby and sad. Whatever spirit
had animated the flat when she first moved in, caught up
with her new job and the frisson of returning to America,
had evaporated like mist in the sun. Through the window, she
could see her Honduran neighbour playing with her baby on
the grass. Celestina she was called. Later, when things settled
down, Erin would stop by their flat with a gift.

She sank into a chair on the balcony and examined the

envelope, front and back. A creamy oblong addressed in an elegant cursive. A printed label provided a return address. *Mrs KG Hartley, 57 Old School Road, Carvill, Massachusetts.* Erin had no idea who that might be. She slit open the envelope and extracted a single sheet of heavy paper embossed with the Meadows' logo.

Dear Dr Cartwright,

I hope this finds you well. If you're feeling up to it, would you be so kind as to meet me at the Meadows on Sunday afternoon, September 19th, at 3.00 pm? There's an important matter I would like to discuss with you. No need to send a reply, as I shall be there in any event to take care of some other business. As you may recall, the staff and patients will be away on their end-of-summer camping trip to Lake George, so we shall have the place to ourselves.

Yours sincerely,
Katherine Hartley

Erin dropped the letter in her lap. She hadn't the slightest idea who Katherine Hartley was. A member of the board, perhaps? If that was the case, the important matter likely meant a public dressing-down before they tossed her out on her ear. Surely, they wouldn't keep her on staff when the lies about who she was became known. But it didn't matter. She'd been planning to resign anyway. Where she would go wasn't clear, though back to London seemed the obvious choice. If she were lucky, or begged, the Thornbury Clinic might take her back. Though she dreaded the thought of working for Julian again.

Her fingers sought the quetzal around her neck. It wasn't there, of course. Lost at Stern's farmhouse in the storm. The chain must have broken during her struggle on the roof, or shortly afterwards, only to be trampled in the mud by the police and paramedics. She'd briefly mourned the loss. But whatever power it once had to protect her from harm seemed no longer necessary.

Lying in the hospital bed in Burlington, with her arm taped up and her body bruised, she'd composed her resignation letter in her head. How could she teach her young patients that leaving their childhood behind to step boldly into the world was something to celebrate, when, in truth, it was full of betrayal, loss and death? Who was she to teach them about courage when she'd been hiding in the shadows of her own childhood fears? Whatever strength she now felt, or how much she'd grown, she had yet to come clean about masquerading behind a new name and invented history, with her past locked in a vault. She was a fraud. Not fit to tell others how to live.

At least Tim was safe. Lydia called yesterday to say that things were still going well at the group home. After Erin had given her statement to the police, and the investigation into Stern's death was closed, Tim was exonerated of all charges. In a week or so, Erin would drive up to Albany to see how he was getting on.

As for the matter of her father, the shock of knowing he was alive was something she had yet to grapple with. Why he'd made no attempt to find her after all these years was a question she would like to ask him. But he must have changed his name long ago and tracking him down would be difficult, if not impossible. And the truth was, a part of her preferred they never find each other. Dead or alive, the man she'd built up in her mind, loving and wise, was nothing but a figment, best left in the past. It might be kinder for them both to leave him undisturbed in his fictitious grave.

* * *

At the Meadows, the gardens shimmered like a moving tapestry in the amber light. The clumps of lavender bordering the drive hummed with the murmur of bees, and the great drifts of blue delphinium glowed like cobalt against the yew hedge.

As Erin passed through a gate in the boxwood, a vision of the house and grounds as they'd once been rose before her eyes. Sylphlike women twirled in sequinned gowns as stylish men with brilliantined hair sipped champagne from slender flutes. At the edge of the terrace, a dark-eyed woman in a green dress kicked off her silver slippers and ran barefoot on the grass. Erin blinked and the vision was gone.

She entered the clinic through a side door and made her way to the staffroom. By the fireplace, a pot of orange asters heralded the end of summer. A creamy white petal from a bouquet of late-blooming roses drifted to the floor. Erin waited, but no one came to greet her. Whoever this Katherine Hartley was, she had yet to arrive.

Upstairs, Erin's office was shrouded in darkness. She pulled up the blinds and flung open the windows. Without the buzz and chatter of the girls, the manor was oddly quiet. She ran her fingers across her mahogany desk, trying to imagine sitting there again, writing up her case notes.

Sunlight filtered through the chestnut trees, and the graceful river shone like pewter. It was a view she would sorely miss. She slipped her resignation letter under the desk blotter. First thing tomorrow, she would hand it to Niels.

As she descended the broad staircase, scattered notes from the music room drifted into the hall. Sonorous and slow, a refrain from a distant age. She followed the sounds and peeked through the gap in the door. The woman who played for the girls was seated at the piano, her fingers moving gracefully over the keys.

Without lifting her hands, she turned her head and smiled. 'Please come in.'

Embarrassed, Erin hung back, as if she'd caught the woman in a private act. 'I didn't mean to disturb you.'

'Do you know this piece? It's one of my favourites. Beethoven's Pastoral. The sonata, not the symphony.' She played a few more notes, clear as drops of water from a mountain stream. 'So fitting on a day like this, don't you think? With the gardens awash with flowers and the lawns so deliciously green.'

Behind the piano, the tall windows framed the majestic pair of copper beeches. A blue jay splashed in the fountain and darted away.

'When the Meadows was still a private home,' she said, playing a few more bars, 'this used to be the morning room. When I first came to this house as a young bride, I would get up just after dawn and run down here to look at the gardens. There were rabbits in those days, perfectly tame and white as snow, hopping about on the lawn, nibbling the grass. I was nineteen, just a girl, and thought they were enchanting.'

Erin's palms tingled. 'I'm sorry, but did you say you lived here?'

In a single, graceful motion, the woman rose and floated across the floor, her hand outstretched. 'I'm Katherine Hartley. Though everyone here knows me by my maiden name, Gillman. Kay Gillman. And, yes, I used to live in this house, once upon a time. It's a pleasure to meet you properly at last.'

Erin clasped the woman's hand, her confusion complete. This was Katherine Hartley? So, their music teacher was, what, a member of the board? And the name, Hartley. Wasn't there a foundation…? She gasped as it came to her. 'You're the anonymous benefactor.'

Katherine's eyes were merry. 'Is that what they call me?' She squeezed Erin's hand before letting it go. 'I'm afraid I've given you a shock. Let's go into the staffroom and make a pot of tea. It's not too hot for tea, is it? We can drink it on the back terrace and revel in the view. Just like in the old days.'

Erin's mind raced ahead as she followed Katherine into the great hall, their shoes clicking like castanets on the stone floor. The identity of the person whose money made all this possible, the first-rate medical care and the exquisite surroundings, was a carefully guarded secret. Why would she reveal herself now?

Katherine plucked a box of loose-leaf tea from the back of the cupboard and filled the kettle with water.

Erin shook herself awake. 'Here, let me do that.'

Katherine tossed her an amused look. 'Don't be silly, I'm perfectly capable of making a pot of tea. And, for what it's worth, that's one of the reasons I prefer to stay anonymous. I shudder at the thought of special treatment, or having anyone bow and scrape before me like I'm some kind of saint.' She waved her hand to take in the room. 'I married into this, and most certainly am not to the manor born.' Her smile was infectious. 'Truth be told, I come from the other side of the tracks, as the saying goes, and have never been a stranger to hard work.'

As the kettle boiled, Katherine arranged the tea things on a tray. A quick rummage through the cupboards turned up a box of vanilla wafers.

'Come. The gardens await,' she said, lifting the tray with a practised flair.

In the shade of the greened-striped awnings on the terrace, they settled into a pair of lounge chairs. The heat from the flagstones warmed Erin's feet through the soles of her shoes. She would have liked to kick them off, but perhaps Katherine would think it impertinent if she exposed her bare feet. This was meant to be a formal meeting, and she was expecting to be made redundant. When Katherine announced she was being relieved of her duties, Erin wanted to have her shoes on.

But Katherine seemed not to have business on her mind. She poured out the tea and added a splash of milk. Her smile was sympathetic as she handed Erin a cup. 'How are you getting on?' She slipped off her shoes and flexed her pale freckled feet in the sun. 'I hear you've been through quite an ordeal.'

Did everyone know? She'd told only Niels, and the barest of details at that. But perhaps Katherine kept a close eye on the goings-on at the clinic. It was her domain, after all.

'I don't mean to pry,' Katherine said, 'but I overheard Dr Westlund say something about an emergency leave of absence, and I put two and two together. I have a summer home in the Berkshires, and the news about Warren Stern's death made it into the local paper.' Her brow creased. 'I'm so terribly sorry.' She touched Erin's hand. 'That patient, Tim? He was lucky to have you in his corner.'

It was too much to take in at once. Erin's head throbbed in the afternoon heat and from the buzz and whir of the gardens, alive with bees and beetles, and the chirp and rustle of birds.

'I do get wind of things on occasion,' Katherine said, shifting in her chair, 'but you mustn't think I'm pulling strings behind the scenes. It's true the money comes from me, but I have nothing to do with how the clinic is run. The board sends me an annual report by way of the Hartley Foundation, but that's all.' She added more milk to her tea. 'As far as everyone's concerned, I'm the sweet old lady in the cardigan and loafers who plays the piano twice a week. It's a perfect set-up. I get time with the girls and the added assurance that this house, and the money I inherited from my late husband, is being put to good use.'

She paused to refill their cups.

'I do hope you'll feel well enough to return to work soon. I hear such good things about you. Though I'm no expert, the girls seem to blossom under your care.'

Return to work? If Katherine wasn't the messenger, she supposed it wouldn't hurt to confess her plans. 'I'm not coming back.' Erin pulled the sleeves of her blouse over her wrists. 'Tomorrow, I'll be handing my letter of resignation to Dr Westlund.'

'I'm sorry to hear that.' Katherine turned her head to look at the fountain. 'Where will you go, back to London?'

'I'm not sure yet.' Erin watched a dragonfly, iridescent as a jewel, as it hovered above the fish pond.

'For people like us,' Katherine said, 'our first instinct is always to flee, isn't it?'

Erin was taken aback. Katherine didn't know the first thing about her.

'Before the board approves a new staff member,' Katherine said, taking a delicate bite from a vanilla wafer, 'they undertake a rigorous vetting procedure. It's the only time I'm ever involved in the business of the clinic. A file is created for each potential candidate and a copy forwarded to me.'

Erin found this hard to believe. If that were true, how did Greta make the cut?

As if possessing unusual powers of perception, Katherine didn't miss a beat. 'You're thinking of Dr Kozani, I presume? It's true she's a bit of an odd bird, but for a certain type of patient, I understand her no-nonsense approach is exactly what they need.' She paused. 'Partly due to my own difficult history, the safety of the girls has always been my first concern.' She sought Erin's eyes. 'People aren't always who they seem to be. So, I'm sure you'll agree, we can't take any chances.'

Erin's teacup slipped from her hand and smashed on the flagstones. 'You know who I am?'

'It's one of the reasons I thought you'd be a perfect addition to the staff.' Katherine met Erin's eyes, ignoring the smashed teacup beside them. 'You have personal reasons to fight for these girls.'

Personal reasons. That could only mean one thing. 'So you know about Danfield?'

Katherine nodded.

'And that my real name isn't Erin Cartwright?'

'That too. But I don't know the name you were born with. Danfield wouldn't release that information, of course. They only acknowledged that a girl from New Hampshire with the initials EM was a patient there in the late 1970s.'

A flood of anger threatened to choke her. Who was this woman to rummage through her past?

Erin collected the broken pieces of porcelain and dropped them on the table. 'I don't know what your game is,' she said, preparing to stalk away, 'but digging into someone's medical history is a major violation of trust.' Her ankle, still bruised from the desperate scramble across Stern's roof, throbbed as she struggled to her feet and stumbled inside.

50

'I didn't mean to upset you,' Katherine said, following her into the staffroom. 'You'd better sit. I can see your ankle is painful.'

She helped Erin over to the sofa.

'What I was trying to say, clumsy though it was, is that you and I are birds of a feather. And I tend to believe that people like us recognise each other. Even across space and time.' Her face was flushed from the heat, and she clasped Erin's hand. 'The memory of that early abandonment, the sadness and the terror… it stays with us always, doesn't it?'

Erin looked away, unsure of where this inquiry was headed.

'The girls will be coming back soon,' Katharine said, glancing at her watch, 'so I'll get right to the matter I mentioned in my letter. Effective immediately, Dr Westlund has been removed from his position as medical director of the Meadows.'

At the shock of this announcement, Erin's head jerked up. Niels, fired? 'I don't understand.'

'Dr Westlund was arrested for forging prescriptions,' Katherine said. 'Narcotics, I believe.' She paused, as if debating how much more to say. 'In lieu of jail time, he's been ordered to enter a rehab facility for three months. When he gets out, the board will vote on whether or not to reinstate him in his current role. In the interim, they would like you to take over as director. If things work out, and I have no doubt they will,' Katherine said, with the hint of a smile, 'it would become a permanent appointment.'

Niels, a convicted felon. It was impossible to take in.

'Due to mitigating circumstances,' Katherine continued, 'and Dr Westlund's exemplary record to date, the judge was willing to be lenient. The board may be as well, but I don't believe they'll reinstate him after he gets out of rehab. It wouldn't do to have a convicted felon at the helm of the Meadows. Regardless of the circumstances that brought it about.'

'Circumstances?' Erin sat up straight. 'I don't understand.'

'It's not my place to say anything, but I suppose it will all come out anyway, as these things tend to do.' Katherine twisted the gold ring on her finger. 'Dr Westlund had a younger sister who was diagnosed with schizophrenia as a teen. About three months ago, she was found dead in a run-down house in Los Angeles. I don't know the details, but it must have hit him very hard.'

Her ankle began to throb again. Erin had trouble taking it all in. She had no idea that Niels had a sister. Or much of anything about him, beyond what he cared to show. Perfectly bland and largely unruffled, with a happy family life. That's what she'd always thought.

'Please tell me you'll think about it,' Katherine said, touching Erin on the arm. 'It would be a wonderful opportunity. Not just for you, but for the girls, as well. With you at the helm, I have no doubt the clinic would soar to new heights.'

In spite of herself, Erin's mind buzzed with excitement. The chance to head up a clinic like the Meadows was more than she'd ever imagined. She studied Katherine's face, and absorbed the kindness in her eyes. There was no malice there. What harm would it do to tell her who she was?

She sucked in her breath. 'For the record, I thought you might like to know what my real name used to be.' She smiled wanly. 'I was born Euphemia Mae Marston. Mimi for short. A terrible name to give a child. I was teased mercilessly at school.'

Katherine reached for her hand. 'If you were my daughter, Erin is the name I would have chosen for you, right from the start. I can't imagine you as anyone else.' She stood and dabbed moisture from her eyes. 'Time to make myself scarce,' Katherine said. 'But before I go, it may interest you to know that a girl named Cassie is being admitted on Monday to the clinic's three-month residential programme. Dr Westlund mentioned you'd taken a particular interest in her.'

'Cassie Gray?'

'She contacted the clinic herself to ask for help. Dr Westlund wanted to be sure you knew that.'

As they left the staffroom, the crunch of tyres sounded on the gravel drive out front. Car doors opened and closed. Excited chatter floated in the air.

'I'll leave you here,' Katherine said. 'It's time for me to sink back into the shadows.' She gave Erin a conspiratorial smile. 'Think it over, won't you?'

Before anyone could see them together, Katherine slipped through the door to the music room, transforming herself once again into Kay Gillman, the quiet, unassuming woman who played piano for the girls.

In that moment, as she listened to the first notes of a lively tune with an up-tempo beat, Erin decided to accept the board's offer.

* * *

In the soft light of early morning, Erin stood in the shade of the stone portico as Lonnie Tyler drove her beat-up Chevy through the gates. From behind the wheel, she looked coolly at Erin before sliding on a pair of dark glasses. As soon as Lonnie stopped the car, Cassie tumbled from the passenger side, lugging a blue suitcase, scuffed with wear.

The gravel crunched underfoot as Cassie approached. To

someone standing outside the gates, it might appear as though Erin were welcoming the girl into her home as a cherished guest. And in a way, she was. The Meadows was hers now, to oversee as she saw fit. Her head was filled with the novel ideas she wanted to try, and the processes she'd like to streamline. Treading slowly at first and including the staff in her plans. Her greatest wish was to create not just a successful clinic, but a community, and to offer the girls in their care – and perhaps, someday, boys – the gift of wholeness to carry them through life.

As she came closer, Erin stepped forward to meet her. Cassie's hair had grown in the past few months, but something else had changed. The girl clutching the suitcase looked vulnerable and lost. The mask of defiance and anger was gone.

Cassie's mother leaned out the window. 'You should know this was my daughter's choice,' she said. 'Not mine.'

'We'll take good care of her.'

Erin stood at Cassie's side as Lonnie's car passed through the gate. *Out in the world, that's where the trouble began*. But it didn't have to be that way.

There was no doubt that Cassie had a treacherous road ahead, but Erin was confident she was ready to make the journey. While her first instinct had been to take over Cassie's care, Erin knew in her heart that someone with a firmer hand, at least initially, would be a better choice. So, for the first thirty days, she would place Cassie into Greta Kozani's capable hands. After that, anything was possible.

Erin turned to Cassie and smiled. 'I'm so glad you're here.'

Acknowledgements

I am indebted to the many people who helped guide this book along the road to publication:

My wonderful literary agent, Charlotte Seymour, and the whole team at Andrew Nurnberg Associates, without whom this book would still be a gleam in my eye.

The team at Legend Press, UK, with special thanks to my editor, Lauren Parsons, whose keen editorial eye helped bring into focus the smallest details and big picture alike.

Rosie Jonker at Ann Rittenberg Literary Agency, USA, for her comments on a previous draft, and for looking after my interests on the other side of the pond.

John Goodman, Eve Seymour, and Jilly Woodford, for their input and encouragement. Jason Donald, and participants at the Swiss mountains retreat, for lively conversations on the art and craft of writing.

Norah Perkins and Anna Davis, as well as members of the CBC online writing class, for the inspiration to finish what I'd started.

Ginny Rottenburg and Allie Reynolds, writing friends and creative muses, for their tireless support and close reading of earlier drafts; and to Shamala Hinrichsen, my longtime friend across cultures and continents, and first reader from the early days.

Finally, to the people over the years, too many to list, who have inspired me to keep reading and writing; and to the kind souls who offered a guiding light, whenever I was lost in the dark.